try
not to
breathe

Holly Seddon is a freelance journalist whose work has been published on national newspaper websites, magazines and leading consumer websites. As a mother of four, Holly divides her time between writing articles, walking her miniature Schnauzer and chasing homework-evaders around the room. And then doing some more writing when night falls.

try
not to
breathe

HOLLY SEDDON

CORVUS

First published in hardback in Great Britain in 2016 by Corvus, an imprint of Atlantic Books Ltd.

4 5 6 7 8 9

A CIP catalogue record for this book is available from the British Library.

Hardback ISBN: 978 178239 945 2
Export Trade Paperback ISBN: 978 178239 668 0
EBook ISBN: 978 178239 669 7

Printed and bound by CPI Group (UK) Ltd, Croydon, CR0 4YY

Corvus
An Imprint of Atlantic Books Ltd
Ormond House
26–27 Boswell Street
London
WC1N 3JZ

www.corvus-books.co.uk

For Boo and the babies

CHAPTER ONE

Amy

18 July 1995

Music thudded through Amy's body and seized her heart. Music so loud that her eardrums pounded in frenzy and her baby bird ribs rattled. Music was everything. Well, almost everything.

Later, the newspapers would call fifteen-year-old Amy Stevenson a 'ray of sunshine', with 'everything to live for'. Her headphones buzzed with Britpop as she trudged the long way home, rucksack sagging.

Amy had a boyfriend, Jake. He loved her and she loved him. They had been together for nearly eight months, walking the romance route around the 'top field' at school during break time, hot hand in hot hand, fast hearts synchronized.

Amy had two best friends: Jenny and Becky. The trio danced in a perpetual whirlpool of backstories, competition and gossip. Dizzying trails of 'she-said-he-said-she-said' preceded remorseful, sobbing hugs at the end of every drunken Saturday night.

Nights out meant lemon Hooch in the Memorial park or Archers and lemonade at The Sleeper pub, where a five-year-old wouldn't have been ID'd. School nights meant 6 p.m. phone calls once it hit the cheap rate. She would talk until her step-dad, Bob, came into the dining room and gave her *that* look: it's dinner time, get off my phone. Thursday nights were *Top of the Pops* and *Eastenders*; Friday nights were *Friends* and *The Word*.

Amy's Kickers bag grew heavier with every step. She shifted it awkwardly to the other shoulder, tangling her wires so that one earbud pinged out of her ear, the sounds of the real world rushing in.

She had taken the long way home. The previous day she'd got back early and startled Bob in the kitchen as he stirred Coffee Mate into his favourite mug. At first he'd smiled, opening his arms for a hug before realizing that she'd made it back in record time and must have gone across the field.

She'd had to sit through half an hour of Bob's ranting and raving about walking the safe route home, along the roads: 'I'm saying this because I love you, Ames, we both love you and we just want you to be safe.'

Amy had listened, shuffled in her seat and stifled yawns. When he'd finally stopped, she'd stomped upstairs, flopped onto her bed and smacked CD cases around as she made an angry mix tape. Rage Against the Machine, Hole and Faith No More.

As she'd surprised Bob the day before, Amy knew he was likely to be home already. Waiting to catch her and have another go at her. It wasn't worth the hassle even though the longer walk was especially unwelcome on Tuesdays. Her bag was always really heavy as she had French and History and both had stupid, massive textbooks.

Amy hated learning French with a passion; the teacher was a dick and who needs to give a window a gender? But she liked the idea of knowing the language. French was a sexy language. She imagined she could seduce someone a bit more sophisticated than Jake by whispering something French in his ear. She could seduce someone older. Someone a lot older.

She loved Jake, of course, she meant it when she said it. She had his name carefully stencilled onto her bag with Tippex, and when she imagined the future, he was in it. But over the last few weeks she had begun to see the differences between them more and more.

Jake, with his wide smile and deep-brown puppy-dog eyes, was so easy to spend time with, so gentle. But in the time they'd been going out, he'd barely plucked up the courage to put his hand inside her school shirt. They spent whole lunch hours kissing in the top field, and one time he'd climbed on top of her but she'd got a dead leg and had to move and he was so flustered he barely spoke for the rest of the day.

It had been months and months and she was still a virgin. It was getting embarrassing. She hated the idea of being last, hated losing at anything.

Frustrations aside, Amy hoped Jake had skipped judo club so he could come and meet her. Jake and his younger brother, Tom, were driven home from school every day because his snooty mum worked as the school secretary. His family lived in the double-fronted houses of Royal Avenue. He was always back before Amy reached the two-bedroom terrace house in Warlingham Road where she lived with Bob and her mum, Jo.

Jake's mum, Sue, didn't like Amy. It was like she saw her as someone who would corrupt her precious baby. Amy liked the idea that she was some kind of scarlet woman. She liked the idea of being any kind of woman.

Amy Stevenson had a secret. A secret that made her stomach lurch and her heart thump. None of Amy's friends knew about her secret, and Jake certainly didn't know. Jake could never know. Even Jake's mum, with her disapproving looks, would never have guessed.

Amy's secret was older. Absolutely, categorically a man. His shoulders were broader than Jake's, his voice lower, and when he made rude remarks, they came from a mouth that had earned the right to make them. He was tall and walked with confidence, never in a rush.

Her secret wore aftershave, not Lynx, and he drove a car, not a bike. Unlike Jake's sandy curtains, he had thick, dark hair. A man's cut. She had seen through his shirts that there was dark hair in the shallow dip at the centre of his chest. Her secret had a tall, dark shadow.

When Amy thought about him, her nerves exploded and her head filled with a bright-white sound that shut out any sense.

Her secret touched her waist like a man touches a woman. He opened doors for her, unlike the boys in her class who bowled into corridors like silver balls in a pinball machine.

Her mum would call him 'tall, dark and handsome'. He didn't need to show off, didn't need to boast. Not even the prettiest girls at school would have thought they stood a chance. None of them knew that Amy stood more than a chance. Way more.

Amy knew that he would have to stay a secret, and a short-lived one at that. A comma in her story, nothing more. She knew that she should keep it all locked in a box; perfect, complete, private, totally separate from the rest of her soundtrack. It was already a memory, really. Months from now she would still be snogging Jake at lunchtime; bickering with her friends; coming up with excuses for late homework; listening to Mark and Lard every night on Radio One. She knew that. She told herself she was cool with that.

The feeling Amy got when he touched her hip or brushed her hair out of her face was like an electric shock. Just the tips of his fingers made her flesh sing in a way that blocked out everything else in the world. She was both thrilled and terrified by thoughts of what he could do to her, what he would want her to do to him. Would they ever get the chance? Would she know what to do if they did?

That kiss in the kitchen, with the sounds of the others right outside. His hands on her face, a tickle of stubble that she'd never felt before. That one tiny kiss that kept her awake at night.

Amy turned into Warlingham Road and the ritual began. She

put her bag down on the crumbly concrete wall. She unrolled the waistband of her skirt so it was no longer hitched up. She decanted her things, finding her Impulse 'Chic' body spray and cherry lip balm.

Amy shook the spray and let a short burst of sweet vapour fill the air. Then, after looking around self-consciously, she stepped into the perfumed cloud, like she'd seen her mum do before a night at the social club.

She ran the lip balm along her bottom lip, then the top, kissing them together and then dabbing them matt with her jumper. On the off-chance that Jake was waiting, she wanted to be ready, but not make it obvious that she'd tried.

Amy's Walkman continued to flood her ears. 'Do You Remember the First Time?' by Pulp kicked in and Amy smiled. Jarvis Cocker smirked and winked in her ears as she set everything back in the bag, shifted it to the other shoulder and continued down the road.

She saw Bob's van in the road. Amy was twelve doors away from home. As she squinted, she could make out a figure walking towards her.

She could tell from the way the figure walked – confident, upright, deliberate – that it wasn't Jake. Jake scuttled around like a startled crab, half-running, half-walking. Amy could tell from the figure's slim waist that it wasn't Bob, who was shaped like a little potato.

When Amy realized who it was she felt a rush of nausea.

Had anyone seen him?

Had Bob seen him?

How could he risk coming to the house?

Above everything, Amy felt a burst of exhilaration and adrenaline thrusting her towards him like iron filings to a magnet.

Jarvis Cocker was still talking dirty in her ears; she wanted to make him stop but didn't want to clumsily yank at her Walkman.

She held her secret's gaze, biting her lip as she clicked every button until she crunched the right one down and the music stopped.

They were toe to toe. He smiled and slowly reached forward. He took one earphone, then the other from the side of her head. His fingers brushed her ears. Amy swallowed hard, unsure of the rules.

'Hello, Amy,' he said, still smiling. His green eyes twinkled, the lashes so dark they looked wet. He reminded her of an old photo of John Travolta washing his face between takes on *Saturday Night Fever*. It had been printed in one of her music magazines, and while she thought John Travolta was a bit of a knobhead, it was a very cool picture. She'd stuck it in her hardback Art and Design sketchbook.

'Hello...' she replied, in a voice a shade above a whisper.

'I have a surprise for you... get in.' He gestured to his car – a Ford Escort the colour of a fox – and opened the door grandly like a chauffeur.

Amy looked around, 'I don't know if I should, my step-dad's probably watching.'

As soon as her words were in the air, Amy heard a nearby front door, and ducked down behind the Escort.

A little way up the pavement, Bob set his tool bag down with a grunt. He exhaled heavily as he fumbled for his keys and opened his van. Unaware he was being watched, Bob lumped the tool bag into the passenger seat and slammed the door with his heavy, hairy hands. He waddled around to the driver's seat, heaved himself up and drove away with a crunch of gears, the back of his van shaking like a wagging tail.

As excited as Amy was, as ready as she was, a huge part of her wanted to sprint off up the road and jump into the van, safe and young again, asking Bob if she could do the gears.

'Was that your step-father?'

As she stood up and dusted herself down, Amy nodded, wordless.

'Problem solved, then. Get in.' He smiled an alligator smile. And that was that. Amy had no more excuses, and she climbed into the car.

CHAPTER TWO

Alex

7 September 2010

The hospital ward was trapped in a stillborn pause. Nine wordless, noiseless bodies sat rigidly under neat pastel blankets.

Alex Dale had written about premature babies, their seconds-long lives as fragile as a pile of gold dust.

She had written about degenerative diseases and machine-dependents whose futures lay in the idle flick of a button. She had even detailed every knife-twist of her own mother's demise, but these patients in front of her were experiencing a very different living death.

The slack faces in the Neuro-disability ward at the Tunbridge Wells Royal Infirmary had known a life before. They were unlike the premature babies, who had known nothing but the womb, the intrusion of tubes and the warmth of their parents' anxious, desperate hands.

The patients weren't like the dementia sufferers whose childlike stases were punctuated by the terror of memories.

These rigid people on Bramble Ward were different. They had lived their lives with no slow decline, just an emergency stop. And they were still in there, somewhere.

Some blinked slowly, turning their heads slightly to the light and changing expression fluidly. Others were freeze-framed; mid-celebration, at rest or in the eye of a trauma. All of them were now trapped in a silent scream.

'For years patients like this were all written off,' said the auburn-haired ward manager with the deepest crow's feet Alex had ever seen. 'They used to be called vegetables.' She paused and sighed. 'A lot of people still call them that.'

Alex nodded, using scrappy shorthand to record the conversation in her Moleskine pad.

The ward manager continued. 'But the thing is, they're not all the same and they shouldn't be written off. They're individuals. Some of them are completely lacking awareness, but others are actually minimally conscious, and that's a world apart from being brain dead.'

'How long do they tend to stay here before they recover?' Alex asked, poising her pen above the paper.

'Well, very few of them recover. This summer we had one lad go home for round-the-clock care from his parents and sister, but that was the first one in years.'

Alex raised her eyebrows.

'Most of them have been here for a long time,' the manager added. 'And most of them will die here too.'

'Do they get many visitors?'

'Oh yes. Some of them have families that put themselves through it every single week for years and years.' She stopped and surveyed the beds.

'I'm not sure I could do that. Can you imagine showing up week in, week out and getting nothing back?'

Alex tried to shake images of her own knotty-haired mother, staring blankly into her only daughter's face and asking for a bedtime story.

The ward manager had lowered her voice; there were visitors sitting at several beds.

'It's only recently that we've realized there are some signs of life below the surface. Some patients like these ones,' she gestured to the beds behind Alex, 'and I'm talking a handful across the world, have even started to communicate.'

She stopped walking. Both women were standing in the centre of the ward, curtains and beds surrounding them. Alex raised her eyebrows, encouraging her to continue.

'That's not quite right, actually. Those patients had been communicating all along, the doctors just didn't know how to hear them before. I don't know how much you've read, but after a year, the courts can end life support if they're being kept alive by machines. And now with the cuts...' the manager trailed off.

'How terrible to have no voice,' said Alex, as she took scribbled notes and swayed, nauseated, amongst the electric hum of the hospital ward.

Alex was writing a profile piece for a weekend supplement on the work of Dr Haynes, the elusive scientist researching brain scans that picked up signs of communication in patients like these. She hadn't met the doctor yet and was skidding towards her deadline. A far cry from her best work.

There was one empty bed in the ward, the other nine quietly filled. All ten had identical baby-blue blankets within their lilac-curtained cubicles.

Inside those pastel walls, nurses and orderlies could hump and huff the patients into a seated position, wipe their wet mouths and dress them in the clothes brought in from home and donated by arms-length well-wishers.

A radio fizzed from behind the reception area, as chatter and 'golden oldies' alternated with each other. The barely audible music jostled with the sighing breaths of patients and the beeps and whooshes of machinery.

In the furthest corner of the ward, a poster caught Alex's eye. It was Jarvis Cocker from Pulp, limp-wristed and swathed in tweed. She strained to see the name of the magazine from which it had been carefully removed.

Select magazine. Long-dead, long-forgotten, it had been the magazine of choice throughout Alex's teens. She'd deluged the editor with unanswered letters begging for work experience, back when music seemed to be the only love anyone could possibly want to read or write about.

The dark-blue uniformed manager who'd been showing Alex around had been snagged. Alex spotted her talking quietly and seriously with the watery-eyed male visitor of a patient in a stiff pink house-coat.

Alex soft-shoe shuffled closer to the corner cubicle. Her shins seared with pain from her morning run, and she winced as she quickened her steps. The thin soles of her ballet pumps ground into her blisters like grit.

Most of the patients were at least middle-aged, but the cubicle in the corner had a queasy sense of youth.

The curtains had been half-pulled across haphazardly, and Alex stepped silently through the large gap. Even in the dark of the cubicle, Alex could see that Jarvis Cocker was not alone. Next to him, a young Damon Albarn from Blur mugged uncomfortably at the camera. Both had been carefully removed from *Select* some years ago, dust tickling their thumbtacks.

The scene was motionless. The bed's blanket covering a peak of knees. Two skinny arms lay skew-whiff on top of the starched bedclothes, tinged purple, goose-pimpled, framed by a worn-in blue T-shirt.

Alex had avoided looking directly at any of the patients so far. It seemed too rude to just stare into the frozen faces like a Victorian at a freak show. Even now, Alex hovered slightly to the side of the Britpop bed like a nervous child. She gazed at the bright-white equipment that loomed over the bed and scribbled needlessly in her notepad for a bit, stalling until she could finally let her eyes fall on the top of the young woman's head.

Her hair was a deep, dark chestnut, but it had been cut roughly around the fringe and left long and tangled everywhere else. Her striking blue eyes were half-open and marble-bright. With Alex's long, pony-tailed dark hair and seaside eyes, the two women almost mirrored one another.

As soon as Alex let her eyes fall on the full flesh of the woman's face, she recoiled.

Alex knew this woman.

She was sure of a connection, but it was a flicker of recollection with nothing concrete to call upon.

As her temples boomed with a panicked pulse, Alex built up the courage to look again, mentally peeping through her fingers. Yes, she knew this face, she knew this woman.

It wasn't that long ago that Alex's powers of recall would have been razor sharp, a name would have sparkled to light in a blink. A mental Rolodex gone to rust.

Alex heard thick flat soles and heavy legs coming towards her apace. The penny dropped.

'So sorry about that,' the ward manager was saying as she puffed over. 'Where were we?'

Alex span to look at her guide. 'Is this..?'

'Yes it is. I wondered if you'd recognize her. You must have been very young.'

'I was the same age. I mean, I am the same age.'

Alex's heart was thumping; she knew the woman in the bed couldn't touch her, but she felt haunted all the same.

'How long has she been in?'

The manager looked at the woman in the bed and sat down lightly on the sheets near the crook of an elbow.

'Almost since,' she said quietly.

'God, poor thing. Anyway,' Alex shook her head a little. 'Yes, sorry, I have a couple more questions for you, if that's okay?'

'Of course,' the nurse smiled.

Alex took a deep breath, gathered herself. 'This might sound like a silly question, but is sleepwalking ever a problem?'

'No, it's not a problem. They're not capable of moving around.'

'Oh, of course.' said Alex, pushing strands of hair away from her eyes with the dry end of her pen. 'I guess I was surprised by the security on the ward – is that standard?'

'We don't sit guard on the door like that all the time, just when it's busy. Other than that, we tend to stay in the office as we have a lot of paperwork. We do take security very seriously though.'

'Is that why I had to sign in?'

'Yes, we keep a record of all the visitors,' said the manager. 'When you think about it, anyone could do anything with this lot, if they were that way inclined.'

Alex drove slowly into orange sunlight, blinking heavily. Amy Stevenson. The woman in the bed. Still fifteen, with her Britpop posters, ragged hair and girlish eyes.

As Alex slowed for a zebra crossing, a canoodling teenage couple in dark-blue uniforms almost stumbled onto the bonnet of her black Volkswagen Polo, intertwined like a three-legged race team.

Alex couldn't shake the thought of Amy. Amy Stevenson who left school one day and never made it home. Missing Amy. TV-friendly tragic teen in her school uniform; smiling school photo beaming out from every national news programme; Amy's sobbing mother and anxious father, or was it step-father? Huddles of her school friends having a 'special assembly' at school, captured for the evening news.

From what Alex could remember, Amy's body was found a few days later. The manhunt had dominated the news for months, or was it weeks? Alex had been the same age as Amy, and remembered the shock of realizing she wasn't invincible.

She'd grown up thirty minutes away from Amy. She could have been plucked from the street at any time, by anyone, in broad daylight.

Amy Stevenson: the biggest news story of 1995, lying in a human archive.

It was 12.01 p.m. The sun was over the yardarm; it was acceptable to begin.

In the quiet cool of her galley kitchen, Alex set down a tall glass beaker and a delicate wine glass. Carefully, she poured mineral water (room temperature) into the tall glass until it kissed the rim. She poured chilled white wine, a good Reisling, to the exact measure line of the wine glass and put the bottle back in the fridge door, where it clinked against five identical bottles.

Water was important. Anything stronger than a weak beer or lager would deplete the body of more moisture than the drink provided, and dehydration was dangerous. Alex started and finished every afternoon with a tall glass of room-temperature water. For the last two years, she had wet the bed several times a week, but she had rarely suffered serious dehydration.

Two bottles, sometimes three. Mostly white, but red on chilly afternoons, at home. It had to be at home.

As Matt had stood in the doorway of their home for the last time, carrying his summer jacket and winter coat with pitch-perfect finality, he had told Alex that she 'managed' her drinking like a diabetic manages their condition.

Alex's rituals and routines had become all-encompassing. Staying in control and attempting to maintain a career took everything. There was nothing left for managing a marriage, much less enjoying it.

Alex hadn't expected to be divorced at twenty-eight. To most people that age, marriage itself was only just creeping onto the horizon.

She could see why Matt left her. He'd waited and waited for some inkling that she would get better, that she would choose him and a life together over booze, but it had never really crossed her mind to change. Even when she had 'every reason' to stop. It was just who she was and what she did.

They had met during Freshers' Week at Southampton University, though neither of them could tell the story. Their collective memory kicked in a few weeks into the first term, by which time they were firmly girlfriend and boyfriend and waking up in each other's hangovers every day.

Drinking had cemented their relationship, but it wasn't everything, and it became less important to Matt over time. They talked and laughed and did ferociously well throughout their courses, (his Criminology, hers English Literature) partly through frenzied discussion, partly through competitiveness. From the very first month, it was *them*. Not he or she, always them.

It had been nearly two years since the decree absolute, and she still defaulted to 'we', her phantom limb.

Every afternoon, before the first glass touched her lips, Alex turned off her phone. She had long closed her Facebook account, cleaned the web of any digital footprints that could allow drunken messages to Matt, his brothers, his friends, her ex-colleagues, anyone.

Alex had a few rules come the afternoon: no phone calls, no emails, no purchases. In the dark space between serious drinker and functioning alcoholic, there had been no rules. Cheerful, wobbly pitches had been sent to bemused editors; sensitive telephone interviews had taken disastrous, offensive paths; Alex had vaporized friendships with capitalized, tell-all emails and blown whole overdrafts on spontaneous spending sprees. And far worse.

Things were better now. She was getting semi-regular work, she owned her own home. She'd even taken up running.

At least once a week she planned her own death, and drafted an indulgent farewell letter to Matt and the child she'd never planned, the child they would now never have.

She sat down at her desk and opened her Moleskine notepad. 'Amy Stevenson'.

Alex had a story, and it was far more interesting than the one she had been sent to write.

CHAPTER THREE

Jacob

8 September 2010

Jacob loved his wife, he was sure of that most of the time, but when she talked for forty-five unbroken minutes about an extension they didn't need and couldn't afford, the lies felt slightly softer on his conscience.

He watched Fiona's mouth moving, forming the words so resolutely. There were just so many of them, so many bloody words, that they blended into one, ceaseless noise.

Her pink mouth was now entirely for talking. How long had it been since those lips had softened for a kiss? Or whispered something sweet in his ear?

'Are you even listening to me?' Her fierce brown eyes filled with salt water, ready to burst their banks without notice. How long had it been since they'd made each other laugh until tears squeezed from the corners of their eyes?

'Of course I'm listening.' Jacob pushed his half-finished cereal bowl away, trying desperately not to be outwardly aggressive, or passively aggressive, or break any other unwritten golden rule.

When Jacob and Fiona had first met, they talked about everything. Well, almost everything. She had fascinated him, she always had so much to say and he liked to hear it.

As boyfriend and girlfriend they had sparred, joked, talked into the next morning. On their wedding night, they had failed to consummate the marriage, wrapped in each other's words until they realized it was the next day; Fiona's legs tangled in her ivory dress train, faces sore from smiling and laughing, sobering with the sun.

But Fiona had stopped asking about his work, stopped expecting to be told anything. Now they wrangled over inane household topics, and not much else.

When had it happened? At the start of the pregnancy? Before?

She had certainly been myopic about ovulation dates and optimum positions, but she had still been Fiona, they had still laughed and talked.

It went beyond disinterest.

Fiona used to grill him, question the who, where, when of meetings and social activities, cross-referencing what she was told with diary dates, previous conversations, outfits he'd chosen, throwaway remarks.

'So exactly who is going to this Christmas party then? How come it's not wives and girlfriends? It's normally wives and girlfriends... are any *wives and girlfriends going?'*

Maybe she didn't care now. Fiona had her little nugget growing in her belly, and nothing else mattered. If so, that flew in the face of the Fiona he had fallen in love with, the Fiona he had married. And for all the pressure that had led to it, he had been over the moon when the second blue line appeared on that fated stick many months ago. Terrified, but over the moon.

Now, sitting at the tired breakfast bar, he watched his wife unsteady on her feet. Her sense of balance had been eroded over the last few weeks as her belly had ballooned with a new urgency.

Jacob sighed. Every conversation nowadays led to this topic: the small, hellish kitchen.

The new kitchen extension would fix everything: the storage problem, the tricky access to the garden, where to keep the pram, tension in the Middle East.

The new extension was everything. And if Fiona didn't get it, however impossible the sums were, the world would explode. He couldn't be entirely sure that it was his baby in that cartoon belly, and not a ticking time bomb.

The 1930s semi in Wallington Grove, Tunbridge Wells, had seemed like a palace when they moved in, just two years ago. It had taken prudence, abstinence and overtime to save a deposit, and the newly-weds had agreed that work and salary had to be the main focus for at least three years; they had to feed the machine. Fiona had agreed wholeheartedly, absolutely, that the mortgage was a stretch; it would take two full-time salaries to service it, and they both must do their bit.

Some eighteen months later, after a concentrated campaign veering from the subtle to the tearful, they had started to try for a baby and conceived almost instantly. And now the baby needed an extension.

'Fi, look, I'm sorry, I'm not trying to be shitty but I really have to go. I've got some really awful meetings today and my head's all over the place.'

'Sure,' she said, 'whatever.'

She didn't ask for more than that. Why didn't she ask for more than that now?

They both needed to leave. Fiona for work as a graphic designer, Jacob for the hospital, where he did not work.

CHAPTER FOUR

Amy

18 July 1995

Amy buckled into the passenger seat and looked across at him. He caught her looking and smiled, just briefly, the corners of his mouth twitching as he looked back to the road. As he changed gear, he brushed her skirt further up her thigh with the palm of his hand, sending a shiver across her shoulders.

Amy wasn't used to such direct attention. Jake would skirt around while he built up courage until the frustration became so loud in her head that she had to make the move instead. What she really wanted, what she was pretty sure she wanted, was for someone to desire her, to really want her. Someone to just *take charge*.

She looked at his hand clamped on her knee as he stared dead ahead at the road. Dark hairs were peeking out from the end of his shirt cuff, and his fingernails were clipped into perfect straight lines.

He had been her knight in shining armour just weeks before. Appearing around the corner and whisking her away from that bloody man. Jake had already zipped past in the back seat of his mum's car, strapped in tightly. Her friends had gone off cackling about something and she'd been left to run the gauntlet of that creep and his pleas. Again. Amy had sworn at him and told him to leave her alone. Eventually he'd slunk away, hissing under his breath and kicking loose pieces of grit into the road. Her shoulders had sagged with a mixture of relief and regret, tears falling hot.

And then her secret had appeared, right there in the street near her school, bold and tall and striding towards her. He'd swept an arm around her waist and led her into a gateway, brushed the hair out of her eyes and asked, 'What's wrong? Can I help?'

'It's my dad,' she'd said, and started to cry.

'What about your dad?' he'd asked, gently lifting her chin so her wet eyes were gazing up at his frown.

'Does he hurt you?'

'No,' she'd sobbed, 'no, it's nothing like that. It's not my dad I live with.' She'd wiped her eyes with her fingertips. 'Bob's my step-dad. I'm talking about my real dad.'

'Listen, fathers are complex beasts. It's not your fault, okay? Let me give you a lift home and you can tell me all about it. Alright, Amy?'

'Alright.'

He'd opened the passenger door for her, and she'd melted into the seat.

He hadn't laid a finger on her that day and she'd not stopped wishing he had.

CHAPTER FIVE

Alex

8 September 2010

Alex Dale woke up with dead legs and a clammy forehead. She didn't remember throwing her duvet off the bed, but it was discarded between the mattress and the wall.

She was lying on the side nearest the door. 'Matt's side'.

In the abandoned space next to her was a dark, wet oval, sharp to the nose. She was wearing her pyjama top, not her bottoms, which lay further down the sheet in a wrinkled, dank pile. She had absolutely no recollection of putting them on, or taking them off.

Alex didn't feel ashamed any more, it was too commonplace to keep reacting. As long as she was correctly 'managing' herself, no-one would be in her bed so there were no reflections of disgrace to worry about.

The morning routine of stripping the bed, binning the Dry-Nites pad, bundling everything into the washing machine, double-dosing the fabric conditioner, padding naked back up to the bathroom to flannel wash her legs… it was normal now. Autopilot.

Before she could talk herself out of it, she pulled her running things over still-damp skin, grabbed her water bottle, tucked her key into her bra and ran out the door.

Putting one leg in front of the other, then the other leg in front of that. If she could do it once then she could do it for half an hour.

As the morning grew in front of her, she jogged slowly and steadily along the narrow pavements of her quiet corner of Tunbridge Wells. Little dogs skittered out of her way and she jumped into the road to avoid pushchairs dangling with changing bags and other weaponry.

She'd done them all: 5Ks, 10Ks, half-marathons. Never a marathon, though. Marathons deserved respect. Sobriety. On jogs and races she ran slowly and steadily, competing against no-one but the desire to stop. Her name was listed on hundreds of race results. Alexandra Dale, unaffiliated senior woman.

Back home and showered, Alex made poached eggs on toast for breakfast. Lunch would be liquid, and dinner would be light. Sometimes, dinner was whatever she could tear with her hands and shove into her mouth, swaying in the kitchen.

At 10.20 a.m., Alex pulled her Polo into the Tunbridge Wells Royal Infirmary car park and found a space in the furthest corner, under the shadow of an old oak tree. Still seated, she dug around in her bag, enjoying the smell of rich leather that rushed to greet her.

She controlled her condition fairly successfully now, but the divorce two years ago had thrown her from the wagon and straight onto the centre of the tracks, where she stayed for three or four weeks.

Several spending sprees had ripped through the last of her savings before she finally grabbed the reins back, although the

Chloé Paddington handbag was one drunken Net-a-Porter purchase she didn't regret so much; it was beautiful.

Alex blanched as she flicked the driver's mirror down to reflect her grey face. She rubbed a palm's worth of moisturiser into her sallow skin and painted on a complexion. She added a rosy blusher glow along her sharp cheekbones and used a pink and brown eyeshadow palette to fool the mirror that she had warm, sparkly eyes rather than black holes.

Lip gloss, powder and paint; she was ready to do her job.

'Alex, thank you so much for your patience, I'm sorry we've had to break arrangements the last couple of times.'

More like five times, thought Alex, as she smiled warmly and shook Dr Haynes's hand.

His hands were perfect doctor's hands: cool and soft.

'No problem, I know you're very busy.'

Dr Haynes, the leading expert on vegetative states, closed the door softly and gestured to a battered leather chair in front of his paper-strewn desk.

Alex sat down, jumping as a rush of air trumpeted its way out of a hole in the upholstery.

Dr Haynes's office was the professional equivalent of a teenager's bedroom. On a sagging office chair in the corner lay a pile of abandoned, crumpled clothes. A CD player perched precariously on a shelf, its drive drawer open like a yapping mouth. Various certificates and awards were dotted around the walls, the skewiff frames taking the edge off any gloating.

On the dark wooden desk sat a dusty laptop with a tangled cable and a photo frame with its back to Alex. Piles upon piles of paper teetered like jerry-built skyscrapers.

Aware that she had been staring while Dr Haynes sat waiting, Alex hurtled into her prepared spiel.

'Dr Haynes—'

'Call me Peter.'

She smiled. 'Peter, the hospital were kind enough to send your biography over and, of course, I've read up about your work. But I'd love to know what drives you to explore this area of medicine?'

Peter Haynes exhaled and leaned back in his own battered leather chair. He looked Alex in the eyes, breathing deeply before raising both his elbows and cupping the back of his head.

Alex knew that the doctor was forty-one, but he looked older. He had deep ridges under his bloodshot eyes and his eyelids were a translucent dove-grey. His sort-of-curly, sort-of-straight hair resembled a guinea pig sitting on his head, digging its paws into his face.

'The thing is, Alex, I don't really think about my work as an area of medicine to be explored. I think it's more about exploring people. It's important because people are important and you don't become a doctor if you don't value human life.'

Alex nodded and gestured for him to carry on.

'The stuff I'm doing now fascinates me because it challenges our understanding of the line between consciousness and death.'

When he spoke, the twitching and awkward grimaces that had punctuated his small talk disappeared. Peter Haynes lowered his hands again and flexed his fingers on the scratched desk.

Alex wondered if this was a rehearsed monologue. She didn't care if it was, so long as she got the quotes she needed and could push on to asking about Amy Stevenson.

'When it comes to our understanding of the mind, we're doing a poor job. I don't mean psychology, I mean the nuts and bolts biology of the brain and how that governs behaviour, thought and communication. There's so much we don't know, but as soon as someone loses the ability to communicate in the ways that we're prepared to accept, they're lost to us.'

The fire in Peter's eyes cooled, he slumped back in his chair and seemed to look through Alex to the door.

'Is it true that about forty percent of diagnoses of vegetative states are incorrect?' Alex asked, hoping to show that she had done her research.

'Oh, numbers, you journalists are obsessed with headline numbers.' He waved his hand dismissively through the air.

'We don't know. But we do know that a large chunk of people who used to be called "vegetables" actually have functioning minds. Maybe a fifth, maybe more; for every scientist you find that thinks it's a fifth, you'll find another who dismisses the whole damn idea.'

'I'd love to understand how you actually recognize communication. You say they can communicate, but not in the way we're accustomed to, so what does their communication look like?'

'Well, they have the capacity to think and to want to project those thoughts. It's a little like a computer intranet – do you know what I mean by an intranet?'

'Yes,' Alex said, hoping the explanation only required a very basic understanding.

'Okay, so within an intranet you have information moving around and you can interact with that data – or memories, thoughts – but you can't share that data outside of the intranet. It's a closed loop, if you will.'

'Got it,' Alex said.

The doctor paused. 'Have you? Yes, well, these patients have data in there, they have memories, and they have a network of thoughts whizzing around, they just can't share them outside of that closed loop. So it's down to us, if you'll pardon the stretched analogy, to hack into that network and see it working for ourselves.'

'And how do you do that?'

'Brain scans – MRIs mainly. We take a look at the patients' brains at rest and we capture which of the parts of the brain are lighting up. Very few of them, generally. So then we start to ask things of the brain. We ask it to imagine and to remember. We ask simple things that will be easy for even a mildly functioning brain with some everyday memories to work from. Sometimes, especially in the younger patients who were active more recently, we'll ask them to imagine playing a sport such as tennis.'

'And can all the patients do this?'

'No, and it's really sad when you see that all the lights are out. But on the other hand, you can't imagine the sheer joy of seeing a supposedly vegetative brain light up and show imagination, memory and willingness to take part. And you see, Alex, that's what I'm in this for.'

'So can you tap into any of their original ideas and memories or just watch them reacting to stimuli?'

'Well, here is the really exciting stuff, especially for the patients' families. Once we identify a number of different parts of the brain and how to generate a response in those, we can start to ask questions and tell them to imagine playing tennis for 'yes' or lying in warm water for 'no'. Essentially, they can have a conversation with us, albeit a simple one.'

'That's incredible. So can all the patients that show this cognitive function communicate like this?'

'Sadly not, in fact very few can, but the more we understand about the process, the more we can help the others.'

Alex bit her lip and the tingle of blood helped to focus her mind. 'Peter, I'd like to ask about a specific patient of yours. When I was last in the ward, I noticed that you were treating Amy Stevenson.'

She glanced at his face for signs of a reaction, but he remained impassive.

'I'm the same age as Amy,' Alex continued, 'and I grew up here, so I remember her abduction really vividly now. I feel bad admitting it, but I had forgotten all about her.'

'That's perfectly normal,' the doctor interrupted. 'All life can possibly do is move on around these patients.'

'Well, yes, I suppose... But when I left here the other day, I couldn't stop thinking about Amy and her situation. I'd really like to write a follow-up piece on her case and I'd love to ask you or your staff some questions about her story.'

Alex held her breath.

'That wouldn't be a problem in theory,' he paused, looking briefly at the door. 'There are lots of limitations on what my staff could tell you about Amy though, as she's protected by confidentiality like any other patient.'

'I'm not interested in muckraking or upsetting her family. In fact, if you've got contact details for her parents, I'd really like to talk with them too.'

Dr Haynes fixed his eyes on Alex. Tilting his head slightly quizzically, he said: 'Amy doesn't have any family.'

Alex sat back in her chair. She had hoped the hospital staff would act as a go-between and give her a leg up with the relatives.

'I remember her mother on the news though. What happened to her?'

Peter stood up suddenly so that the wheels of his chair squawked sharply.

'Her mother died some years ago, not long after Amy was attacked. Maybe a year...'

'Oh... Oh, I'm sorry,' Alex said, offering condolences to no-one, 'what about the step-father?'

'I have no idea. But if you'd been accused of trying to kill your step-daughter, would you stick around?'

The doctor was blunt, but he was absolutely right; precious few families could survive having a child torn from them, much less like that.

'Would you be able to pass my details to her next-of-kin?' Alex asked, reaching into her bag for a business card.

'Amy doesn't really have a next-of-kin. She's the responsibility of the hospital trust and, ultimately, the local authority.'

The more Alex learned, the more crushed she felt. Amy had been a normal, healthy teenage girl, walking back from school to her family home.

'God, this is just so sad,' Alex blurted. 'I suppose you become desensitized to these sorts of details in your job?'

Peter Haynes was edging closer to his door, work clearly on his mind, but he seemed affronted. 'I don't think you become desensitized. I haven't, anyway. There are weeks I want to lock myself in my office and not face them.'

'You keep things in boxes though. You have to or you couldn't do your job properly. I suspect being a reporter is much the same, psychologically speaking...'

Alex wanted to make it clear that she really wasn't a reporter, but thought better of it.

'What I *can* tell you about Amy,' continued Dr Haynes, 'is that she breathes by herself, she has awake time and she sleeps, she is off the feeding tube and we've registered a degree of brain activity that shows she is not "brain dead" as the papers used to love calling her.'

Alex scribbled on her notepad. 'So has she done the yes and no tennis experiments?'

Peter Haynes frowned a little. 'We've tried. We registered an ability to imagine, but the brain responses were somewhat haywire, and she became extremely distressed. You certainly couldn't interview her via an MRI scan, if that's what you were getting at. Not in her current condition.'

'No, I hadn't even thought of that at all. I mean, it would be amazing if it could happen but I understand if it can't.'

'It can't,' he said emphatically. 'Now we have visitors who come and sit with the patients and talk to them and that seems to have a slight effect on Amy, but having gone through such a high level of trauma, we haven't run many more tests on her. We're still taking things slowly as she's prone to shock. Having no next-of-kin slows things down too.'

Something buzzed sharply on the doctor's belt.

'Sorry, Alex, but I'm wanted in another part of the hospital.'

'I really appreciate you giving me your time. I'll let you know when the article is published.'

As Alex shook Peter's perfectly dry, smooth hand again, she wondered if he ever read his own press, if he would read her piece on Amy Stevenson. If she managed to get it published. If she managed to get it written.

The doctor had bolted in the opposite direction, and Alex headed to Amy's ward before she could talk herself out of it.

The doctor's office lay at the heart of a coil of corridors, which eventually opened out into a main walkway. The shiny floors squeaked under every footstep, and the smell of chemical hand cleanser prickled Alex's nose. She couldn't begin to calculate how many ill people there were right now, all coughing and complaining into this same block of warm air.

As she came to the thick double doors of Bramble Ward, Alex dropped a big gloop of disinfectant hand gel so it sat like ketchup in her palm. She rubbed it slowly and carefully into her skin.

Alex pushed the doors open, passed the empty reception desk and tiptoed quietly up to the open office door. Giving a gentle knock, she waited for the nurses inside to finish their conversation. Inside, the radio was burbling with mid-morning local news updates. A breezy voice announced the arrest of a wanted rapist, the results of a successful school fundraising event and the timescale for extended roadworks on the A21.

After a minute or so, she knocked again. Eventually one of the nurses came out as Alex had made a fist to knock one last time.

'Oh, sorry, you should have knocked,' said the nurse, despite looking straight at Alex's unfurling fist.

Alex tried to peer into the office to see if the ward manager she'd met last time was in there, but she was nowhere to be seen.

'I don't think we've met. I'm Alex Dale, I'm a journalist. I visited before because I'm writing about Dr Haynes's work.'

'I'm Gillian Radson, and I wasn't aware there'd be journalists on my ward today,' replied the nurse, pursing her lips.

'I've just been interviewing Dr Haynes and he's agreed that I can write a piece on one of your patients, Amy Stevenson.'

'I'll have to check that with him,' replied the nurse.

'Sure,' said Alex, 'but while I'm here I wondered if I could sit with Amy?'

'She has someone with her at the moment.'

Alex tried to see into the corner cubicle but there were pillars in all the wrong places. 'I didn't think she had any relatives?'

Nurse Radson crossed her cardigan over her chest, folding her thick flat arms. 'He's not a relative. He's one of our sitters.'

She sighed at Alex's blank expression. 'Volunteers. They come and spend time with the patients.'

'Oh, okay. Maybe I could speak with him?' Alex suggested, opening her bloodshot eyes as widely and innocently as she could manage.

Alex sensed the answer was no, and that if the nurse could speak freely, the answer would be more like 'fuck off.'

'Wait there,' she sighed, 'I'll go and ask.'

Nurse Radson, with her apple tummy upholstering the tight, sexless striped blue uniform, marched off towards Amy's cubicle.

Inches at a time, Alex shuffled along so that could see Amy's curtains clearly, noticing the man's foot tapping under the gap.

The nurse pulled the curtain back sharply and Alex could see that a tall, sandy-haired guy was sitting on the bed, holding Amy's hand. He was wearing a blue hoodie with a hospital-issued visitor's badge dangling from his neck. As the sitter dropped Amy's hand, Alex could see the nurse stooping to talk in his ear. The man and the nurse both shot Alex a look at the same time. After a minute, the nurse came back over to where Alex was trying to look nonchalant.

Perhaps weighing up whether to complain about Alex moving from her original spot, the nurse shook her head and said, 'I'm sorry but he says the volunteering he does here is personal and he'd rather not talk to you.'

'Can I have a quick word and explain that I can interview him anonymously?' Alex tried.

'No, look...' The nurse took a deep breath, her irritation barely concealed. 'I'm sorry but that won't be possible. He gives his time out of the goodness of his heart and he's a nice man.' She rolled the words around her mouth slowly. 'I'm not going to risk his goodwill by letting people bother him when he's already said no.'

Knowing when to call it quits, Alex passed the nurse her card to give to the sitter, just in case, and slinked back out of the ward. It was almost noon now anyway, and she needed to get home.

CHAPTER SIX

Jacob

8 September 2010

Jacob's heart raced. He had been sitting with Amy for too long, he knew that. Nonetheless, he hadn't expected that nosy nurse to yank the curtains back so suddenly.

He hoped it wasn't obvious that he was holding Amy's tiny hand, something he didn't do with most of the patients he sat with.

As casually as possible, Jacob uncurled their fingers and dropped her hand, palm facing up, fingers bent.

Gillian Radson was full of her usual bluster: 'I'm sorry to interrupt but there's a journalist over there and she wants to talk to you,' she puffed.

Jacob was still recovering from the interruption. 'A journalist wants to talk to me? Why would a journalist want to talk to me?'

'Don't worry,' soothed the nurse, 'she's writing an article about one of the doctors and she's interested in this one's story. She wanted to sit with Amy but I explained that you were with her so she asked to speak to you.'

In unrehearsed synergy, Jacob and the nurse both shot the journalist a look.

Jacob had been thoroughly unprepared for this. He stared at the nurse, waiting for her to tell him what to do.

'Don't worry, you don't have to talk to her, I can get rid.' Nurse Radson smiled.

'No-one knows I come here,' he faltered. 'Volunteering is a private thing and, to be honest, I come here in work hours and I could get in a bit of bother if it got back to my boss.'

The corners of Nurse Radson's mouth twitched.

As he watched her thick buttocks heave up and down like piston engines, marching back to the visitor, Jacob finally exhaled. He stood up, and slowly and quietly tugged the curtains to a close again. Then he sat back down, picked up Amy's skinny hand and pressed its cold skin to his face.

He said nothing because there was nothing new to say, but he closed his eyes and drank in her almost vanished smell. With the lightest touch he kissed her paper-thin skin and slowly laid her hand palm-down on her stomach.

After stroking her newly brushed hair and coughing away the lump in his throat, Jacob backed out and took a long blink.

He was ready to leave, but Jacob couldn't let Amy be his last patient. There were currently nine patients, so he let Amy be his seventh and chose the two nearest the door as penultimate and final.

There was an extra incentive to do it this way, as patient number eight – Claude Johnson, sixty-two – had an incredibly devoted wife. Nine times out of ten she would be there, holding Claude's red-raw hands, talking to him about last night's Coronation Street or rolling her eyes about the neighbours. Jacob would offer to sit with Claude, to give Julie Johnson a break, but she never accepted.

Patient nine, Natasha Carroll, was a happy ending. She was forty-two, and still striking. Her hair was a light gold, with delicate greying strands that sparkled silver in the sunlight.

Natasha had been in this ward for a few years and before that she had been in intensive care. Jacob remembered the day she was transferred in. At the time, he had been sitting with Joan Reeves, since deceased. It wasn't long after he and Fiona had returned from their honeymoon and the fading tan on his hands had looked ridiculous against Joan's lilac-white skin.

Today, Jacob sat down on the chair next to Natasha's bed. He placed his vending machine Dr Pepper bottle – its inch of brown liquid now warm and unwanted – on the small beech bedside cabinet.

Natasha had been propped on her side slightly, her eyes open and peaceful. Her knees pointed towards Jacob's chair. Golden hair lay slightly matted at the back but curled in waves around her neck and mouth. With the sunlight oozing through the nearby window, she looked like a stained-glass Madonna.

'Hello, Natasha,' Jacob said in hushed tones. He pulled the curtains casually, leaving them askew so that the nurses could see him going about his business, behaving breezily.

He knew more details than he wanted about some of the patients' backgrounds, mainly from their abandoned partners. About others, like Natasha, he knew very little.

She looked so peaceful bathed in the pastels and whites of the hospital. She wore a dressing gown that looked like cashmere or something similar, and silk pyjamas from a collection of similar pyjamas that he knew was several pairs deep.

Some of the patients Jacob had sat with over the years had faces filled with trauma. Gargoyles bearing the weight of witness. Not Natasha, who looked like a contented house cat, totally assured of comfort and safety.

Over the years, Jacob hadn't seen anyone else visit Natasha, but every once in a while a new vase of incredibly expensive-looking flowers would appear at her bedside, and birthday cards would tumble over themselves annually.

He talked in his hushed but sing-song hospital voice, telling Natasha all about Fiona's baby bump, and his job. Talking to her about things he never broached with Amy.

Natasha lay coiled, silently purring while Jacob listed the names Fiona was currently favouring for the baby (Archie and Harry for a boy, May and Elvie for a girl). Time passed easily, and the steady flow of one-way conversation and the simplicity of Natasha's expression helped take the strain out of the overall hospital experience.

It was past noon and his time was up. Smiling at Natasha a final time, Jacob swept up his Dr Pepper bottle and breezed to the clunky yellow bin, swinging its lid up and dropping the bottle inside with a thud.

Attracted by the noise, Gillian Radson bustled over, cardigan flapping.

'Jacob,' she puffed. 'I'm glad I caught you.'

She smiled knowingly into Jacob's frown, waiting just a few seconds too long.

'The journalist left this card for you. She seemed quite insistent that you might change your mind about talking to her.' The nurse pressed the sharp corners of the business card into Jacob's sweating hand.

'Well, okay. I'll see you next week then.'

As Jacob paced out, pushing the double doors of the ward with some force, he looked down into his palm. The card was thick with slightly embossed lettering in a thick black typeface.

ALEX DALE
Freelance journalist
Tel: 07876 070866
Email: alexdalewrites@gmail.com
15 Axminster Road, Tunbridge Wells TN2 2YD

CHAPTER SEVEN

Amy

18 July 1995

Amy bit her lip, tasting the tiniest trace of cherries. She stared up at him from under her hair. Still wearing her uniform, she could feel her knickers cutting into her leg where they'd been pulled out of shape, a new sting between her thighs, the smell of rubber and sweat on her fingers. Under her legs she felt a baby-soft duvet.

This was without a doubt the worst thing she'd ever done. The meanest, the most secret.

Poor Jake. He didn't deserve this; he was such a gentle, trusting boy. Just a kid, and she punished him for not treating her like a woman. She hadn't really enjoyed being treated like a woman.

She heard the soft patter of socked feet in the hall and gasped. A shadow crept under the door and scurried away, and the distant sound of bedsprings twinkled. Amy looked up at him for reassurance.

'Don't worry,' he said, in his deep drawl. 'The others won't be back for hours.'

Amy sat up, snapping her knees together. 'I thought we were alone.'

'Don't worry,' he smiled, 'he knows what's what. We won't be disturbed.'

Her secret was out of place in this room. A dog-eared box of Lego sat on top of the wardrobe, a framed *Star Wars* picture hung above the bed. It was pretty neat, and smelled like sweet musk mixed with a tinge of new sweat.

Amy stood up with a sigh and straightened her skirt. It had happened. Finally. And now she just really wanted to be with her mum, to have a bath and pretend to be a kid for a little longer.

'I need to get home or I'll get in trouble.'

'Let's get going then.'

'It's fine, thanks. I'd like to walk.'

'No, Amy,' he shook his head. 'Let's give you a lift.'

CHAPTER EIGHT

Alex

8 September 2010

Alex made it home at 12.28 p.m. and parked just outside her terraced house. She was painfully late. Her feet throbbed. Her eyes and throat were dry from concentrating in the strip-lit hospital air.

The stone path to her crimson front door was short, but every step pinched her ankle bones while her black dress tangled around her knees. All she wanted in the world right now was to sink into the cool dark behind the closed curtains.

The house had belonged to her mother but Alex hadn't been raised in it. Her mother had moved back to Tunbridge Wells from Spain when the first cracks appeared in her memory, and dementia was whispered about in breathy, broken English.

Alex's mother had wanted to be on home soil, wanted to be near a hospital whose name she could pronounce, and near familiar roads and avenues that she thought she'd be able to find her way around, no matter how bad it got.

It got bad very quickly.

Alex had moved in for the last months, while dementia punched permanent holes in her mother. She watched her only parent turning inside out, while Matt stayed in their rented flat in south London. When her mother moved into the hospice on the hospital grounds for her bitter end, Alex went too. She'd chronicled the experience in a weekly column for the *Sunday Times Magazine*, 'Losing Mum'. Her most intimate, private agonies were also the most lucrative.

After Alex's mother died, Matt moved in and the couple had tried to make the terraced house in Tunbridge Wells their home.

Leaving London was easy. For Alex, at least. She only lived in the capital because the newspapers were based there, not out of any affection for the place.

But Matt had loved living in London, working for the Met Police, surrounded by the constant hum of crime and punishment. He relished buzzing around in an anonymous hive, where nobody outside of his home or station knew his name.

Alex couldn't bring herself to sell the place. The house was all that was left, apart from a few bits of jewellery and clothes. Her mother had shed everything else when she had packed up and moved to Andalucia some years before.

Coming back to England and choosing that house was the last major decision Alex's mother had made. The last major decision she had been capable of making, and Alex couldn't overturn it. Not yet.

The furthest Alex could go was remodelling the two-up, two-down with some of her inheritance money. Matt unhappily but dutifully followed.

They'd barely lived there six weeks before Matt was back in London.

Alex had pored over every microfilm clipping she could find on Amy Stevenson, then printed and organized them into sections. So much of it was identical agency copy, topped and tailed for the different papers, but even excluding duplicates, the clippings from the first two weeks after her disappearance filled a whole archive box.

The *Mirror*, 20 July 1995

MISSING TEEN FEARED ABDUCTED

Scores of local residents are searching for missing schoolgirl, Amy Stevenson, 15, who disappeared on her way home from Edenbridge Grammar School in Edenbridge, Kent on Tuesday.

Amy's parents, Jo, 34, and Bob, 33, raised the alarm at 9 p.m. on Tuesday but were told by police that the teenager was likely to have run away.

Jo and Bob told the *Mirror* that their daughter was a happy teen and would not have run away, claiming that none of her clothes or belongings were missing.

Police began searching the nearby area after Amy failed to appear at her home in Warlingham Road, Edenbridge, the next morning.

Fears are mounting that Amy may have been abducted and police are appealing for any witnesses who saw a man, woman or several adults approaching Amy between 3.30 p.m. and 4.30 p.m. on Tuesday, 18 July.

Amy is five foot four inches tall, slim with long brown hair and blue eyes.

Amy was wearing a navy-blue skirt, short-sleeved white blouse and black shoes with a wood-effect wedge heel. She was carrying a black nylon and rubber Kickers rucksack, and was last seen with her navy Edenbridge Grammar School jumper tied around her waist.

If you have seen Amy or saw anything suspicious in the Edenbridge or wider Kent area, call Crimestoppers on 0800 555 111.

Amy's parents were initially treated as a unit. Within a day or so, Bob had become 'Amy's step-father'.

'It's always the step-dad,' Alex remembered a nicotine-yellow news editor telling her once, 'sure as death and taxes, abductions are the step-dad, robberies are an inside job and bodies are found by dog-walkers'.

The Times, 22 July 1995
POLICE ARREST STEP-FATHER FOR ATTEMPTED MURDER
Amy Stevenson's step-father, Robert Stevenson, has been arrested for questioning about the teenager's disappearance. The arrest follows the discovery of an unconscious young woman in woodland near to where Amy went missing.

Police are yet to make a formal statement, but several sources claim it is the missing girl.

Mr Stevenson, 33, had taken part in the search party. It is believed he was less than 100 metres away when the young woman was found...

There had been hundreds of clippings about Bob's arrest, from scathing right-wing columns focusing on step-families and the disintegration of the traditional British community, to flimsy 'eyewitness' interviews with unnamed neighbours presented to all but say guilty in blood-red letters.

The *Star*, 25 July 1995
TRAGIC AMY'S STEP-DAD IN HIDING
Step-dad Robert Stevenson, the main suspect in Amy Stevenson's abduction, has gone into hiding following his release by police...

The clippings thinned out considerably within weeks of Amy being found. The box containing clippings spanning nearly fifteen years was the same size as that for the first two weeks.

The *Sun*, 14 August 1995
STEP-DAD DID NOT ABDUCT AMY
Police investigating last month's abduction and sexual assault of Amy Stevenson, 15, have announced they are formally dropping all charges against her step-father, Robert Stevenson.

The unusual move comes amid fears that fresh witnesses will not come forward if they believe Stevenson, 33, is to blame...

Alex remembered the *Crimewatch* episode about Amy's abduction. By then it was fairly old news.

Alex had watched the programme with her mother, who had taken the opportunity to point out that she had been wholly correct to drill stranger danger into her own daughter from a young age. 'Why was this girl making these bad decisions? How could she have just disappeared in broad daylight?' Her mother had sloshed her whiskey sour as she concluded: 'No, Alexandra, you mark my words, she went off with someone'.

Alex set her two glasses down on the glossy white sideboard. She filled the tall glass with bottled water until it threatened to spill. Carefully, she filled the wine glass with a millimetre-perfect measure of chilled, crisp Chablis. She replaced the heavy-bottomed bottle in the fridge door alongside five identical bottles.

Alex had decided this morning, as she carefully wrote out her to-do list for the day, that she would have just one drink first.

Then she would go to the landline in her bedroom, which was

fixed and not wireless. This would tether her away from the rest
of the wine for the duration of the conversation.

Stalling in the kitchen, Alex stood by the Belfast sink while she
drank. Slow medicinal gulps.

She walked slowly to the carefully arranged desk, picked up
her Moleskine notepad and pen, then an extra pen, and stepped
silently up the staircase.

The dove-grey bedroom was, of course, exactly as Alex had left it,
but its empty chill still surprised her. The wine and the anticipation
brought a giddiness to Alex's gait, and she sat down heavily on the
stripped mattress.

In her notepad, in careful thick black writing, was Matt's mobile
number. She had deleted it from her own phone long ago and had
no memory for numbers, but had managed to track it down on an
old joint insurance policy.

If she was deadly honest, this was her chance to prove that she'd
moved on. Show that she was in control, that she was getting better.
But more than any of that, she just wanted to hear his voice again.

Her stomach lurched as she pressed the keys on her retro
handset. The oppressive dial tone burst repetitively. If he didn't
answer quickly she would—

'Hello?'

For a moment all that came from her mouth was air, a noiseless
whoosh.

'Hi, Matt, it's Alex,' she heard each word echo as she forced
them out.

'Oh... okay. Hello, Alex, how are you?'

'I'm okay, thanks, and I've only had one glass, before you ask,'
she joked, maybe more spikily than intended. As Matt's polite laugh
crackled down the line, she winced.

Matt's low, gentle voice used to be hers whenever she wanted
it. Until two and a half years ago, his voice was on tap for her ears,

whenever, wherever she needed it. She missed him daily. Of her two great loves, he was the healthy one.

'I'm really sorry to bother you, but I thought you might be able to help me with something...' Alex was doing her best impression of professionalism, keeping her register high and clipped. But she knew all too well that Matt would know all too well that her bottom lip was shaking and tears were pooling inside lower lids.

'Okay, well, what's the thing?' he didn't sound overly disturbed; curious if anything. A contrast to the nightly post-breakup calls that Matt had eventually ignored altogether, leaving Alex to babble, hiccup and sob incomprehensibly into his voicemail.

'Well, I've been writing about coma patients, well, they're not really in comas, they're... well, you'd call them vegetables. They're not brain-dead but they can't move or talk. They're not on life-support machines or anything. It's called persistent vegetative state.' she drew breath.

'Okay, I think I've heard of that, we watched something on Five a few months ago,' said Matt.

We? Who are we? Not her right to ask. Not her right any more. Her chest hurt. Alex wished she was on the wireless handset and could run downstairs and gulp down a second, third and fourth drink.

'Ooh, we, eh?' she tried to be breezy as tears fell fat and hot onto her lap.

Matt laughed politely, more of a snort than a laugh. An acknowledgement.

'Well, while I was in the ward I saw a girl I recognized. It was Amy Stevenson, do you remember her from the news? The girl who was kidnapped and attacked and then they found her half-dead a few days later. She lived near me but it would have been on the national news too. Back when we were teenagers.'

'It rings a bell... but what has this got to do with me?' In the background she heard a door slam as Matt sighed.

Alex imagined her mother, hand on hip, eyes rolling. 'Oh this is a sad sight,' she'd say, shaking her head. 'You must learn when to walk away with your head held high.'

Alex had weaned herself off Matt once before, cutting off all contact for both their sakes. Now she was putting the gun in her own mouth and pressing his finger onto the trigger. But there was no-one else to ask. She'd burned all her bridges with his police friends. She tried to tell herself that was why she was calling him.

'Well, it's an interesting one. Her attacker has never been caught, the step-dad was taken in and released, the mum died soon after... This girl has just been stuck in this state for fifteen years, while everyone else has moved on around her. I know it would make a great story, and I know that cold cases are notoriously hard to solve, not that I'm trying to crack the case, but I wanted to see what I could do, see if I could find any new angles to write about.' Alex drew a long breath.

'But where do I fit in?' Matt asked, a slight disquiet to his voice.

'Well, I've got some newspaper clippings from the time, but it would be really good to know things from a police perspective. The lead detective on the case has left the force and I can't find her anywhere. I wondered if you could look up the case for me, see if there's any information that might be useful? Any suspects they didn't track down or—'

'Christ, Alex! You're asking me to pass you confidential documents. I'm a detective! I'd get myself sacked, or worse. What the hell?'

'Sorry, Matt. I didn't mean to put you in an awkward spot, I don't expect you to pass me documents or anything.'

'Well, what are you actually asking?'

Alex didn't know. She'd sorely misjudged Matt's willingness to help her. After everything she'd put him through, she'd still hoped that he'd open himself up like this, just because she asked. She cradled the embarrassment in her belly. Because she still thought of him daily, still dreamed of them together (when she ever dreamed), she'd imagined a mutual connection that was apparently entirely one-sided.

'Just take a look with your detective's hat on. Have a look at the case. It was a long time ago; policing has moved on, so has technology. You might see something that seems iffy.'

Matt made a sort of 'hmn' noise.

'Just have a look, see if you think it's worth exploring, tell me what you can – if anything – and I'll let you know anything I find out before it goes anywhere near an editor. And I won't mention your name to anyone.'

'Oh God, Alex, look, it doesn't really work like that. I can't look up police records and then pass them to a journalist.'

A journalist. She was just 'a journalist'. Of course he couldn't pass information to a journalist. Foolishly, she'd allowed herself to imagine a gradual working relationship emerging. As she'd passed out the night before, she'd even allowed herself to imagine some kind of reconciliation. Memories of her nocturnal naivety made her cringe deeply. After everything she'd done, as if he'd come back.

'Okay, I'm sorry, I got this wrong. I fucked up, I didn't mean to put you on the spot. Look... You don't need to tell me anything that isn't already out there. I'm not a proper reporter, Matt, you know I've not done this stuff before. There must be a lot of information, clues even, just out there in the public domain, but I don't fully know what I'm looking for. Perhaps you could just take a look at the details I've found, and let me know what jumps out at you?'

A pause. 'Maybe.'

'Do you have a pen, Matt?'

Matt always had a pen. Well, he *had* always had a pen. A Montblanc she'd bought him as a wedding gift.

'Her name is Amy Jeanette Stevenson. Date of birth 28 February

1980. She lived on Warlingham Road in Edenbridge, Kent. She went missing on the 18th of July in 1995. Her mum was Joanne Stevenson. Father was unknown, step-dad was Robert Stevenson. He was fingered for it the day she was found but police released him. No-one else was pulled in, according to the press, but I'm guessing they actually grabbed every paedo in a thirty-mile radius.'

'And the rest,' Matt murmured, audibly scribbling on some paper.

Alex's stomach fluttered. As artificial as the situation really was, it felt good to be focusing, digging around. It felt good to be talking to Matt.

'Okay, Alex, I'll see what I can do,' he said. 'Look... you know I said "we" earlier?'

It was a clumsy segue. Alex didn't want to have this conversation.

'It's fine, you don't need to tell me anything.'

'I know I don't, but I'd rather it came from me, I wouldn't want you finding out from someone else.'

'I never see any of your friends or family, I don't see anyone. Don't worry.'

He ignored her protestations and blurted out his news.

'I'm getting married, Alex. I'm getting married and I'm having a baby.'

'With the same woman?' Alex countered, while her heart shattered and her throat furred.

More awkward laughter.

'I'm really pleased for you. Congratulations. What's her name?' She really, really didn't want to know.

'Her name's Jane, she's a police officer at my station so...' Matt stopped.

So she understands.

'So she understands the hours then?' Alex helped him out.

'Yeah, something like that.'

'And when's the baby due?'

'Next month. We're having a girl.'

'Matt, I'm so pleased for you, that's lovely news. Congratulations to you both. So... do you have my number or is it easier to drop me an email if you find anything out about Amy?' Alex dragged her nails along the mattress, moving them up to her leg and digging them into her skin to stay focused. She had to hold it together.

'I've still got your mobile number,' he continued, oblivious. 'And your email address if it hasn't changed?'

'I've never got round to changing it, even though it is a bit cringey.'

'Oh it's fine, it's who you are – Alex Dale Writes.'

'At gmail dot com.'

'At gmail dot com. Anyway, I'll be in touch. It was good to hear from you, Alex.'

'Thanks, Matt.'

'Alex?'

'Yes?'

'What about the... about you, are you looking after yourself? I mean properly? Are you going to appointments?'

'Matt, you don't need to worry about me, okay?'

'Okay.'

Alex put the phone down with a prim click. She lay on the bed, grasped the bare duvet in her fingers and pulled it up over her legs, her belly, her chest, her face. A baby. He was having a baby. With his new wife. A healthy baby and a nice normal wife. Everything he ever wanted and always denied needing.

Twisting the unsheathed duvet around herself until she was completely swaddled, womb-like. Crying, bucking her body, swallowing tears. Howling, Alex contorted and writhed, trying to twist herself away from the pain until she was spent.

Exhausted and nauseous, she threw the duvet from her face and dragged herself from the scratchy mattress like it was cartoon quicksand. She was determined not to think about Matt and his new wife and their new baby. Determined but damned.

The shadows were so long, she didn't know what time it was, or how long she had been lying there.

Alex paced into the bathroom. She peed, washed her face with expensive cleansing wash that made her grey skin squeak, and then cantered quickly downstairs. Down to the glass and the bottle, and the bottle next to that. And a 'fuck it' number of bottles after that too.

CHAPTER NINE

Jacob

8 September 2010

Jacob had spent an hour in the ward and it hadn't been enough. Time is not a good healer. Time is a blank page on which those left behind scribble their regrets and their confessions.

This weekly trip to medical purgatory was taking its toll.

Jacob had sat with Natasha Carroll as his final patient. He had held her expensive porcelain hand in his and felt his eyes grow watery and heavy. She had kept her peaceful expression, a sacred statue with its face up to someone's God.

Natasha Carroll was in a better place. Not philosophically, or religiously, but mentally. Her thoughts were elsewhere, a summer's dream, set somewhere far more cheerful than this clinical tomb.

Jacob, on the other hand, was very much stuck here. After saying goodbye to Natasha and waving to the nurses, he had stumbled out of the hospital and into the bright sunlight. He was not sated but utterly spent by his time with Amy.

Jacob caught sight of his wrung-out reflection in the window. His sandy hair was speckled with a new grey, the skin around his squinting eyes shrivelled like burned plastic. Guilt was rotting him from the inside out.

He'd staggered just a few feet and then sat down heavily on the gravelly, uneven floor outside the old hospital block, which loomed over him like a prison tower.

Cross-legged and perfectly still, shoulders slumped, Jacob's lower back brushed the cool of the crumbling brickwork building. His spine felt anchored. So rooted that if an ambulance suddenly veered towards him, he'd be incapable of moving out of its path.

The morning before the hospital visit had been tough. Fiona was allowed half days off work for midwife appointments, and she'd wanted Jacob to take her for brunch after they went for the check-up. The check-up would finish at around 10.45 a.m. and the surgery was at least ten minutes by car from the hospital, not including parking time. If he'd had brunch with Fiona, he'd not have had any time left to visit. It was that simple. Fiona or Amy.

He had decided that he would avoid the hospital this week. He would avoid Amy. He told Fiona that, yes, it would be lovely to go for brunch together before they both returned to work.

But in the midwife's room at the surgery he had watched Fiona's tummy shiver as the cold gel was dolloped onto the bump; he had held his breath in the half-second before the fetal doppler whooped into life; he had felt his eyes prickle at the runaway heartbeat of his unborn baby.

In a room filled with the very sound of life and potential, he had thought of Amy.

He had thought of Amy's heartbeat, weak and whispering. He thought of her years ago when her broken body was threaded with wires and drips and sustained by great hunks of machinery. Back then her heartbeat was barely audible, the needle that recorded it skittered so sporadically up and down the lined paper that every pause seemed like an end.

Right now, Jacob's unborn baby was gearing up for life, armed with this thundering heart, determined little fists and unspoilt mind.

Meanwhile, Amy lay trapped, souring like milk on a window sill.

Jacob's phone trilled, scattering his thoughts away. Fiona. Jacob shook his head, slapped his face a couple of times and answered. 'Hi, sweetheart, what's up?'

As he spoke, the liquid-gold sunshine prickled all over his bare arms.

'I'm sorry to bother you, I was just a bit worried.'

He cleared his throat. 'You're not bothering me, Fi, why are you worried?'

'You just seemed so choked up at the surgery this morning, and then when you rushed off you were so funny with me. I'm not accusing you or having a go, I honestly don't mind about brunch, but you were off. It was like you needed to be away from us as quickly as possible.'

Jacob swallowed hard. None of this was Fiona's fault, but at least she was an adult; what kind of man was he to run away from his tiny son or daughter?

'Fiona, I'm so sorry. You're right.' He slowed down. He had to remember to pick his words carefully.

'It really got me this morning,' he continued, slowly. 'It was the heartbeat, it was so strong. I was so amazed and so scared at the same time. I don't know why. The closer it gets to the due date, the more I worry that I'm going to let you both down.'

Grey clouds swooped out of nowhere and rushed the sun away, like minders. Shadows raced across the hospital yard and Jacob heard Fiona's voice, 'Jacob, J, don't cry, it's okay, don't cry.' Before he realized it, he was gargling on huge salty sobs and wiping his gritty eyes with his free hand.

'I'm so sorry,' he heard himself burbling, 'I'm so sorry.'

———

Jacob had a scheduled face-to-face in half an hour's time at a client's office near the Sussex border. As he made his way into the hospital car park, coughing away the last of the sobs and wiping his eyes with the flesh of his thumb, he called Marc, his colleague – his junior – and asked him to call the client to postpone.

'Thanks for doing this, mate, I owe you,' Jacob told him. Marc didn't ask what was wrong – of course – but Jacob knew he'd assume it was something to do with Fiona and the baby and Jacob didn't put him straight. Another guilty notch on the cot bed.

He called Fiona again as he was about to start the engine. He told her to blow work off that afternoon – that he was coming home. She sounded so genuinely concerned that Jacob started sobbing again, head on the steering wheel, and had to wait another five minutes before turning the key.

Jacob turned slowly into their road, his black company Audi purring its low whirr. He could see that Fiona's car – their car – was already in the driveway. A big black shining example of another expense they didn't really need and couldn't afford. A seven-seater Volvo XC90, bought on tick the day after their twelve-week pregnancy scan.

They were only having one baby, he'd protested; they were future-proofing, she argued. And before he knew it, he was signing the hire purchase agreement while she stroked her barely there belly and smiled adoringly at the huge car.

His job in field sales for a specialist software company was well paid, but not as well paid as their spending would suggest.

When Jacob and Fiona bought the house, before the baby was a twinkle in its mother's eye, they just took care of their respective bills. He earned more, so he paid a few more. A few months after that, fuelled by two-for-£10 white wine, Fiona had initiated an almighty row, bemoaning the unromantic financial arrangements.

The marriage and the mortgage were not, Fiona had declared, worth squat. The real mark of a life-long commitment was a joint account. Jacob had argued that this would obliterate the romance of secrecy. That he couldn't buy her a present without it coming off their shared balance, printed clearly on a shared bank statement.

'When was the last time you bought me a present?' she'd yelled. 'You just don't want me to see your bank statements!' And with an adolescent flounce, she'd run upstairs, thrown herself on their bed and howled dramatically.

At the time, Jacob was terrified. Who was this woman in their house? The Fiona he'd first met was so cool and in control, and would have rolled her eyes at anything resembling a tantrum. If she ever cried, she cried in secret, in the bath. Only her eyes would give her away, and it took him a long time to learn that. Was that other woman, the Fiona he had fallen in love with, just a siren, drawing him onto the rocks?

After a while, the tantrum had died down and he had heard Fiona moving frantically around their bedroom. He heard drawers open and close, heard the wardrobe sliding open. It took a few minutes to realize that she was going through his things: she was looking for a bank statement.

Jacob had been mystified. He regularly gave her his bank card to get cash out with, or pick something up for him, she could have easily checked the balance or got a mini-statement, so why would he hide his bank statements?

After pouring himself a large whiskey from the expensive Christmas bottle his father, Graham, had given him, Jacob had thrown it to the back of his mouth and trudged wearily up the stairs. He wasn't a whiskey man, and the spirit had burst across his forehead and fogged his thoughts.

He had seen Fiona on the floor on her knees in their bedroom, surrounded by bits of paper, old receipts and bills.

'Where the fuck are your bank statements?' she'd demanded, with eyes so fierce he'd had to look away.

'Fiona, look...' he'd begun, trying to shake the whiskey mist.

'Don't say anything! Don't tell me anything other than where your fucking bank statements are!' Her eyes had burned red and her face was so wet with tears that her shining auburn hair had stuck to it.

He had walked out of their newly decorated bedroom and into their smaller spare room, which had been appropriated as a makeshift office. Slowly, so that he didn't make any mistakes, he wrote down a web address, username, password and PIN.

He walked back into the bedroom, placed the piece of paper next to Fiona's foot and said carefully, 'I haven't been sent paper statements for years 'cos I get them online. Here are my internet banking details so you can see my statements for the last few years and can check my account any time. If that's what you need to do, then that's what you need to do.'

Jacob had hoped this would snap Fiona out of it. Put a stop to this and realize how sad an end to their honeymoon period this would represent.

It didn't work.

For the next three weeks Fiona had audited his every transaction, calling him over to the screen frequently so he could explain every pound and penny. They got a joint bank account after that.

Financially, at least, Jacob had nothing to hide.

————

Jacob didn't know how long he had been sitting outside his house, staring at the back of the big Volvo and gripping his steering wheel with white knuckles.

He knew that Fiona was waiting inside. Jacob opened the front door and walked slowly into the hall. The Fiona on the phone earlier had sounded like his Fiona. Now, with her back to the door so her bump was invisible, she even looked like the old Fiona.

Jacob stayed standing in the hallway. Fiona span around a little unsteadily so that the bump swung into view.

'Hey,' he called quietly, and as she walked to his open arms he saw that she had been crying.

'Fi—' he started, pulling her into a hug.

'Don't,' she answered quietly, 'just cuddle me.'

They stayed locked in a tight hug for a long time, saying nothing.

CHAPTER TEN

Amy

18 July 1995

'You're very quiet, Amy.'

'I feel really bad.'

'You don't need to feel bad, no-one will blame you.'

Amy closed her eyes and turned her head towards the passenger window. Her shoulders faced the door and the seatbelt cut into her chest. No hand on her knee, no murmuring in her ear. Tears began to form and she struggled to hold them in.

'He shouldn't have been there, why was he there?'

No answer came.

'I shouldn't have done this. You won't be able to help me now.' She started to sob again.

'You're overthinking this.'

Sniffing, she scrunched her eyes as tight as she could. These could be her last few hours before the shit hit the fan and she wanted to sink into the darkness of them as much as she could. What would the others say when they heard? Everything was about to change. No-one would keep her secrets for her.

She should never have got into the car. She should never have gone there and she should never have had sex with him. So many things she shouldn't have done in such a short space of time.

Amy opened her eyes and saw the dull brick outskirts of Edenbridge falling away.

'Where are we going? I need to get home.'

'Somewhere nice, you'll like it.'

'I have to go home though, please. Can you just turn the car around?'

'That would spoil the surprise.'

His voice was once the source of such dizzying excitement. That voice, her hanging up the phone with seconds to spare as Bob's key clattered in the lock. Leaving her so flustered she had to scuttle to her room to hide.

Now the voice just sounded mean and patronizing.

'I'm sorry,' she said, turning to face him but unable to make eye contact. 'I don't want to spoil whatever the surprise is but I really have to go home. You can just leave me here if you have to, I can walk.'

'I can't do that, Amy,' he said, and turned to flash her the briefest of smiles.

CHAPTER ELEVEN

Alex

9 September 2010

Alex woke early, a surge of adrenaline forcing her to sit upright before she had a chance to slip back under. Her bed was dry for once and she checked her emails on the phone as she sat on the loo.

As soon as she opened the inbox, she saw Matt's name. The email had been sent at 5.32 a.m., presumably after he returned home from a night shift. Where was home, Alex wondered, realizing she knew so little about Matt's life. His name in her inbox seemed so right, barely exciting ...just... normal.

From: Matthew Livingstone
To: Alex Dale
Subject: Amy
Hey Alex,

Good to talk to you yesterday, forgot to ask what you're up to, sorry about that.

Like I said, I have to be careful, but here are some bits and pieces I found to get you started. Please keep this confidential, I'm trusting you with this.

It seems like there were three main suspects:

1. The step-dad, who you know about. Robert Stevenson, known as Bob, born 22-01-1962. You know as well as I do that it's almost always someone who knows the victim. It's more often birth dads than step-dads, depending on who you listen to, but the step-dad is always going to be in the frame unless he has a cast-iron alibi. They would have bugged him, followed him, gone through every job he'd had, spoken to ex-girlfriends, all sorts. Looks like he was squeaky clean, because they made a big thing of publicly clearing him later, but I suspect the damage was done and most people thought 'no smoke without fire'.

2. A neighbour in the road Amy lived in, John Rochester, known as Jack. Local nonce, peeping Tom, long track record of low-level child abuse, taking pictures in parks, flashing, that kind of thing. He was eliminated as a suspect because he was physically too frail to have assaulted a healthy young girl. The Sex Offenders Register wasn't around in 1995, but he's on it now.

3. Amy used to go to a church youth club. Obviously, we hauled everyone in that was involved with that group: a reverend and quite a few volunteers from the church. It came to nothing, but the investigations turned up some unspent convictions for one of the old boys and he was booted out. There wasn't anything to tie him to Amy, plus he couldn't drive, and it's unlikely Amy was abducted on foot or more people would have seen her.

She had a boyfriend, but he was cleared early on. They'd not even slept together, all very innocent.

Doesn't look like there was anything to find along Amy's walk home. No witnesses once she left her friends in the road outside the school and nothing in her room that offered any clues (although the photos will exist somewhere, but I really can't look for them).

There was a lot less CCTV back then, and no-one reported a car acting suspiciously.

Did you know they'd done a *Crimewatch* re-enactment? Might be one to look into.

The mum, Joanne, killed herself a year or so after Amy was abducted.

The step-dad left the area and changed his name. He's now living in Devon and is known as Robert Bell. You CANNOT tell anyone where you got that from though, seriously. I doubt he's particularly savvy – he changed his name himself, I didn't get that from police records, I got it online – so you may turn up his info on 192.com.

Good luck. And please do look after yourself.
Matt.

As hard as it was not to reply and say everything, Alex sent Matt a friendly but brief thank-you and tried to put the source of the information out of her mind. She knew that he was putting himself on the line just by talking to her about this stuff. No doubt out of pity, which stung.

The paedophile neighbour was almost certainly a red herring, the church guy just sounded unfortunate. And it wasn't the step-dad.

Alex had never been a roving reporter, never wanted to be. But there was something about this static victim that chewed away at her, something that sat just outside of her eyeline at all times.

She had wanted to find out what really happened out of journalistic curiosity. But now that Matt was involved in a whisper of a way, she wanted to nail it. To present him with proof that she still had something about her, besides the whiff of ethanol and ammonia.

Alex carefully worded a letter to Robert Stevenson/Bell, asking him politely to put his side across and help her fill in some gaps for a sensitive feature on Amy. There was one Robert Bell with the right date of birth listed in Uffculme, Devon. With no phone number, no email address and none of the tools of the trade her crime reporting peers would employ, it seemed the only route to reach him.

Two days later, at 2.45 p.m., a man's voice spoke carefully and quietly into Alex's voicemail.

'This is a message for Alex Dale. My name is Bob. You sent me a letter about my daughter Amy. I might be willing to answer some questions but I'd like to talk to you first... I don't use the name Stevenson any more and I'd need to know that you wouldn't publish my name now. I mean, the name I have now. Can you call me back, please, on 07781 257 539? Thank you.'

Bob spoke in an oddly formal voice that sounded rehearsed. Alex wondered how long it had been since he dealt with 'the press'.

''ello?' Bob's voice was gruffer and less practised than on his voicemail message.

'Hello, it's Alex Dale here, returning your call.'

'Thanks for calling me back.' A long pause. 'I got your letter. I don't wanna talk about any of this but I know what you journalists are like and I don't want you turning up at my door.'

Alex was taken aback. Writing her fluffy features and navel-gazing pieces, she tended to forget that to most people 'journalist' meant 'doorstepper'.

'Thank you, but I would never do that. I hope you don't think I'm trying to do anything disrespectful to Amy or your family.'

Bob murmured something.

Alex took a deep breath and trudged on. 'Mr Stevenson, I'd really like the chance to interview you.' She waited a second to gauge his reaction, but silence was the stern reply. Alex realized she'd used his old name.

'I would really like to sensitively portray what happened in your life after Amy was found and get a better understanding of Amy's life in general.'

No reply, but she could hear breathing; she knew he was still there.

'I could transcribe our interview afterwards and send it over for you to look at, to make sure you were happy that I'd written everything accurately? Give you what's called "copy approval"?'

The deeper the silence Bob held, the more Alex was giving up to him. She could never be a tabloid hack, she'd be eaten alive.

'Alright,' came the gruff voice, finally. 'That sounds alright.'

They arranged to meet the following Monday, halfway between Tunbridge Wells and Uffculme, just off the A303. Didn't want it hanging over him, he'd said. Bob didn't want to be seen talking to a strange woman near his home in case his new wife saw, but he hadn't returned to Kent since Jo's funeral, and wasn't about to now.

Alex sat in the arbitrarily chosen Little Chef, convinced she would be stood up.

If she were Bob, would she turn up? Almost certainly not. She'd probably drive up and down the road outside trying to peer in, or perhaps she'd sit in her car in the car park, heart jangling, hiding behind a magazine whenever the Little Chef door swung open. She wondered if that's what Bob was doing now. He was already late.

It was 10.20 a.m., and Alex could feel the dry rot settling in her throat and creeping to the back of her mouth. She had emailed Matt after putting the phone down to Bob. She had kept Matt up to date in a breezy, neutral email that had taken nearly three hours to write and rewrite. He hadn't replied.

While she waited, Alex repeatedly clicked the refresh symbol on her iPhone inbox, but the number of unread emails stayed the same. Zero.

She felt out of place. She was out of place. Her trusted Moleskine notepad and Cross pen at perfect right angles to the table. With her iPhone positioned equally anally next to them, her Ted Baker dress and Chloé handbag, she knew she stood out like a dismembered toe.

The plastic coating on the chairs was peeling off, the table corners looked like they'd been chewed. Discarded nappies had been piled in the corner of the toilet cubicle that she'd used upon arrival.

A doughy-faced young woman of around nineteen was walking around with a warm pot of thin coffee, refilling cups and glaring at people.

Behind Alex sat a foursome of pensioners, all thick middles, nylon T-shirts and red-raw hands.

Three middle-aged men in badly fitting suits sat alone on three different tables, all throwing back coffee, tapping away at old-fashioned mobile phones and shuffling dog-eared bits of paper around. Alex wondered who would ever buy what they were selling.

Bob was now forty-five minutes late, and Alex had received no emails apart from unwanted newsletters and irrelevant press releases. She didn't want to harass Bob, but she wanted him to know she was waiting, and that she understood and would be patient. She sent a text message:

Hi Bob, it's Alex. Just to let you know I'm at the Little Chef so just get here when you can, don't worry if you're caught in traffic, I'll wait.

As she set her iPhone back down on the yellowing table, a short, dumpy man in overalls barrelled through the doors. His greying dark hair had visible comb-marks where he had used gel or pomade, and he had a speckled doormat moustache.

After waiting unattended at the 'wait here to be seated' sign, he walked into the middle of the seating area, obviously looking for someone.

'Bob?' Alex asked quietly, doing the half-stand half-stoop standard to these situations.

Bob span around. His overalls were tight around his buttocks and his belly was like a block, swinging around slightly later than the rest of him. He half-smiled and walked towards Alex.

'Alex? Sorry I'm late...' he trailed off.

Alex gestured for Bob to sit down and looked around for a waitress. The plump, pudding-faced girl with mousy hair was nowhere to be seen but a friendly older woman with a blonde bouffant walked slowly over, smiling.

'What can I get you, sir?'

Bob smiled, warmly. 'Hello, er, yes, can I have a pot of tea and some Jubilee Pancakes, please?' He looked awkward, 'I've not had breakfast yet.'

The waitress – Valerie by her name badge – turned to Alex, 'Can I get you anything else?'

'Actually,' Alex smiled, 'I'll have some Jubilee Pancakes too.'

The room seemed brighter, more sunlit. Alex had finally recovered from the nappy-filled toilet. She'd stopped scowling long enough to remember how she'd loved stopping at Little Chefs on childhood journeys to stay with her mother's various boyfriends and, rarely, to visit her father while his wife was away.

She'd adored the Jubilee Pancakes, and the orange lollies by the till. As a seven-year-old she hadn't even known what a calorie was.

As Valerie left them to it, they both sighed a little, at nothing, as if perhaps they could make this meeting about pancakes and grey tea. A nice little rest stop.

'I'm really pleased you agreed to meet with me, Bob,' Alex started. 'I want you to know that I'm not out to do a hatchet job. I've never written about crime or anything like it before. I mainly write about health, and that's how I came to see Amy.'

In her hopeful letter to Bob she had explained her chance encounter with Amy, but she wasn't sure if he had believed her. She wondered how many offers to 'tell his side' to the tabloids he'd received in the immediate aftermath.

Bob cleared his throat. 'Do I have your word that you're not going to stitch me up or tell everyone where I am?' he asked. His voice still had its gruff edge but he had shrunk a little smaller in his chair.

'You have my word.'

She tried to imagine how Bob would have fared in a police interview. Snarled up with grief over his step-daughter, probably terrified about his wife's ability to cope, being accused of crimes he couldn't comprehend.

Alex and Matt had never seen eye to eye on police matters. Fairly early on in his career he'd stopped talking to her about his shifts, about the terror on interviewees' faces, about the casual decisions he made or the acts he witnessed.

'Bob, I have a recorder on my phone and I'd like to use that because I'm not very fast at shorthand. Would you mind if I did?' Alex asked.

'I s'pose not. I'd rather you recorded it than wrote it down wrong. That's what's done for me in the past.'

Drawing a deep breath, Alex pressed record.

CHAPTER TWELVE

Jacob

10 September 2010

Jacob frequently drove past the shop where he'd first met Fiona. It had changed from a printer's into a pet shop but it still made him smile. Sometimes.

As he drove past today, he tried to shake the memory of this morning, tried to think of the Fiona he'd first met and not the Fiona who demanded to know why he'd deleted the internet history on the computer in the home office. Jacob had just stood there, dumbfounded. He had thought he was being paranoid deleting his Google Map searches, and everything else.

'It's a surprise,' he said.

'What surprise?'

'Well, I didn't want you to see what I'd looked at because I was ordering a present for you,' he said.

She'd rolled her eyes and turned away quickly. 'You should have said you were looking at porn, I'd have believed you then.'

Six years ago, he'd been rushing in to collect some business cards for his boss. Fiona had been manning the till in the print shop, although she told him several times within that first conversation that she was just covering. She was actually a designer and she even had a desk. She designed the business cards and leaflets for local hairdressers and plumbers.

Fiona had astonishing flame-red hair back then. That first day she was wearing a kind of floral patterned dress, a half-cardigan he didn't understand and Converse trainers. He'd have guessed she was eighteen but found out later she was twenty-two. She'd passed him the business cards in a box with a flourish, and before he could stop himself he said, 'You remind me of someone'.

'Someone awesome and hot?' she'd deadpanned, without cracking a smile.

'Yes, that's the one', he'd smiled, and she'd laughed.

'Want to take me to lunch?' she'd asked, without showing a shred of the anxiety she later admitted to hiding really well.

'Um, right now?' he'd asked.

'Yeah, why not, I'm owed a break.'

He'd been running late as it was but he didn't say no. That was the part of the story she loved to hear again and again.

They had paninis and bottles of beer in the Wetherspoons pub near the shop. Nothing like that had ever happened to him before, or since. It was like a cheesy film and he'd not stopped smiling for the rest of the day, partly in bewilderment.

Fiona had listened to bands he'd never heard of, and would push CDs into his car stereo when he picked her up from work. Bands with complicated, ironic names that made him feel out of touch.

'You're such an old man', she'd say, kissing him on the cheek.

'How did a cool kid like you end up in a town like this?' he'd asked her on their first evening 'date' to the bowling alley, where teenagers were throwing chips at each other in the next lane.

'Uni', she said, sipping beer from the bottle as she sat back down after toppling three pins. 'I did my degree at Rochester and then moved here for my shitty job. Don't get me wrong, I'd hate to live here forever but Tunbridge Wells is alright. It's quite arty, not that far from London, the rents are reasonable.'

'You're not as cool as you look,' he told her. Laughing, she'd acted mock-offended.

'No, I'm definitely not.' She'd smiled and rested her head on his shoulder as she took another big gulp of Rolling Rock.

She'd stopped acting quite so cool after that too. The flame-red hair that he loved was replaced by auburn hair with highlights and lowlights and other things he half-listened to her talk about. She looked less like a teenager then, more sensible. He was disappointed and relieved.

She moved into his one-bedroom flat and they spent the weekends and evenings in bed. She made him laugh from his gut. Almost nothing was off the table, and they talked and laughed so late that he was often late for work despite living five minutes' drive away.

Fiona was late for work constantly because she hated her job intensely. She'd made a mistake, she said, doing a marketing degree. She'd applied because it was a sensible thing to do, not because she wanted to do it. She had wanted to do graphic design, be a 'proper designer', but her parents had talked her out of it. So she ended up doing an approximation of the job she wanted, and it seemed to cause her a lot of bitterness.

'I wish I had ambition, or a dream or something,' he told her one night as they quipped over cheap TV and drank even cheaper wine on the sofa. 'I'm so jealous of you for knowing what you want to do.'

She'd laughed sadly. 'I don't know,' she'd said. 'I think it's worse to know what you want and not be able to get it. I envy your crushing lack of ambition.'

'What should I want to be when I grow up?' he'd asked her, mostly joking.

'You're fine as you are,' she'd said. And kissed him for a long time.

A few months later, when he'd walked in on her crying in the bath, he'd offered to lend her the money for a post-graduate graphic design course.

'I've been saving money for years for no real reason. I'd like to use it for something that matters so much to someone that matters so much to me.'

She was speechless for several minutes. For the first time since he'd met her, she stopped talking.

'I don't know when I'll be able to pay you back,' she'd said eventually.

'Then you'll have to stay with me for the long haul,' he'd said, smiling.

Jacob pulled into the car park near the old print shop with more force than he expected. He didn't have long before his next appointment, and he needed to buy a present for Fiona.

CHAPTER THIRTEEN.

Amy

18 July 1995

A thick, instant sweat coated her skin and Amy became slowly aware of her own hair – wet and sharp – digging into her skin and eyes. A trivial discomfort compared to her broken ankle and smashed skull, but it was this scratching pain that made her the most desperate.

She lay on the soil, unable to move, unable to talk her way out of this, sweat cooling in the dip of her back. The dusky scent of the trees filled her broken nose with a thick perfume.

She considered trying to scream. She had tried and abandoned pleading with her eyes as the noise neared her again. There was no hope to be had; if he had wanted to help, he would have. No matter how many footsteps, she was alone.

Her eyes fell upwards as the great murky bruise of blues and greys tumbled overhead. Deep-grey clouds slid across the sky as two white-gloved hands gleamed in the sunlight. Slowly they crept onto her neck. She closed her eyes, waiting for the relief.

CHAPTER FOURTEEN

Alex

13 September 2010

Alex held Bob's gaze as long as she could bear, trying hard to think of this as *just another interview*. After checking the iPhone was recording properly, she looked into her lap at her notes.

'Thanks for agreeing to answer some questions, Bob.'

Bob leaned in towards her, distrustful of the technology, 'It's okay. You know my reasons for talking and I hope you'll respect them.'

Alex nodded.

'Bob, I'd like to go back to the beginning, and ask you a few questions about your first years as a family with Jo and Amy. Are you okay with that?'

'Yes... but you'll have to bear with me if I get a bit upset.'

'Of course I will.' Alex swallowed. 'Could you tell me when you first met Jo?'

Bob smiled. 'It was in the spring of eighty-four, and I was an apprentice plumber at the time. Tony, the old boy I worked for, used to drink in a pub called The Castle and I'd go in there with him lunchtimes and sometimes after work. Jo worked behind the bar and we used to have a bit of banter with each other. She was a bit older than me and I knew she had a little girl, but...' Bob ran a thick hand over his face.

'It's okay, there's really no rush. So Jo was a little bit older than you?'

Bob cleared his throat, leaned in again. 'Yeah, Jo was twenty-two when I met her. We had about eighteen months between us, which doesn't sound like anything now I'm an old codger but at the time we used to joke about it.'

Alex smiled. 'So where was Amy when Jo was working?'

Bob paused, looking upwards briefly. 'Jo was good friends with her neighbour at the time, a girl called Carole. Carole had a little boy who was a few months younger than Amy so they'd take it in turns minding the kids so the other one could work. Things were different then, you left your kids with people. You trusted them. Jo couldn't have afforded to pay anyone to look after Amy.'

Alex looked down at her notes. 'Did Amy's birth father have any contact with her?'

'No. No, he didn't. He'd never met her. He was a brute, a really nasty piece of work. Vicious and violent. When Jo found out she was expecting Amy, she upped and left him, moved to Edenbridge and started again, just her and the baby. She'd told him she was pregnant, and he'd said he didn't want nothing to do with it, with her. And that was for the best...' Bob stared at the cars whipping past the window. 'Anyway, I don't want to talk about that scumbag. It makes my blood run cold just thinking about him.'

'Okay, that's okay. So when did you move in with Jo and Amy?'

Bob tilted his head and leaned in. 'Looking back, it was quite quick but it never seemed it at the time. We'd been going out for about three or four months before I met Amy...'

'It's okay, take your time, it's okay.' Alex found the sight of men crying difficult, and hoped to God Bob held it together or she'd end up in tears too.

'Jo didn't want her to meet anyone that wasn't for real, you know. She didn't want to disrupt Amy's life or get her attached to anyone.

She was such a good mum.' Bob spluttered the words a little. Alex had to stop herself reaching across to hold his hand.

Bob cleared his throat again. 'What was I saying? Yeah, when I met Amy for the first time, I thought she was brilliant. She done me a picture and I read her a story and me and Jo took her to the park down the road from their house. I was skinny as a rake back then, and I showed off walking on my hands. You probably can't imagine that now. We got on straight away and I think that sealed it for Jo really.'

Alex smiled at the image. 'So you moved in?'

'Yeah, well, sort of. I started staying over, and after a few months we decided we should make it permanent. I moved in with them and we all lived in the house that Jo rented. I was doing a bit better by then 'cos I was qualified, and after about a year we'd scraped up a deposit to buy a little place.

'We wanted to do things right, and I got down on one knee, you know, and we got married on the Monday because it was cheaper than the Saturday. Amy was the bridesmaid and Carole and her fella were the witnesses. We moved into Warlingham Road on the Wednesday. We never had a honeymoon but Carole had Amy for the wedding night. Other than that, it was always the three of us. Always. Jo couldn't have any more kids so Amy was everything to us.'

'Did Amy call you Dad?'

'Sometimes, yeah. That's one of the things the police kept asking me. I don't know why but they kept on and on about it. At first she called me Bobby, 'cos that's what Jo called me, then when Amy was about six or seven she started to notice that all her friends had dads or daddies, and she started to call me Dad in front of them. I never pushed for that. At home she still called me Bobby, and then Bob when she got older. She'd call me Dad when she knew she'd done something wrong, or she was...' Bob's voice broke, 'or when she was scared.'

Alex lowered her voice, hoping to hold herself and Bob together. 'How did you get on as she got older?'

Bob leaned back in. 'We always got on great. I know I did her nut in sometimes 'cos I was on at her about things, but deep down I think she knew it was because I cared. She was a bright girl, our Amy, and I didn't want her to piss it away like I did, if you pardon my French. She could be a bit of a daydreamer, and she did silly things sometimes, but she was a good girl.

'She had a nice boyfriend, and I know she and Jo had the talk about all of that, but we didn't have to go on at her much.'

Bob's mouth smiled but his eyes drooped. 'We were always laughing too. Right from when she was small, she'd always have us in stitches. I'd take her out in the van with me when she was little, let her do the gears and all that. Have a little chat. She always cracked me up. They were special times.'

'I know this is really difficult, but you said that Amy was silly sometimes. What did you mean?

'Oh no, I don't want you getting the wrong idea, I just mean the stupid stuff that teenagers do. Walking home in the dark, a bit of drinking, nothing worse than what I done.

'She and her friend Jenny cobbled this plan together once. Jenny said she was staying at ours, Amy said she was staying at Jenny's, and the pair of them got a train to Redhill and went to a disco there.

'Well the reason I know this is because we got a call from Amy about midnight. They'd read the timetable wrong, missed their last train and had nowhere to stay. It was bloody freezing and she was crying and she asked us to pick them up. Which we did, obviously. We was cross with her, don't get me wrong, but I was so glad that she phoned, 'cos a lot of girls wouldn't have. Amy could always be honest with us.'

'She sounds a lot like me and my friends,' Alex lied. 'I know this is really hard but I'd love to hear more about Jo. All I know is what

I've read in the newspaper clippings and what I saw on television at the time.'

'Jo was a diamond, I loved her to bits. She was a brilliant mum and a brilliant wife. We didn't have much but she loved our house and she was proud of everything we did have. And she loved that girl to death. She'd talk about how Amy would do all the things she'd never done. She'd go to college, university even, she'd have a career. She had high hopes for Amy, we both did. But more than anything, we wanted her to be happy.'

'Where was Jo when Amy went missing?'

'She was at work. She worked in a ladies clothes shop in town. She got back at teatime and Amy wasn't there. I got back from a job not long after and Jo was already worried.'

'When did you realize she was missing and not just running late?'

'It got to about seven, and that just wasn't like her. She knew not to miss dinner.' Bob gulped his tea.

'We knew something was wrong, we just knew. There's nothing like it. It's like this icy-cold feeling in your belly. Anyway, I started driving around, knocking on friends' doors that I remembered, driving to school and back, not really knowing where to go. Jo rang all the mums she could think of, got her boyfriend's number and called over and over until someone answered. I think she was hopeful that whole time, you know, thinking they must be together 'cos no-one was there either. Then someone answered and told her they were having some kind of celebration meal and Amy wasn't invited.'

'When did you decide to call the police?'

'It was when I got back from driving around. It was getting dark, probably about nine o'clock by then. They told us to check her clothes and look for a note to say she'd run away. We knew she hadn't run away. Next day, they came over.'

'Did you sleep at all that night?'

'Not a wink. I don't think anyone can understand what it's like for a child to go missing.'

'Did you continue living with Jo after Amy was found?'

'If you can call it that. I don't think Jo really carried on living after she was told Amy was brain dead. That's what we were told, an' all. As for me and Jo, well, I loved her with all my heart, but when the police took me away... the look in her eyes... I don't think any marriage can survive that. What they made her think I'd done.' Bob stared out of the window and rubbed his eyes. A young woman was trying to feed her toddler into its booster seat in the back of her car, little legs rigid in protest.

'When I finally left, Jo barely noticed. The papers said I was hiding, but I wasn't running away from them. I pleaded with her not to do anything stupid but I don't know if she even heard me. And then a year after Amy was found, Jo couldn't take it any more. There was no-one there to stop her and she took her own life.'

Alex stopped the recording and held Bob's hand, trying to ignore the depth of her thirst.

CHAPTER FIFTEEN

Jacob

12 September 2010

Jacob pressed hard on the accelerator and slipped through the junction just as the amber light gave way to red.

Fiona took a sharp breath. 'What's up with you today?'

Jacob didn't answer. He locked his jaw and squinted at the road.

'J?'

'Sorry, what?' He flicked his eyes at her for a split second before turning his frown back to the road.

'J, what's wrong with you? Are you even listening to me?'

'I'm fine, why?' he tried to smooth his expression out.

'You're not fine,' she said quietly, looking dead ahead. 'You're all over the place. I wish you'd tell me what's up.'

'You're worrying about nothing, just relax.'

Swinging the car into Royal Avenue was always difficult.

He wished his parents had left Edenbridge, wished he didn't have to return to its streets. The town had wrapped around him like a duvet when he needed it the most, but leaving home for good was like ripping a plaster off, and the old wounds seeped every time he visited.

He felt guilty that he frequently turned down invitations from his mum, who had always loved him so completely, so protectively. He was the only one left, in any real sense.

As he parked on the crunchy, wide drive and slowly took the key out of the ignition, Jacob wondered if his younger brother, Tom, really would be here for the family lunch. He tried to imagine Tom perching on the edge of his chair, picking at his roast dinner, his black head with its scowling eyes nodding politely at the conversation and asking Fiona if she was having any twinges yet. The picture didn't work.

Tom lived and worked in the Midlands. Within the family, it was referred to as 'Birmingham', but in reality it was a West Midlands wasteland no-one had heard of, burrowing into the backside of Walsall. They'd not visited. Jacob had often texted to offer to drop in when a planned trip took them along Tom's section of motorway. Tom would invariably make excuses, or only receive the text once the trip was over. Each time, Jacob wondered whether Tom was as slow to reply to the teenagers he worked with. Then he would stop himself going down that line of thought.

The last time any of them had seen Tom in the flesh was at Jacob and Fiona's wedding in Lancashire. Several of Tom's planned visits to Kent had fallen by the wayside since. Tom hadn't seemed comfortable in the pretty Lancastrian countryside that framed the wedding. He'd been clearly – and inexplicably – itching to get back to his adopted urban mess.

Jacob loved visiting Lancashire. He loved the warmth and openness of Fiona's family, the work-to-live attitude, the pubs and the big knotty open spaces. He loved the drystone walls in the villages, and he especially loved how relaxed and happy he felt away from Tunbridge Wells. Until he thought of Amy, and then his chest would hurt and his eyes would darken and guilt would pull him back under.

'Hello, darling, come in,' said Sue, Jacob's mother, who was standing on the hall doormat wearing lambskin slippers and kissing Fiona on both cheeks.

As soon as the heavy front door had swung open, Jacob picked up that distinctive smell of 'home'. The Fairy liquid and Comfort fabric conditioner his mother had always used, the dark-pink pot-pourri in the porcelain dish, the Shake 'n' Vac on the carpet, the Pears soap in the downstairs loo, his mother's buttery cooking.

'Hello, Mum,' Jacob said, stooping down to kiss her cheek. Sue was five foot two; he – like both of his brothers – was more than a foot taller.

'Is Tom here yet?'

Sue looked away, her ears turning pink at the tops. She smiled awkwardly and explained that Tom wasn't coming after all.

It's because I'm here, thought Jacob. He couldn't pinpoint exactly when it had happened because there were whole months, years maybe, when Jacob had been completely wrapped up in himself. But at some point, his younger brother who had just always been there, whose loyalty he would never have questioned, had pulled clean away.

Jacob remembered the afternoon Tom moved out with a wince. Although Jacob was eighteen at the time, it had been sixteen-year-old Tom who left home first. Jacob barely noticed. His brother's spiky silhouette had appeared in Jacob's doorway, black dyed hair drooping in front of his eyes. He'd had a big duffel bag over his shoulder, a couple of carrier bags in each hand. Tom had just stood there, waiting, possessions hanging off him. Jacob had looked up and said, 'You off?'

'Yeah,' Tom had said.

'Where you going?'

'New Cross.'

'Oh, right.'

It was only later that night when he walked into the kitchen to find his tear-stained mum eating cold cherry pie from the foil and splashing wine over baby photos that he realized Tom had gone for good.

Jacob's memories of teenage Tom before that night were thin. The remains of toast crumbs in the morning, the sound of mopey music seeping from one bedroom to the next, a door slam. A shadow who had become a lone wolf and stalked away.

Years later, Jacob had tried to build bridges. He had asked Tom by text message to be his best man, had insisted upon it. To his surprise, Tom had agreed, the only condition being that he didn't have to do a speech.

The stag do was held in their home town, a small night with several half-friends from work and university. Many pints into the night, the others drifted away. Jacob had staggered to his feet in the corner of a bar and asked his brother outright what the problem was, did he blame Jacob for something.

'I don't blame you for anything,' Tom had said, looking away.

'I never hear from you, mate.' Jacob had said, without expecting eye contact. 'I don't know what I've done wrong.'

'You've not done anything wrong. Look at you. You've done everything the right way.'

'How do you know that?' Jacob had asked, louder than he'd intended. 'You're not here to see how I'm doing anything.' He'd scuffed his shoe along the sticky floor, pushing himself away and pulling himself back on the brass rail around the bar. 'I miss you.'

Even steeped in beer, the words were awkward.

Tom had paused for a long time. 'You're better off without me,' he said, his words slurring like they were too big for his mouth.

Defeated, Jacob had sloped out of the bar and to the kebab shop next door. After tramping up and down the main street in Edenbridge looking for a taxi without saying another word, the brothers had called their mother. Cradling their cold food, they had been driven to Royal Avenue in silence.

That night, Jacob lay queasily in his childhood bedroom with the sounds of Tom's snoring rattling through the wall. He'd stared into the black, listening as Tom had risen to pee, heard the creaks and sighs as Tom had tried to get comfortable in the narrow bed again. Jacob had closed his eyes and tried to work out what he could say the next day to change things. In the end, he had said nothing.

'It's so good to have you both here.' Sue clasped Jacob's hand over the table, surprising him. Fiona took a deep sip of her faux-wine grape drink.

'I wish we could see you more often,' Sue said, the tip of her nose belying her Sunday dinner tipple.

'We're just up the road,' Fiona interrupted, 'you're always welcome to come over.'

'Thank you, darling,' Sue lifted her hand from her son's and placed it carefully back in her napkinned lap. 'Newly-weds need their space though.'

'Oh God, we're hardly newly-weds,' Fiona said, her eyes struggling not to roll. 'We've been together forever, we really don't need any more space.'

Sue smiled in Fiona's direction for just a moment.

'Well, perhaps I could pop round when you go on maternity leave?' she said, directing her question more to Jacob, who looked at his wife uneasily.

'I'm sure she'd love that, wouldn't you, Fi?'

'Come round any time, Sue.'

'You're welcome too, Dad, now you're retired,' Jacob added, taking a shallow sip of his blood-red wine.

'Thank you very much, Jacob,' Graham answered, swirling his drink. 'Thank you, Fiona.' The older man smiled at Jacob and then, for a little longer, at Fiona, until she blinked first and looked down to carefully cut a roast potato.

'I'm on the court every day at the moment,' Graham continued, looking back at his son. 'Maybe you could join me for a game?'

The court. When Jacob was a young boy, before he'd seen that 'the court' was in reality a slab of ground with white painted lines on it, he'd imagined it to be some grand building where only the brightest, fittest and most manly were allowed to go. Simon had been allowed to go. The next in line to the court's throne. As the eldest, taking his position seriously, he had stood in the hallway, matching white socks with green trim, an upright, silent, knock-kneed version of his father with a miniature racquet.

Jacob had thought it might become his turn at some point, but his turn never came. He remembered Tom joining them a handful of times, but Jacob had judo by then and tried not to feel left out. He'd never mastered any ball sports.

Of course Graham was on the court every day. Graham was a see-saw of health and overindulgence. He drank far too much whiskey and wine but put in hours of intense tennis practice every day. He scooped chunks of gooey gourmet cheese onto yet bigger chunks of white bread for elevenses, but took nine hours' sleep a night, every night. Graham watched any sort of television show, almost indiscriminately, but never had Jacob seen such an appetite for books of every kind. Russian fiction, crime thrillers, academic papers, manuals for cars he no longer owned and had never serviced himself.

Jacob's mother said it came from all those years of commuting, consuming books to make the time pass. Today, of course, an executive's work would start the moment the train left the station – emails on phones, laptops with dongles hanging out – but back then Graham had an hour on the train and half an hour on the Tube, each day, each way.

But Jacob had no interest in any of those things. He didn't trust what he read, for one, and the thought of whacking a ball back and forth, especially against someone with a ruthless instinct and years of training, appealed like a bed of nails.

'Sure thing, Dad.'

CHAPTER SIXTEEN

Sue

18 July 1995

Girls. When Sue first married Graham, she'd imagined them having two little boys and two little girls, alternating like good dinner party table settings. The boys would be rosy-cheeked and handsome like their father, with bright grass stains on their knees. They'd tumble around, kicking a ball and getting up to mischief. The girls would wear matching pinafore dresses, with rosebud lips and bright-blue eyes like little china dolls. While the boys would play football with Graham in the garden, Sue would sit and brush the girls' long hair, tying the tightest, neatest of plaits in matching ribbons.

The girls that her sons had brought home were nothing like her girls would have been. As brash as boys, they flicked their hair around and seemed to have a staggering ability to use their bodies to get their own way, from a ridiculously young age.

Her girls would have been different. Her *girl* would have been different.

Every once in a while she felt a pang for the missing number four. The one that, maybe, finally, would have been pink. But she couldn't complain – she had three strapping sons. Graham had been happy to stop at three anyway. More than happy. But since her first pregnancy, Sue had planned the second, third and fourth.

She'd loved carrying the babies, but Simon's pregnancy held a special magic. The only one bathed in ignorance and plans, nothing but hope.

She'd expected the baby stuff to come easily once he arrived. She'd intended to have him sleeping through the night after a month, planned to snap back into her old clothes thanks to the Jane Fonda workout tapes that she would use while the baby napped. Potty-training, she'd thought, would be done during the baby's second summer and then the next baby would come along. And so she had planned to continue until there were four shiny-faced children, lined up in height order like the von Trapp kids. Boy, girl, boy, girl.

From the agony of his breach birth to Simon's first reluctant day at school, it hadn't gone to plan. Sue had lived in her flannel jumpsuit until six o'clock, barely finding the time to apply make-up before Graham's car pulled into the drive.

A baby with endless needs, Simon would absorb every shred of attention throughout the day and, at the same time, reject it outright. He wanted her eyes on him at all times, until Graham would appear in the doorway and then Simon would frantically look for his gaze.

All the while, Sue had crumbled into a world of loose clothing while Graham's career was in an upswing. He remained handsome and controlled, while she was becoming hollow and scatty.

It had taken two hours of the baby's tears, and sometimes Sue's, to vacuum a room, so she would put the task off again for weeks at a time.

Graham never once complained at the state of the house. But he surveyed it with a slower gaze through narrowed eyes each night, and started to catch the later train home, losing the haste of their early married years.

Eventually, Sue had resorted to carrying Simon under one arm as he suckled milk feverishly, pushing the Hoover with the other, lactic acid shooting up to her shoulders.

She'd relied on Lean Cuisine in the day and Vesta meals at night, and the rest of the time she had drunk tea by the bucketload and blown smoke out of the window and just stared at her angry, red-faced infant.

It got easier with Jacob, easier still with Thomas, aside from the secret sadness at another blue bonnet. And when Thomas approached play school, talk – Sue's talk – turned hastily to the final piece in the puzzle. The one that would be a girl.

Then, just as Graham appeared to soften toward the idea of having more children, the letter had arrived. Written in calm text on cold paper, it spoke of 'abnormal changes' and 'repeat smear tests'.

'Don't worry,' Sue was told, 'these things often correct themselves, the next smear could be completely clear'.

Six months later, the calm letter was replaced by an urgent phone call from the surgery. From mild to severe changes. Cells were removed and Sue walked home from the cottage hospital tenderly, gingerly, with Thomas clawing at her legs to be carried.

After two years of repeated, failed treatments, Sue made the decision one day while all the boys were in school. Sitting sore in the empty house after another painful outpatient operation. Graham later described it carefully as 'cutting our losses'. The thought of him raising the boys alone was inconceivable. She had to forgo future fertility, the stakes were too high.

The preparation for the hysterectomy was as brutal as the operation. Fistfuls of pills every night, nightmares about being scooped out like a soft boiled egg, crying fits behind closed doors, following women with baby girls around supermarkets, nothing in her basket.

When she woke up after the surgery, head thick with morphine, she just felt empty. She'd stayed that way for a long while.

CHAPTER SEVENTEEN

Alex

14 September 2010

Alex's heels raced to meet their mirrored counterparts, colliding with a loud click. The hospital had recently been the subject of a media-friendly 'deep clean' and everything shined as if polished beyond practical use.

Alex had called several hours before, and with surprising ease had been granted a little more time with Peter Haynes. She was already regretting the high heels, which pinched at her running blisters and slowed her walk.

She knocked on the closed office door, the space inside sounding hollow and empty. After a couple of polite coughs, followed by some not-so-polite coughs and a sharper knock, the door finally opened. The doctor looked a mess. His hair seemed to be clambering over itself and his eyes were wild. As he showed Alex to the worn leather chair again, she noticed that the room was immaculate.

'I'm sorry, Alex, I've been tearing my hair out trying to find something but I don't know where anything is any more.'

Alex wondered if in this case, 'tearing my hair out' was more than just a saying.

To no-one in particular, Peter Haynes muttered, 'Bloody cleaners.'

He sat in the other leather chair, fidgeting like a child with worms.

'Thanks so much for seeing me at such short notice, Peter.'

'That's okay, but I really have squeezed you in, so I don't have long. How can I help?'

'I just have a couple of questions about Amy, then I promise I'll leave you in peace.'

'Alright, Alex, shoot.'

'Well, after Amy was found, some of the newspaper reports seemed to contradict each other. A few say there was no evidence of sexual assault, but others allude to recent sexual activity. That's only via unnamed sources though, never official statements. More or less all of them say there were signs that she'd fought off her attacker.

'I just wondered if – medically – you know which story is correct?'

The doctor held her gaze for a few moments and then walked to a dull-grey filing cabinet next to the brilliantly sparkling window.

Muttering, he opened and closed each of the four drawers in quick succession before returning to the desk empty-handed.

'I'd rather not do this on the computer,' he said, hovering his fingers above the keyboard, 'but I can't put my hands on the hard copies right now.

'Okay,' the doctor continued, 'so let's think this through. You need to know about the examinations that were undertaken when Amy was first found, yes?'

Alex felt her pulse quicken. 'Yes, I suppose so, if that's okay?'

'Well,' Peter Haynes began, 'it's rather a grey area. Amy has no known next-of-kin so she's under the care of the health authority,' he paused, catching up with his thoughts, 'and that means we can take decisions but we can't be seen to abuse that authority.'

He looked up and fixed his eyes on Alex's lips, 'I would never abuse any position of trust,' he said.

Alex sat in silence, unsure what she was supposed to say. Meanwhile the doctor tapped cautiously at the keyboard, like he was cracking a safe.

He cleared his throat. 'I shouldn't give this information out liberally, so anything I say needs to be handled with absolute discretion.' He paused, and Alex held her breath. The doctor was frozen, fingers over the keys. His eyes were locked on Alex in a way that made her wiggle awkwardly in her seat.

'Okay,' he lowered his gaze, half-smiling, 'I'm doing this for you because I think the more people know about these patients' stories, the better. But that relies on you doing a sensitive job, so I'm taking a leap of faith.'

'I promise I'm not out to sensationalize, that's not the kind of writing I do.'

Peter Haynes's neck was newly flushed and he seemed unsure where to start.

'Okay.' Alex scanned her notes. 'Was Amy a virgin?'

'No.'

'Oh, really? Had she recently had sex before she was found?'

'Yes she had, sometime within the previous seventy-two hours, according to this report.'

The secret information thrilled Alex. It was at once revolting and exhilarating.

'Okay, so, were there signs of sexual assault?'

'There were no signs of trauma to the genitals.'

'So she'd willingly had sex?'

'It would appear so.'

'Were there signs she had fought off her attacker?'

'Oh God, yes.' Peter Haynes looked Alex in the eye, furrowing his brow slightly. 'I don't need to look at the records to tell you that. She was still black and blue when she reached me, and I can remember what a state her fingers were in. Most of her nails were broken off and she had a missing tooth where she had tried to bite something. Or someone.'

Alex felt the exhilaration subside; now she just felt sick. Amy had managed to fight just enough to condemn herself to purgatory.

'And there were signs of strangulation?'

'Yes, strangulation, deep bruising, some internal injuries to the abdomen, splintered bones, several cracked ribs...'

'Was she beaten with something or did the examiner think he'd done it with his bare hands?'

'It doesn't go into that here, but from what I saw, I'd say she'd taken everything he had. Kicks, punches, whacks with objects, who knows?'

'Christ. So Amy was as close to death as the papers made out when she was found?'

'Probably worse. There's a lot of information on her record that was marked as confidential and wouldn't have been in the papers.'

These details would have been gold dust to a prosecutor, thought Alex, and they wouldn't have given them away in case that jeopardized a trial. It felt like just another quiet injustice that Amy never got her trial. 'Do you think her attacker thought he'd killed her when he left the scene?'

'Who knows?' the doctor held her gaze. 'I mean, really, who knows what a person like that thinks?'

Alex nodded. The uncomfortable facts were seeping through her notes like a dark ink blot. It appeared that Amy had willingly had sex with someone, and been attacked soon after. She was there, in part, through trust and choice.

'So she wasn't raped or sexually assaulted – it was a non-sexual attack?' Alex clarified.

'That's what it looks like on paper here, but there would be far more details in the police forensic reports, I'm just looking at the bare medical facts, just the stuff we needed to know to treat her.'

'Could the person she had sex with, and the person who attacked her be two different people?'

'Yes, possibly,' Dr Haynes said, looking at his watch, 'it's possible that she willingly had sex with someone then toddled off and ran into someone else who attacked her, but—'

'But no-one ever came forward who'd had consensual sex with her,' Alex finished, 'right?'

'Right.'

Alex continued: 'So she had a boyfriend, but apparently they hadn't slept together, so—'

'I can't really help there. I wouldn't have the first clue about my patients' love lives. I can barely get my own on track.' Peter Haynes looked up briefly and then back down at his hands.

'Oh yes, of course,' Alex said, feeling her cheeks flush a little. 'Just one more thing. Last time we spoke, you said that Amy had shown signs of brain activity. Does that mean there's a chance she might wake up?'

'Well, she's not asleep, Alex. That's an important distinction. This isn't a coma. She's in there somewhere, to a small degree at least. But after fifteen years, and with such slow progress, I think it's highly unlikely she'll ever improve.'

'But it's possible?'

'Well, it's not entirely impossible. But it's highly unlikely. Alex, I'm sorry to rush you but I really need to get to another meeting.'

'No problem at all. And thanks so much, you've really helped iron things out. It's been hard to piece together from news clippings alone.' Alex stood up quickly and grabbed her bag.

'Well,' said Dr Haynes, extending a hand to shake. 'You can't trust everything you read in the newspapers.' And he smiled, holding Alex's hand for a little too long.

———

The chill of Dr Haynes's touch stayed with Alex long after she'd left the office and made her way, blinking, out of the hospital and into the sunlight.

She walked with sore feet to her car which was parked in the furthest corner, shaded by a thick tree. She sat down with a heavy 'hmph' and placed her bag, notepad and phone on the empty passenger seat. She yanked off her shoes and lobbed them into the back footwell. For just a few moments, she closed her eyes in the cool quiet. Her head thumped and she was sweating last night's Sauvignon Blanc.

Her conversation with the doctor had stitched together some assumptions – and scorched some guesses where they lay. As grotesque as she found the crime, the challenge of unpicking Amy's final conscious moments stirred a small part of her, buried beneath the rubble.

Once upon a time she had been a bright young thing, a celebrated writer, a 'voice of her generation'. She'd had fire and ambition and ideas... now, most of the time, she felt dry. Her moment had passed, and she'd spent it wasted.

Alex slipped her flip-flops on and headed home. Her mind churned over her conversation with the doctor as she drove slowly past the white villas of Tunbridge Wells's moneyed 'village' area.

Amy Stevenson was not a virgin. Apparently she'd willingly had sex in the run-up to her attack, and it must have been protected sex. According to the clippings, there was no forensic evidence, no semen. That word only used in Biology class and sex crime reporting. He – they – must have used a condom, but that would have been long lost or long hidden.

Police had been satisfied that Amy and her boyfriend hadn't slept together. So it looked like Amy had been unfaithful to him.

Poor kid, thought Alex. Did he know one of her last decisions was to betray him? Would he have known that her 'rape' wasn't rape? Or perhaps he did find out, and was so angry that he attacked her? It seemed far-fetched, but it was foolish to discount anything.

It had become a standard phrase in the later newspaper clippings, 'the rape and attempted murder of Amy Stevenson'. But that wasn't the real story. The police couldn't have known that when they brought Bob in, could they?

Alex shook her head; it was a far knottier story than she'd thought. The best article she could produce would be found in the kinks left behind from unpicking those dusty knots. She wished she could skip to the end and find out what those kinks looked like.

As she pulled up outside her brick terrace, heaved her bag out of its seat and walked along the path, Alex checked the time: 11.22 a.m. The deadline for her piece on Dr Haynes loomed in a few days and she had thirty-eight minutes of work time left today.

Getting to sleep wasn't a problem for Alex. Her eyes tended to shut as the final sip tingled her lips. It was often a battle of will over fatigue just to get the glass of water down her neck before passing out in a deep, throaty sleep.

It was staying asleep that was hard.

Since Matt had left, the witching hours were wakeful. As the tide of alcohol washed away, a heightened sense of self-preservation kicked in. Every night brought different creaks and groans to the little house, a variety of imagined terrors creeping in the shadows.

Alex's night nerves were almost as irrational as her childhood fear of ghosts. It was always possible that someone could break in. If they did, it was possible they'd get up to something really sadistic, rather than look for easily pocketed, high-value goods. But it was incredibly unlikely.

By day, Alex recognized her paranoia for what it was. By night, she often spent the darkest hours rigid and dripping with sweat.

After a late supper of toast dipped into a half-eaten tub of hummus, she'd fallen into a hot, dreamless sleep at around 10 p.m., chickpea residue on her hands.

At 1.37 a.m., Alex burst into total wakefulness, on high alert, convinced that someone was in the house.

Downstairs, the polished floorboards creaked in rhythm with the wind and the trees tapped warnings on the windows.

She heard slow, deliberate movements around her living room. She heard the first three steps of the staircase sigh underfoot, then nothing. Alex remained paralyzed, making no moves to investigate or protect herself. She just lay prone, peeping from under the covers, coated in thick sweat.

A few more noises echoed through the house. A little way up the street a car door slammed, and a cat shrieked as gears crunched and tyres drove away.

Two hours passed, with Alex dry-eyed and sweating. Finally, having braved a trip to the bathroom and finding no harm on the way, she was able to fall back into a just-below-the-surface slumber.

The morning found Alex red-eyed and agitated. Since her mid-twenties she'd lost the ability to lie in, and felt a strong pull to the thick black coffee her kitchen offered.

Her bed was dry, but the bedding still smelled bittersweet. Out of habit, Alex stripped it all off and padded downstairs. As she set the coffee machine off with a sigh, something caught her eye.

Her Moleskine notepad was closed. She was sure she'd left it open on the first blank page, weighted by her pen. Now it was tightly shut.

The sudden sound of blood in her temples drowned out clear thought as Alex thundered back up the stairs and into the bathroom, locking the door as quickly as her shaking fingers could manage.

Was she imagining it? It had been a heavy night. Could she have returned to her notes before bed, thumbing through and then closing the notepad tight? It was all possible but it didn't feel right.

Alex stepped into the scorching shower. Nothing added up, but she was an unreliable witness. Supper was a blur and she definitely didn't remember coming to bed. She couldn't be sure of anything. Fuck.

As the thick steam and the sharp, citrus zing of the shampoo cleared her sinuses, Alex's heart rate slowed and she became more sure that she must have been the nightcrawler. Thinking logically, there really was nothing else to suggest anything undue had happened. The pen could even have rolled out and the notepad snapped closed all by itself.

Leaving her hair wet in the Indian summer heat, Alex threw on knickers, sweatpants and a vest.

Back in the kitchen the coffee was ready, the rich chicory fragrance turning Alex's delicate stomach almost as much as it comforted her. She needed food and had started to make toast when something else caught her eye and made her stop dead, butter knife in hand.

When Alex had inherited the house, she had remodelled the kitchen and the bathroom. She'd stripped the floors herself, painted every inch of wall and replaced the front door. She'd had enough money left to replace the windows at the front of the house and keep a little cash in the kitty.

The back windows were the old sash variety, thick wood with a brass hook and catch. No-one could see them from the street so she'd left them as they were, with some vague plan to update them eventually.

She never opened her kitchen window. Never. But her kitchen window was open. It was definitely open.

The little garden at the back of Alex's house had been untouched for years. It was really just a yard, with a few dead sprigs of once-were-plants and a lopsided whirligig dripping with cobwebs.

Still reeling at the window, Alex jumped as the toast popped up, spinning around instinctively. There was no denying it, the window was definitely open. She fumbled in the 'stuff drawer' by the sink for the back door key.

The lock was stiff, but once outside she could see that the back gate was shut at least, and the catch was down.

She tiptoed closer, her eyes focused on the bolt. With the laughter of neighbours' children in the near distance, Alex inched forward. The bolt had clearly been pulled back, a spider's home broken in the process. But when?

She didn't dare open the gate, but instead yanked the bolt back across and ran straight into her kitchen. She slammed the door, locked it and reached for the cordless phone, unsure who to call.

It didn't look like anything had been taken. Her laptop was on the sofa, her TV was where it always was and she had precious little jewellery anyway. She ran upstairs to check it, but everything was present and correct; even her engagement and wedding rings lay where they had long lived, in the mirrored box on her night stand.

She had to get her head together. It was a long time since she'd felt so vulnerable and violated. But nothing had been taken, and she'd not been touched. As far as she remembered.

As she scrabbled for the back page of her Moleskine and that number in thick, black writing, she knew she was making a mistake.

Alex dialled with shaking hands and walked into the kitchen to pour another strong black coffee.

She lifted the mug to her lips just as Matt answered.

'Hello?'

'Hi, Matt, it's Alex.'

'I know, your number came up on my screen again. What's up?'

'Matt, I'm so sorry, I didn't know who else to call,' she started, her wobbly voice barely more than a whine.

'Oh God, Alex,' Matt hissed. 'It's eight in the morning, what's wrong with you?'

'No, no, I've not been drinking, I'm not... I... Look, I don't know what to do, I think someone's broken into my house.'

She heard a sigh.

'Alex, if you think someone's broken into your house then you need to call the police. Your local police. They'll send someone round.'

'No, Matt, you don't understand, nothing's been taken. I know they won't believe me because nothing's been stolen, but the kitchen window was open and the bolt on the back gate has been moved.'

'Nothing's been taken?'

'Well, no, but I'd left my notepad open last night and it was closed this morning...' she trailed off.

'Alex, no-one has broken into your house. What you're saying is your back gate's unlocked, just like most of your neighbours' back gates are probably unlocked, and your kitchen window isn't closed. It's still warm at night, you probably opened the window yourself and forgot.'

Alex was as certain as she could be that she'd not opened her own window; she'd never opened that window to prevent this precise scenario. She was petrified about forgetting and going to bed with the outside able to get in.

'The police won't be interested unless you've had something stolen or there's actual evidence that someone's been in.'

Matt's measured tone only loosely disguised his annoyance. It was breakfast time at the weekend; he'd probably had to leave his fiancée and step outside of the room, she'd put him in a difficult spot.

'I'm sorry, Matt, I thought you'd understand but—'

'Alex, enough. We're not married any more, and I thought you'd finally got to grips with that. I'm not the one you call now. I was very understanding when you asked me to help with this wild goose chase. I've helped you more than I should have because I felt sorry for you. And if I'm honest, I knew that nothing would ever come of it but—'

'Why not? Why would nothing come of it?' Alex squeaked down the phone.

'Why? Because you haven't seen anything through in years, Alex. Look at yourself.'

'Matt, there's no need to be cruel, I just didn't—'

'Alex,' he hissed. 'I thought we'd stopped all this, I hoped you'd sorted yourself out.'

A pause. A breath.

'You drank away your career, you drank away our marriage, you drank away – you know what you drank away – and now it looks like you've drunk away your fucking sanity. Do yourself a favour and get some help before it's too late. You have to move on. Like I have.'

'Like you have,' Alex repeated.

She'd just started to apologize, as the phone clicked. He'd gone. Again.

Alex tore out the page with his number on, screwed it into a ball and ran it under a blast of cold water until it stuck together in a clump. She threw it into the bin with the cold toast, too embarrassed to acknowledge to herself what had just happened, ignoring the chill creeping up her chest.

CHAPTER EIGHTEEN

Jacob

15 September 2010

Jacob knew from the flash in Fiona's eyes that he was in deep trouble. Not just 'forgetting to put the bins out' trouble, but something genuine. At least to her.

He remembered the first time he'd seen that flash. They'd been together for nearly six months, no longer 'dating', just always with one another. Her toothbrush was in his bathroom and her underwear was in his laundry basket. She hadn't moved in officially, but she had one foot in the door and he liked the way that felt.

Until that point his visits to the hospital had been sporadic, maybe once every couple of months. But the tighter he felt bound to Fiona, the stronger he felt a sense of duty to Amy.

He'd arranged to go to work late one day so he could have a lie in and then visit the ward for a little longer. He wanted to tell Amy that he had found someone and that he was sorry. Just in case she was in there somewhere, waiting for him. He wasn't going to drop her, like everyone else had, but he was going to level with her.

Jacob had waited until long after Fiona had left for the print shop, snoozing his alarm and sleeping fitfully. He'd spent the rest of the morning in the ward, sitting with Amy and trying to build up the courage to tell her he had moved on in a way she couldn't.

He'd stared at her face. She was still wired up back then and her body frequently rejected its drip, convulsing with an automatic determination at odds with her passive condition.

As a result, Amy had been incredibly thin; her beauty hidden behind razor-blade cheekbones and dark dips under her eyes. He'd held her hand in lieu of her gaze, then bottled out. Rather than tell her he was moving on, Jacob had committed to coming back to visit sooner next time – imagining a glimmer of eye movement as he whispered his promises.

When he'd been back at work for a couple of hours, Jacob had realized that he'd forgotten to switch his phone back on. As soon as it sprang to life, he found several texts and voicemails. He'd called Fiona straight back but got no response.

That night he saw the flash in her dark eyes for the first time. 'Where were you today?' she'd asked.

'I was at work, why?'

'I called and you weren't there.'

'When, this morning?'

'Yeah.'

Jacob paused for just a split second. The truth, as it stood, was half-told and did no-one any favours.

'I was visiting a client.'

'You said you had loads of paperwork to catch up on.'

'I did, I still do, but I had to go out to Sussex at the last minute, why?'

The fire in her eyes had cooled. 'Shit, I'm sorry. I'm acting like a crazy person.'

That time they'd laughed about it. When it happened again a few months later, again due to a clandestine hospital visit and a number of missed calls, the fire had taken longer to put out. They'd channelled it into bed, not knowing what else to do with the friction.

'I'm sorry, J,' Fiona had said afterwards, lying in the nook of his arm and staring up at the ceiling. Her hair had been stuck to her forehead and clothes lay strewn on the floor.

'Dan was such a fuckwit for this kind of thing. I felt like such a mug when I found out he'd been cheating on me. And it wasn't just once or twice. I can't handle the thought of that happening again. That's not fair on you though, I know you're not him.'

'I'm sorry I worried you.'

'Don't apologize to me, I'm being an idiot. It's a stupid trap that everyone falls into, isn't it? Bringing old relationships into new ones.'

He hadn't said a word.

'Except you,' she'd teased. 'Look at me, taming a stud!'

'Oh, Fiona,' he'd laughed.

'You know those girls you *think* were just flings probably didn't see you that way. You probably broke their hearts,' Fiona's eyes twinkled mischievously.

'Oh God, stop. Actually, carry on. No, I mean stop,' he'd smiled.

'You really didn't have any proper girlfriends at uni or college?'

'No, not really, just the odd thing that fizzled out.'

'So I'm your first proper girlfriend, really?'

'Yes, for the fifty millionth time, you're my first proper girlfriend *since school*,' he'd said.

'School doesn't count, that's a fact. So I'm your first proper girlfriend. La, la, la, look at me,' she'd sung. 'Your first proper girlfriend. The one you ditched your womanizing ways for.'

He'd pulled her into him and kissed her, laughing. 'You're so silly.'

Other times she would ask him about his university affairs, only to stop him the moment he started to cobble a description together.

'Actually, don't tell me anything. I don't like thinking of you with other girls.'

'You're my number one girl,' he'd say, and kiss her with relief.

Jacob hated to see that flash in her eyes, and he'd seen it more and more in pregnancy. He was meticulous about doctor's appointments, midwife check-ups, antenatal classes, ultrasounds and everything else marked in thick pen on the kitchen calendar. He'd never missed a single meeting with his future son or daughter.

It wasn't their wedding anniversary, her birthday or any other important date. Everything had been fine when she'd kissed him goodnight and gone to bed, but this morning Fiona wouldn't even meet his gaze.

'Do you have any plans today?' he asked, trying to sound light.

'No.'

'Are you doing anything at lunchtime? Meeting any friends?'

'No.'

'How do you fancy having a nice lunch somewhere, then? Maybe we could drive down to Rye?'

'Why?'

'No, Rye,' he'd smiled, trying to crack her mood, but she had just glared harder.

'Okay, because you're my wife and I love you and we don't have much time left for long lunches on our own.'

'Hmn.'

'Okay, Fi, I give up. What's wrong?'

'Ha!' the snort-come-laugh sent a chill through him – ordinarily she was spilling words when she had a problem.

'What is it? You're worrying me now.'

'I'm worrying you, am I? I'm worrying you?! That's rich, Jacob, that's fucking rich.'

'I have no idea what I've done, so why don't you just tell me?'

Fiona sat down heavily, sinking into the oatmeal armchair. Gesturing to her belly, her eyes filled with tears. 'I'm thirty-five weeks' pregnant, Jacob, thirty-five weeks' pregnant with *your child* and I have to pee a lot.'

And with that, the tears came in gulping fat sobs.

Jacob knelt by his wife and gently placed one hand on her shoulder, and one hand on the enormous bump.

'There's no need to be upset. I know your body's changing and that must be weird for you, it's weird for me too, but—'

Fiona brushed his hand from her stomach, lifting a face black with yesterday's mascara.

'Jacob, you really are stupid sometimes. I'm thirty-five weeks' pregnant and I have to pee all day and all bloody night.'

She sniffed, wiping her nose on her sleeve as she staggered to her feet. He reeled back from kneeling, steadying himself with a hand.

'I had to get up and pee in the early hours last night and you weren't in our bed. I checked downstairs in case you'd fallen asleep on the sofa, but you weren't there. I checked the whole fucking house, J, and then I checked your car and it was gone.'

She drew a quick breath, hands on hips. 'Where the fuck were you?'

'I didn't know you'd woken up.'

'Where the fuck were you?'

'I was just driving around.'

'You're lying to me.'

'I'm not lying to you.'

'You're lying. You think you can just lie to me now and it doesn't matter any more.'

'That's not true. I just drove around for a bit. I wanted to clear my head, I was feeling stressed about stuff, about work, about the baby, I just wanted to get out for a bit.'

'At half one in the morning?'

'Yes, at half one in the morning! I thought you were fast asleep, I didn't mean to worry you.'

'So where did you go then?'

'I just drove around.'

'Where did you drive around?'

'I don't know really, just around town.'

'So you stayed in Tunbridge Wells, you only drove around Tunbridge Wells?'

'Yes, mostly.'

'Mostly?'

'Yes, totally then – I just drove around Tunbridge Wells.'

'Did you stop anywhere?'

'Did I stop anywhere?'

'Stop repeating what I'm saying and answer the flaming question. Did you stop anywhere?'

'No, I didn't stop anywhere.'

'You didn't pick up any petrol, or maybe a snack, or maybe another fucking woman?'

Fiona's body sagged but her eyes were ablaze.

'Oh for God's sake, Fiona, I just drove around.'

'I give you the benefit of the doubt so much, Jacob, but you've just rammed it in my face this time—'

'Jesus Christ, this is so unnecessary! You don't give me the benefit of the doubt, you interrogate me like you're doing now. I'd never have gone for a drive if I'd realized the trouble it would cause, I just really needed to get out.'

'Do you know what, Jacob? Fucking snap, that's what. I just need to get out.'

With a sputter of energy and still wearing her maternity pyjamas and slipper-boots, Fiona stormed out of the house, snatching her car keys off the hall table as she went. And with a door slam and a shriek of revs she was gone.

Jacob had nowhere to go and nothing to do. He sat on the stairs and stared at the front door. Who was there that he could call, really? University friends he'd spent the three years of his degree avoiding? Marc from work? Barely above an acquaintance.

Jacob thought of his younger brother, Tom, so far away. Who

did *he* call? He'd been popular as a kid, there were usually one or two friends back to play from primary school. Tom usually had a little cluster around him during break times at the grammar. But Jacob didn't see him for his last years of school and didn't remember anyone coming to call. All he remembered was the dyed hair and the dark music and a permanently shut bedroom door.

The last time Jacob had seen Tom was the wedding, where he'd been painfully quiet, blending into the background and hovering around their mother.

Did that same shy man have a ferocious social life that kept him from thoughts of home? Was it really just about work? And his other brother, Simon, what did he do in his 'down time'?

With a threesome of boys, it was probably to their parents' credit that no-one was piggy in the middle. Simon, the spit of his father in so many ways, had also shared his interests and demeanour. They would pair off, playing tennis, running errands or sitting quietly, frowning slightly as they read or watched television. And that left Tom and Jacob to bob around together, comfortably jostling and playing. They were pals, both young for their years, making dens, wrestling and building Lego constructions far longer than was normal.

Until Amy came on the scene. Then Jacob would close his door quietly but resolutely if she was over to see him, leaving Tom to his Game Boy and the sound of Lego tipping onto the floor. And then afterwards. What did Tom do after Amy's attack, when Jacob retreated even more? Was Tom taken under his father's wing while Jacob lay alone on his bed, staring into space for those long months? It was a blur, and one he didn't really want to explore.

Taking his keys from the hall table, Jacob slammed the door on the silent house and opted instead for the loud music and growling engine of his car. With nowhere specific to go, he went where he increasingly headed in spare moments – to the snug red brick terraces of Axminster Road.

CHAPTER NINETEEN

Alex

15 September 2010

Alex pushed the trolley along each Sainsbury's aisle in turn, although her list was short. She lingered amongst the vegetables, hesitating between two organic cucumbers for over five minutes.

Eventually, with a little food in the corners of the trolley and a fresh pack of Dry-Nites pads, she wheeled her way down the wine aisle, trying to quell the acceleration. She hovered by the rosé: *Should I? For a change?* Then immediately reversed back to the same white section she'd plundered for the last few weeks.

As Alex loaded the bags into the boot of her car, arms aching, the sound of her phone's ringtone burst out of her bag. This was rare enough to make her jump, and she answered suspiciously.

'Hi, Alex, it's Andy Bellamy from *The Times*. Can we arrange a time for you to come in?'

Alex's knees clattered together as she shivered on the narrow Wapping pavement, craning her neck to look up beyond the tall grey walls. She breathed deeply, the cold air wrapping itself around her lungs as Alex drank in the huge tower. It was still the colour of wet newspaper, rising up out of the east London mess.

News International's 'Fortress' was a lot bigger than she remembered. Or perhaps she was smaller now. Unable to move, Alex rummaged in her bag for a tissue she didn't really need, and tried to wipe away the memories of her last day here.

A different time. A different person. No-one will remember me.

Couriers bustled in and out of the security office, incredibly fresh-faced men and women whooshed in and out of the turnstiles, jabbing their security passes, jaws tight with their own deadlines. *Was I ever that young?* Alex wondered. But it was rhetorical; she was younger.

She remembered the initial call-up so vividly. Scuttling out of the *Mizz* magazine office and hiding from colleagues in the stairwell, hand shaking so vigorously she thought she'd drop her phone. 'Calling from *The Times*... Would you come in for a chat? Maybe meet some of the team? Talk about opportunities?'

The first visit to the Fortress. Deep-breathing exercises on the ride over, a stiff slug from the handbag for Dutch courage, a strong mint, the arched eyebrow of the taxi driver in the smeared rear-view mirror. Twenty-four and hungry.

Waiting and waiting and waiting in the security office, visitor badge dangling, brand-new shoes tugging at newer blisters. Couriers buzzing in and out, the lazy laughter of bored desk staff. And then the phone ringing behind the desk, the clipped tone from the woman leaning over, 'They want you on the red sofas. Do you know where they are?'

'I'm sorry, I don't.'

Accompanied at painful speed along the cobbles by a sighing security temp. Behind the velvet rope. The 'inkies' rushing in and out of the dirty bits on the lower floor, where execs and columnists would never deign to go.

The editor's parking space as close to the main doors as a white line could ever hope to be.

Once inside, Alex had drunk in the smells of the newsroom, the leather of the executive lift and the Styrofoam coffee. She'd walked tall along corridors papered floor-to-ceiling with famous headlines. Holding her head as stiff and straight as her mother's late-night deportment lessons had taught her years before. 'Just walk with the books on your head, Alexandra, it's not that hard! My God, what have I done to deserve this?'

The unstoppable gush of excitement, creativity, that hunger again, spilling from Alex as the smiling faces nodded from the other side of the walnut table, as polished as a bowling alley. 'Zeitgeist', 'generation', 'ahead of the curve'... all the right phrases. And – Alex recognized looking back – her then-beautiful face smiling openly, a face that would look *just so* above a byline.

The handshake, the sealed deal, the sweats. The shits in the foyer bathrooms on the way out, barely making it. Glimpsing an oil painting of Rupert Murdoch in the reception as she walked giddily by, smiling so hard her cheekbones hurt. The burbling water feature. So eighties and ridiculous, and everything she'd ever wanted to see in the flesh.

On the taxi ride home, Alex had called her mother in Spain. It had seemed like the right thing to do.

'A columnist?' her mother had sniffed. 'It's a shame they didn't put you on the travel desk. At least then you might make the effort to come and see me.'

And then Alex had phoned Matt.

'Oh my fucking God, seriously?'

'Seriously.'

'Seriously?'

'Seriously!' she'd squealed, kicking her legs in the back of the taxi, shoes flying as she'd slid slowly from one side to the other as the driver shook his head in the mirror but not unkindly.

That night they'd put buttery lobster on a credit card. Delicate flutes of champagne, clinked with wild abandon, tears in their eyes. Matt had carried her home. She'd felt light as a feather. And he had made love to her so gently that she couldn't bear it. She'd sunk her nails into his flesh and dug him into her so she could be sure she was feeling everything. And his gargled voice had proposed in her ear. She'd cried: 'Yes, oh my God, of course, yes.'

The next day, he'd woken her up with a strong coffee, kissed both her eyelids and said, 'I meant it.'

If she had known how it would end, would she have taken the job?

Yes. God, she was hungry then.

A different time. A different person. No-one will remember me.

'Do you know where to go?'

'Yes, it's fine, I used to work here.' Alex smiled at the security temp and pushed out into the grounds. As she walked along the familiar cobbles, Andy Bellamy came out of one of the side doors, shirt flapping around his big belly.

'Alex, thanks for coming in.'

'No problem, it's good to see the old place.'

They met awkwardly. She went for a one-cheek kiss, he for two, and they clashed mid-air.

'I thought we could grab a coffee.'

The coffee shop in a chilly corner of the newspaper complex had been a thinly disguised Starbucks franchise in Alex's time. Now it appeared to be a thinly disguised Costa franchise.

'No more caramel macchiatos?' Alex asked.

'No, now it's the same old shit with a different name,' Andy said. 'Thank our friends at the *Sun*, they did an exposé on Starbucks wasting water and the whole thing kicked off. Anyway, take a seat.'

Andy had worked on the City pages when Alex left. He hadn't

been in the meeting room that last time. But he'd looked over the rim of his newsroom monitor as she'd been escorted out, flanked by Security. A hundred pairs of furtive eyes had looked over their monitors that day.

'So d'you miss it here?' he asked.

'I miss the money,' Alex laughed.

'Yeah... there's not so much of that about now, eh?'

'Hey, don't get me wrong. I'm grateful for every commission I get now, but *damn*. When I think about how much I got then, and how little I had to write in comparison...'

'What was the name of the column you did again?'

'Which one? There was the main column on Tuesday and then "Losing Mum", on Sunday.'

'Ah yes, of course.'

Alex could see a guy in the queue that she dimly recognized, and immediately worried why.

'Shame that stopped.'

'Well, my mum died so it sort of reached a natural end.'

'Oh God, I'm such a twat,' Andy said, aghast. They both laughed.

'It's fine. Ha, it's really fine.'

'Look, I wanted to talk to you about the Amy story you pitched and I thought it would be easier to have a face-to-face. It's an interesting case but I have a few misgivings. Put it this way, we couldn't make a story out of it yet.'

'There's definitely a lot more to be done.'

'Make no mistake, it's interesting. Very interesting. I remember it happening, the step-dad being nicked, the mum. It's awful what happened to that family, but I'm still struggling to see how we could legitimately make a valuable article out of it now.'

Alex swallowed hard. 'Okay, I see what you're saying. But what if new evidence was found about the person that attacked Amy? That would warrant a full feature, surely? Whoever did this is still out there. Someone capable of attacking a young girl and leaving her for dead. People don't tend to do things like that once and then retire – they tend to get worse.'

Alex looked around at all the caffeinated eyes peering out from behind giant cardboard cups of coffee. She lowered her voice.

'I think the key to the story, is, y'know, where is this guy? And what are the police doing about catching him?'

'Who knows.'

'Right, no-one knows where he is and the police aren't doing anything. It's just another cold case for them. It would only be opened up if something very similar happened.'

Andy Bellamy folded his arms over his barrel tummy and cocked his head to the side.

'I mean,' Alex carried on, quietly. 'Is that okay? Should someone else's family be ripped apart before this is solved?'

'Okay, yeah, you've made your point.' Andy said. 'I'm not totally convinced, Alex, and to be frank your last few pieces haven't really done it for me like they used to...

'Here's what I'll do. You bring me something with a tangible exclusive, similar cases that hadn't been put together before, police reopening the investigation, some suspect they overlooked, girl waking up and dancing the tango... something, and we've got an interesting double-page spread. Bring me something vintage Alex Dale and you've got yourself a full four-pager.'

Andy Bellamy's words had gnawed away at her all night and she thought of them as soon as she woke up the next morning. Parallel cases, overlooked suspects; she'd not started on anything like this. Other than rifling through all the clippings, pissing off her ex-husband and bothering a wary step-dad, she'd not done very much at all.

It was a battle of willpower over fatigue to pull her running things on, but Alex knew it was the best method for clearing her head.

As her trainers thumped heavily along the pavement, chest pumping and stomach gurgling, she tried to order her thoughts into some kind of plan.

Retracing the police inquiry was largely pointless. They'd spoken to Bob and ruled him out. She'd spoken to Bob and ruled him out. The police had done the same to the boyfriend, the neighbours and her teachers at school. All were incapable or elsewhere.

The net needed to be widened. In 1995, there was no obvious way to pull together the social network of any one person. Apart from any help the school might have given, it would really have been up to the parents to provide a list of friends and contacts.

Amy had no friends at all in 2010, but in 1995 she was still at school, she still went to youth clubs, she had had friends. Amy may not be able maintain those connections, but her friends from 1995 would still be around, linked together by their shared school years. Alex sprinted all the way to her front door.

Still panting and coated with salty sweat, she fumbled her key in the door and jogged straight over to her laptop, flipping it open and clicking into the browser window.

For the first time in years she typed: www.friendsreunited.com.

A quick search on 'Edenbridge Grammar School' brought up 2,047 members, but to see them, Alex had to register or log in. After deliberately stepping away from this kind of thing ages ago, signing up felt dangerous. She added herself to Amy's school, in Amy's year, and filled in scant information.

'Alex Dale' now nestled amongst Amy's classmates, right where Amy Stevenson would have sat. Between the out-of-date biographies.

Referring back to her transcript of the interview with Bob, Alex had jotted down some names: Jenny, Becky and Jake.

There were three Rebeccas (Harris, Limm and Simpson) but only one potential Jenny – Jennifer Cross. No Jake, but a Jacob Arlington.

Alex's tummy fluttered. Jennifer Cross and Jacob Arlington. That had to be Jenny and Jake, surely? Everyone signed up to Friends Reunited back in the day, it *had* to be them. She called Bob's number, chewing the end of her pen.

''Ello?'

'Hi, Bob, it's Alex Dale here.'

'Oh.'

'I'm really sorry to trouble you, Bob, I just had a quick question.'

'Alright, what's the question?' Alex pictured him shuffling around, one hand in his overalls pocket.

'You mentioned Amy's friends Jenny and Becky when we spoke. I just wondered if you could remember their surnames?'

'God, bloody hell... I don't remember at all.'

'Oh that's okay, don't worry... perhaps if I read out the surnames I've found you could say if they sound familiar?'

'I s'pose so.'

'I'll be really quick. The Jenny I've found is Jenny Cross – does that ring any bells?'

'I honestly don't know.'

'What about Becky Harris, Becky Simpson or Becky Limm?'

'Oh, yeah, I do remember Limm, Becky Limm, 'cos it's a funny name, isn't it?'

'Do you remember any other friends' names, even vague memories?'

'No, not really I'm afraid. Sorry, Alex.'

'Don't be, that's so helpful, thank you. Bob, there was one other thing actually, do you remember the name of Amy's boyfriend, Jake?'

'Yeah, I do,' Bob paused. 'We used to take the mickey out of Amy 'cos we'd found a load of little signatures she'd done, testing out her name as if they was married. We used to call 'er Mrs Arlington. As a joke, y'know. Jake Arlington he was, poor sod.'

'That's brilliant, thanks, Bob.'

Alex clicked on Jacob Arlington. Generic blue avatar, no photograph. 'Living with Fiona in Kent. Sells software.'

Short and practical. But then the boys' profiles were often far more functional and factual than the girls'.

Jacob Arlington still lived in Kent, at least up until the last time he updated his profile, in 2007.

Rebecca Limm's profile was comparatively upbeat. 'After Edenbridge, I went to Mid Kent College, then uni in London. Did English Lit and now work for a PR agency in Soho. Life is good!'

Jennifer Cross's profile spoke of working as an estate agent in Surrey, living with her partner, expecting her first child.

'You must be our Jenny...' Alex muttered.

Opening her working document, Alex typed 'Jacob "Jake" Arlington' under the 'Possible Suspects' heading. She knew she'd need to approach him. She'd have to try to interview him. But not until she knew more about the run-up to Amy's abduction.

She sent a brief message to Jennifer Cross, asking if she had been friends with Amy and would consider answering a few respectful questions. She stressed that it was for a possible article with *The Times*, not a tabloid. Friend or not, she was in the same year at the same school and would surely remember who Amy was.

Who Amy is, Alex corrected herself.

Alex clicked on Rebecca Limm again. An English Literature graduate working in PR. Their paths could easily have crossed before.

Hi Rebecca,

I hope you don't mind me contacting you like this. I'm a freelance journalist and I recently became interested in Amy

Stevenson's story. I know you were friends with Amy at school, and I don't want to upset you but I'm writing a piece for *The Times* and I'd love to know a little more about Amy. I was hoping you'd help by answering a couple of questions?

I'm quite local to Edenbridge (I went to school in Tunbridge Wells and live there again now) and I would like to assure you that I'm not trying to do anything disrespectful or sensational.

I hope you can help.

Kind regards,
Alex Dale
alexdalewrites@gmail.com
Tel: 07876 070866

Send.

Alex gave her email inbox a final refresh before switching off for the day at just gone noon. A Friends Reunited message from Rebecca Limm was waiting.

Hi Alex,

I got your message through Friends Reunited. I don't use it any more so the email was a bit of a bolt from the blue.

I was very good friends with Amy but what happened was a long time ago and I've tried to forget it. I don't know if you've spoken to other people from school but I suspect they've all moved on as well.

I don't see anyone from those days and my parents have moved to France so I never go back to Edenbridge. I don't know how much help I could be.

I would like to talk to you though. I always wanted to work in magazine journalism but I ended up in PR. I know this is crass, but I'm due to go on maternity leave soon. I really want to go freelance when my baby's born and I want to move away from press releases and into content.

I do have press contacts but they all know me as a PR and I need some help. If you're willing to give me some pointers and a few introductions, then I'm willing to answer questions about Amy, on the record.

Let me know,
Becky x

Alex sent a hurried response, then switched off her phone.

A reply had been waiting when Alex switched her phone back on first thing. Perhaps eager to wrap things up before maternity leave, Becky had suggested coffee that day.

Becky Limm was the epitome of what some of Alex's male colleagues had called 'a PR chick'. Bubbly and smiley with wavy blonde hair, crystal-blue eyes and discreet determination. She was wearing a trouser suit that was perfectly tailored around an enormous bump.

They met in the Fleet River Café, a pretty little tearoom away from the noise of High Holborn. They split a slice of hummingbird cake and drank lattes. A PR and a journalist meeting for coffee. The scene was so generic, so replicable across the city.

'She wanted to be a journalist too, you know, Amy did.'

'Oh really?'

'Yeah, well, a writer. We both did. She wanted to write about music and I wanted to write about fashion.' Becky smiled. 'We used to write short stories and stuff, y'know, silly poems in letters. We'd give them to each other the next day. There was a bit of one-upmanship, but sometimes that's a good thing.'

'Did you keep any of Amy's letters?'

'No, I didn't. After Amy was, you know, after she was found, I just got everything that had anything to do with her, stuck it in a box and took it round to her mum's house.'

'What did her mum do with it?' Alex asked, trying not to let hope tickle her voice.

'I have no idea. After she died, the house was sold; I remember my mum and dad talking about it. I suppose whoever bought the house just chucked it all.'

'Do you miss her?'

'Not now, no. There are plenty of people from back then that I don't see. You just grow apart and move on, so I have to put Amy in that category in my head and not think about the reality.'

Becky sipped her decaf latte slowly.

'Look, the day they found Amy was just... I mean it was unbearable. The whole time she was gone, I'd told myself that she'd run away. I was almost cross that she'd done it without me. I thought she was doing something amazing and brave. Like she'd run off to join the circus or something. She was always so fun and daring. I convinced myself that she was bigger than Edenbridge and bigger than school, that she'd just gone out there into the world to take it by storm.

'So when she was found,' Becky swallowed hard. 'And I realized she hadn't got away, I had to just block it all out.' Becky wiped her eyes with a napkin. 'Sorry, I'm so much more emotional now I'm pregnant!'

Alex forced a smile.

'It was horrific. We were so young. It's just too much to be confronted with at fifteen, you can't process it. I had to try really hard not to get sucked in by that and lose sight of my own plans. I couldn't let it mess with my head. I was as desperate to get out of Edenbridge as she was and it would have been disrespectful to Amy if I'd wrecked my own chances. I think she'd agree. I hope she would.'

'Did you get counselling at school?' Alex asked.

'God no, not at all. And at that age it's amazing how quickly you move on, as awful as it sounds. We had this godawful special assembly where the head teacher read passages from the Bible and the TV news cameras filmed us crying when we came out. That obviously wasn't helpful.

'I used to go to see the school nurse when I got upset about it from time to time, but that's it. She didn't really know what to say or do either, but the sick bay was somewhere quiet away from the others.

'I suppose in a way it helped that we had the summer holiday so soon after, and could get our crying done and just come back and start over. It's not something you're ever prepared for, because who in their right mind would expect that to happen to a school friend?'

'What do you think Amy would be doing now if she hadn't been attacked?'

'I've been thinking about that since you got in touch.'

Becky picked her words carefully. 'I know Amy's worst fear was ending up like her mum. She loved her mum and dad to bits but their life was just so... meh. They lived in a tiny house, did crappy jobs and always had to worry about money. Amy didn't want to be stuck in Edenbridge working in a shop – she wanted to do all the stuff that her parents didn't get the chance to do.

'She was uni material, you know, she was smart. I don't know if she would have been a writer in the end but I'm sure she would have done something creative. Maybe she'd have been a music PR,' Becky sniffed and smiled. 'She loved music, she knew more about it than any of the boys. And she was always up for a laugh, up for a challenge. I don't know about settling down but, y'know, probably. She tended to have steady boyfriends, I think she was wired that way.'

Alex turned her notepad to a short list of names.

'Can I ask about Amy's other friends?'

'Sure, though I really don't see anyone these days.'

'I'm just trying to eliminate some names at this stage, anything you can add is helpful. Is Jennifer Cross the same Jenny that Amy was friends with?'

'Yeah, that's her.'

'Do you have any contact details for her?'

'Jenny? No, sorry. We grew apart years ago.'

'It must have been a horrible time for you both.'

'Yeah, it was. But we dealt with it differently, you know? She liked to wallow and talk about Amy constantly and that just made me feel worse.'

'And what about Amy's boyfriend? I know Amy was going out with Jake Arlington, he must have been heartbroken?'

'Jake, yeah, I think he really struggled. When Amy was attacked it was close to the end of school term... Well, you know that, don't you? He came back really briefly after she was found but we never saw him again after that. I don't blame him. There were rumours. Kids are horrible.'

'What kind of rumours?'

'That he was somehow involved. Stupid things like she was pregnant and he'd beaten her up so she'd lose the baby. Did you know his brother went to the school too? He seemed like a sweet enough boy but there was even a rumour about him and Jake, y'know, hurting her together and the brother left the school too.

'Every scenario that stupid little minds could dream up did the rounds. There were rumours that Jake had helped someone do it, that someone had helped him, that he was really violent because he knew karate or something like that,' Becky half-laughed. 'Just mean, unhelpful stuff. Totally untrue. And then by the next year, no-one was talking about it.'

'You're sure there was no truth to any of them?' Alex asked.

'God no! I mean, come on. He was cleared by the police and they'd never even had sex. She couldn't have been pregnant. It would have been all over the papers if she was.'

Alex had prepared a list of section editors, many of whom she'd burned her own bridges with. She placed the list, with contact details and a few notes, on the table. Becky smiled.

'You must have plenty of contacts already,' Alex said.

'Yeah, but not in commercial mags. Besides, I'm an annoying PR chasing coverage – they don't see me as a writer, right?'

Alex smiled. 'Right.'

'I know it's going to be tough to move across but I'm excited.'

'Good. Freelance life is a mixed bag though. I can go days without talking to anyone.'

'Oh I know. But I'll have my husband home in the evenings, and then there's the little one – once he can talk.'

'Of course.'

'Do you have any kids?' Becky asked, smiling and rubbing the side of her bump gently.

Alex paused.

'So you know you're having a boy, then?'

'Yes, I couldn't wait to find out. We needed as much time as possible to work on names. Anyway, thanks so much for this, Alex, do you have everything you need?' Becky stood up to go, glancing at her mobile.

'I think so, can I call you if I think of any other questions?'

'Yeah, of course. Can I do the same?'

'Absolutely. Good luck with the baby.'

'Good luck with your story. And listen, if you do get to talk to Jenny Cross, be careful. She was always a little bit, I'm not sure how to put it. A bit much.'

The stopping service to Tunbridge Wells picked its way through the grey outskirts of London and out to the little brick stations of West Kent. As cottages started to replace factories and high rises, Alex spread her things out on the table in front of her.

Based on her conversation with Andy Bellamy, she'd made a list of bases to cover. She was awash with notes and decided she needed to approach it like any other feature: background, interviews, facts and figures. She'd just started to cobble together a mind map when the phone rang. Blocked number.

'Hello, Alex Dale?'

'Hey, Alex, it's Matt.'

'Oh hello.'

'I just wanted to check you were okay, I felt bad about the other day.'

'I'm fine, don't worry about it.'

'Yeah, I know, but I have been worried. You called at a really bad time and caught me off guard, I know you get nervous at night and I was being really up my arse.'

'It's fine, let's not get into a big thing.'

'Just 'cos I can't be there like I used to be doesn't mean we can't be civil and I should have been civil to you.'

'I appreciate you calling, Matt, but I shouldn't have rung you in the first place, especially at the weekend, especially when your fiancée's pregnant and could do without your ex-wife harassing you!' Her eyes welled up, and her laugh gurgled out unconvincingly.

'Oh, Alex...'

'I'm fine, I'm so sorry, it really is fine.'

'I really don't think you've got anything to worry about at your place, but if it happens again, the local boys won't mind coming round to check. Just give them a call.'

'I will do, I was probably imagining it anyway.'

Outside the window, green fields and knotty hedges whipped in and out of view.

'Before I go, how are things going with your coma girl?'

Alex resisted the urge to snipe about 'never finishing anything' and instead gave Matt the briefest overview.

'And Andy Bellamy, remember me mentioning him? From *The Times*? He's interested in running it as a big feature if I can find a new angle.'

'That's great news, sounds like you're doing all the right stuff. Let me know if there's anything I can do to help.'

Matt was almost certainly just being polite and trying to wrap up an awkward conversation, but the moment was too tempting.

'Well... there is one thing you might be able to do for me.'

'Oh?'

'Yeah, I need to look for parallel cases. I've been thinking about the Rachel Nickell and Samantha Bissett thing, where police didn't tie the two up for ages and Robert Napper was able to carry on under the radar—'

'That type of thing is very rare, Alex. Generally the police are on to any kind of similarity long before the public are aware of it.'

'Oh I know, you don't need to defend the Almighty Force, I just thought with it being such a long time ago, maybe something could have happened recently that hadn't been connected? Is there any easy way for you to check?'

A pause.

'I'll see what I can do, but no promises.'

'Thanks so much, I really appreciate it. And if you do find anything, just email it over. I won't call you again, I promise.'

'Alex, it's fine, just don't pick first thing on a Saturday.'

'I won't, I promise.'

'Take care, Alex – please look after yourself.'

'And you.'

Alex turned to look out the window. Her pale reflection appeared ghostlike in the window.

At home, Alex's Friends Reunited inbox offered up a stern rebuke from Jenny Cross.

'Damn right Amy was my friend and that's exactly why I don't want to talk to you. Contact me again and I'll call the police.'

Okay, thought Alex, *I'll leave you for now, Jenny. But anyone that reacts so fiercely has something to say.*

Alex nipped upstairs to use the loo and slip her pyjamas on. Back down at 12.01 she unscrewed the bottle of very nice Pouilly-Fumé and let it trickle gently into the delicate, tall glass. She still enjoyed the romance of a cork, but this was certainly more efficient. She span the cap back and popped the bottle back into the fridge door, turning it slightly so all the labels lined up.

Phone off, computer clamped shut, she picked up a book she'd been trying to read for months and slumped into the corner of the sofa. Within a few lines she knew she wasn't absorbing a single word and flicked the TV on with the remote. A rerun of a rerun of a rerun of *Columbo*. Alex smiled – perhaps she would pick up some tips.

CHAPTER TWENTY

Jake

18 August 1995

Jake's socked feet dangled off the end of his single divan. Downstairs his parents rowed in sharp little bursts. No yelling. Flurries of words, scrapes of bottles, ice being smashed out of trays and into glasses. The sound of the conservatory doors sliding open as his mother stepped outside for another of her poorly hidden cigarettes.

Through the wall, Jake could hear the sound of Tom's Game Boy. Jake lay back and let his eyes fall closed as the sounds blended. A ding from Super Mario, the sharp tone of his mother's voice. He'd given up trying to listen to music. Every song he played reminded him of Amy. He wasn't even that bothered by music anyway; most of the CDs that he'd bought had been to impress his girlfriend.

His girlfriend.

Did he still have a girlfriend?

Boyfriend and girlfriend stuff was hard enough to work out when everything was normal, let alone now.

It had been twenty days since he'd left the house. Seven since he'd washed. He couldn't remember the last time he'd spoken to either of his brothers. One had left gladly on some worthy trip that had never really interested Jake, the other scuttled into his room and slammed the door whenever he heard Jake coming. He didn't blame him; he didn't have anything to say back either. How could a thirteen-year-old boy understand this any more than a fifteen-year-old?

At one point, he'd asked to call Rob and Dave from school, but his mum said it was a bad idea. Besides, they'd not called him. No-one had.

Another scrape of the conservatory door. His mother's voice was louder than usual, and Jake rolled over to face the wall, picking lethargically at the wallpaper seam.

There were exactly twelve miles and eight hundred yards between Amy's bed and his. He lay still and imagined himself raised up two feet higher in the air, stiff pillows under his neck and machines all around, beeping and whizzing. Probably a blood bag thing as well. He'd not seen her: his mum had said no, absolutely not. So he had to imagine what she looked like based on *Casualty* episodes. He imagined a room as white as heaven, with more plug sockets than anyone could ever need.

Part of him just wanted to get to her, to crawl on his knees if that's what it took. To stride downstairs and say to his mother, 'I love Amy and she loves me and you can't keep us apart.' He'd snatch up the keys to the Ford Fiesta and say: 'Either you drive me, or I'll drive myself'.

The bigger part of him was anchored to his bed, eyes raw. He wouldn't do any of those things. He wouldn't stand up to his mother, or demand to see Amy. He wanted to see *his* Amy, the one who loved him, not the bashed-up, unconscious girl twelve miles and eight hundred yards away. And he probably couldn't remember how to drive the car now anyway. It had been years since he and Tom had been shown how on the old air strip, and he'd barely got out of first gear then. He'd gone so slowly, Tom had been able to run alongside the car, laughing at him, his eleven-year-old legs flying.

Where was Tom? Jake strained to listen for Game Boy sounds but all he could hear now was muffled talking that was getting faster and louder. His mother's soprano rising up through the floor far sharper than his father's deep baritone.

'We sent them back to school far too quickly. Louise said—'

'Who is Louise?' murmured his father's weary voice.

'Louise Waters, Jake's form tutor, she said he struggled. Couldn't focus on the work, looked close to tears all the time. She said there was lots of whispering and finger pointing.'

'That stuff will pass, Sue. By the time they go back in September, there'll be something else to talk about.'

'Really, Graham, you really believe that? You honestly think that something will happen in the next few weeks that trumps *this*?'

Silence. His father's unique brand of silence. Jake flipped over onto his belly and sniffed his pillow deeply. How many pillows did Amy have in intensive care? Did they bother, if she was unconscious anyway? His own bedding had been changed several times since Amy last sat here with him. He was desperate to smell her cherryade scent once more. He started to cry again.

'It's not your tennis buddy we're talking about here, Graham. He's safe and sound, he's doing what he wants. We need to focus on the little ones now, and I know what's best for *these* boys. Jake will *not* be going back to that school, Louise can send his work for him and I can help him with it. We need to find somewhere safe for Tom, somewhere with no distractions and no bloody girls.'

CHAPTER TWENTY-ONE

Alex

22 September 2010

Alex walked the staggered corridor to Bramble Ward. She carefully opened the door, hoping to avoid that busy little nurse.

No luck. The reception was unmanned, but the office door was open and Nurse Radson bustled out at the sound of Alex's shoes.

'Can I help you?' she asked, looking Alex up and down.

'I hope so. I came before, I'm not sure if you remember me?'

'What can I do for you this time?'

'I was wondering if I could sit with Amy Stevenson today?' Alex asked.

Nurse Radson stayed silent for a couple of moments, then looked over at the roughly closed cubicle in the corner – Amy's cubicle. Alex, who was standing further into the ward than last time, had a clear view of the curtain. Under the gap she could see the sitter's shoes and the denim of his jeans.

Nurse Radson turned back to Alex. 'I can ask. Again.'

'I don't want to trample over anyone's feelings. I know that guy doesn't want to talk to me, but I'd really like to sit with Amy. I don't mind waiting for him to finish.'

'Well, he tends to sit with them for a while, and he's only been in there a couple of minutes.'

'Does he sit with all of them?'

Nurse Radson paused, heaving her expansive bosom up and down and breathing deeply. 'Yes, he sits with all of them.'

'So has he sat with all the others yet today?'

'No, not all of them. Can I take your name again?'

'It's Alex, Alex Dale.'

Alex was still sounding out her surname as Nurse Radson bustled across the ward towards Amy's bed and wrenched back the curtain. Alex saw the man recoil in surprise as the nurse stuffed her head in like a bear ransacking a picnic basket.

The nurse and the sitter talked with their heads close together for under a minute before the nurse marched purposefully back to where Alex was standing near the office.

'I explained how keen you were and he's agreed to move on to a different patient so that you can sit with Amy.' The nurse handed over the visitor's badge like the key to the city.

Alex glowered at the striped blue uniform in front of her. 'Okay, thank you.'

The nurse insisted on writing Alex's name on the log herself in curly round lettering, and buzzed back into her office. Alex waited while Amy's cubicle spat out a tall, sandy-haired man. He stood blinking for a moment.

Rubbing his eyes and surveying the beds, he plonked down with an audible 'oof' on the chair next to a blonde, female patient a few metres from the reception desk.

He had short, scruffy hair and was wearing a V-neck T-shirt of the slightly 'distressed' type Matt used to buy in All Saints. The sitter's jeans sat low on his hips, like school uniform at the start of term.

He was within earshot of Alex, and she stayed rooted to the spot waiting to see how an experienced sitter opened their monologue.

Alex realized the sitter was probably waiting for her to move away. As she stepped gently towards Amy's bed, she heard him exhale, followed by a gentle, 'Hello, Natasha, how are you today?'

Natasha, of course, did not answer, but Alex was too far away to hear the man's follow-up patter.

Alex reached Amy's cubicle, where she had stood so intrusively just a few weeks ago. Back then, when Alex saw that 'ghost' for the first time, she could remember very little about the woman in the bed. Now, Alex wondered with a shiver, there was a chance she knew much more about Amy Stevenson than Amy herself did. Maybe more than Amy ever could.

Taking her cue from the sitter, she sat down on the chair and pulled the curtain almost to a close.

She picked Amy's hand up cautiously. For its tiny size it felt cold and heavy. It was too much. Alex couldn't bear the intimacy of their touch, a touch Amy had no say in. She placed the little hand back down and instead clasped her own clammy hands together.

'Hello, Amy,' she said, 'how are you today?'

She paused for an uncomfortable moment before plunging in.

'Amy, I'm a journalist. I saw you in here a while ago when I was speaking to Dr Haynes and I wanted to get to know you better. I grew up in Tunbridge Wells and we probably went to a lot of the same places because we're about the same age. I've spoken to Bob and read a lot about you and I sort of feel like I know you. I know that you can't answer me, but I was hoping to ask you some questions, as I don't really know what else to try.'

Did Alex just imagine the tiniest flutter of an eyelid? Perhaps it was an involuntary twitch. It was enough to elicit a shiver of expectation, however absurd and illogical that was. She remembered what Peter Haynes had told her, that there was brain activity somewhere deep down. That Amy recovering was highly unlikely, but not impossible.

'Amy, can I tell you what I've found out so far?' Alex felt conspiratorial, almost whispering the words. The two women were close enough to smell each other's breath. Alex wondered if Amy could still process smells.

Amy had been laid out on top of the blankets, her patterned gown fanning over her knee-high DVT socks. Alex had often wriggled similar socks up her mother's thinning calves. On Amy, they created a disquieting schoolgirl image.

'What did I do first?' Alex asked herself. 'Well, I came here to talk to Dr Haynes about his work for an article I was writing. I asked him a little bit about you, but he couldn't tell me very much so I also spoke to my ex-husband because he's a policeman. He's called Matt.

'He's the same age as us, so he wasn't in the police force when you went missing. He didn't want to do too much digging around and get into trouble but he's found out a few things.'

Alex paused; it felt so unnatural to just talk and talk and talk like a relentless radio DJ. She realized that she was skipping over moments where the other person would normally ask for clarification like 'who is that?' or 'what do you mean?'

In the silence, Alex studied Amy's face through the tiny pieces of dust sparkling in a sunbeam.

Fine lines around Amy's eyes showed her thirty years, but other than that she looked exactly the same as she had at fifteen. And, Alex thought, if Amy could hear anything, she was listening as a fifteen-year-old. She was not really a thirty-year-old, dashed into her third decade onto the rocks of heartbreak, work fatigue and parental decline.

'So, Matt,' Alex continued, in the same hushed, conspiratorial tones. 'He got me a few details about the main, er, the main suspects.'

Alex realized that if Amy could hear, down at the bottom of her well, this could be the first time she'd heard talk of 'suspects'.

If there was anything of her in there, did she remember what had happened? Was there a chance she could ever name her attacker, somehow?

'I mean,' Alex faltered, 'the people that the police thought might know what happened to you, and why you're here now.'

Alex couldn't help but talk in a sing-song way, like she was soothing a child.

'The police found out that one of your neighbours liked to do mean things to children, but he was too old and frail to do anything nasty to you.'

Not a flicker. Amy's breathing stayed the same: shallow and slow. Alex wondered if this was a 'sleep state', and how anyone could really know.

'And they looked into the youth club that you went to,' Alex continued. 'And they found someone there who had told a few fibs, but they didn't think he'd hurt you at all.'

Nothing, Amy's eyelids were closed and their creamy skin lay still.

'And the day that you were found, they, um, they arrested Bob,' Alex paused, holding her breath in anticipation of... something, she wasn't sure what. But Amy's breathing stayed the same, her eyelids stayed smooth. Alex took a breath as she noticed a tiny sliver of moisture curling in the corner of Amy's left eye. A tear? No, that was silly, her eyes probably watered all the time in this cloggy air.

'Well they let Bob go really quickly, they knew he hadn't done anything wrong.

'I met him recently, Amy, and he was so sweet. He loved talking about you and your mum.' Alex realized too late that she'd mentioned the one person she hadn't wanted to bring into this.

Amy's eyes moved, there was no doubt about it; both her eyes moved the tiniest, tiniest of twitches and, before she had a chance to stop herself, Alex had jumped up and knocked over her plastic chair.

The clattering of the chair bouncing along the floor snapped Alex out of her daze. She sat the chair up, smoothed down her vest and rearranged the waistband of her jeans. Clearing her throat, Alex sat back down and held her breath before continuing, embarrassed.

'I spoke to your friend Becky Limm too. She was nice. She works in London now and she wants to be a journalist, so I've tried to help her with that. She told me that you'd wanted to be a writer. She said you wrote brilliant short stories.

'Amy, I don't want you to be upset but I'm just going to say it and stop beating around the bush. I know that you'd had sex before you were attacked. And I know it wasn't with Jake.'

Amy's breathing stayed level and shallow, her eyes stayed relaxed.

'I'm wondering if you met someone when you were walking home...'

No reaction.

'I think you went somewhere with him but the situation changed...'

A tiny, tiny ripple spread across the top of the nose, almost like Amy's skin was trying to shake off a butterfly that had perched there.

As Alex stared intently, suddenly Amy's mouth smacked open and closed, open and closed, like a beached fish.

In the blink of an eye the curtains were open and a small group of angry faces rushed in as Alex realized too late that she had just screamed at the top of her voice.

CHAPTER TWENTY-TWO

Amy

Sometime in late 1995

I've been trying to look down, but I can't get my stupid head to move. I just want to know what I'm wearing, because I don't remember choosing anything. Did I go out last night? Was I at The Sleeper? I need to talk to Jenny because I'm having a massive blackout. I hope I didn't make a wally of myself; I'm not very good when I'm drunk. I get louder and louder until I throw up. It's like I can see it's going to happen, but once I'm on that path I know I'll follow it to the end anyway.

I must have just slept funny, cricked my neck or pinched a nerve or something. It happened last summer too, maybe that's my summer thing. Maybe I'll have to work around a few days of paralysis every summer for the rest of my life. That'll make it hard to book holidays when I'm older. 'I'd love to elope with you, Damon Albarn, but it'll have to be in August, I'm stiff as a post in July.'

Last year it happened just before the summer fête. I woke up early and tried to sit up and I've never felt pain like it. Mum reckoned I'd pinched a nerve in my back. Bob had to carry me to the toilet, I've never been so embarrassed. He'd plop me down and turn around while I went. Mum would come in and wash my hands for me and then Bob'd carry me back to bed while Mum flushed the chain behind us. I'd hold it for so long that I'd feel like an overfilled hot water bottle ready to burst. I barely ate or drank for two days.

Jenny had rung while I was in bed and my mum told her what had happened so by the time I turned up back at school, shuffling in painfully to make a grand entrance at the fête, Chinese whispers had declared me a full-blown wheelchair-bound cripple.

I was the talk of the school for a few hours and I'm not going to lie, I totally milked it. But it was just a trapped nerve. Maybe that's what I've done this time, but at least my bladder doesn't feel like it's bursting. That's something to be grateful for.

CHAPTER TWENTY-THREE

Jacob

22 September 2010

Fuck. It was her again. Alex Dale. Jacob felt her eyes boring into him, as if she was scanning him for data, taking down his vitals. What did she know? Why had she wanted to talk to him before, but didn't want to talk to him now? Had she found something out since he last checked? What game was she playing?

Jacob had been scared for so long. The fear he had when Amy went missing had never fully gone away, it had just ebbed and flowed into new places. He had been so scared that he would be arrested, and then he was scared that no-one would be arrested. He'd been scared to see her and then he'd been scared to stop.

Fear was the undercurrent, always threatening to whip his legs from under him. Fear was a secondary heartbeat only he could hear, that could get so quiet it was almost imperceptible, or so loud it drowned everything else out.

But it was always there.

It was there on his wedding day.

It was there in the seconds before he first saw his grey splodge of a baby on the sonographer's screen.

It was there today as he plunged his right hand into his pocket and fingered the worn corners of the business card, the details of which he knew off by heart.

Jacob really hated journalists, almost as much as the one person he hated above all else. Journalists had taken unbearable pain and printed it over and over again, thousands of times. Lies about Amy, accusations about her poor dad, photos of her in school uniform, to be gazed upon and speculated about. Day after day. And then dropped when the next lost schoolgirl came along.

Jacob's index finger was raw from being dragged over the rough corner of Alex's business card, which had remained in his pocket like Kryptonite, ever since he'd been given it.

So far, he hadn't found anything to either quash his fears or give shape to them. He needed to look again. He needed to know what she knew. Did she know who he was? Did she know about his lies?

Jacob had moved on to lovely Natasha, and yet the journalist had lingered nearby, eavesdropping. If she had really wanted to see Amy, why had she stayed there, craning her skinny neck to the side of his shoulder?

He stayed with Natasha just a few minutes, just long enough so that it didn't look like he was fleeing the scene. As he pushed out of the ward, Jacob looked over to Amy's cubicle and saw the curtains tugged shut.

As Jacob stood in the corridor, trapped by indecision, he heard a smash from inside the ward. A tray of drinks had probably been dropped, but it unnerved him. The ward, with its mechanical whistles and hums, was his quiet place. When he was in a situation he felt hemmed in by, he would close his eyes and take his mind back to the quiet of the cubicle, and the cool of Amy's skin.

Jacob stayed just outside the double doors to Bramble Ward, unsure what to do. He would have stayed there even longer, worrying and panicking, if it hadn't been for the scream. Before he could catch a hold of himself, the surprise had sent him bursting through another set of double doors and half-flying, half-running down the bleached stairs.

He could feel the blood throbbing in his head, and he was too dizzy to think about anything but getting to daylight and away from bloody Alex Dale.

He could hear doors above and below swinging open onto the stairwell. He had absolutely nothing to be afraid of, really, but he was running helter-skelter. He was running for his life.

And then he wasn't.

He was in a heap, teetering on the edge of the next set of speckled grey, highly bleached stairs, a full flight down from where he had been seconds before.

Blood whooshed around his ears and his face was wet. Jacob felt cold. Then hot. Then freezing. He slowly reached up to his face like he'd forgotten how his body was put together and couldn't find the controls.

He tentatively touched his temples, then looked at his fingertips. They were thick and sticky with the brightest blood he'd ever seen. Then the pain came.

There was a deep throbbing in his face, but far worse was the agony of his leg. From his right ankle to his knee surged a pain so intense that he needed everything he had to cope with it; he couldn't use a single unit of energy for calling or crying out.

After a few moments the double doors nearest to him flew open and a middle-aged woman with a visitor's badge sauntered out, took one look at Jacob and screamed.

And that's when he saw his leg. And passed out.

Apart from the days following his own birth, Jacob had never so much as sat in a hospital bed. *On*, many times, but never *in*.

Waking up strapped to a stretcher bed in A & E was never part of the plan.

Jacob's leg wasn't as badly damaged as they had first thought, the doctor said cheerfully, his bright-white hair framing his jolly face.

Oh, the leg was still broken, he chuckled, but it could be fixed and it would eventually be as good as it ever was. And then he'd frowned and leaned in, asking, 'Unless you're a sportsman?'

Jacob shook his head, looking down at the patterned hospital robe, identical to the ones Amy was dressed in day-in, day-out, and wondered who had stripped him.

'Oh good. Then yes, you'll be good as new.'

'When can I leave?' Jacob asked, suddenly putting two and two together and making Fiona. He tried to sit up, but he was strapped in.

'Oh, soon, soon,' said the doctor, unstrapping Jacob's torso and subtly moving the unforgiving hospital robe where it had ridden above the crotch.

'We had to strap you in to make sure you didn't wake up and try to move. You could have done yourself even more damage.'

Jacob nodded, as if this was something he encountered all the time.

He looked past his drip and up at the clock. It was nearly 1.30 p.m. – he'd lost several hours.

'Will I be able to leave before five?'

The doctor looked at Jacob like he had asked if he could still catch his shuttle to the moon.

'Most certainly not. We'll move you up to the ward and then you'll need to stay in for several days at least. You fractured your lower leg and you need to keep off it entirely. Even a fit and healthy young man like yourself needs to be careful.'

The doctor clasped his hands together.

'Right then, we do have a couple of forms that we need you to fill in.'

'I see. Christ. Okay. I'll need to ask someone to come and get the car. I'll need to call work and let them know, and my wife. Oh God.' Jacob looked up at the chipped ceiling tiles. His car was in the hospital car park. He'd fallen down the stairs in a building in which he had no reason to be spending time. And then there was work. He was at a dummy meeting at a made-up prospective client's office. Oh God...

The little doctor was still smiling but with his mouth only.

'I'll ask an orderly to bring you a payphone and we'll get you up to a ward later this afternoon. I'll have those forms brought over in a little while.' And with that he swept the curtain to one side and left.

Without waiting for the payphone, Jacob leaned over to the chair that had his clothes piled onto it. Who had done that? Who had folded his socks and underpants? His underpants. He tugged his jeans until they came away in his hand. He could sense from their weight that his phone was still in place as he worked his hands around carefully until he found the right pocket.

Work was easy enough – he told Marc that he'd gone to the hospital to pick something up for Fiona on his way back to the office when he'd fallen down the stairs. He'd made it as absurd and funny as possible, lots of wincing and sighing. True to form, reliable, laid-back Marc had laughed and passed the phone on to Geoff, their boss. Geoff had sighed and told Jacob his appointments would be taken care of and to get well soon.

And now for Fiona. He couldn't exactly tell her he was picking something up for her.

The blood beat faster in his temples.

It had to be unquestionable. He had to have been here, in the hospital, for a reason that was *unquestionable*.

He pressed 'Favourites', then 'Fiona' on his BlackBerry.

Jacob swallowed away the taste of sick and blood. The pain in his leg, while dulled, was still creeping up his body. His head swam from the morphine trailing into his arm.

'Hi, J.'

'I don't want you to freak out but—'

'What's wrong?'

'It's nothing serious but I'm in the hospital.'

'The hospital?'

'Yeah, I didn't want to worry you, but a while ago I thought I'd found a lump... you know... down there.'

'Oh my God! A lump?'

He could hear her breathing hard.

'It's okay, it's okay, it's fine.'

'Why didn't you say anything? Why are you still in hospital?'

'Oh, Fi, I'm really embarrassed. The consultant practically laughed with my nuts in his hand because it was so obviously not a lump. It was just a normal part that I'd not noticed before.'

'Oh, thank God!'

'Well, I was so relieved that I just ran down the stairs instead of taking the lift and I fell and broke my leg.'

'What?' Fiona was laughing. Thank fuck, Fiona was laughing.

'I'm still in A & E. They've strapped my leg up and I've got some nasty cuts but nothing that won't heal.'

'Oh my love, I'm so sorry, I don't know what to say. Let me come over there—'

'They don't want anyone to come and visit me while I'm in A & E but you can come and see me in the ward later this afternoon.'

'Which ward?'

'I'm not sure yet but I'll text you as soon as I know. I have to go, I'm not supposed to have my phone on.'

'But Jacob—?'

The curtains suddenly ballooned towards him, so he hung up and stuffed the phone under the covers.

He could feel the phone vibrating as Fiona called back but he tried to keep a neutral expression while the orderly was wheeling the payphone into position next to his elbow.

'There y'are, I'll come back and get it in a few minutes,' the thin young orderly mumbled from under some kind of ratty, trendy hairstyle.

'Okay, cheers.'

As soon as the curtains were still again, Jacob pulled his phone back out. Three missed calls in the last two minutes.

He called Fiona back. The call connected: 'Can't talk, I'm driving. I'll be there in a minute.' Click.

CHAPTER TWENTY-FOUR

Alex

22 September 2010

Amy was absolutely still now, her eyes and mouth giving nothing away. Alex was still frozen next to the clunky bed, mouth agape. Besides her heartbeat thumping in her temples, the only sound was from barely there radio reception crackling out from the abandoned desk. Three nurses and an orderly were standing at the open curtain staring at her, while in the background a middle-aged female visitor lurked, trying to look casual while straining to see what was happening.

For a moment, no-one spoke. Then the orderly with the ponytail stomped away, prompting the visitor to shuffle back to her shrine.

The remaining nurses stood in height order, with dumpy Nurse Radson at the front. The other two turned to one another, muttering and commenting behind cupped hands.

'What on earth was that about?' Nurse Radson hissed, her face just a few centimetres from Alex's collar bone.

'I'm so sorry. She was... I think she was communicating with me.'

'You what?' the tallest nurse asked, half-laughing, while Nurse Radson, for once, looked at Alex sympathetically.

'She, I... I'm sorry.' And with that, Alex grabbed her bag and her notepad and walked briskly out of the cubicle, out of the double doors and down the corridor.

It had all gone wrong. It had all gone horribly wrong.

Alex had behaved like a total ass, probably blowing her chances of being allowed back. Just as she was getting somewhere, she had completely embarrassed herself.

Alex rushed to the lifts, both of which had their lights parked at the top floor of the building. Keen to just keep moving until she was out of the building, Alex walked back to the stairwell and started down, careful not to slip on her flip-flops and break a toe.

The highly polished stairs were a sort of faux marble that dated this wing of the hospital firmly in the 1980s. The flecks reminded her of a suit belonging to a short-lived boyfriend of her mum, back when Alex was too small to wonder why she was calling an almost stranger 'Uncle Stephen'.

The steps felt freshly clean. Her adrenaline was seeping away, leaving the odd swoosh of hot flush and sweat licking Alex's temples.

She could feel that dry rot creeping up the back of her throat. That desire to drown, stronger than it had been in months. The need to flood herself and to spend the afternoon with a thick ink blot over all her thoughts.

Alex needed a drink, and she needed it as soon as possible. She had to get home fast or she wouldn't make it, and pulling her car into a pub car park and spending the afternoon raw, wasted and vulnerable was not a situation she wanted to revisit.

Her quickening footsteps slid to a stop almost immediately, as a piercing cry shot up from the stairs below her.

Alex's first thought was 'mental patient'. At one of the last outpatient appointments with her mother, they had encountered a 'wandering resident' from the nearby community health ward. The confused man had been scratching at his face and muttering impenetrably. Her mum, dancing close to the rim herself, had shrieked loudly and yelled about gypsies stealing the radiators. The man in turn had started screaming. Alex had stood frozen until nurses came running.

This scream had been incredibly loud and incredibly brief. Spooked, Alex raced back up the stairs to the floor above, crashed through more double doors, scuttled through a reception area and out into another windowless corridor.

Heart thumping and feeling under siege, she skittered around oblivious outpatients, visitors and whistling orderlies until she came across another pair of lifts. She had to get home.

One set of lift doors was open, the big grey box inside empty. Alex ran in, hammered the buttons until the door closed, and sank to her knees. As the lift started to move, Alex gathered herself up, took a deep breath and pressed the 'G' button.

A few people got in and out along the way, all of them ignoring the skinny woman at the back smiling nonchalantly while gripping her handbag with white knuckles.

Alex knew she was just reacting to the panic of the moment, but all she cared about right now was getting out. Getting out and getting a drink. Fuck the routine.

As the lift doors opened to a secondary foyer at the back of the ground floor, Alex stepped out as lightly as she could and looked around for the exit.

Taking the visitor badge from around her neck and slipping it into her bag, she pushed through a fire escape and ignored all the signs to the car park.

Stepping onto the pavement and away from the hospital grounds was wrong. She knew that, but right now that wasn't important. Softening the edges, stamping down on the panic, that was what she needed to do. Many years ago she could have had one brandy for shock, then a cab home. Not any more.

Alex knew full well that the second she chose to roam around the streets, looking for the nearest pub without discrimination, she would be sunk knee-deep into a bender within the hour.

The Elephant's Head was what her mother used to call 'an estate pub'. It wasn't actually on an estate, but it serviced a nearby block of council flats, a garage, a tyre place, a builders' merchant and, of course, exhausted hospital staff.

The floor inside was a sticky red carpet, with pre-ban cigarette burns and blackened chewing gum in abstract shapes.

The flock wallpaper helped make the optimistically named 'lounge' even more suffocating, and the dark wood chairs looked as inviting as a fist in the face.

Alex had ordered a double brandy as soon as she'd got to the bar. Throwing it back medicinally, she'd followed up immediately with whiskey and Diet Coke in a glass bottle, no ice.

Tipping just a thumb's measure of Diet Coke into the cheap bourbon, she'd sunk three in quick succession, still standing at the bar.

She'd run out of cash and knew she was walking a tightrope, but there was no way back now, she had to keep going and pray she didn't fall to her death.

Trying to keep her voice level, she asked the indifferent, middle-aged landlord, 'Can I put my card behind the bar? I'll be staying a while.'

He smiled for the first time, and gestured to a more comfortable-looking chair just around the corner from an 'out-of-order' jukebox. A familiar figure appeared in the doorway, caught her eye and waved.

Alex woke up with a start. A thick, sticky night still hung outside. She was lying on her bed with her vest and bra on, no knickers or jeans. One flip-flop sat next to her.

The room was spinning, and it took Alex five minutes of seasick crawling to find her phone. She'd almost given up, assuming she'd lost another one, when her groping thumb felt the cool of its touchscreen. She pressed the round indent and the time flashed up: 4.31 a.m.

She could feel that tell-tale raw feeling. She wasn't sore so much as *aware*. Her heart sank. Why did bloody Peter Haynes have to show up then? Why then?

She was coated with sweat and her heart thumped sporadically, unevenly. Eventually she found a window in the vertigo to make her way to the bathroom. She knew as soon as she sat down, the contents inside her tumbling into the bowl, that she'd had unprotected sex.

A fucking doctor should have known better, thought Alex.

Back to a pharmacist for the morning-after pill. Sober Alex would need to clean up Drunk Alex's mess. Again.

But for now she needed to do whatever it took to get back to sleep then wake up in the morning and not drink. Hair of the dog was a dangerous thing, the doorway to forty-eight hours of oblivion and weeks of mess. She threw up several bowlfuls of acrid bile before swaying her wobbly way downstairs to follow the well-worn procedure of paracetamol, ibuprofen and a half-pint of Berocca.

She'd done what she could for her morning self, now she just needed to sleep and feel relieved that at least she hadn't choked on her own vomit.

———

Alex woke again at 6.41 a.m., eyes stinging, head humming and stomach eating itself. A brief memory bubbled up of being carried through her front door, laughing wildly. Another of the doctor's red face above hers, sweating with concentration. Her laughing that maniac laugh and grabbing his awful, awful haircut. When had he left?

She barely had a second to wonder before running to the loo to throw up gallons of Berocca.

Considering everything, she could have felt worse. Perhaps she'd gone so far around the hangover wheel that she'd made it back to 'feeling alright'. Perhaps she was still drunk.

She eased into her loosest-fitting pyjama bottoms and slowly felt her way downstairs to put the kettle on. No running today. She'd had the wherewithal to plug her phone in when she'd woken at four-something. Now to perform the stomach-churning checks.

No emails sent.

No text messages sent.

She moved to her laptop. Internet banking, deep breath. Balance of bank account about £200 lighter; not great, but it could have been a lot worse.

The kettle eventually reached its climax, spluttering noisily. At first more water splashed along the glossy sideboard than in the mug, but eventually a cup of strong, sweet builders' tea was ready. Coffee would be too punishing today. As she turned to put the teaspoon in the sink, Alex spotted two shot glasses on the side and realized they'd sunk the last of her emergency cistern whiskey.

The sun was full, blasting orange light into every corner of the room. Most people would be leaving for work soon, and the showers up and down her road would be pumping away for the next hour. In moments like this, it was painfully clear that she could never handle an office job. Freelancing suited her lifestyle, however corrosive that may be.

Her handbag was on the arm of the sofa, purse and notepad intact. No cash, but at least all the cards were still there.

Opening her notepad, she slumped into the well-worn dip of the once-luxe cream corner sofa. Hugging her knees and sleepily reaching for the mohair throw, she started to flick through the notes.

Another wave of nausea crashed over her and she squeezed her eyes shut. She wasn't getting better, she'd just mistaken survival for progress. It didn't matter how many times Alex had convinced herself she could get well, it wasn't actually happening. She was treading water. Or maybe wine.

'Hello, Mount Pleasant Medical Centre?'

'Hello, I'd like to make an appointment to see my GP.'

'Name, please?'

'Alexandra Dale.'

'Axminster Road?'

'That's right.'

'May I ask what the appointment's for?'

'I had some tests taken a while ago and I think I need to do something about them.'

CHAPTER TWENTY-FIVE

Amy

Sometime in summer 1996

I don't know what to do. I can hear my mum sobbing, but what she's saying doesn't make a lot of sense. She's not a big drinker, but every Christmas she necks Babycham all day and me and Bob take the mickey out of her because she laughs at the stupidest stuff and talks nonsense. She sounds a bit like that now but with the opposite of laughter.

'I should have got you a cat,' she's saying. 'All your life you wanted a little kitten but I always said no. Every time no. Just no, no, no. Not for any good reason, Ames, just because I didn't want to have to look after it. I thought you'd get bored with the hassle and I'd be lumbered. And now I wish I had your cat to look after, my love. I wish I had something that you cared about, something special, so I could look after that at least.'

I don't know what to say. I never know what to say if she's upset. I get so choked up and it's like, making her happy again matters so much that it freezes me to the spot. I want to make everything better *so much* that I can't move.

'Oh this is pointless,' my mum says so quietly I can barely hear it.

I know she's angry now. Unlike most mums, when she gets

angry she gets quieter and quieter until I have to lean into her breath to catch what she's saying.

'This is all completely pointless,' she says again. 'It's just pointless.'

She sobs louder than she talks and I hear the chair hiss as she moves on it. But I have no answer for her and I don't know what I've done so I don't know how to make it better. The one person I never want to upset, hate to upset. I'll walk the other way round the Earth just to avoid crossing that line in front of us. But somehow, without realizing it, I've done it anyway.

Does she know I lied? Does she know that I let those phone calls turn into meetings and hearing his side of the story? Even though it was short-lived, it still wasn't right. I told her it had stopped before it got that far, that I'd listened when Bob put his foot down. I should have been honest, I should have listened to them.

She says she has to go and I call out to her, 'Mum! Mum!' 'Cos I can't play it cool with her, not my mum. But her footsteps don't stop, not even for a second, and I'm crying 'Mum! Mum!' as loud as I can and thinking, *shit, what the hell have I done wrong? I don't remember anything. I'm so sorry, Mum.*

CHAPTER TWENTY-SIX

Jacob

26 September 2010

Since leaving the hospital two days earlier, Jacob had now spent more weekday time in his Englishman's castle than ever before.

It wasn't so long ago that he and Fiona more or less shared one room in his tiny flat. They'd spent most evenings wrapped in each other. Sometimes they would lie on the living room floor between two duvets, like a sandwich. They'd watch cooking shows and *Coronation Street* and eat crisps from a big bag and drink too much wine. But then they'd got married and they'd bought a whole house into which they could spread. And they'd untwined.

The transition from boyfriend to husband probably hadn't been very fast in reality but, looking back, Jacob felt a lurching, roller-coaster whoosh. From the time he'd fumbled with the ring box in the restaurant to saying 'I do' in front of a congregation that was ninety percent the bride's side. It had whizzed by. But before the roller coaster set off, there was Amy. Two days after proposing, he'd gone to see her.

Now that he was to hobble around the house for the next few weeks, Fiona had insisted on looking after him with gusto. 'It'll be like the old days,' she'd said when he came out of hospital. 'We can lie around all day eating crisps and I can blame the weight gain on the baby.'

It was 10.43 a.m. He should have stayed in bed, he should have pulled her back under the duvet with him. Just talked nonsense all morning like they used to, mucked about as the day fell away. But lying down was agitating and he'd done nothing but lie flat in the hospital.

The painkillers had knocked some fight out of him, leaving just a throb in his limbs and peppery itches on his healing face. His leg had been plastered and bound in a bright-blue invalid sock. The whole thing weighed heavily and sweated like fury.

'Oh, J, you look miserable,' Fiona said, surveying him warily. 'I'm popping out for a bit. Will you be okay?'

'I'll be fine.'

'I've got my phone if you need anything.'

'Okay. I love you.'

As the front door clicked shut with a jingle of keys, Jacob reached into his pocket, squeezed his phone out and ordered a taxi.

'This'll do fine.'

'That's £8.60, please.'

The taxi driver left the engine ticking as he came round to open Jacob's door.

'Keep the change.'

As the tyres crunched away, the sudden cool and quiet of the road halted him. Jacob was alone in Beadminster Road, where the alleyway to the back of Axminster Road slashed two blocks of terraced houses.

This part of town was a beehive. Identical, neat and full of workers.

Most of the houses were empty by day, their occupants working in shops or answering phones somewhere. Alex Dale's house had also looked abandoned when the taxi had driven through as requested. The black VW nowhere to be seen.

The alleyway was cool and a little dank. Jacob's painful movements forced him to take in every brick, twig and stench as he slowly laboured his way through to the back of the journalist's home.

An ant house writhed around under the gate of number fourteen, and behind it he could hear children shrieking and bickering.

Alex Dale's gate didn't hide any children. The little garden inside was more of a yard. A graveyard of pots.

Jacob peered through a crack in the gate, blistered with green paint. The yard was empty, as ever, its lopsided clothes drier partially obscuring his view of the kitchen window.

Taking a last look up and down the empty alley, Jacob leaned on his crutches, struggled up onto one tiptoe and reached over the gate to grapple and swipe at the bolt. Eventually it squawked back.

Softly, holding his breath like a safe-cracker, Jacob flicked up the catch, pausing for a moment to quiet his panic. While this was not his first time, it was his first attempt to get inside in the full glare of sunlight, with crumpled legs slowing him down.

The rucksack he'd brought kept slipping off his shoulder as he swooped the gate open as quickly and quietly as he could manage.

Jacob shuffled and swung on his crutches, hunkering down, along the gravelly concrete.

He hobbled to the kitchen window, pausing briefly at the semi-paned back door, and leant his crutches against the sill. This wouldn't be easy.

The window opened just as quickly as before, but pulling his broken bottom-half up and through it required a level of athleticism that Jacob had never needed before. In the end, he shoved his way through and flopped like a decked fish.

Pulling his crutches through was comparatively easy. Blood pumping and adrenaline surging, he finally got to work.

CHAPTER TWENTY-SEVEN

Alex

26 September 2010

'Hi, Amy, it's Alex, I hope you don't mind me visiting you again.'

Alex looked at her hands, which were shaking. 'I can't tell you how sorry I am for freaking out last time I was here. I'm so embarrassed. I honestly thought they wouldn't let me back in.'

Sunshine streamed through the tall windows, the dust particles danced and a nearby visitor was snoring rhythmically next to her loved one. Alex could see the nurses training their eyes on her from the doorway of the office.

'Amy, I've been finding out a little bit more about you and what was happening in your life before you came into the hospital.'

Alex swallowed; this hackneyed monologue didn't come easy. The ward lay still around them and the smell of bedpans and antiseptic curdled at the back of Alex's throat.

Amy's small breasts rose and fell slowly, her skinny wrists at her side, palms open and upward. Her seaside eyes were open. Amy was 'awake', but her skin had a sheen of sleepy sweat on it. She looked like she'd been wrapped in cling film.

'Amy, I still feel like I'm intruding a bit, because you don't know me but I know so much about you. I hope I'm not upsetting you by being here.'

Alex looked around at the other beds. The blonde woman with the satisfied look lay next to a huge bouquet of flowers wrapped in gold ribbon, which spilled out of the hospital vase. An old couple sat entirely motionless, he in his checked pyjamas, propped up with pillows, she holding his hand and hanging her head, like her batteries had run out.

'We might have been friends if we'd known each another in our teens, you know. And I can definitely imagine you going on to do something like journalism, like Becky said.'

Amy's chest continued to rise and fall softly.

'Amy, I know that you were going out with Jake for quite a while before you were attacked.'

The steady 'shhh shhh' of breath continued, unchanged. Alex put her head in her quivering hands, running her hands up and through her hair.

'But I've had some time to I think about it, and I have a feeling you might have been seeing someone else, as well as Jake. I just don't think you're the kind of girl who would have met someone for the first time, gone off with them and given them your virginity.' Alex squinted to look for a reaction. 'I just don't.

'I think things must have been building up for a while and I think this other person might have been older. You probably felt like you had to keep it all very secret.'

Alex held her breath and tried to tell if the tiny twitch she saw on Amy's nose was a trick of the light.

'Amy, I'm sure that he made you feel special, like you could trust him.

'If it was me and if I'd started seeing someone in secret when I was fifteen, especially if he was older, I'd have been so excited and at the same time I think I'd have been quite scared. Especially the first time.'

Amy's breathing was half a beat faster, Alex was sure of it.

'At some point, Amy, I think this guy changed. I think you saw something in him that you'd not seen before. Maybe you didn't feel special any more or maybe he stopped treating you nicely. Perhaps the guilt was too much. And I think something happened and this guy hurt you really badly.'

Was Amy's breathing quicker? Alex tried not to get carried away. Perhaps it was her own fast breath confusing things.

'Amy, I've thought about this a lot, and whatever else this guy was, he was smart. The police combed the area, they went through all your things, they had your clothes and your fingernails,' she lowered her voice, 'but they found nothing. I just don't think an event like that would be possible on the spur of the moment.'

Amy's sleepy sheen had faded and her eyes were wider than ever.

'I think he planned this meticulously, Amy. And you couldn't possibly have known that. He tricked you and *none of this is your fault*.'

Alex scraped her hair back into a ponytail and rubbed her eyes. She had been sitting and talking for about an hour, but the one-way flow had sucked more out of her than she anticipated. Had she been allowed, she could quite easily have slipped under the covers of the spare Bramble Ward bed, lay perfectly still and drifted away.

In the corner of the ward, Alex could see Nurse Radson washing the face of an older, male patient. Alex could just make out that the nurse was singing quietly while she wiped away the tiny suds. An old Frank Sinatra song or something similar.

Alex watched as the nurse lifted the patient's chin slightly. Then she dipped her fingers into a little red pot and worked the contents into her palm. The nurse smoothed the man's hair, using a tortoiseshell comb to create a sharp parting.

'There,' she said, standing back to survey her work. 'You look like a young Cary Grant, Burt.'

She folded the comb into a small black case, straightened Burt's collar and gave his eyebrows a final tidy with the tip of her finger. The comb and pomade were tucked away, Burt's hands were patted and the nurse went back to her office.

The sun was still high as Alex drove back, and her clothes felt close and uncomfortable. She was irritable, rattled by Amy's almost-there anxiety as much as she was excited by it.

Everything felt awkward and aggravating. Alex's bag slipped hard off her shoulder, her car door didn't shut the first time – clanging against the seat belt, she had a tiny stone in her shoe and a deafening headache.

As she backed through the front door with her various belongings dangling painfully, something stopped her dead, as still as a held breath.

She reopened the front door with a quiet click, and placed her stuff down silently. And then she stepped carefully down the hall.

'Hello,' she said to the sitter. 'What the hell are you doing in my house?'

'Oh shit,' said Jacob Arlington. 'Oh shit.'

'Well? What are you doing in here?' Alex asked, heart banging in her chest.

'I'm so sorry.'

Jacob sagged to the side, leaning heavily on his right crutch and sinking his face down to his chest.

'How did you get in?' Alex Dale kept one eye on her front door.

'I climbed through the kitchen window. Fuck, I'm so sorry. I just needed to know what you knew. About me.'

'Well, what is there to know about you?'

'About me and Amy.'

'Go on,' Alex said.

'I'm married,' Jacob sat quietly. 'I have a baby on the way.'

Patting her phone in her pocket and making sure her door was still open, she gestured to the living room.

'Look, sit down. I'll get us both a drink. Let's start this again.'

'So I'm Alex. Which I guess you know already. And you are?'

'I'm Jacob.'

'Jacob Arlington? Amy's boyfriend?'

'Yes. Amy's boyfriend. But you knew that already.'

Alex sighed. It was all so obvious. Why would a young guy choose to visit a ward stuffed with people he didn't know, every single week, for no reason? He was there for Amy, and Amy alone.

'Jacob,' Alex started, groping for the right words. 'Have you been going to see Amy for the last fifteen years?'

'No, not the whole time. At first, my mum wouldn't let me out of her sight.' He trailed off, looking at the door and then at his crutches, askew on the floor.

'Go on,' said Alex, chewing her lip.

Jacob sat back, wincing and lifting his ankle to rest it on the coffee table. 'May I?'

'Of course you can, it looks very painful. So what happened?'

'I fell down the stairs. Stupid really.'

'No,' said Alex gently. 'I mean, what happened after Amy was attacked? When did you start visiting her?'

Jacob sighed. 'I suppose I don't have a choice but to tell you, right?'

Alex looked at the open kitchen window and then back at Jacob's red face. 'Under the circumstances, I think it's only fair.'

'Okay,' Jacob conceded. He took a deep breath, and exhaled sharply.

'After they found Amy, the police called my mum and told her what happened.'

'Where were you when they called?'

'At home. I was sitting on the stairs when the phone rang. Mum wouldn't let me answer it. It'd been a couple of days and things weren't looking good. She answered and immediately turned her back. I just knew. She sort of did this weird little sound.'

Alex sat down slowly at the other end of the sofa.

'My mum got off the phone and she just stood there with her back to me. Then she came and sat on the stairs and put her arm around me and I knew it must be really bad. She couldn't get the words out. I just sat there. I didn't cry, I didn't know what to do. Eventually my mum told me that Amy was in a bad way and that the police needed to talk to everyone close to her.

'I didn't get it at first. I told Mum they didn't need to talk to me because she'd had already told me. I just wanted to go to see Amy and see how she was, be there for her. I didn't realize that the police wanted to talk to me to find out if I was involved.' Jacob turned to look at Alex, coughing to clear his throat.

'I was a fifteen-year-old kid, I didn't know what to do. I was in shock, I guess. And then I was really scared.

'My mum was beside herself. The police turned up that night and carted me off to the police station. She came with me and I'll never forget the look on her face. Or my brother's. Tom was watching from the living room when I got into the police car. He just looked horrified. I felt like I'd really let everyone down, even though I hadn't done anything wrong.

'Mum denied it afterwards, but she must have thought I was going to be charged with something. I'd never seen her so worried.'

Alex bit her lip to stop from prompting him. Interviewing 101: shut the fuck up and let the interviewee fill the silence.

'The questions the police asked were pretty full-on,' Jacob carried on, looking at Alex and then looking away. 'That's their job, but it must have been obvious from the start that I couldn't have done any of those things.'

'So did you go to see Amy once the police released you?' asked Alex, trying her damnedest not to rush her uninvited guest.

'No,' said Jacob. 'I went back to school. Just for one day. My parents had said to just carry on as normal,' he laughed.

'My mum worked at the school, and she'd spoken to all my teachers at the end of the day and asked how I'd coped. Well, I hadn't coped, of course. So that was it. We left.'

'We?'

'My brother Tom and me. He was a couple of years below me and I guess kids had been hassling him too.'

'That must have been tough on him?' asked Alex.

'Yeah, I think so. He moved to a private school up the road. He didn't like it, but I was too wrapped up in everything to notice.'

'So did you go on to a new school as well?'

'No, the teachers sent work home for me and I took my GCSEs at a nearby college. After that, I went to the same college to do my A-levels. I did them at night, with all the stay-at-home mums.'

'Why?'

'My mum was worried I'd be in a class with someone from school otherwise. She didn't want me to be bothered, but I never saw any of them again.'

'So did you start visiting Amy while you were at college?'

'Yeah, just now and then. After Jo died, Amy didn't have anyone. I didn't really want to go but I felt I should. Amy was still wired up to machines when I first went in. She was so fragile... I don't

know, it seemed like some kind of duty or something. So I just...
I haven't stopped.'

'Did anyone go with you?'

Jacob shook his head. 'I went alone. In secret.'

'Every week?'

'No, not straight away. Each time was so hard that I really had
to force myself to go. I went every few months. Every time I had to
gear up for it. That was when she was in intensive care. It got a bit
easier when she moved to Bramble Ward. I gradually went more
and more and started to, kind of, need to go. So I became a sitter,
and that took some of the pressure off. That probably sounds weird.'

'Not really. It sounds really tough. There must have been times
when yours was the only voice she heard. That's a real kindness.'

'I don't think of it like that but that's nice of you to say.'

'So how long ago did you become a sitter?'

'A couple of years. I'd actually gone in to tell her that I couldn't
keep visiting so much, and...'

'Why was that?'

Jacob looked down. 'Because I was getting married.'

'Oh.'

'Yeah.'

'So what happened when you went to tell her that?'

'It's going to sound ridiculous. I'd been going about once every
few weeks by then, sometimes more. I told Amy that I was getting
married the next week and that I'd always love her but that it wasn't
right for me to keep seeing her as often as I did.

'Like I said, it sounds ridiculous, but Amy looked like she was
going to cry. She didn't cry... I mean she can't, can she? But her
eyes welled up. That's how it looked.

'I felt so bad that I told her I didn't mean it and that I'd still see
her. On the way out I saw a poster about volunteering to sit with
the patients. And I figured it wasn't quite so dodgy, you know, I

was doing something for the patients, plural, I wasn't just hanging out with my old girlfriend.'

'Are you the only person from her past that visits her?'

Jacob faltered. 'I think so...' he trailed off. 'Yes, I am now.'

'So what was your plan today? What would you have done if I hadn't come home and found you?'

'I just wanted to look, you know, at what you really knew. I got so worked up, imagining some kind of exposé in the paper, me and Amy, accusations or something. I know I'm in it up to my neck here. I've really fucked up.'

'Jacob, that's not the kind of journalism I do. Look, what's in the bag?'

'USB sticks.'

'For taking stuff from my computer?' Alex asked, not able to conceal her shock.

Jacob started to panic. Downing the rest of the tea Alex had made despite his protestations, he tried to stand up.

'Please don't – you'll hurt yourself. I'm not going to call the police.'

'Really?'

'Yes, really. Just as long as you're honest with me.'

'My wife's pregnant and she has no idea that I visit Amy. She has no idea about Amy whatsoever. She's not from round here and my family doesn't talk about what happened, it's just this huge secret.

'We've been having a tough time, together I mean, my wife and I. I thought you were going to write about me and Amy and I thought it was going to ruin everything. I guess you're still going to write about me, and I've given it all to you on a plate.' His head was in his hands, thumb thumping his forehead.

'I didn't even know it was you at the hospital,' Alex admitted. 'I'd not thought that far ahead.'

'Great,' said Jacob, 'so now I really have fucked it all up.'

'I don't want to make things difficult for you, but why don't you talk to your wife about this? You've not done anything wrong.'

'You don't know my wife. Lies are her thing, the line you can't cross with her. Especially lies about another girl.'

'But Amy's not a bit on the side, she's a victim – she's not in a position to do anything wrong.'

'It doesn't matter, believe me. I've kept this from Fiona since the beginning when I barely saw Amy, and it's just snowballed. The longer time's gone on, the bigger the secret's got. We're talking years. She won't think I've done nothing wrong,' Jacob shrugged. 'I mean, I have done something wrong, haven't I? I've lied to her.'

'I know what it's like to keep secrets from the person you love,' Alex said. 'And I know that the damage is done by the secret, not by being honest.'

'With all due respect,' said Jacob, looking up, 'I can't imagine that you've kept a secret like this. I've been sneaking around for years to sit with my half-dead teenage girlfriend. You're honestly telling me that you can match that? Try me.'

Alex tried to shake a memory. The look on Matt's face when he found a bottle in the cistern.

'What?' she'd laughed. 'Oh come on! I hide my emergency credit card in the freezer so I don't buy things I won't need. Are you telling me that makes me a spendaholic too?'

Matt had said nothing. He'd placed the bottle on the tiny sideboard of their London flat and washed his hands, slowly and carefully.

Alex hovered nearby, trying to decide whether to put the bottle back or open it to make a point.

'The flush works now, anyway,' he'd said. 'I need to get ready for my shift.'

Alex looked at Jacob. She thought about his healthy, sober wife full of a healthy, plump baby, wondering where he was right now.

'Maybe another time,' she said. 'Let me get your number and I'll call you a cab.'

CHAPTER TWENTY-EIGHT

Amy

Sometime in summer 1996

I woke up this morning and Bob was in my room, sitting on my bed. I knew it was him from the weight, even before he spoke. The whole of my bed was sagging like a little boat caught in a big wave.

I think he'd just woken up from a bad dream or something because he wasn't making any sense. His voice was all gargled like it gets when a West Ham game doesn't go the way he wants, or one of his elderly customers pops their clogs. Actually it was worse than that, it was like his mouth was full of pickled onions and he couldn't get his words out.

'Ames, love,' he'd said, but I hadn't answered and I don't know why. Then there was a long pause and if it wasn't for the weight I'd have thought he'd gone.

Eventually he said, in one breath: 'I've got some bad news about Mum, sweetheart.' He always says it like 'swede heart' and I imagine little swedes carved into heart shapes, bobbing along on a chorus line, kicking their legs up and down like showgirls.

He said that Mum had been poorly for a while and struggling to cope. That's how I know he was wrong because my mum's fine, she's not called in sick to work for as long as I can remember. We even went shopping just the other weekend. She took me up to

Camden, after a hell of a lot of nagging. She'd been promising for a long time and we finally went on the train. I was like a little kid, nose pressed to the window, steaming it up. Mum was nervous. London always makes her nervous. She had her handbag clutched to her chest the whole time and when we got off the train and walked down to the Tube, she wouldn't touch the handrail because of all the germs.

I loved it. The noise and the smells and all the different people whizzing about. You had faces from everywhere, languages I'd never heard being spoken all around us on the Tube, every kind of outfit, every kind of shoe. Buskers playing the sixties and seventies songs Mum and Bob like, but even those didn't seem to make Mum relax. It's a young person's place, I guess. Though she's not really that old. She's probably the youngest mum out of all my friends. I hope I'm not so scared when I'm in my thirties.

We'd made our way out of Camden Town Tube station and down past the lock, my mum spinning around and jumping at every bloke that walked past. Thankfully none of them seemed offended. I'd got my purse out to count my money at one point and she'd thrown an absolute epi. Next time I'm just going to go up with Jenny or Becky, tell Mum and Bob I'm going into town for the day and be done with it. Camden's for the young.

I bought some really cool second-hand jeans and a couple of T-shirts from different stalls while I was there. One T-shirt had a picture of Jarvis as if Andy Warhol had painted him and the other was a knock-off Smashing Pumpkins top. Not really a favourite but I'm trying to move across into rockier stuff and I do like some of the songs off *Siamese Dream*.

I also got some little hair clip things for twisting your hair up in cool sections like Björk. When we got home, I showed Mum a picture I'd cut out of *Select* and we tried to do it together but I think my hair's too long.

I always knew I wanted to live in London but I only really knew it as a big glob of London-ness, red buses and Buckingham Palace and Oxford Street and all of that. I knew that wasn't where real people lived. Now I can picture everything more clearly.

I'll go to uni in London and I'll live in halls for the first year and then I'll find the friends for life who'll be my flatmates and we'll live in Camden. Maybe I'll still be with Jake and we can get a flat together. Deep down, I think I know he'll still be living in Edenbridge with his mum though. Maybe that's unfair on him, we'll have to see.

I'll be editor of the uni newspaper and be known for my bravery and cutting-edge style. People at real magazines'll be like, 'we've been watching your work for a while and you have what it takes'. *NME*'s the prize though; if I can get in there, I'll have died and gone to heaven.

Fast forward a few years and I'll be the *NME* editor, the first ever woman – I think – and living in my own place overlooking Camden Lock. I'll be going out with Damon Albarn by then; we'll have met when I go to interview him and convince him to leave that druggy Justine from Elastica. Or maybe I'll still be with Jake, and Damon'll just be my bit on the side. Ha! I know most of that won't happen but I will go to uni in London at least, and I'll meet a whole bunch of new people. I definitely know that.

Bob was wrong anyway. I think my mum's here now. I can hear her humming an old song, 'Fly Me to the Moon', I think. She's washing my face and stroking my hair. He must have had a really bad dream to get so worked up. Poor old Bob.

CHAPTER TWENTY-NINE

Jacob

26 September 2010

The house was quiet when Jacob got home, the big car conspicuous by its absence. He swung into the living room and flicked the TV on to a rugby match he might have watched had he stayed put.

Could he really trust the journalist to keep her word? It had all sounded so stupid when he'd said it out loud. She hadn't even known who he was. At least she didn't know how many times he'd broken in.

He looked at the mantelpiece, over which hung a huge photo of their wedding day in a silver frame. Fiona had never looked so beautiful. What was it about a big white dress? On no other occasion would that make a woman look good, but she had appeared other-worldly that day. Even Jacob looked like a better version of himself, smiling so widely his face looked cut in two.

Beneath the wedding photo sat two new frames. One with a twelve-week scan of their black and white prawn. The other at twenty weeks, the watery grey picture showing an actual baby shape. A real human, that he'd co-authored. There really should be some kind of vetting process, he thought.

Along the mantelpiece was a picture of Fiona and her parents on holiday when she was a teenager. Fiona staring moodily at the camera from under dyed red hair, her parents beaming through sunburned faces. There was a photo of Fiona at her postgraduate ceremony, and another of them both as tanned newly-weds, peering over huge cocktails on their honeymoon.

Soon, like his mum's house, the mantelpiece would be overflowing with baby photos. The photo collection would grow with their family. Jacob thought of Amy's mum, who must have collected her own photos so eagerly and then, no more. No-one would take a camera into Bramble Ward to capture that moment. The whole ward was a captured moment.

Fiona's car pulled up outside and Jacob's heart thumped as he waited to see if his face gave anything away.

'Hey, J,' she said, holding carrier bags and looking pleased with herself.

'Hey, you.'

'Whatcha watching?'

'Rugby.'

'Ugh,' she groaned. But remained standing on the spot, grinning.

'You look pleased with yourself,' Jacob smiled.

'Well, I am. I drove to Waitrose and got us some nice bits for tea tonight. I thought you might need cheering up.'

'Why?' he frowned.

Fiona looked at him, puzzled. 'Because you broke your leg.'

'You're so good to me.'

'Yeah, I am. Got you some posh beer and everything.'

'I love you so much.'

'Oh, calm your knickers down, J,' she said, but looked delighted.

Could he really trust Alex Dale?

CHAPTER THIRTY

Alex

27 September 2010

The sun streamed through the window into Alex's bedroom, dappling her crisp white duvet with playful sunbursts and shards of rainbow. A few little dewdrops clung to the window and she could hear children playing nearby.

She sat up slowly, expecting her brain to slide against her skull at any second, but the headache didn't come.

For the first time since she started this pet project, she felt like she might actually be getting somewhere. She had tugged at the pieces of thread and finally one of them had been attached to something.

Jake.

She half-smiled at the memory of his words. Such sad words. As she played back the recording from her iPhone, she allowed the smile to become a full-blown beam.

Jake. Jacob Arlington. The sitter. And he might have told her far more than he realized.

It was still early, way before visiting hours, and Alex knew she was chancing her arm. But she had nearly two hours to kill before her doctor's appointment and was desperate to make headway with her investigations.

She stepped out of the big grey lift and strode confidently to the Bramble Ward door, rapping on it loudly.

The door opened ajar and a nurse she didn't know peered out. 'Can I help you?'

'Hi there, I'm writing a story about your patient Amy Stevenson and I have a couple of questions.'

'I'm sorry?' the nurse creased her forehead as if she didn't understand a single word.

'I'm a journalist, my name's Alex Dale.'

'I'm not sure about this. I'll have to speak to Dr Haynes.'

Alex swallowed hard and tried to ignore the fragments of memory. Peter Haynes buying a round of drinks. Peter Haynes in her bed. The awkward weight on top of her. His tongue poking out of the side of his mouth as he concentrated on what he was doing.

'Well, I really do just want to check one thing with you, I'll be really quick.'

'Wait there,' commanded the nurse. Alex stepped back, leaning lightly against the pale pastel wall. Flyers for self-help groups and fundraisers fluttered by her ears as she waited. She could hear one half of a conversation, the nurse sighing. 'You're the boss,' she said, wearily.

The door opened wider and the nurse ushered her inside.

'I'm not very happy about this,' she said to no-one. 'So then, what do you want to know?'

'How far back do these go?'

'I'm not sure.'

'Might they be archived somewhere?'

'I doubt it. They're probably just shredded.'

Alex flipped the heavy pages to the first lined entry, just over three years ago.

'Could I take this to the café to look through? I'll bring it back before visiting hours.'

'I'd sooner you didn't. You can sit here for as long as you like though.'

It took sixty-seven pages of records to find what she was looking for, but when Alex saw it, a bolt of excitement whipped her spine.

Afterwards, she sat in the car and scribbled urgently, too scared to drive straight to the GP surgery in case it all seeped away before she had a chance to capture her thoughts. That feeling was back, for the first time in who knew how many lost years. The feeling she'd get when she found that killer line. Or that shock and awe set-up, or that zinger of a wordplay. That perfect point. How she'd chased that feeling. It became ever harder to catch. She would get closer and closer to deadline until the paper was due to be off stone in mere hours and Alex was still sipping wine from a plastic cup and ignoring her desk phone.

She couldn't remember getting this feeling when sober for many, many years.

'Alexandra.' Dr Evans peered over his glasses. 'I'm glad you've come in. Looking at your notes, we don't have the luxury of time.'

'I've cut down a lot,' Alex told the doctor. 'And I'm a lot more in control than when I was last here.'

'My dear, it's not a case of cutting down. Cutting down was what needed to happen years ago. You need to stop altogether. And if you cannot stop—'

'I can stop.'

'If you cannot stop by yourself, it's a case of getting some help to stop. And as fast as possible.'

'It was only in the early stages when I was tested, and it wasn't that long ago. I feel fine, I'm pretty fit and active so—'

'Are you incontinent?' the doctor asked, cutting her off.

'Well, I mean I have the odd accident, but I drink a lot of water.'

'Are you still having periods?'

'My periods have never been regular,' Alex replied quickly.

'And sleep? How is your sleep?'

'I fall asleep easily,' Alex said.

'But do you stay asleep? Do you feel rested in the morning?'

'Who does?' Alex tried to smile.

'Do you have nausea throughout the day?'

'Well, yes, I mean...' Alex trailed off.

The doctor took off his glasses and looked directly into her eyes. Heavy bags tugged his lower lids towards his whiskered mouth.

'We know that the organ started to lose function some years ago, Alex. This started even before your loss. The loss tells me you're not able to stop because you would have stopped before then. I'm sorry to be blunt.'

He passed her a thin tissue.

'And even if you have reduced your alcohol intake, you are still drinking, which will be accelerating your condition. As your doctor, I have to urge you to seek help.'

'I am seeking help, that's why I'm here. And I've already cut back and my work is improving. I'm still running most days, I have bags of energy.'

'Here is a list of local meetings. If you don't manage to stop, coming around the corner will be hair loss, sickness, jaundice, memory loss, confusion—'

'Confusion? Do you mean dementia?'

'No, similar but not the same.' Dr Evans had been her mother's doctor. 'You may start to stagger when you walk. You could even get ascites, where fluid builds up in your abdomen until you look heavily pregnant. Really, Alex, you need to take this seriously.'

'How far off are these new symptoms?'

'Don't obsess about those, because those aren't the main issue here. You need to understand that you are facing a potentially fatal condition.'

'How long do I have?'

'That depends on whether you make some significant changes.'

'I'm a journalist, I deal in deadlines.'

'Okay, Alex, here it is. If you don't stop drinking, you'll be dead in a year.'

Alex sat back in her chair and exhaled deeply.

Dr Evans spoke softly and slowly. 'This leaflet has details of all the meetings in the area. They are completely anonymous, and they're free. And, most importantly, they can work. But you have to take that first step.'

'I thought I had.'

CHAPTER THIRTY-ONE

Amy

Sometime in 1998

I still can't quite believe it, but Jake's mother came to see me today.

My heart was thumping like a drum when I heard her voice. I instantly felt like I was in trouble. I don't know if it's the school secretary thing or the fact that she seems to despise everything that I say, do and am, but either way I was in bits by the time she left.

I think she might have wanted to say something important but bottled it. I think she wanted to warn me off Jake, to be honest. To tell me that he was too good for me or that I was distracting him and she could make things difficult if I didn't bow out graciously. She didn't say that though. She said in her haughty telephone voice, 'Amy, I'm sorry to say—' And that was it. She stopped dead.

Sorry to say what?

Eventually, she started up again but she just made pointless chit-chat. She said something dull about the weather and about Jake's dad's train being cancelled due to the weather and about choosing the wrong coat for the weather. And when I woke up again, she was gone.

I don't know if she's coming back. I can't believe my mum let her in and didn't check if I was okay while she was here. She could have said or done anything and no-one checked. I don't know what's up with my mum any more, nothing seems right.

CHAPTER THIRTY-TWO

Jacob

28 September 2010

Jacob hadn't wanted to meet when she called, but Alex had him by the crutches and they both knew it.

He'd arrived early to grab a table as far towards the back of the station café as possible. His heart raced as she walked in, ordered a cappuccino and sat down lightly in front of him.

'Hello,' she said.

'Hello,' he said.

The distant sizzle of bacon fat thickened the air; the chinking of cups and tinkling of glasses softened the silence. Alex wore a hard stare, blowing lightly on her coffee and holding Jacob's gaze.

'Jacob,' she began, before taking a sip. 'Thank you for meeting me.'

'I didn't really have a choice.'

'I meant what I said, I won't go to the police about the break-in. I know you were there out of fear.'

Jacob didn't smile. Not even with relief.

'Jacob, you said you were the only person who visits Amy now, didn't you?'

'I said that I thought I was. As far as I knew...' His voice trailed off but his heart was charging like a horse.

Alex took a sip of her coffee and smiled slightly. He couldn't tell if she was trying to be reassuring, or smug.

'Don't worry,' she said, 'we're on the same side. I'm not trying to screw you over. I really feel for you.' The fingers on her spare hand stirred. He wondered if she was considering laying a reassuring palm over his far bigger hand. But the hands stayed where they were.

'Jacob,' Alex carried on with a softer voice. 'I have a feeling you already know what I'm about to tell you.'

He stared at her bony hands as they twitched again.

'I asked to see the visitor records for Amy's ward. I didn't know exactly what I was looking for until I found it.'

'My mum.' Jacob looked at his hands.

'Your mum.' Alex said.

Jacob had known for some time that his mum had visited Amy. He'd found out the same way Alex had, his mother's careful signature in the log book, curling perfectly on the line. Because this wasn't television and because he was his mother's son, he hadn't said a word.

His mum had disliked Amy in a way that he'd never seen from her before or since. His mum wasn't a hater. She was a worrier; overprotective perhaps. She could seem haughty to outsiders, but she wrapped her family in unstinting love and affection. When Amy came on the scene though, Jacob had seen something new in his mum's expression. Amy had been convinced of Sue's hatred, and would rarely come to the house if his mum was there.

'I just don't know what I've done!' Amy would say, alternating between welling eyes and outrage.

'Is it because she thinks I'm common? Or thick? Because I'm at the grammar school, too! And we don't have a lot of money, but my mum raised me to know how to behave. It fucks me off so much, Jake!'

And he'd go red. Because he knew that Amy was right, and he didn't yet have the words to reassure a girl.

For all that, his mum had been devastated when Amy was attacked. Perhaps Amy's fate had reduced her back down to size, leaving his mum hollow with guilt. Jacob had watched her fumbling in her handbag not long after it happened. 'I'm just popping out to the car,' she'd say, before sliding into the driver's seat, lighting a cigarette with clumsy fingers and leaning back to exhale.

She'd come back in, sucking an Everton mint, red blotches circling her eyes.

Until Amy was attacked, he'd never seen his mum smoke. In fact, she had never admitted that she did smoke. Not to this day.

'Did your mum not tell you she'd visited Amy?' Alex asked.

'No, she didn't tell me.'

'Why do you think that was?'

'I don't know.' He turned around to look out of the window and shook his head. 'I guess she wanted Amy to stay in my past. She didn't want me to dwell. She'd told me to move on almost as soon as it happened. I guess she couldn't say that and then openly wallow in the past herself.'

'Was Amy close to your mum?'

'No. They didn't like each other. Amy thought my mum was stuck up and looked down on her. My mum thought Amy was a bad influence.'

'Perhaps your mum felt guilty about that?'

'I don't know, maybe.'

'Why did she stop visiting?'

'As far as I know she only went a few times, and not for years now. I always cast an eye over the book but I've never seen Mum's name again.'

'She's visited occasionally by the looks of things – the last time was two Augusts ago.'

'That's when I got married. Perhaps she was sure I'd moved on enough.'

'Perhaps. But what's really puzzling me is why she took your brother Tom with her.'

Jacob woke early with a dry throat. Next to him, Fiona lay on her side, snoring. One of the less endearing traits she'd acquired in pregnancy, but he was grateful for it this morning. The low rumbles told him she was still at the bottom of sleep's well.

He sat up and swung his good leg and then his bad leg out of bed. The sun had just started to appear along the bottom of the blinds like an orange frame, but the day had barely started.

He had always struggled to get up in the morning, a trait his brother Tom didn't suffer. They were Jack Sprat and wife in that respect; Tom bounding out of his room at first light, crashing soon after dinner, Jacob lying frustrated and twitchy until the early hours, then heavy-lidded until late morning.

What the hell were you doing there, Tom?

He wished they had the kind of relationship where he could just grab his brother, give him a wedgie and all the secrets would come tumbling out. Secrets they could just laugh off.

They'd been best friends once upon a time. And then Jacob just dropped him like a wet stone when Amy came along. Instead of playing with Tom like before, Jacob had spent his afternoons and evenings in his own room, listening to music and trying, failing, to write a note in reply to Amy's love letters.

Those love letters. Jacob wished he'd had the balls to keep them, but he'd thrown them away as soon as he read them, like James Bond destroying MI6 briefing notes. Except in his case, he wasn't hiding spy stuff from the enemy, he was getting rid of anything of which his mum might disapprove.

Before Amy disappeared, Jacob would often hear Tom rustling

around in his own room, playing his Game Boy or doing his homework. Sometimes, Tom would knock on Jake's door and stand there expectantly. Sometimes Tom would nod at the paper on the bed and say things like, 'Are those from *her*?' or 'I s'pose your girlfriend's coming round now Mum's gone out?' but he rarely said any more. Jacob would wave him away and Tom would walk off, looking wounded.

He didn't remember Tom or Amy saying more than two words to each other. She was nothing to Tom, nothing more than his brother's inconvenient girlfriend. She wasn't ever that comfortable in their house, becoming agitated when she thought an adult was due home. So they hid in Jacob's room and shut the rest of the house out. They'd only sneak onto the sofa if they knew they were alone.

What had Tom done instead? Jacob vaguely remembered him spending more time with Simon, passing the Game Boy back and forth or watching TV in silence.

Jacob and Tom would probably have grown closer again, had Amy's abduction not derailed everything. As it was, Jacob then had new reasons to lie in his room without talking. By the time he surfaced, his brother was no longer a cheerful thirteen-year-old, but a full-blown teenager. He wore black eyeliner and a long leather jacket that smelled like a charity shop. He listened to Nine Inch Nails and the Manics and read gloomy books like *The Catcher in the Rye*. From being peas in a pod, they were suddenly night and day. And Jacob barely noticed it happen.

Tom hadn't known Amy though, they didn't have any shared friends and had barely ever met. They were civil, that was as far as it went.

Jacob stood in his kitchen, drinking tea and watching the orange light creep through the garden towards the house.

———

Tired from his early start and with half of his lunch still languishing on the plate, Jacob looked up decisively.

'Fi?'

'Yeah?'

'I need to go out for a bit.'

'Where?'

'I just need to clear my head.'

'Why do you need to clear your head? You needed to go out to clear your head yesterday too, so what's up?'

'Please don't interrogate me, I'm finding this really hard.'

'This is hard for you?' Fiona pushed her plate away and sat back. 'Okay.' She nodded to herself. 'You're in a world of your own and all I'm trying to do is help you...'

Her head sagged as Jacob held his breath. When she lifted it again, tears were pouring freely and silently.

'No,' she said quietly, 'no.'

'Fi—'

'No.' She swallowed hard. 'Enough.'

Fiona struggled to stand up from her stool and rested a wobbly arm on the breakfast bar. 'I can't do this any more. I can't do this. Fuck knows, I've tried.'

'Why are you being so dramatic? I just wanted some fresh air.'

'I've tried and tried to push this over the line but I can't do this any more. This isn't who I am.'

'What are you talking about now?' Jacob struggled up after her and tried to grab her hand but she snapped it away.

'I said I would never be one of these women. Not me, no fucking way. Yeah, you're a liar. You're a cheat and a liar—'

'What the fuck? Is this about the other night again? I told you where I was, I *told* you.'

'Don't! Don't you dare!' Fiona took a deep breath and closed her eyes.

'There's the other night,' she said, her voice wobbling. 'There's the fictitious present buying—'

'I did buy you a present! The bracelet, remember? You're wearing it right now, I can see it.'

'Yeah, J, but you bought it the day after you said you had. From a shop in town, not online. I saw it on our statement.'

'I tried to buy one online but I—'

'Jesus, Jacob, stop. Please. You're making this way worse for both of us. You're a liar and I'm pretty sure you're a cheat, and that's on you.' Tears trickled freely down to her jaw.

'But I've played my part too,' she sniffed. 'I didn't see it, did I? I didn't see what was right in front of me until it was too late.

'I overlooked stuff, I tried to see the best in you. I fussed around you like you were a wounded animal but you just carried on retreating, shutting me out and lying to me. I can't do this any more. You just need to go.'

Jacob winced and tried to find a better resting place for his leg. He leaned on the suitcase next to him while a sports bag acted as a makeshift leg rest in the footwell. Jacob wiped his eyes, pinched his temples and wondered what Fiona had shoved in the case for him. He was almost too scared to look.

'Just here, thanks, mate.'

His mum's car was in the drive as the taxi pulled in, his dad's car was gone. Probably at the court, as usual.

'Darling!'

'Hi, Mum,' Jacob said, leaning on his suitcase on the doorstep.

Sue's smile dropped. 'Oh,' she said.

'Mum,' Jacob started, swallowing tears away, 'do you think I could stay for a few days?'

'Of course you can, but what's going on?'

'We're just having a few problems, Mum,' he said, and his face folded.

'Oh, J.' Sue pulled Jacob down to her level, hugging him to her chest as he crouched awkwardly on his crutches. 'I'm so sorry,' she soothed. 'We'll work it out though, don't worry. We'll work it all out.'

CHAPTER THIRTY-THREE

Alex

29 September 2010

Alex had her plan. Her new plan. Self-devised and not exactly on doctor's recommendations, but a plan nonetheless. Baby steps. She'd written it down although she really didn't need to. Thirty minutes later each day, 100ml servings, one day at a time. She'd bought a new measuring jug for the occasion, a personal talisman chosen after nearly an hour of wandering around the sprawling kitchen shop in the posh Pantiles part of town.

It was 12.30 p.m. and overcast. Alex wrapped a cardigan around her pyjamas and opened her bottle of Faustino VII. She poured it slowly into her new jug, 100ml precisely, then transferred it into her favourite black wine glass.

After all this time, the central heating still followed the temperature and timings that her mother had set up; it was stone cold and would be for several more weeks. Alex drew a blanket up over her legs and settled into the sofa dip. Moleskine in her lap, she closed her eyes and tried to do her deep-breathing exercises. Just knowing that she would be leaving a third of her second bottle of wine tonight was making her heart race. What if she forgot when that time came? What if she couldn't stop herself? If she couldn't leave a third of a bottle untouched tonight then she would never be able to stop.

She breathed out and counted *two... three...*

———

Alex woke early and dry. Her cardigan lay next to her under her duvet, and an empty water glass lay on the bedside table. The morning was crisp with a sharp yellow sun streak underlining the curtain's edge.

Bursting for the loo, she threw the cover back and paced into the bathroom for a wee. She trotted downstairs, trying to contain her pride.

In the kitchen, with a perfect purple ring sitting under it and a tatty drip-covered label stood her second wine bottle from last night. The cork had been left out and there wasn't quite a third of the liquid, but there it was. Wine. In the morning. Left from the night before.

Alex allowed herself a wide smile as she pulled the tap on to a full gush. After filling the coffee machine and flicking it on, she picked up the bottle of wine cautiously. She moved it onto the draining board and spritzed a stern burst of kitchen cleaner onto the drip stain. She scrubbed the whole time the coffee machine burbled, working the stain away until only she would know it was there. As she wrung the cloth under the warm water, without giving herself thinking time, she emptied the cold, stale wine down the plughole. She watched the water destroy the purple trickle of Rioja and drag it away.

As she drank her coffee and pondered a run, Alex flipped open her notebook to the penultimate page. She ticked the line marked '12.30 p.m., 100ml servings, leave one-third'.

Today's line read '1 p.m., 100ml servings, leave one-third'.

She had a lot of time to kill.

She hadn't written next week's plan down yet, though it was there in her head, looming large. The thought of leaving half a bottle of wine made her chest sweat and her temples beat so she tried not to think that far ahead.

Alex left the bed unstripped and pulled on her running things. She tucked her key into her sports bra and popped in her headphones. With renewed faith in her willpower, she kicked herself out of the door and into a slow, steady run.

She ran past the tight terraces and out into the open spaces of Mount Scion – the 'village' of Tunbridge Wells – with its blocky white villas, fraying at the edges despite their grandeur. She paced towards the welcoming green of the Calverley grounds and up towards the hospital.

How dare I consider not running? Alex thought as she imagined Amy's legs, DVT stockings covering the light downy hair that grew like baby moss.

It was Wednesday. Jacob would be there soon, holding Amy's hand like it was made of glass and worrying about who was watching. For a moment, Alex thought about going in, buoyed by runner's adrenaline and the success of the last night. But she ran straight past and out towards Southborough, wind behind her and brain clearing with the breeze.

CHAPTER THIRTY-FOUR

Amy

Sometime in 2000

Jake came to see me earlier, and while he was here he brushed my hair. It felt like he'd done it before, but I don't know how he could have. Whose hair would he have brushed? He doesn't have any sisters and I'm his first girlfriend. Unless he's been lying to me about that, but we've been friends since year seven, I would have known. And he's a rubbish liar.

He knew what to do this morning, though. Holding the hair in clumps and working the knots from underneath so it didn't pull. I didn't like it. We're not that kind of couple. When we hold hands on the field, I'm always painfully aware of our skin being crushed together, our fingers tangled up and sweaty. We're still working out how to be physical, and it's so intimate, having your hair brushed. Even my mum has barely brushed my hair in the last few years, apart from when we tried and failed to make it look like Björk's hair, or the handful of times when she's blow-dried it dead straight and shiny for a school disco.

When is the disco? We haven't had the letter yet. They're cutting it fine an' all, it's nearly the end of term, I think. I can't have slept through summer, after all. I need to get hold of Jenny and Becky, work out what we're going to wear. It seems like an age since I've even spoken to them. I hope they're not phasing me out.

CHAPTER THIRTY-FIVE

Jacob

30 September 2010

Jacob woke up in his childhood bed. His feet dangled off the end of the mattress and his arm hung out of the bed frame like a shipwreck survivor.

For a moment, he forgot where he was and why. When he remembered, he sat up with such a start that he nearly snapped his leg again.

His mother rushed in to his exclamation, 'Are you okay?'

Jacob rubbed his leg gingerly and pulled the duvet up over his bare chest.

'What time is it, Mum?'

'It's about 9.30.'

'9.30? Shit! Sorry, sugar! Why didn't you wake me?'

'I thought you needed the sleep. Is something wrong?'

'No, it's fine.' He attempted a reassuring smile. 'Don't worry, Mum.'

He wondered if the nurses would notice. If they would remark on it next week. It's not like Amy would know. He hoped.

'I'll bring you a cup of tea. Do you fancy a dippy egg or some toast?'

'Tea would be good. Thanks, Mum.'

He was surprised he'd been left to sleep in. As a teenager, it was probably the only thing they had properly rowed about. He was a natural night owl who could happily have slept the day away, but his mother had taken huge umbrage to any 'wasting' of the sunlight.

She'd disallowed it right up until Amy had been found, and then Jacob had been left to stalk the corridors at night, making himself endless cups of tea into the early hours, drifting between his bed and the sofa, letting the television screen dance around in front of him, then sleeping through lunch. Doing his A-levels at night all but formalized the arrangement. He was the night and Tom was the day, and they rarely overlapped.

He hardly remembered seeing his father during this time. Perhaps, under normal circumstances, Jacob would have been invited to fill the void left by Simon, his father's sidekick. Or perhaps no-one would ever have moved up into that golden slot.

And so from a household full of people just a few years before, their numbers had been slashed until the silence was exhausting.

Jacob looked around the kitchen. The same kettle, the faded basket of wheat on the same toaster, the ceramic hen egg holder with the dent at the back.

'It's amazing how powerful hormones can be,' Sue said. 'It's easy to underestimate the effect they can have on a woman. And pregnant women are completely at the mercy of the changes in their bodies.'

Sue reached over and stroked Jacob's cheek. 'I was horrible to Dad at times.'

'It's not that she's horrible, or even that she's being completely unreasonable,' Jacob shrugged. 'It's bigger than that. She says she doesn't know what's going on in my head. She reckons I shut her out.'

'Do you shut her out?'

'I don't share every thought that runs through my head but I talk more than Dad does.'

'Your dad's from a different generation. I'd like to think I raised you to talk about your feelings when you need to.'

'We do talk, don't get me wrong. I guess maybe I do live in my head a bit but it's not just me either. We seem to be bickering and misunderstanding each other all the time. She's more emotional now she's pregnant but this has been building for a while and getting stuck at home after my accident has just accelerated things.'

'I wish you'd called me when you fell, I could have come to help.'

'I'm a grown man, Mum.'

'Not to me. You'll always be a little boy to me. Even when you have your own little one.' She smiled into Jacob's frown.

'Both of you are new to this, love. You've not dealt with a pregnancy before or the changes it brings. I know things will get better and it will all be worth it when the baby's here,' Sue said. Jacob stared at his tea.

'And if it helps, it was very different the second time, with you. I was more relaxed, Dad was more relaxed and we knew what to expect from the pregnancy and from each other.'

'Right now,' Jacob sighed, 'I honestly don't know if we're going to sort this out, let alone have more kids. I just thought we were more solid than this, but it's like even when things are good, they can crumble really easily.'

'Jacob, that's marriage. That's life. It takes work. Even when you have a family, it doesn't mean things can't be rocked or shaken by what comes along. That's why you keep trying – you have to put the work in.'

Sue poured them both another mug of tea. 'You'll sort this out. You have to, for the baby. Just give yourselves a couple of days and make sure Fiona knows you're not going anywhere.'

Jacob took a biscuit and ate it slowly, without tasting a crumb.

'Are you looking forward to being a grandma?'

'So much, J. Although I'm struggling to accept that my baby is having a baby. I know it's a cliché, but it feels like only yesterday that you three were little and I had you all safe and snug, tucked up where I could see you and look after you.'

Jacob brushed crumbs from his hands and onto the plate of other biscuits.

'Have you heard from Tom since he cancelled on lunch the other week?'

'No, not since then, but I'll give him a call soon. I speak to him when I can but he's so busy with work. He's really excited about meeting his nephew or niece though.'

'Really?'

'Of course he is. I know he's not one for talking about his feelings, but you can tell how much he cares. You remember how much he looked up to you and wanted to be just like you. He always wanted to have everything that you had.'

'I don't know, Mum. I think you've got rose-tinted spectacles on a bit there.'

'Maybe.' Sue smiled. 'I can certainly remember a lot of wrestling too. But he does love you and he'll love being an uncle.'

'Hmn, it feels like he's been off with me for a long time. I hope he doesn't cancel on his niece or nephew like he does on us. I'd find that hard to forgive.'

'You know Tom, he dances to the beat of his own drum. I'm sure it's not about you.'

'He could already be an uncle, of course. So could I.'

Sue snapped her head around to look at him, 'What do you mean?'

'Well, it wouldn't surprise me if Simon had left a couple of reminders behind—'

'Jacob!' Sue half-laughed, but shock crinkled her forehead skyward. 'Don't be so crude!'

'And I'm sure he's met his fair share of pretty volunteers out there.'

'Oh, stop. He'd have been in touch if there was any news to share, thank you very much.'

The key rattled in the sticky lock, then the door squeaked open.

Moments later, his upright father appeared around the door in his pristine whites. A surprising amount of dark hair, framed with distinguished grey, sat above those familiar unreadable green eyes.

'Hello then, you're still here?' Graham said. Then came the light clinking of ice falling onto thick cut glass. Amber liquid swilled in the tumbler, swallowed in one.

When the youngest brothers were little, the clink of ice had been an early warning system, telling them that they should immediately stop wrestling and dismantle the den made from sofa cushions.

'I think I might need to stay a few more days,' Jake told his father's back as it retreated to the freezer. More clinking of ice.

'You can stay as long as you need, Jacob. Fiona will calm down though. It's just her hormones. It's best to stay out of it altogether and wait for her to sort herself out.' Two swallows.

Sue looked away from her husband. As Jacob watched Graham open his mouth to continue, his mother cut his father off.

'Graham,' she said. 'Would you two mind picking up some wine for dinner? I completely forgot.'

As Jacob limped out of the front door after his father, he heard his mother in the kitchen opening up the teapot.

CHAPTER THIRTY-SIX

Alex

1 October 2010

'Hi, Amy, it's Alex.'

Alex waited for the nurse's footsteps to move away before she picked up Amy's hand. It was cold and still, but delicate blue lines were busy under her skin.

'I don't know if you recognize my voice or if you can even hear me, but I'd like to think you can.'

Alex smiled in surprise as she thought she saw a twitch spread from the corner of Amy's mouth and up to her cheekbone.

'I used to spend a lot of time in hospitals, in this hospital actually, but I still don't feel very comfortable here. I feel like I'm intruding.' Alex paused. 'I guess I am intruding.'

Alex bit her lip and looked around the quiet ward. She was the only visitor today, and that lay like a burden. In the background, the radio played 'Wonderwall' by Oasis.

Alex remembered hearing this for the first time.

'I used to love this one,' she said. More to the ward than to Amy. 'You probably didn't,' she added, remembering that Oasis's rivals Blur adorned Amy's cubicle.

Amy's breathing was quick and quiet, her narrow chest shaking slightly as it rose and fell. Her arms were covered in goose pimples, so Alex pulled the blue hospital blanket over them, tucking it around Amy's shoulders without thinking.

'I used to visit my mum every day here at the end of her illness, y'know. I probably shouldn't have bothered.' Alex laughed and sniffed. 'She didn't know who I was anyway. I could have saved all that time.'

Alex chewed the inside of her cheek and looked around the ward. 'I wonder what else I could have done with those months. Written a book, maybe.' She sighed. 'Stupid thing is, Amy, I could write a book now. Or learn to paint, or do cookery classes. I have hours free every day, just like I could have had then.'

Alex wanted to be asked what she spent her time doing. She realized that, even after all this time, all this practise, she was still craving a two-way street that would probably never come.

She tried to imagine Amy's voice in her ear, her soft Kentish accent, a songbird's version of Bob's gruff speech. 'Well, Alex, what *do* you spend your time doing?' she'd ask. *Oh*, Alex would sigh, *I just drink and I stare at my hands and sometimes I gaze around the room and I read my notes and stare at the TV and I just kill the time. I just kill the day. Sometimes I get my wedding album out and I fall asleep crying, and then I wake up covered in my own piss.*

Visiting hours were nearly over and there was a sudden sense of activity and urgency seeping out from the nurses' office. Nurse Radson came over, and Alex was all set to leave in a cloud, but the nurse put her hand on Alex's shoulder.

'I'm not coming to boot you out,' she said. 'It's okay, stay where you are. We're just having a shift change.'

'I should probably get going anyway,' Alex said, slipping her shoes back on and gathering her jacket. 'Can I ask you something?'

'Okay,' the nurse said warily.

'Do you think Amy can hear me? I mean, do you think any of this gets through to her?'

'I'm certain of it.'

'Really? You think she's taking this all in?'

'Good grief, I couldn't have done this mad job for so many years if I didn't think so. I sing to them sometimes, you know.'

'Really?'

'Oh yes. Music can be very powerful, don't you think? I wish more visitors sang to them.'

'Well, I'm not going to torture her with my voice,' Alex smiled, 'but maybe some of her own music would help?'

'I'm sure it would, love. And between you and me, I don't care what anyone says, you can tell the ones that are still in there, and the ones that've gone. No matter what the tests reckon. And she's still in there, listening. I can feel it in my bones.'

'I think so too,' Alex heard herself saying, 'I feel like we're building a connection, I really do. Does that sound nutty?'

'Not at all. It's probably doing her the world of good to have a new friend visiting.'

'It's doing me good too,' Alex said, and the nurse gave her a strange look.

'Glad to hear it.'

'Okay,' said Alex, embarrassed, 'I'd best get going. Nice talking to you.'

The sun was over the yardarm, but the bottles stayed in the fridge. They would chill there for over an hour.

On her list of suspects, Alex had circled the name 'Tom Arlington'. He had been a teenager, barely, and was too young to drive. But it sent shivers through her that a man now in his late twenties would secretly visit his brother's teenage sweetheart fifteen years after she was attacked. For no reason.

Alex's instinct used to be her greatest gift. The ability to be counterintuitive, to follow a hunch in the seemingly wrong direction and create a fresh new take on a situation. That ability had been long lost. Alex didn't trust her rusty toolkit any more, and was frequently paralysed by second-guessing herself and deleting everything.

Jacob answered in two rings. 'Hello?'

'Hi, Jacob, I'm sorry to call you like this.'

'My mum's in the other room, I really can't talk to you.'

'I'm sorry, but I have some questions and I really need your help to understand some things.'

'Alex, I have to go.'

'Perhaps I could talk to your mum instead?'

'Okay, what questions?'

'I just want to understand a bit of background. I want to get to know Amy better.' It sounded weird when she said it so overtly.

'I don't know what you want from me here,' Jacob started.

'Okay, like, what was her favourite film?'

'I don't remember,' Jacob said flatly.

'Okay, well, what about music? What was her favourite band?'

'Look, Alex, I don't have time for this so if you're skirting around something important please just come out and say it.'

'I'd like to know more about your brother, Jacob.'

Jacob didn't say anything, but Alex could hear him breathing, she could almost imagine his nostrils flaring.

'Are your mum and your brother close?' she tried.

'Not especially – he's a grown man who lives miles away.'

'But your parents must be in touch with him at least?'

'Of course they are, they talk to him from time to time. He keeps himself to himself though. He's very busy with work.'

'When was the last time you spoke to Tom?'

'A couple of years ago at my wedding.'

'Where does he live?'

'You mean you haven't already found out?'

'Look, I'm just trying to piece this all together and I need some help. I have found a few things out – I know he works in social care, something to do with kids. I don't think he's married, he's in his late twenties and he lives in the Midlands. That's pretty much all I know.'

'That's pretty much all I know.'

'Were Amy and Tom close?'

Jacob drew breath. 'He was thirteen.'

'But were they close?'

'I know what you're implying and you're way off. He was thirteen and he was just a kid. They'd barely ever spoken.'

'I know it's tricky for you, but can we meet?'

'No. Look, I'm genuinely sorry about your house, about what I did. But you promised you wouldn't do this.'

'Jacob, I don't know how to prove to you that I'm on your side.'

'How are you on my side?' Jacob whispered. 'You're calling me at my mum's house, you're digging up stuff about my brother, you're disrespecting Amy's memory—'

'I'm trying to get justice for Amy!'

'You're trying to sell newspapers.'

'I'm not some tabloid hack!' Alex spat the word as if it was a shot of vinegar. 'This isn't my beat, but no-one else is trying to find out what happened to her any more.'

Jacob tried to interrupt but the words were flying. 'And if I don't find out what happened and if you don't help me find out what happened then somewhere out there, there is a man, or two men, or seventeen bloody men for all I know, who seduced a young girl, seriously assaulted her and left her for dead. And if they've done it once—'

'*Seduced?* Amy wasn't *seduced*, she was raped. Raped, beaten and strangled.'

'I... yes.' Alex's temples pulsed.

'Seduced implies consent. How fucking dare you imply consent!'

'I didn't mean to imply anything, Jacob. I'm just trying to... oh fuck it, do you know it was rape? Do you actually know it was rape? Because that's not what the evidence suggests and maybe this was more than a random attack.'

'Amy and I had never slept together, she was a virgin. And that meant something to her. It meant something to me.'

'Okay, but what if I said she wasn't a virgin any more? What if it was consensual?'

In the background, Alex heard a woman's voice saying something about tea.

'Wrong number,' Jacob said fiercely.

Click.

Alex took a cold bottle from the fridge and stared at it for as long as she could.

She woke early, sticky with dream sweat. The tang of ammonia perfumed her sheets. Her legs were wet, and the dark round mark under them was still warm. This was the first 'accident' in a while, and it sat heavily in a way that it hadn't before.

The shower felt too hot and the coffee felt too cold and she was considering blowing it all off and taking a bottle to bed – because what was the fucking point – when the phone rang.

'Blur.'

'Sorry?' Alex said, baffled.

'Amy's favourite band. It's Blur, she loves them. But listen, I've been thinking about what you said,' Jacob said.

'And?'

'And I need to move past this and I'm not getting anywhere on my own. It makes less sense now than it did fifteen years ago and it's about time something changed.'

'I still don't know how much I can help you.' Jacob looked around Alex's living room as if he'd never seen it before.

'Everything is falling apart around me and I can't carry on in limbo. Things have got so bad with my wife that I'm staying with my parents. It's all getting really messy and I can't seem to get my head together.'

'I'm sorry,' Alex said, 'I know I've brought this to the fore.'

'It's not your fault, it was becoming a bigger and bigger issue as time went on. I just need something to change for the better, you know? It's been fifteen years and I need to move past this. I'm being a crap husband because of it and I can't be a crap father as well, I just can't.'

'I know you don't think you can help much but you never know what little detail was overlooked back then that might be really useful now. Let me get my recorder going again and let's just have a chat and see what comes up. Okay?'

'I guess.'

'Let's start at the beginning. How did you and Amy get together?'

'We were in most classes together throughout school. I'd had a crush on her since year seven, when we were paired up for Biology. She was a pretty girl and she made me laugh. She was really sweet to me, even though I wasn't one of the rowdy boys that most of the girls seemed to go for.'

'Who asked who out?'

'I asked her,' Jacob smiled. 'She'd been out with a couple of other lads in school over the years. I was always jealous but I never said anything. They weren't particularly nice to her. Most boys that age are morons, I guess.'

Alex sipped her tea. Her own teen memories were pretty sharp, even after all these years. The time she'd woken up in a flat above a shop, two boys from the year above her at school slobbering all over her body as the party carried on in the room next door. Losing her virginity blind drunk, holding her hair out of her own face as she threw up onto the floor, a fleshy boy from year nine working busily behind her, in his own drunken trance.

'When we were about fourteen,' Jacob continued, shaking Alex from her sour memory. 'Amy was going out with a lad called Steve Dixon. He'd been mouthing off in the changing rooms after PE, bragging about how he'd seen Amy's bra and done this and that with her. He said he was going to break up with her as soon as he'd, y'know, as soon as they'd gone all the way.' Jacob rolled his eyes.

'She told me later on that Steve had never even kissed her, but at the time I was furious, I thought she deserved better. I called him out on it right there and then, which was unlike me, but I was just incensed. She was so lovely and she was being disrespected by a total plonker. And then, afterwards, I told her what he'd been saying. I said I thought she deserved to be treated better, like a lady,' Jacob laughed. 'I mean, she wasn't a lady, she was a fourteen-year-old kid, but *I* thought she was a lady.

'She dumped him at break time in front of everyone, one of those big whole school dramas on the front lawn. I asked her out as she marched off. My heart was thumping but I just went for it and she said yes. I couldn't stop smiling for weeks.'

'How long had you been going out when Amy was attacked?'

'About seven or eight months. I don't know how I got away with it for that long, she was totally out of my league.'

Alex smiled.

'I know we were stupidly young but I really did love her. I'd loved her since I was eleven.'

'Jacob, who did you think hurt Amy?'

'At the time, I didn't have a clue. I thought it must have been one of those random, unlucky things. A kidnap by some nutcase. Then they arrested Bob.'

'Did you ever think he might have been guilty?'

'Well yeah. As soon as he was arrested, I thought he must have done it. The police only arrest bad people, so he must have been a bad person. That's what you think when you're fifteen.'

'That's only human. It's a gut reaction.'

'I guess. I know it wasn't him now and I was really shocked, obviously, but there were a few little things that sort of made sense.'

Alex put her mug down and flicked her eyes at the recording app, still glowing red.

'How did it make sense?' she asked as calmly as she could.

'I feel awful saying it now, but he was very affectionate with Amy. That sounds horrible, and now I'm an adult and I have a baby on the way, I know that it's a *good* thing for dads to be affectionate. But because he was her step-dad and I didn't really know many step-families then, I thought maybe that wasn't how it was supposed to be.'

Jacob looked at Alex's raised eyebrows.

'I know, like I say, I don't think that any more.'

'So was that it, just what you thought might be misplaced affection?'

'He could be a little bit possessive, I guess.'

'With Amy's mum?'

'No, with Amy.'

'Go on.'

'I don't know, like he didn't like her talking to boys on the phone, didn't like her dressing up too much. And she said he used to get a bit funny about her coming to my house, used to say things about our house being bigger than theirs and make little digs about what my dad did for a job.'

'I imagine that's normal when there's a disparity in income.'

'Yeah, probably. Also, Amy had the chance to meet her real dad once, but Bob stopped her. I didn't think that was right.'

'I didn't think her birth dad knew where she was?'

'He'd got in touch once—'

'He'd got in touch? When?'

'Oh, ages before, you know, a long time ago. Months before she was attacked.'

'But there's nothing about him anywhere in the reports. I've read *everything*, Jacob, I mean everything.'

'Well I guess there wouldn't be. She didn't get to meet him because Bob stopped her.'

'Are you sure?'

Jacob narrowed his eyes and looked at his lap.

'They never met; Amy would have told me if they had. He phoned out of the blue one day and said he was her dad. He wanted to see her but Bob said no.'

'Are you sure? This guy just phoned out of the blue and that was it? Nothing more happened?'

'Yes, definitely. Don't get the wrong idea, it was nothing. He called her after school one day, said he was her father and that he wanted to see her. She called me afterwards. She wasn't sure whether to even mention it to her mum and Bob or just forget it.'

'But you don't think they met?'

'No. She wasn't even sure he was telling the truth, he could have been anyone. She told him she'd think about it just to get him off the phone, but she never met him. Bob put his foot down and that was the end of it.'

'And you're sure?'

'Positive.'

Alex looked at the kitchen clock out of the corner of her eye. A deep thirst was crushing her chest as the afternoon rolled around.

'I'm confused,' she said. 'Bob told me Amy's dad didn't want to know about her. That he was a thug and her mum ran away from him when she was pregnant.'

'I don't think her dad was on the scene at first, but I'm pretty sure he'd come looking for her when she was little.'

'So she did see her dad?'

'No, from what I remember, she said he'd turned up at their house one day but Bob saw him off.'

'Bob?'

'Apparently, yeah. Amy was inside the whole time with her mum. She was just a little kid.'

'When did she tell you about this?'

'I don't know, she mentioned it once or twice when we were going out. It wasn't a big deal though, honestly. She was much more bothered about the constant in-fighting between her and her friends.'

'Do you remember her real dad's name?'

'I don't have a clue. I don't even know if she told me his name.'

'Why didn't you mention any of this to the police?'

'They took Bob in for bigger reasons than jealousy. Anyway, it was months earlier and they never met. It was just a phone call. I'd forgotten all about it until a little while after Bob was arrested. The police knew Bob wasn't Amy's real dad, anyway. I'm sure they looked into this at the time.'

'I wouldn't be so certain about that,' Alex said. 'The police miss stuff all the time. They cut corners, they prioritize leads, they lose evidence...'

'Sounds like you don't have a great view of the police, Alex.'

'I'm just saying they're human and they make mistakes. That's all.'

Jacob's taxi pipped its horn at 1.30 p.m. on the dot. Alex was dialling with one hand as she closed the front door behind him.

Bob picked up after two rings, his voice immediately echoing down the line.

'Hello?'

'Hi, Bob, it's Alex Dale. I'm sorry to disturb you.'

'That's okay. I'm just on a job though, what do you need?'

CHAPTER THIRTY-SEVEN

Amy

Sometime in 2002

I woke up desperate for my mum, in this piercing way I haven't felt since I was tiny, since before Bob was around.

Back then, though I barely remember it, it was just me and Mum. Every day. The only hand I remember holding was hers, and more often than not I slept in her bed, cuddling up to her while she snored slightly. Especially in the winter when it was cold. I think we both liked that feeling, having each other there, wordless and happy. Although I can remember a time without Bob, I'm glad he came on the scene. But I don't remember a time before Mum because there wasn't one, it's always been us.

People underestimate my mum. They see her... actually, they don't really see her. She doesn't stand out, she doesn't seem remarkable in any way. She potters along, not asking for much and happy with her lot. But she is remarkable. She did it all by herself, she gave me this whole world she never had. These possibilities. Every single day of my life I've felt like she was proud of me, even if I couldn't tell you why or for what. And without her, I just feel so small. I feel like a little speck suspended in space. I can barely feel the bed under me, or my nightie, like I'm almost part of the air.

I just want my mum.

It's physical. A feeling in my chest that's somewhere near fear but also a sort of longing and a desperate sadness, all at the same time. And it's like something from a dream, because it doesn't make sense, the feelings are out of proportion.

She'll be at work, and Bob'll be at work, and they must have let me sleep in because it's the summer holidays.

I'm lying here, hours later, still waiting for the last of this feeling to slip away. It's like when you have a dream that sticks to you and the only cure is going back to sleep the next night. I once dreamed that Becky had told Jake all this horrible stuff about me that wasn't true, and he'd dumped me in front of everyone in the middle of the canteen. And even though it was just a dream, I couldn't look at her all day. Couldn't look her in the eye, I was that livid. And we ended up falling out anyway because I was 'being funny' with her.

I've been telling myself that this dream situation is as stupid as that one. But I can't shake the last little drops of it. And it's making me question things. Like, *when did I actually last see my mum? What conversations did we have?* I can't place them. Was it yesterday or the day before, did I get in after she'd gone to bed? Did I drink last night? Did I drink and do something wrong and embarrass myself? Is she ashamed of me? Does she not want to see me because some of that pride has been punctured and she can't bring herself to show that?

The more I think about this kind of thing, the more scared I feel. My mum calls it 'going down the rabbit hole'. We both do it, especially at night if we can't sleep. We start thinking about things, and before you know it, we've jumped to the worst-case scenario and are obsessing about it. Along with her smile, her voice and her long legs for her height, that's the biggest gift my mum gave me. I wish I could give it back.

CHAPTER THIRTY-EIGHT

Jacob

2 October 2010

It felt wrong knocking on his own front door, but Jacob knew that barging in unannounced would be a gross misdemeanour. He slumped to the side on his crutches, lifting his fist to knock for the third time as the neighbours to the left looked on.

He slipped the key in and turned it to the right, meeting resistance. He tried to turn it to the left, it didn't give at all. Right again. Jiggle. Turn. No. He staggered back, punch drunk. She'd changed the locks. She'd actually changed the locks on his own house. Their home.

He banged on the door, louder this time. 'Fiona! It's me!'

'Fuck.' He sat down on the doorstep, propped against his own front door. She could be hours. He tried to call her mobile again, just as he had this morning when he woke up. Was it an echo of a memory or did he really hear Fiona's phone ringing inside the house?

The voicemail cut in, he hung up and dialled again. And again. As he tried calling for the fourth time, he heard a voice behind him.

'What are you doing?' Fiona hissed through the letterbox.

Jacob scrambled to a stand, wincing as he stood on his bad leg, fumbling with the crutches.

'Fiona,' he said, head bowed into his chest, forehead resting on the door. 'We need to talk. Please let me in.'

'No, Jacob. You don't live here any more.'

'Fiona,' Jacob felt his hands clenching into fists. 'Fiona,' he said again quietly.

'Just go away, Jacob, don't do this now.'

'No,' he said, pushing upright from the door and standing as straight as his crutches would allow. 'This is my house too.'

Fiona swung the door open, but stood blocking the entrance.

'We're beyond that now, J, you've come out with so much bollocks, I find it hard to even look at you.' She was angrier than before. 'You're better off staying with your mum.'

'Fiona, I moved out to give you some space, I did what you asked and you've changed the locks. Do you not see what a massive overreaction that is?'

'I'm just trying to be sensible. Everything I thought we were building just wasn't good enough, was it? I really tried, but you're obviously not going to change, you're not going to tell me the truth, you're not going to magically reappear as the old Jacob. We need to be realistic.' She wiped her eyes on her cardigan cuff.

'So what is it now, then? You don't know me and I keep my thoughts to myself and *that's* the problem?' Jacob said, grinding his jaw. 'Or you think I'm cheating on you and throwing away everything we have because I dared to go for a drive at night when I couldn't sleep because of your snoring! Which is it?'

'The two aren't mutually exclusive, Jacob. It's both of those things and more. And thank you for twisting this so it's somehow my fault for snoring when I'm heavily pregnant. Jesus.'

'Fiona, you're wrong about so much of this. And you're choosing to see the worst in me. After all this time, don't I deserve some benefit of the doubt?'

She said nothing, hands on hips, her eyes searching his face.

Jacob's voice got louder. 'I've never hurt you, never cheated on you, never laid a finger on you. I know I'm not always easy to live with, but neither are you. How about a little mutual understanding?'

'How can I understand you when you're never honest with me? I don't know what I'm supposed to understand! Who are you, Jacob? What's going on in that fucking head of yours? You sneak off, you lie to me, you can't look me in the bloody eye. If you're not cheating, I dread to think what you are doing.'

'You want me to be totally honest with you, Fiona?' He laughed and looked at the neighbouring house, whose curtain suddenly snapped back into place.

'You want me to be totally honest so you can twist everything and use what I say to beat me around the head? Some things are too precious for that,' he spat. 'You don't know me at all, you said it yourself. I thought you knew me better than anyone, but that was just wishful thinking. Fuck it, I don't even think you like me.'

He pressed his hands against the wall as she glared at him. Her silence more deafening than her yell.

'Fiona, I love you. But right now I don't like you very much either. You're like a coiled snake all the time. I can't ever relax, I'm walking on eggshells and I can't do it forever.'

'You made me this way,' came the strangled reply.

'I probably did, yeah,' he said, with a softer voice.

'I hate you for that. I don't want to be this person.'

'We are who we are. If we can't get past this, then maybe we *should* call it quits.'

He hadn't meant to say it. He hadn't even thought it until it fell out of his mouth. And when Fiona said nothing, he swung away on his crutches before he could say anything else.

CHAPTER THIRTY-NINE

Alex

4 October 2010

Alex gave her eyes an almost cartoon rub as she barrelled down the M5, blinking into the morning light.

The night before had been restless and the small servings of wine had slipped down too quickly. After her preliminary water, she'd drunk her first two glasses in quick succession. She had stood and stared into the sink, almost in disbelief, as if that's where the wine had disappeared. It had taken every shred of her will to step away, sit on the sofa and slow things down.

After a fitful few hours' sleep, it wasn't a good morning to be driving, but at least she was out of the kitchen and taking charge.

The first and last time she'd visited Devon was in secondary school. A school trip aged twelve, riding ponies on Dartmoor and learning to do brass rubbings. She'd taken a bottle of cheap, watery vodka from the back of the cabinet – the emergency stash – and she and two friends had got so drunk on cartons of orange juice and slugs of vodka that the other girls had ended up half-naked. They weren't used to alcohol. One girl, Anne, had to be sent home.

Since hanging up on her, Bob hadn't answered any of her calls, so she'd decided to drive down at first light. To distract herself from how much she wanted to sink another big glass, Alex had spent the previous evening cross-legged on the floor, rifling through her CDs. With the nurse's singing in mind, she'd decided to put together a playlist for Amy. She didn't know where to start, and eventually just spread them all around her like sweets. She'd forgotten she had so many albums until she pulled them off the shelves and scattered them. Thousands and thousands of songs. Albums covered in dust, edges frayed, abandoned. Music had been everything when she bought some of these. What else do you have to care about at fifteen?

Blur had been Amy's favourite band, Jacob said, so eventually she started there. And now, iPhone dangling from the MP3 slot of her car stereo, Alex's heart pounded with the familiarity and sadness of so many long-forgotten favourites.

By the time she reached Uffculme, Bob's village, Alex was desperate for the toilet and a shot of caffeine. To stop and wander around was too risky; the four-hour journey would be a total waste if Bob spotted her and got spooked. She turned the music off and followed the satnav past the church, down a lane just wide enough for one vehicle. She bumped over a cattle grate, bladder close to bursting with every jolt.

Bob's van was outside, his new name stencilled in dark blue on the side.

The little cottage was more cardboard box than chocolate box. Meeting the road side-on, it was hemmed in on all sides by thick wedges of fields divided by jagged blackberry bushes. The cement-covered walls had turned green at the bottom, and only one small window faced the road. The low metal gate swung open towards her.

'You promised you wouldn't do this!'

'You lied to me, Bob,' Alex said, climbing out of the car and standing carefully on the uneven ground. 'You said you'd never met Amy's birth dad.'

'What the hell are you doing here?' Bob looked around frantically.

'I didn't want to do this. I really didn't want to drive four hours to surprise you but this is serious.'

Alex leaned against her car and Bob sagged.

'Bob, you didn't just meet Amy's dad, you attacked him.'

'You've got it all wrong.'

'No, I haven't.'

'You've got it half right. Okay? He came looking. Alright?' Bob puffed like he was reaching the end of an uphill run.

'He came looking. Just... look, come in, Judy's out on the school run. She's not gonna be long, so you need to promise me you'll go afterwards.'

'After you tell me the truth?'

'Yeah.'

'Okay. I promise. Again.'

They walked in silence through broken pots and bright plastic trikes in the garden. Bob shoved the sticking porch door and took his shoes off carefully. Alex followed suit.

Inside, Bob flicked on the kettle in a kitchen with patterned floral curtains instead of cupboard doors.

'Judy did this all herself,' Bob said.

The downstairs bathroom Alex had almost pleaded to use had little net curtains hanging in front of the frosted, scalloped window. A couple of lazy spiders rolled in the furthest corner of the ceiling and the small hand towel was slightly cold and damp. It was deathly quiet outside of the door, and had Alex been any less bursting, she would have felt self-conscious at her own noise.

After picking her way through a corridor of toys leading back from the bathroom, Alex sank into the tired velveteen sofa. She splashed a little of her tea and apologized profusely. The detritus of family life was dotted on shelves and in corners. Stacks of wicker baskets with toy limbs poking out, children's shoes lined up by the door.

'How old are they?'

'I don't want to... They're young. Primary school. Judy's... I've been lucky.'

'Tell me what happened, Bob. When Amy's dad came looking for her.'

Bob took a rattly breath and cleared his throat.

'Amy was only small. I'd not long moved into Jo's and he turned up.'

'When was this? During the day, middle of the night?'

'It was evening time. Jo had just given Amy her bath and they were in our room with the hair dryer.'

'So what happened, did you let him in?'

'He didn't knock. He was banging on the door with both hands, yelling, threatening... saying he'd get custody, that he'd come back and take her in the night, all sorts. Jo was terrified.'

'Was he alone?'

'No, he had his mum with him, and she was a vicious old bat.'

'So he didn't try to talk sensibly to you? You didn't try to talk to him?'

'He was pissed as a fart. There was no talking to him. Jo was shaking like a leaf, sobbing. Amy was scared stiff, she was only little. I sent him away. I was protecting my family.'

'And he never came back?'

'We moved.'

'He never found you again? You didn't exactly move far, one bit of town to the other.'

'No.'

'I know that's not true. He called Amy at your house when she was a teenager.'

'How do you know about that?' Bob sat up and put his tea down fast.

'She told her boyfriend.'

'Shit,' Bob said under his breath. 'Yeah, alright he got the number. God knows how. He called and tried to confuse her. She didn't really want to meet him.'

'Are you sure about that?'

'Definitely. She could have told us if she wanted to see him.'

'And you don't think she just went ahead and met him anyway?'

'She didn't meet him. She wouldn't have kept that a secret, she was a good girl.'

'And the police knew he'd been in touch?'

Bob shook his head.

'Why not, Bob? Don't you think he might have been involved?'

'No.'

'How can you be so sure? Jo told you he was a thug. Surely you wanted to tell the police that Amy's violent birth father had tracked her down? Surely Jo wanted to tell them that? A history of violence...'

'Oh, blimey. Look, he wasn't exactly violent. Not to her, that wasn't true. I told you that stuff so you wouldn't start down this line. I didn't want you writing about that, connecting me and him again. He was just a waster. He was a mouth-ache, a petty criminal, he smoked grass, he nicked things.

'He treated Jo like muck on his shoe, had her shoplifting things, giving him her wages. He'd have done the same to Amy, dragged her in, pulled her down. She was going to be better than that. Better than us. And definitely better than him.'

'What's his name, Bob?'

'Do I have a choice?'

'What time's Judy coming back?'

'Alright, alright,' Bob sighed. 'Paul Wheeler.'

'Do you know anything else about him?'

'I've told you everything. Please, Alex, I just want to protect what I have now.'

'I don't want to cause problems for you and I'm sorry it came to this. Just please let me know if you think of anything else.'

'St Mary Cray,' Bob said with a sigh, and rose quickly to show her out.

'St Mary Cray near Orpington?'

'That's where he lives. Arsehole of a place. St Mary Cray, I doubt he's had enough about him to move.'

'Thank you, Bob.'

'Just please, love, don't get sucked in by him. And, Alex?'

'Yes?'

'Please don't come back.'

The last hour of the drive was a blur of dry throat, inane radio chatter and slamming her brakes on through traffic cameras. Finally home, Alex threw the front door open and ran into the kitchen, holding the sideboard to steady her. She had to stay level-headed, the plan had to hold. Two days of gulping in a row would have been risky.

She poured her first serving of Rioja into the jug and back out into her smallest glass. She bit the inside of her lip to slow herself down as she poured a tall glass of bottled water. She sank the water fast, out of sheer physical need. She sipped the wine, then lapped at the dregs with her tongue until even the sheen on the inside of the glass had been replaced with tiny drops of saliva.

Placing the empty glasses carefully on the sideboard, she opened her laptop's browser.

Paul Wheeler of St Mary Cray. Amy's birth dad. Fucking hell.

Within seconds, a bunch of Google results belched up on the laptop screen. By the looks of things, Paul Wheeler was still in St Mary Cray. Bob was right.

Paul Wheeler of St Mary Cray, giving his opinion on a local

election in an old newspaper article. 'They're all on the take.'

Paul Wheeler of 42 Eden Court, St Mary Cray, representing himself in the Crown Court on charges of benefit fraud. Suspended sentence.

Her phone blinked with a text from Jacob.

'How did it go?'

'Hi, it went well. Think I'm getting somewhere. Do you fancy a road trip tomorrow?'

'Depends. Where are you going?'

Paddock Grove, leading to Eden Court, looked much the same as the rest of St Mary Cray in the rain. Tight little red bricks burrowed into dirty walls, white plastic balconies sagged under flat roofs.

The twin hums of the M25 and A20 underpinned the town's soundtrack, cars rushing past the place in great voice. Just a few souls dotted the pavements. An overweight woman spilled from the sides of a motorized scooter, a crumpled man zigzagged towards the road, waving a short stub of rolled-up cigarette at no-one in particular.

'Thanks for coming with me, I really appreciate it,' Alex told Jacob, flicking her eyes briefly from the road to try to make eye contact. 'You're the only person that knows about Amy's dad. Besides Bob, I mean.'

'I still don't think he's connected, but it didn't feel right you going on your own. Besides, I'm at a loose end right now.'

'Turn left into Eden Court,' the satnav barked.

They parked a few doors down and sat in silence.

'Come on, let's get this done and then I'll drop you straight back to your mum's.'

There was absolutely nothing to mark number forty-two out from the rest of Eden Court. As tired as the rest, it nudged up to number forty, with a dark alleyway tunnelled out between the two. A 'beware of the dog' sign hung impotently on an open gate and the neighbouring garden had a moped propped up in it, casting a diagonal shadow across the patchy brown grass. Nothing moved.

No sound came when they rang the bell. Alex rapped on the dull blue door with a prim fist. As the sound of the television stopped abruptly, she shot a look at Jacob, who was leaning on his crutches. He didn't smile.

The door swung open. A tall man of about fifty had a toddler perched on one hip as he held a boxer dog back with his leg. His sharp emerald eyes narrowed in the thin light.

'Yeah?'

'Are you Paul Wheeler?' Alex asked.

'Why?' came a low, rumbling voice.

'I... we—'

'We've come to talk to Paul Wheeler about his daughter, Amy. I'm pretty sure that's you 'cos you look just like her,' Jacob interrupted.

'Fuck's sake. And who are you two?'

'I'm Alex and this is Jacob. I'm writing a story about Amy and Jacob is—'

'An old friend of your daughter's.'

'Offer 'em a cup of tea then,' Paul said to a boy of about eight, as he kicked the boy's socked feet off the footstool and gestured for him to put his Nintendo gadget down.

The boy flopped off the sofa, sighed, and asked the side of Alex's head if she wanted a tea.

'Oh, I'm fine, thanks. What's your name?'

The boy looked at Paul. 'It's alright, you can tell 'er.'

'It's Matty.'

'My husband was called Matt.'

'Okay,' said the boy. Alex blushed.

'Do you want a tea?' he asked Jacob.

'I'm good, thanks,' said Jacob.

The boy flopped back down.

'What about old Dad?'

'Wanna tea, Dad?' the boy asked.

'Yeah, make it a good strong one. Don't rush it.'

Paul narrowed his eyes as the boy slumped out of the living room door. 'You two are a bit dense, aren't you?'

'Sorry?' Alex and Jacob said in unison.

'I was trying to get rid of him. I don't want him hearing this. He doesn't even know he had a sister. Other than this one.' He gestured to the toddler sucking on a dummy in the corner of the battered sofa.

'Oh, sorry, I didn't think,' Alex said, feeling flustered. Paul Wheeler seemed entirely calm.

'It's alright. What do you want, then? Want me to sell my story?'

'Well, do you have a story?' Alex asked.

'You tell me.'

The small living room was neat and tidy. One bar on the gas fire flickered blue, and the boxer dog lay contentedly on his belly in front of it, absorbing all the heat.

'Let's start again. I'm Alex Dale and I'm a journalist. I write about health issues and I'm writing about your daughter's condition. Jacob was close to Amy in school and he's been helping me build up some background to her story.'

'I know who 'e is.'

Jacob sat up a little on the grey sofa. 'You do?'

'I know all about you, Jake.'

'I don't understand.'

'No, don't s'pose you do.'

The dark curls of the small girl next to Paul started to tremble a little as she slipped into a snoring sleep. Brief bursts of unconscious suckling came from her mouth until, with a final half-hearted suck, the plastic dummy fell from her lips into the crook of the sofa. A spit trail followed it.

'She told me all about you,' Paul continued, holding Jacob's gaze without blinking.

'Amy did?' frowned Jacob.

'She told me about how you was her boyfriend, she told me about her little friends, she told me about the grammar school, what teachers she hated. All of it.'

'I thought you only spoke once?'

'Did you now?'

The boy sloped back in and put his father's mug on the arm of the sofa.

'Good boy, Matty. Go to your room for a bit.'

'All this happened in one conversation?' Alex asked, as the boy shut the door behind him.

Nodding at Alex's hands, Paul's eyes narrowed again.

'Notes, is it?'

'I'd really like to interview you on the record, Mr Wheeler. Would that be okay? I don't have to name you in the published article, but I'm sure it would be helpful to get your side across.'

'Oh, you can name me. You can say whatever you like so long as you pay me.'

'I don't think you understand. I've not been paid yet. I'm a freelancer and I'm writing this off my own back. *The Times* are interested in running it when it's finished, but it's not guaranteed.'

'Then I don't think there's anything else for us to talk about.'

'Oh, well I'm sorry you feel that way. You're the first person to ask me for money. I mean, maybe if I place the story, I could—'

'Bob's helping,' Jacob said, fixing his eyes onto Paul's steely blues.

'Is he now?'

'Yep. He's already helped a lot. He told Alex his side of the story, told her all about Amy. Told Alex what it was like raising her.'

'Has he now?'

'Yes,' Alex joined in, 'he's given me some really valuable insights into Amy's life. You know he was accused for a while? Police took him in because they mistook how close he and Amy were. She was a real daddy's girl by all accounts.'

'Not by my account.'

'How so?'

'He controlled her.'

Alex flipped her notepad back open, praying the iPhone hadn't stopped recording in her pocket. 'Go on.'

'He wouldn't let her out of his sight. Wouldn't let her meet my family, *her* family. It killed my mum. Granddaughter she only met once. Killed her cold.'

'Your mum met Amy? When?'

'That's how I found her the first time. I'm not gonna lie, when Jo told me she was pregnant I weren't happy. I was eighteen. I was a kid. No proper job, doing this 'n' that.'

'What do you do now?' Alex asked.

'I'm a single father now,' Paul snapped. 'Me and Jo weren't really together. On and off, you know. She could be a stuck-up little cow. She looked down on me and mine. Not that she came from better. Anyway, we were back on this one time and she tells me she's in the club and it's mine. I didn't know if she was telling the truth or not. Birds are sneaky.'

'So what happened after she told you she was pregnant?' Alex asked.

'I said she should get rid of it. It weren't the right time. She told me where to go and I didn't see her again. Just like that.'

'That seems very extreme.'

'It wasn't a polite conversation like what we're having.'

'Did you threaten her?' Jacob asked.

'No, I didn't threaten her. What's your problem?'

'So she just upped and left?' Alex asked.

'She was a kid herself. Wasn't tight to her family, I don't even know where they lived. She could be a bit... what's the word?'

'Impulsive?'

'Shirty.'

'So when did your mum meet Amy?'

'She was in Sevenoaks one day with my auntie, few years after I last saw Jo. Mum said she was in Tesco and clocked Jo, recognized her straight away. And Jo had a little girl with her. A little blue-eyed, dark-haired girl, the spit of me and my brothers and sisters.'

'Amy.'

'Yeah, Amy. 'Course I didn't know that was her name. Didn't know anything about her then. Mum went over to see Jo and asked her straight out if the girl was mine. She looked that similar.'

'Your mum didn't know?'

'I didn't tell her Jo was expecting. I still lived at home when Jo fell, I'd have got a hiding for getting a girl in trouble. Jo left anyway, there was nothing to tell.'

'So what did Jo say to your mum?'

'Told her Amy was mine, told her she was living with her new fella. Told her I'd known all along. Bloody told her I wasn't interested, really threw me under the bus. Told Mum she lived in Edenbridge and that Mum could see her anytime she wanted. Even wrote down her address.'

'What happened then?'

'Mum came round my bedsit and gave me a clip round the ear. Told me I had a kid. Told me she was being brought up by some other bloke and it wasn't right. We got in the car and she drove us straight round to Jo's.'

'You and your mum went?'

'Yeah.'

'And what happened when you got there?'

'I knocked on the door, respectful like.' Paul shot Jacob a look. 'Waited. Nothing. Knocked again, saw the curtains twitch, you know what I mean, nothing. Cunt comes out, shouting the odds.' Paul was getting more and more animated as the toddler next to him slept on obliviously. 'He's calling Mum all sorts. He shoves me. Tells my mum to get back in her car and never come back. He's swinging at me and threatening her.'

'Bob was?'

'Yeah. Saint bloody Bob.'

'I've met Bob a couple of times now,' said Alex, cautiously. 'He's not a very big guy.'

'I'm not being funny, but I just wanted to get my mum out of it. Yeah, I could have knocked him out cold. But her health was bad and she was upset. I didn't want a row, I didn't even want to see the kid then. Harsh but true. I didn't know her. Didn't have no money, didn't want the headache. I was only there for Mum's sake.'

'So you just left?'

'Yeah, we left. Got in Mum's car and she drove us back.'

'And your mum didn't see Amy again?'

'My mum died a couple of weeks later.'

'I'm sorry.'

'S'alright, it weren't your fault. It was his.'

'What did your mum die from?'

'Broken heart.'

'Okay,' interrupted Jacob, 'but what did the doctors say she'd died from?'

'Heart attack. But she'd still be here today if it wasn't for him.'

'So you were angry with Bob?'

'Of course I was angry with Bob! Cunt had my kid *and* killed my mum.'

'That seems like a bit of a leap; you said your mum was ill already?' Alex said.

'She'd still be here today if it wasn't for him. So would Amy.'

'What do you mean?' asked Jacob.

'He kept her on a tight lead. Too tight. She rebelled and went off with someone. Look what happened.'

'Who did she go off with?' Alex asked. 'Do you know what happened to Amy?'

'I don't need to know what happened to know what happened.'

'You said you knew all about me,' Jacob said. 'How often did you talk to Amy?'

'You know they upped and moved after Mum died?' Paul said to Alex, ignoring Jacob. 'I sent a letter to Jo, told her what happened, asked her to bring Amy to the funeral. Never got a reply. Time I went back round there, they'd moved.'

'When was that?'

'Couple of years later.'

'Years?'

'Yeah, years. I was grieving for my mum, wasn't I?'

'So when did you get back in touch with Amy?'

'When she was in her teens. I saw her in the paper.'

'What paper?'

'She was in the local news for some writing competition. My auntie saw the article, sent it to me.'

'I remember that,' Jacob said, more to Alex than Paul. 'She was embarrassed about her picture being in the paper.'

'Yeah, well my Auntie Jean saw it. Amy was called Stevenson by then but my auntie could see exactly who she was, she looked the spit. Paper said she went to the grammar school in Edenbridge. That's not my genes, to be fair. She was lucky from her mum there.'

'How did you get in touch with her?'

'Phoned the school.'

'The school?'

'Yeah, the school. Well, my sister did. Put on a posh voice, told the bird on the other end that she was calling from a private school. Made out there was this writing scholarship for bright kids and they wanted Amy to apply on account of her winning this story competition. Woman gave out the number. Done.'

'My school gave out a pupil's home number, just like that?'

'Yeah, just like that.'

'I'm sorry, but that seems really unlikely,' Jacob said. 'My mum worked in the school office back then and she would never give out information like that, she was way too fastidious.'

'Whatever, someone gave my sister the number.'

'And you called the number?' Alex asked.

'Yeah. Called after school that day. First time, *he* answered. I just put it down. Next time I tried, Amy answered. I knew it was her, straight away. She sounded like her mum, but posh.'

'Amy isn't posh!' Jacob laughed.

'Maybe not to you. I told her who I was. Said I was her dad. Said I'd tried to track her down and that I wanted to get to know her.'

'What did she say?'

'She didn't say a lot. She was shocked, I think.'

'She told me you'd asked to meet her,' Jacob said. 'She told Jo and Bob too.'

'I wanted to meet her. But I said I'd phone her a few more times first so we could get to know each other. I didn't want it to be tricky when we met.'

'She didn't tell me that.' Jacob said, frowning.

'No, don't seem she did. She told me what times to call so she'd be on her own.'

'I don't think I'd be happy with my daughter telling people when she'd be home alone,' Jacob said.

'Got kids, have you?'

'One on the way,' Jacob said, carefully.

'Well let me tell you, she wasn't telling "people", she was telling her dad. Her real dad. And she knew I was her real dad because I knew so much about her mum. I told her about when we got together and that I knew about Bob and I told her everything. I told her about when I came looking for her before and she told me she remembered.'

'So did you call back again?' Alex asked, pen hovering.

'Most days. At first I did all the talking, and then she started to tell me more. She told me about school, about her little boyfriend over there,' Paul smirked at Jacob. 'All about her friends.'

'But you never met?'

'No. After a couple of weeks of us talking, she told Bob and Jo.'

'A couple of weeks?' Alex's eyebrows rose.

'Yeah, a couple of weeks. She told Jo and him that I'd called. Told them I'd been nice and reasonable – which I was – told them she wanted a chance to get to know me. They told her no. Told her I was this and that, none of it true. Confused her for a while so she wouldn't even talk to me, but she came round. We started talking again. After a couple of months, she agreed to meet me.'

'So you're saying you did meet her?'

'Nope, we hadn't made a formal arrangement, but I wanted to check she was alright. I wanted to see her in her own world, y'know? So I went to meet her from school one day but she was with some fella.'

'What fella?' Alex asked, sitting up straighter.

'How am I s'posed to know? Some bloke, older fella, teacher maybe.'

'When was this?'

'A week or so before she was on the telly.'

'What did this bloke look like?' asked Jacob, his voice wavering.

'Fuck should I know? It was fifteen bloody years ago. It was a bloke. I think he was white, and taller than her. I didn't get a good look but he weren't a schoolkid. And he weren't you.' Paul nodded slightly at Jacob.

'And did Amy speak to you?' Alex asked, staring directly at Paul.

'No,' Paul said, avoiding her eye. 'She didn't see me, I left her to it.'

'Did you tell the police?'

'What do you think I am, a mug?'

'But you had information about your daughter, you'd seen her with someone. And all those phone calls, she might have told you something that could help.'

'She didn't tell me nothing that would help them. And I wasn't sticking my neck on the line. It don't take a genius to see how that would go.'

'You don't seem very upset,' Jacob said, flatly.

'Who the fuck do you think you are?'

The living room door opened and Matty's mop of hair poked around.

'Can I watch telly?'

'Back to your room!' Paul yelled. 'You're s'posed to be off sick anyway!'

Socked feet thundered up the squeaky stairs.

'Tell me I'm not fucking upset, mate, I'm not having that. You don't know nothing about me.'

'I find it odd that you never came forward with any of this, she was on the TV for weeks. And you're describing your daughter going missing like, I don't know, like a dog that ran away,' Jacob's bravado was unsettling Alex.

'You wait until you have your kid,' said Paul, raising his voice to pub row levels. 'You just wait. You can't imagine what it's like yet. Some cunt out there picks up your little girl and kills her. You have to decide, do I pick myself up, dust myself down and block it out? Or do I die with her? That's your only choice.'

'I'm sorry,' said Alex. 'I understand how upsetting this must be for you. But Amy didn't die, she's still alive.'

'No she ain't. Her body's hooked up to some machine, but she's dead.'

'She's not being kept alive by machines any more. She's breathing by herself and the doctors have registered brain activity,' Alex argued, quietly. Jacob frowned at her.

'Amy's dead,' Paul said.

'So your other children don't know about Amy, then?' Alex asked.

'There's never been a reason to tell them. Look at Chloe sleeping, she don't need to know how shit the world is. Let her sleep, let me worry about the world.'

'Where's their mum?' Jacob asked, stretching his fingers out in his lap.

'Mums. Two of them. Matty was a one-off thing with a girl I knew. She was in no fit state to bring him up. Slag. Chloe was with my ex. She sees her weekends.'

'That's quite unique,' Alex said.

'I wasn't letting these ones go. I told both their mums, "You have this kid, this is my kid. You leave me, you leave the kid here." I walked away once, never again.'

Paul wiped his eyes on his sleeve.

'Now, how much can I get for a photo?'

CHAPTER FORTY

Amy

Sometime in 2004

When my mum thinks someone is a bit dodgy, she describes them as 'a case'. It's the kind of mum language that doesn't arouse suspicion, that doesn't sound like she's slagging them off or 'casting aspersions', as she also says. But if you know her, you know exactly what she means.

Bob's dad – Granddad Pete, who died a few years ago – he was 'a case'. And by case, she meant he was a mean old racist and woman-hater.

The bloke in the greengrocer who always makes double entendres about fruit, he's 'a case'. Behind Mum's eye-rolling smile you can see her opinion of him curdle more and more with every shopping trip. Eventually, she'll just go to the Co-op instead.

And old Jack in our road, he's another one. My mum has told me in no uncertain terms to give him a wide berth. She didn't trust him as it was, you could see her invisible antennae go off the moment she first met him. Even I noticed that and I was really young at the time. But when I told her I'd seen him *being a case* in the window when I walked past, she grabbed me by the wrist and told me that I was to walk away if I ever saw him coming my way, and to cross the road whenever he was out and about.

I didn't tell Bob. I just knew, without Mum saying, that it was better not to. What words would I even use? 'Fiddling with himself'? Or maybe I should be all Biology class about it and say that I suspected he was 'masturbating' as he watched me. Ugh, cringe! No, it was better just to avoid him and leave Bob undisturbed. The last thing any of us needed was Bob steaming round to a neighbour's house, kicking off.

Not that Bob's a thug, not at all. He's just quiet and cheerful most of the time. But when it comes to me and Mum, he's very protective. And that's nice, more or less. I mean, it does my head in when he over-worries and that means I can't do something I want to do. Especially if Mum's said I can go out and then Bob's overruled it. But even when I'm at my most pissed off about it, I do get it. Some people don't have a dad who cares that much, and I'm grateful that I do. Not that I'd ever tell him that.

I guess it's like having a bodyguard. A short, fat bodyguard in dungarees. It makes you feel safe. And if you feel safe, you feel brave. Maybe that's why I've always felt brave. Right now though, I feel a little less brave than I used to. I think it's because I can't remember my last conversation with Bob, I can't feel his invisible hand on my shoulder. Has he had extra work on, maybe? I feel a bit foggy-headed today but it feels like it's been a while.

In fact, everything feels like it's been a while. I don't know if that makes sense but I can't really place when I last did *anything*. Even stupid stuff like go to the toilet. When did I last go to the toilet? What did we have for tea yesterday? Or the day before?

Maybe I've been sleeping too much and that's got me all cloudy. Mum always says it's just as bad to sleep too long as too little, your body clock gets scrambled and you don't know where you are.

I'm not a big sleeper. Not like Jake – that boy can sleep. I called him at about 4 p.m. during half-term once and his brother said he was still in bed. At 4 p.m.! Now that's a sleepyhead.

I guess it's easier when you live in quite a big house. In our house, if one of us is up and using the loo, we're all awake and queuing outside the bathroom. The kettle downstairs whistles me awake in the morning. I like our little house though. I like knowing Mum and Bob are right there, and it's cosy. But I haven't been waking up when they've got ready for work, I seem to be asleep more than I'm awake right now. Maybe this is just something that happens at this age. That's the joke isn't it, about students and teenagers and that, sleeping all day? Maybe my time has come. Maybe this is just a part of growing up.

CHAPTER FORTY-ONE

Jacob

6 October 2010

The surgery had no record of an appointment for Fiona Arlington today.

'The midwife is in again next Monday, perhaps she has an appointment then,' the baggy-faced receptionist had told Jacob, brusquely.

'Fiona's my wife so I need to be there. Can you please tell me when I should come back?'

Jacob's hands gripped the reception desk where he had often signed Fiona in as she'd flopped down exhausted in the waiting area.

'I'm sorry, sir, I can't. You'll need to ask your wife for that information.' Jacob pushed away hard from the desk, partly for momentum, mostly not.

Outside, he furiously jabbed at his phone. Fiona picked up after three rings. 'What is it, Jacob?'

'I've come for our appointment but you're not here,' he said.

'It's *my* appointment,' she said.

'Don't punish the baby.'

Silence.

'We're still the baby's parents, regardless of what's happening with us.'

'You should have thought about that before you cheated on us.'

'Did you listen to nothing I said the other day? Sweet Jesus, Fiona, I'm not cheating on you. I've got stuff I need to sort out, and I don't even care if you believe me right now, but I'm not cheating on our baby and you can't shut me out like this.'

He heard Fiona take a deep breath. 'Fine. You can come to the next appointment if you answer me one question.'

'Blackmail now? Fff...' Jacob trailed off and sought a shot of patience from the sky. 'Fine. What's the question?'

'Is there another woman?'

'Not in the way you mean.'

Click.

The phone went straight to voicemail as soon as he tried to call back. As patients shoved in and out of the surgery doors, Jacob kept calling until he had barely any battery left, and no idea what to say if she did answer.

CHAPTER FORTY-TWO

Alex

6 October 2010

'Hi Amy, it's Alex again.'

Amy's breathing made its gentle 'shh-shh' sound like the sea retreating. Her skin was almost luminous in the sunlight and her face looked softer than during the last visit.

It was easy to imagine Amy as a little girl, sitting in the garden pouring water between cups. Or catching ladybirds on the ends of her fingers and pedalling in decreasing circles on a tiny bike. Bob and Jo would have watched her grow from a little thing to a young woman. Did they feel misplaced relief that she was no longer small and vulnerable?

Of course, Alex realized, she was just reimagining her own childhood. When she'd sorted through her mother's things, she'd found a small leather photo album at the bottom of a box. Inside, pictures of Alex on a trike, Alex with a four-leaf clover, Alex sitting in a washing-up bowl playing with a bucket. And one of her father in his sixties, two-year-old Alex folded into the crook of his elbow, both smiling rigidly. She couldn't remember meeting him then, didn't remember any visits clearly except the last one.

She was eleven and about to start secondary school. He had shown up, flustered and irascible, with a My Little Pony sticker book that Alex at once hated for its babyishness and loved because it was all there was.

'I didn't think I missed having a dad, you know,' Alex told Amy. 'I didn't know what it was like to have a real dad anyway. I mean, a dad who doesn't have to keep you secret from his wife. But the older I got, the more I felt cheated, like I'd missed out on something fundamental. I bet it would have been different if I'd had a step-dad like Bob,' Alex said carefully, watching Amy for tiny reactions.

Alex's father was a high court judge, a highly regarded one. He died just after her twelfth birthday, by which time he was nearly eighty. Her mother was left a sum of money, and that's how his wife found out about Alex. It was all there in the will.

'My mum had held out for years, Amy. I think she'd hoped having me would get her a pay bump. Obviously she saw other men on and off, lots of them, actually,' Alex snorted, 'but she was always holding out for that golden ticket.'

Alex closed her eyes. She had absorbed all the talk of 'The Judge' and ignored as much of it as possible. She hadn't asked about her siblings after the first time. Her mother had not reacted with kindness to Alex's lonely questions.

For a while after he died, they would drive to the cemetery at night and her mother would rage about the family plot and the discrepancies on the stone. Her mother would pour red wine from a thermos, and what sometimes started as a toast would fast descend into yelling at the gravestone. After a few months her mother fell in with a new boyfriend, and the mourning abruptly ended.

Alex sat back in the hospital chair and looked around Amy's curtained room. It must have been bigger than her bedroom at Warlingham Road had been. A sort of softened version of it. Alex imagined Jo and Bob carefully removing the posters from Amy's walls at home, rolling them up and carrying them like newborns into the hospital. They would have unfurled them, maybe quarrelled over where best to put them for 'when she wakes up'. Or perhaps they moved silently, tacking the posters up to the one solid wall, working without words.

Thinking about her playlist, she noted the band names from the posters in her Moleskine. Pulp and Blur, she already knew, but there were several T-shirts folded on a chair with pictures on the front. Alex walked over to them, looking over her shoulder to be sure she wasn't being watched. They looked worn and faded, the kind of ageing that makes them soft. Alex touched the first T-shirt gently and eventually picked it up and held it from the shoulders so it unfurled. It had pictures of Iggy Pop on it, in a pastiche of Warhol's *Marilyn Diptych*. Alex folded it carefully and put it to one side. The next T-shirt was a blue Blur T-shirt, possibly the one Amy had been wearing on Alex's first visit to the ward. Without picking up the last, Alex could see the familiar typeface of the Smashing Pumpkins. She folded them all back up and placed them down neatly. From everything Bob had said, she imagined Jo would have taken great care over folding clothes, laundering for her little family.

Chaos and crisis, those were the breeding grounds for bad things to go on unnoticed. Not enough eyes watching. Visitors who should not have been made welcome, slipping in through cracks. Nothing about Jo and Bob's life smacked of chaos, or distraction. The tiny little house, the regular jobs, the one child. What could they have missed? How could they have missed anything? But they missed Paul. And maybe, if Paul was to be believed, they missed an older guy too.

Alex thought of her own mother. She had slept through whole days, leaving Alex to run hungry for the school bus in the previous day's crumpled clothes. So many times she wasn't there. And nothing dramatic had happened. All those dark corners and very little happened. So why Amy?

Alex looked at the posters, and the silence of the ward boomed. She took her iPhone out of her bag, pulled out her earphones and tucked one bud into Amy's ear, the other into her own. She leaned in, cocking her head towards Amy, scrolling until she found the right playlist. She put the volume way down so it was barely audible, and allowed Blur to seep into their ears. Amy's lips ever so slightly parted and a long exhalation seeped out.

Tonight, Alex would add the others: Iggy, yet more Blur, Smashing Pumpkins.

When Alex had listened to the mix on the way down to Devon, she'd allowed herself to mull over her own cultural experiences of that time, *her* 1995. She'd thought about using that imagery to inspire some personal connection, to help open up the article. Until it dawned on her that one of the biggest challenges with this piece wasn't finding her way in, it was unpicking herself from the story altogether. In her best work, she'd always been the story.

As her mother had lain concave as a chicken carcass, whiskey sour untouched on the hospice night stand, Alex had scrawled her thoughts and observations into a notepad on her lap. As her mother took her last, ragged breath, Alex had noted her feelings, the accuracy of the term 'death rattle', her sole situation in a room occupied by two just moments before. She had watched her mother's face wilt as the sun came up. She'd sent her five-hundred word column to her editor in a series of long text messages as the day broke, gulping warm bourbon from the rubber hot water bottle usually tucked in her mother's nook.

The morning after her mother died, Alex had returned to Matt's arms but didn't cry for four days straight. She didn't cry until she read her column that Sunday, and finally knew how she was supposed to feel.

Her compassionate leave was dead time. She spent it sculpting the house into their home. As she prepared to go back to work, she had her own surprise hospital stay. And then Matt left.

She'd returned to her Tuesday column, working on it from home in wine-splattered pyjamas. She stared at the blank page for three nights in a row, head swimming with painkillers and wine. Whiskey was too strong for pills like those. The white space had danced around as she'd tried to catch a line. Finally, twelve hours after her deadline had passed, she wrote:

Question: What have my mum, my baby and my husband got in common?
Answer: I've lost them all.
   It's not a great punchline, but it's the only one I've got...

Four hundred and seventy words later, she emailed the column in, crawled halfway up the stairs and passed out.

Her phone woke her up three hours later. 'Firstly,' the voice had said, 'I'm sorry for your loss.' Then he'd asked, though she'd barely known who he was, 'Can you come in this morning? We need to talk.'

Two hours later, hair still wet from a cold shower, Alex held her head still in the conference room and tried to work out what face she should be trying to pull as they talked.

'We need new ground,' said one of the execs she barely recognized from the other side of the walnut table.

'This miserablist stuff has served us well but it's getting old hat. People become blind to it after a while. You know?'

'I see,' Alex had managed to say, focusing on the basket of fruit at the centre of the table to keep her eyes straight.

'What other ideas do you have?' they'd asked.

'This is all I've got right now.' She'd burped, and coughed the words away.

'Alex, perhaps take a bit longer, you've had a terrible time,' said the woman exec.

'Yes,' the editor had nodded. 'Richard is covering your column and the reception has been good. Very good. There's no rush to return. And when you're ready, we'll look at other opportunities for you.'

Alex had stood quickly, knocking her knee so sharply on the table leg that tears splashed from her eyes without warning. 'Forget it,' she'd said. As the anger swept up her chest, she'd let it out with a 'Fuck it all.' And then she'd screamed it to make certain they'd heard. 'Fuck it all!' and then 'Fuck you!' And she'd wobbled out of the room and into the hands of the summoned security guards. She'd hit the darkness of The Flowers pub minutes later. She'd drunk until she could barely squint, and fucked the glass-washer with the weepy eye in the tiny kitchen off the bar, door open. She'd made it into *Private Eye* that week.

Alex looked at Amy's clear skin. Barely a wrinkle, just a tiny dusting around her eyes and darker hairs on her top lip than she probably would have recognized. There was one sprig of grey hair along her parting. Alex reached up and plucked it out. Letting the hair fall to the floor, she stroked Amy's face and felt the skin give a little beneath her hand. The lightest of light sighs came from Amy's open mouth.

CHAPTER FORTY-THREE

Amy

Sometime in 2006

Okay, I'm just going to say it. I think my secret might be a bit of a case.

I've had some time to think about it. In fact, I've had nothing but time, stretching out in every direction I look. I've run things over and over in my head from every angle until I wonder if I've changed their shape.

But the more I run through them, the more my memories of him sour a bit. Like, his behaviour doesn't really stand up to scrutiny. Not like mine does, but even ignoring why it's obviously wrong, the situation should never have arisen. I mean, he's a *lot* older than me. That's for starters. When we first kissed, I was in my school uniform. A school uniform he knows only too well. That's a bit weird. It is though, isn't it?

I was fourteen when I met him for the first time, fifteen when we kissed, and he knew it. He knows exactly who I am.

He's a good-looking guy. By good-looking, I mean crazy bloody lush. Fit too. You can tell just by the way he carries himself, tall and confident, that he's in shape.

Why would someone who looks like that want a fifteen-year-old girl? He could have the pick of the bunch if he just wanted something easy, so why doesn't he? He has plenty of opportunity to pursue actual women, professional women. Maybe he has gone through them all and he's left to move his finger down the list and start on the teenagers. I don't think so though, but maybe that's wishful thinking. We all want to be chosen, don't we? Want to be someone's special one, the object of desire rather than yet another body in a barrel load. But the more I think about it, mull it over, roll it around in my brain and dissect it, the grubbier it all seems.

And he started it. Oh that sounds grown up, Amy. But he did, and I think that's part of the problem. If I'd pursued him, dressed up to look older and tricked him, met him under different circumstances, that would be different. But he pursued *me*. He took every first step.

From turning to me that day and starting a conversation when no-one else was in the room, holding my gaze too long and sitting too close, he started it. I should have moved away, should have made my excuses and left. But I didn't. It wasn't just because he's, as I've already said, crazy bloody lush, but it was also out of politeness and obligation. An adult talks to you and you talk back.

I guess I'm thinking along these lines to make myself feel better. Trying to wriggle out of it, because the truth is, I should have stopped it before it crossed the line. He shouldn't have kissed me but I shouldn't have kissed him back. I shouldn't have liked it. I should have been upset, or disgusted.

He shouldn't have touched the fabric of my skirt like that, or run his fingers down my back, but I shouldn't have run home with a smile on my face as wide as the River Eden. I shouldn't have run straight into my bedroom, slammed the door and lay on my bed, grinning like a Cheshire cat and running it over and over again in my head like a dirty movie.

He wasn't some letch, either. He gave me a lift home once and he could have tried anything but he didn't. He could have driven us off somewhere else, carried on where we left off in his kitchen, but he didn't. He talked to me kindly, brushed my tears away and took me home. And the dark, nasty truth of it is that I didn't stop wishing he'd taken advantage of the situation. I didn't stop wishing that another situation would arise because I knew, just like I still know, that if it had, I would have grabbed it with both hands and not given a damn about right and wrong.

So if he is a case, what does that make me?

CHAPTER FORTY-FOUR

Alex

9 October 2010

Alex had been putting off visiting the optimistically named 'park' where Amy had been found all those years ago. It was time to brave it, but she didn't like it on sight. The trees were tall as sin, lurching in the fierce wind. Dew hung wet and thick on the ground, twinkling on the spiders' webs and crushing leaves into the grass with its watery weight.

It was still early on a crisp Saturday morning, but there were already several teams of Chinese families gathering early sweet chestnuts, pulling the brown bellies from the spiky green sheaths and stuffing them mechanically into carrier bags.

Mechanically? That was the kind of sweeping-statement racism her mother had frequently oozed, thought Alex.

Kent was full of chestnut trees, but it was 'uncouth' to stoop down to collect them. 'Floor food,' her mother had spat when she'd caught Alex stuffing chestnuts into her pockets as a little girl.

Alex had woken up today haunted by her research the afternoon before. And the feeling was enhanced in this dark, cloudy place.

The visit to Paul Wheeler had left her more confused than ever. He was shifty, and almost certainly lying about something.

Was there any truth to his 'older fella' story, or could this just be a cover story? Could he be the 'fella' in question?

No matter which angle she approached the idea from, it was hard to imagine he could have committed a sex crime on his own daughter and executed the attack well enough to get away with it. The question mark that throbbed brighter than ever was the consensual element, the lack of bruises in the most private of places. As unpalatable as it was, there was one possible explanation, where previously there'd been a de facto alibi for Wheeler in Alex's head. It even had a name. Genetic sexual attraction.

It was such a firm and definite phenomenon that it had an acronym. GSA. And those three letters stood for the possibility of Paul Wheeler and Amy Stevenson engaging in an intense sexual affair. The thought of it, when Alex allowed herself to think while she researched, turned her stomach.

GSA, she'd read, often happened in cases of close relatives meeting for the first time as adults or adolescents. Adoptees, long-lost first cousins... even unknown parents. A few couples had even found they were father and daughter only after marriage and children of their own. It was, Alex had read with a scratchy swallow, felt more keenly when relatives closely resembled each other. Alex thought of Paul with his blue eyes shining. She imagined him fifteen years younger; tall, handsome, his sparkling eyes locking onto Amy's identical irises. His patter irrelevant beside that unfathomable connection. A connection that maybe, just possibly, led Amy here, to this cold, damp slice of nowhere.

Alex shivered. As well as the gangs of trees sprouting haphazardly in acres of ragged wet grass, there was a little lake surrounded by big jagged rocks. With every sinking step into the muddy grass, Alex felt more nauseated. Amy's final resting place, as was intended. It wasn't a nice place to die.

In July, the grass would have been lush and green. The trees would have been stumpier fifteen years ago, standing still in the summer air. Maybe save for a rustle of leaves at night.

Alex imagined the search party, carefully combing the land with sticks, line by line, hoping not to find anything. How many of those trudging through the tall summer grass secretly believed Amy had run away? Until that fateful connection of wood to cooling body, metres from where Bob had been thrashing his own angry, desperate stick.

No, it was not a nice place to die.

As she reached the spot – a dark little enclave surrounded by thorny bushes and guarded over by thick chestnut trees – the wind blew Alex's skinny legs clean from under her and she landed awkwardly in the mud. Unnerved and cold, she scrabbled to her feet.

There was nothing and no-one for miles around. Somewhere in the distance the hum of an A road barely scratched the silence. An off-season wasp buzzed half-heartedly while it waited to die. The only person here today had arrived alone and would leave alone, no-one else was likely to turn up. Not while there was a river to walk along in town and pretty parks tended by committees. This big block of nothingness, 'saved' from development through a quirky green belt by-law, was cared for by the council at arm's length, like a step-child.

Alex took pictures, which all looked the same. Ten or so identical pictures of a dark, spiky place. No plaque, no flowers, nothing to suggest it had been anything special to anyone.

Why here? *Why not here*? It was deadly quiet; someone was unlikely to be seen assaulting someone, or dragging a body. There was a main road nearby, but not so close that anyone could see a car – maybe Paul's borrowed car – in the car park, a generous name for a gravel patch with way more space for vehicles than needed. And not enough spaces when it mattered. Volunteers' cars and police vans would have snaked along the hedge all the way back to the main road.

Alex stared at the horizon, the distant cough of cars still the only sound.

Where had they been when they first had sex? Amy and her 'older fella'. Was it here? Had it built up for days, weeks, longer? Had their first time been that last time, or was that just one encounter in many?

If it was Paul, it all made a screwed-up kind of sense. Of course Amy didn't tell anyone that she was seeing her birth father; if they had a secret that ran so deeply in the wrong direction nobody could hear it. Of course he hadn't admitted to meeting her, finding himself drawn to her in a way he would never have anticipated – no-one would.

Where had she been when she was beaten until blood splattered? Her father's borrowed car? Had she changed her mind about their clandestine meetings? Perhaps she'd tried to end it and he was so enraged he just attacked without thinking. A crime of passion. Alex hated that phrase.

Had Paul brought his daughter here for secrecy as he explored a body he should never have seen like that, before laying that body on the ground as if at random? Or was there some sense of occasion as Amy lay in the grass and felt his hands on her throat and the tug of black sleep nipping at her toes? Did she stare into his eyes? His eyes that are just like her eyes?

Alex pictured Amy foetal on a gurney. Dewy grass under her nails and in her hair. Without thinking, Alex lay down on the wet grass and closed her eyes. The smell of damp autumnal soil was wrong, of course. Amy would have felt the warmth of the summer soil and smelled the stink of the nearby lake, humming with midges and thick with slime. Amy lay right here, on this spot that could be any spot, and thought her last conscious thoughts.

Paul was a sneaky, snaky liar, but he was also a bit of a buffoon. Was he really capable of this?

Alex shivered and got back up carefully. She rushed back towards the car and tried to ignore her thirst, and the thought of the measuring jug and bottle on the kitchen counter.

It was time to talk to Matt again. She was a little dizzy at the thought of presenting him with a new idea. No perfectly wrapped-up case, but something fresh at least. Not criminal evidence, but evidence of her own abilities. Her ability to stay sharp and focused, to work into the afternoon. To accomplish something tangible. To accomplish anything at all.

CHAPTER FORTY-FIVE

Jacob

11 October 2010

Jacob's job at GRX Solutions was the only one he'd ever had. He'd come straight out of university with no plan besides avoiding being a computer programmer. Regrettably, he'd taken a degree in computer programming, which limited his options. Selling software seemed as good as anything.

As Jacob called his boss Geoff to arrange dragging his slightly improved leg back to work, he realized he'd worked in the same office for nearly ten years. At the same desk. Besides Geoff, who owned the company, and Linda, who manned the reception, Jacob was the longest-standing employee.

'Hello, stranger', Geoff answered.

'Hey, Geoff, how's it all going over there? Falling apart without me?'

'It's heavenly, mate, heavenly. No-one's eating all the biscuits and morale's through the roof.'

'You'll be gutted to hear I'm coming back in a few days, then.'

'God, d'ya have to come back?'

The only one-to-one Jacob had ever had was about three years into the job. One of the long-gone account girls had complained about the lack of career progression, so Geoff had made a big show of having one-to-ones with everyone.

'It's a load of old bollocks, if you ask me,' he'd confided in Jacob. 'We all know what we're doing, and if you're not doing a good job, you're out. But apparently Susan needs cuddles, so here we go.'

Geoff had attempted to make notes about each employee. Under Jacob's name was just one word: solid. At the time, Jacob took it as a compliment. The clients liked him, he wasn't pushy with them and he didn't overpromise. In this industry, that was enough to elicit loyalty. He had staying power; that was certainly true. Solid. Dependable. Loyal. He'd thought they were good traits.

Graham Arlington had worked for the same company for decades. It wasn't that Jacob had deliberately aped his father, but it had seemed to work out well enough for the older man. For every year that Jacob could remember, his father had set out at the same time each day, caught the same train, read his books or the paper and worked with a stream of pretty secretaries. He only knew the last nugget from the occasional snatched sniping of his mother, bubbling through the floorboards when he still lived at home.

If pressed, Jacob would have struggled to describe his father's job. It seemed to belong in a past version of London. Not the fast, smart, dirty city of today. More like the bowler hats and red buses of the fifties and sixties, an era that predated his father.

Until his retirement, Graham had worked for a livery company, an antiquated, excruciatingly British institution that would never have existed anywhere else. All Jacob knew, from what little his father had explained to him, was that livery companies are London's ancient trade associations, a sort of olde worlde guild of workers. Now they mostly seemed to dole out cash from their considerable monies for charitable work. The other thing Jacob knew was that his father had managed to avoid having a computer for his whole working life, and that he earned a very decent wage. With no real desire to do anything in particular, this last achievement seemed to be a sensible one to try to emulate.

In that respect, Jacob was the only son to follow in his father's footsteps. To push slightly into the next income tax bracket. He wondered, when he let himself, if this pleased or disappointed his father.

In many ways it was a surprise that Simon hadn't followed his father, given they were so similar. Not that Simon was particularly money mad, but he was women mad. The bevy of secretaries his mother had painted and the kudos of a good City job must have appealed, but he'd rejected that. How many women were there to choose from in the middle of the humanitarian crises Simon picked through?

Both Jacob's brothers were 'helpers' rather than earners, putting the greater good above their own pay packet. In fact, even his father, for all his pin-stripe suitedness, had technically been a helper, dishing out other people's money to a specific sliver of the needy. In contrast, Jacob's form of help was laser precise. His charitable acts began and ended with Amy, and that was hardly pure and altruistic.

Jacob's leg was still painful and his head was still foggy from painkillers, but he'd be able to get by without crutches soon. The routine of work would be good for him, he decided. It would stop him thinking, churning things over so bloody much. Mostly, though, it would get him away from Edenbridge for part of the day, and – maybe – away from his most punishing memories.

CHAPTER FORTY-SIX

Sue

23 August 2010

Sue sat still on her dusky sofa, knees to the side. 'Side saddle', the way she'd been shown to ride a pony as a child. The quiet tick-tock of the carriage clock gave the lounge a heartbeat. The sun danced from the reflection of the clock's gold case and the silver photo frames that surrounded it.

Where had those little boys in the photo frames gone? Their shaggy hair and nylon jackets, always slightly too big for them.

Jacob's first school photo beamed out at her from the corner of the mantel, a gappy smile and his hair flying a little at the sides. How she had raged at him for the shirt collar that was tucked awkwardly into his jumper. A quirk of the photo that she loved to death now. She could barely bring herself to look at his happy little face. His brown eyes bright and clear. He'd cried so rarely back then. And when he did, when he fell and scraped his knee or landed awkwardly from his bike, what sweet luck to be able to rush in and hug him until he was better.

He'd had a big scab on his knee when that photo was taken. Five years old, tumbling down the garden like a sausage roll, clattering into Tom's tricycle and crashing onto the stone path. All these years later, Sue could still smell the iron blood in the air.

Could picture herself wincing on his behalf as she gently cleaned the gritty graze.

Her favourite picture over the fireplace was of the five of them. Standing on a sand dune, the wind blowing them sideways, smiles carved into the boys' cheeks. Graham was standing so tall and handsome, frowning into the lens as he always did, unconvinced that the self-timer would work. And Sue herself looked so young, so strong. Where had the years gone?

Her eldest son was so unbearably handsome: it was almost captured in the pictures, but real life always won. His eyes sparkled like emeralds in a storm cloud. Her two youngest boys had always reminded her of Labrador puppies. One chocolate, one golden. Tom would chase after Jake with boundless energy, desperate to catch him, join in with him, wrestle his ball from him. Just like puppies.

The little two needed wrangling, herding in a way that Simon did not – or would not – allow. He responded more to Graham's silent form of 'handling'. A look from his father, that was enough. He always knew what it meant, like a private code. Had it not been for the needs of the younger two, Sue would have allowed herself to feel shut out.

The windy picture had been taken on the penultimate day of the last family holiday to Sandy Bay. The last time they caravanned and the last holiday that was in Devon rather than abroad. Until then, they'd just caravanned at Sandy Bay because they had always caravanned at Sandy Bay. The gold sand as warm and familiar as her own doormat. And then, of course, there was all that trouble, those misunderstandings. They couldn't go back after that.

It was the push they needed. They'd always wanted to try Portugal though, and from the following summer, holidays were spent in the Algarve surrounded by other Brits.

But even now, Sue remembered the exact layout of the Sandy Bay caravan. A big five-berth beast with a full dining table and chairs, floral wrap-around sofa and three separate bedrooms. You didn't find them like that any more; it was a gem.

The two youngest boys would bunk together in the middle room, wrestling until way past bedtime. Simon would lie alone on his bed, thumbing through *NME* or *Melody Maker* or whatever it was.

Sue remembered their final night with a smile. One of the last times she and Graham had made love spontaneously, wordlessly. That hazy, happy holiday feeling. The boys at the holiday park disco. After days of acclimatizing, and just hours before they had to pack up, Graham had finally seemed to unwind.

They had drunk crisp gin and tonics, silently watching the sun hanging over the sea. A wedge of grass, little beige caravans and colourful washing lines had been all that lay between them and that deep blue water.

CHAPTER FORTY-SEVEN

Amy

Sometime in 2007

I didn't like it earlier. This loud voice came through a speaker or something and told me he was a doctor and that I needed to imagine I was playing tennis. Like that's a perfectly normal, everyday thing. To be told to play tennis in your head by some random doctor. But I couldn't see any reason not to, so I just did as I was told.

I've only played tennis once or twice in my life. The doctor didn't ask and I didn't say anything, but if he'd have told me to play netball, it would have been a lot better. But whatever, I dutifully imagined myself playing tennis. In my head, I threw the hard fuzzy ball up in the air and swung my racquet so the ball smashed down hard over the net. Over and over again, slicing it through the air and firing it away whenever it came close. And I heard the doctor's voice and it had laughter in it. He said things like, 'That's really good, Amy, that's wonderful,' and, 'You must be winning.'

He also said weird stuff about how the tennis bit of my brain was lighting up. Since when does anyone have a bit of brain just for playing tennis? And I thought, *Are you laughing at me? What are you really testing? My honesty, or something like that? Does he know about the Jesus Jones tape I stole from Woolies that time? I didn't even like Jesus Jones, I just went along with what*

Jenny and this lad were doing. I've been quite scared about that ever since.

He told me to relax then but I thought, *no, I need to put this right.* So I imagined myself back on the tennis court and I decided to do it properly, realistically. That time, in my more accurate imagination, the sun was in my eyes and I dropped one ball after another. When my wooden racquet finally connected, I just scooped the ball softly into the net. I watched it flop down into the folds of the material and I could feel my palms and forehead prickling with sweat. After I dropped about seven more balls, I looked up. I think I'd thought I was playing Jake or Becky, but when I realized who it actually was, I was mortified.

Without warning, he threw the ball in the air, far up over his head, leapt into the clouds and sent it shrieking over the net. I just stood rooted to the spot in my own imagination, watching the spinning yellow shape as it landed between my eyes and sent me flying back so hard that I landed on my bum.

I scrambled up and looked at him, hoping for a friendly smile, but his eyes were black. He stayed where he was, looking at me like he'd tasted something bad. I hated how that look made me feel. And I think I must have cried out or something because it got light outside of my eyes and I could hear the doctor's voice in my ear rather than through a speaker. He was saying things like, 'That's enough, that's enough, just relax, Amy, it's okay.' And I suddenly thought, *Hang on, why is this doctor doing tests on me, does my mum know about this?* And I think they must have given me something because I didn't care after that. And I didn't care right up until just now.

CHAPTER FORTY-EIGHT

Alex

11 October 2010

'I don't know, Alex, I think your first hunch was right – Wheeler's just an untrustworthy little worm, not much more. And even if he did have an unhealthy interest in underage girls like Amy, it wouldn't be on his record or he wouldn't have kept his other children.'

'I know, Matt, it doesn't sit right with me either but I want to look under every stone.' Alex ignored the sting she felt at Matt's dismissiveness, like she wasn't seeing a full picture that came easily to him.

'Well, I hope that's true and you're not getting your hopes up about this.'

Alex bit her lip and murmured. She couldn't allow herself to snap or argue, to damage the fragile truce they were working within. She needed Matt to be on her side as a police source. She needed Matt.

'Don't worry, I'm still looking at other angles; I'm talking to Amy's friends and looking into her school life. I want to do this thoroughly.'

'I know you do. I know you'll do a good job.'

For a moment, Alex couldn't say anything; she just smiled widely, eyes dancing. It was a long time since anyone had told her she was doing a good job, let alone the person whose opinion mattered the most.

She took a deep breath and shook her head, trying to ignore her racing heart.

'Thanks, Matt,' she said as professionally as possible. 'Let me know what you find, yeah?'

'I'll let you know what I *can*,' Matt cautioned.

Alex said goodbye and looked at the time on her phone's display. As if she didn't already know it. Her thirst knew it. Five hours, forty-two minutes to go until she could crack that screw cap. She'd almost done it instinctively before calling Matt, her hands leading her into the kitchen and towards the bottle as her heart had beat faster.

But she'd done it again. She'd spoken to Matt completely sober. She'd spoken clearly, keeping emotion out of it. It was fucking exhausting, but she'd managed it. With every conversation she was calmer, more like a normal person. God, she hoped that was how it came across.

If there was more to Paul Wheeler and Amy's relationship, Bob and Jacob had been totally in the dark. The only other people likely to have seen anything were Amy's school friends.

Alex scrolled through her contacts and called Becky Limm. The sound of a baby crying in the background hit before her voice did.

'Hello?'

'Hi, Becky, it's Alex Dale here. Is that your baby I hear? Congratulations!' Alex closed her eyes.

'Thanks,' came a hurried reply. 'Hang on a sec.'

Eyes still closed, Alex could hear mumbled negotiations.

'I'm just running upstairs.' Muffled sounds came down the line until a panting Becky returned.

'Sorry about that, I needed to get my husband to hold Jude.'

'I'm really sorry to bother you, I'll be quick.'

'It's okay, but if you're phoning about any work, I'm not quite ready yet.'

'Work? No, I wasn't phoning about that. I just wanted to ask you something about Amy.'

'Oh, okay. I'll have to be quick as it's mayhem down there.'

'Just one question, did Amy ever tell you her birth dad had got in touch?'

'Um, yeah, he showed up at school a couple of times, why?'

'Paul Wheeler showed up at Amy's school? And you saw him?' Alex's heart beat faster as she circled Paul's name in thick pen over and over.

'I don't know what his name was, but it was her real dad, yeah. Amy just used to roll her eyes. I mean, I think she liked the drama of it at first, the long-lost dad thing, but she got bored of him. He was a bit of a loser.'

'Did you tell the police any of this?'

'No, why would I?'

'But if he was bothering her—'

'No, he wasn't bothering her, she used to laugh about it. Honestly, it wasn't a big deal. I don't want to give you the wrong idea, so please bear in mind that I'm crazy with sleep deprivation and barely remember my own name.'

Alex laughed through her nose. 'Don't worry, I'm not holding you to anything you say. It just really helps to sound someone out who was there at the time. Even if your head's foggy, I really appreciate any help you can give.'

'I mean, I want to help, I really do, but I don't want to un-help, does that make sense?'

'Um, sort of, I think. I know you might think it's unhelpful, but just scratch an itch for me. When was the last time you remember seeing Paul at school?'

'Oh, I don't remember offhand... a while before she disappeared.'

'If I told you that Amy and her birth dad had spoken a lot and may have met up in secret, what would you say?'

'Huh. Really? That's weird. She was pretty dismissive of him in front of me but maybe she changed her mind.'

'Or he changed it for her?'

'What are you getting at?'

'Nothing really, just trying a few ideas for size. Becky, did you know Amy wasn't a virgin when she was attacked?'

'God, Alex, I'm not sure that's how I'd describe it. She was raped!'

'Not exactly. I'm sorry to be insensitive, but can you keep this confidential?'

'Well yeah, of course, what is it?' There was an uneasy excitement in Becky's voice. *Maybe she'll make a decent journalist after all*, Alex thought with a grimace.

'Well, this isn't confirmed,' Alex lied, 'but there's evidence to suggest Amy had had consensual sex at some point before her attack.'

Becky laughed. Just a titter at first, and then a more throaty, tearful sound. Alex imagined her blonde hair bouncing, still shiny despite the baby sick in it.

'I'm sorry,' Becky said, voice wavering. 'It's just that she won and she never got to brag.'

'What do you mean, she won?'

'She won the competition. To lose it,' Becky lowered her voice. 'Me, Amy and Jenny had a sort of serious, sort of joke competition to see who could pop their cherry first.'

'Do you have any idea who it might have been with?'

'It wasn't Jake?'

'No, it wasn't Jake.'

Becky stopped laughing abruptly. 'Oh God,' she said. 'Then I have no idea.'

CHAPTER FORTY-NINE

Amy

Sometime in 2008

Jake came to see me today and it was really weird. It felt like he was distant and we barely knew each other.

He didn't speak for a long time, but I could hear him breathing hard. In the background, this cheesy song was playing from the radio I hear sometimes. It was that awful 'Everything I Do' song by Bryan Adams and I remember thinking, *God, there are actually couples in the world who would have chosen this as their special song.*

I always felt like we should have a special song, but we never did. We sat by the radio once and said the next song that came on would be ours. It was Celine Dion. We said we'd wait and see what the next song was instead. We never picked one in the end, but we've made each other a lot of mix tapes. I wonder if he's kept his. I have all of mine in a box under my bed, but deep down I know that Jake isn't that bothered by music really, he just knows it matters to me. I tried to make my tapes full of surprises; live tracks and B-sides and weird covers. Bands like The Breeders, early Red Hot Chili Peppers from when they were still punk, Pavement. I slipped in some Kraftwerk, Siouxie and the Banshees, Bowie at his most 'Berlin', a whole melting pot. And some stuff I was sure Jacob already knew, a bit of light relief maybe, some Queen for laughs.

I s'pose, if I'm honest, I was trying to educate him a bit. Open his eyes. J's tapes were more... I don't know, more like he'd recorded the top forty off the radio. I loved that he tried though. I wasn't angry with him then.

Anyway, earlier, after a long time, Jake took this big, gross, loud swallow and then started talking about another girl. I mean, c'mon, what? He was saying he was sorry and she made him happy and this kind of thing. I know I'm a massive hypocrite, I really do know that, but my secret is – or was – just that, a secret. A sidestep. There was no way either one of us would have let Jake know, he was totally insulated. I didn't break up with him, I didn't lose my patience with him, I didn't abandon him. I didn't even really do anything with you know who, I just wanted to. Then, out of the blue, today Jake said he couldn't see me any more.

I was pissed off more than anything, then I was gutted. He'd just given up on us, out of the blue like that. I couldn't say anything, I guess I was dumbstruck, but my face must have given it away because he started back-pedalling and saying he didn't mean it and he would see me after all. Then he started to say – actually, scrap everything, he would see me *more*. I'm not sure what that means in reality; he wants more of a commitment?

I'm left not knowing what to do, and I feel quite breathless about it all because I never expected this from Jake. If he was trying to make me jealous – if he's going to start playing games like that – I should probably break up with him. Although, not that I'd admit it openly, it is a bit romantic, in a weird kind of way.

But if he really has met another girl, some tart called Fiona – and where could he have met her, anyway? Judo? – then good riddance, he needs to belt up and break it off with me for good.

I don't mean it. It's me who should have broken it off. I probably should have put him out of his misery weeks before I had my head turned, but I was always going to turn my head right back. I really was. It was only temporary. I hope Jake never finds out about that because I love him. I'll always love him. I hope he feels the same about me, I hope he forgets about this Fiona and we can get back to how it was before.

CHAPTER FIFTY

Alex

12 October 2010

'You could use this space as an office, or a nursery.' Jenny smiled and deep dimples formed on her generous pink cheeks.

'Do you have kids, Kate?'

'No,' Alex answered, though she could have lied, she supposed.

'Do you live in Oxted yourself?' Alex asked Jenny, interrupting her monologue about the shortcut to the train station.

'Yes, I do. We love it. How far would you be moving?'

'I live in Edenbridge at the moment,' Alex lied. 'Do you know it?'

'Yes,' Jenny said, smile dropping briefly. 'I grew up there actually.'

'Oh, what a coincidence!' Alex laughed, clasping her hand to her chest.

'I moved there when I was twenty,' Alex added, 'for a job.' It sounded strange and rehearsed as soon as she said it.

'Would you like to see the loft? There's a proper ladder and it's fully boarded out.'

'Oh, yes please. So did you go to school in Edenbridge?'

'Um, yes. The grammar school there. I just need to grab this.' The loft ladder funnelled down to the landing carpet. Alex waited in the hallway, the other woman's bulk taking up nearly all of the square landing. In Alex's mind's eye, all these people, these characters in Amy's story, were freeze-framed in 1995. Knock-kneed, wide-eyed youngsters at the start of the path. One by one, she had met Jacob with his greying hair and crinkled eyes, Becky with her new domesticity and now Jenny. Although swathed in a long, forgiving skirt, there was no hiding just how large and thick her limbs were.

Jenny put one foot on the bottom rung and the ladder groaned audibly under her weight. The foot was taken off hastily.

'Do you want to just poke your head up there?' she asked, moving out of the way. Alex climbed the steps and looked up into the small loft. 'Handy,' she agreed.

'I'm writing a story about Edenbridge Grammar at the moment actually,' Alex added into the hollow loft.

'A story?' Jenny asked, her hands steadying the ladder. 'What is it you do for a job?'

Alex popped her head back out of the ceiling. 'I'm a writer,' she said.

Jenny looked up hard into Alex's eyes.

'What did you say your name was?'

'I said it was Kate,' Alex said, as she stepped back down to the landing carpet. 'But that's not quite true.'

'You sneaky bitch.' Jenny tried to push past Alex but there was no room.

'I'm sorry,' Alex said. 'I really didn't want to trick you but I had to talk to you. I need your help.'

'I don't care what you need.' Jenny said.

'I'm not trying to hurt anyone,' Alex called as Jenny thundered heavily down the stairs and threw the front door open.

'Out!' she shouted up the stairs to Alex. 'Get out now or I'm calling the police.'

'I know about the competition,' Alex said as she stumbled a little down the stairs.

'What?' Jenny spat.

'The competition to lose your virginity.'

'Who the hell told you about that?'

'It doesn't matter who.'

'Bloody Becky!'

'Look, Jenny,' Alex said, wavering on the mat with one foot in the doorway. 'Do you know who Amy slept with before she was attacked?'

Jenny looked down briefly, then snapped her head back up. She was breathing like a charging bull and slammed the door hard. Alex just managed to pull her foot out of the way to stop it being crunched into the frame.

'Hi, Amy, it's Alex.' In the slight chill of the ward, Alex took Amy's hand into hers and found herself trying to warm it.

'Oh, Amy,' Alex said, her head hanging to her chest. For all the new openings in the story, she was hitting a lot of brick walls.

As she started to tell Amy about how she'd been working with Jake and talking to Becky, there was some kind of commotion in the world outside the fabric. Alex could hear curtains being flapped open, squeaky wheels and numerous footsteps slapping the floor. She tried to tune it all out, but the curtains were suddenly wrenched back and standing with his hips thrust forward was Dr Haynes.

'Oh!' he said, looking at the nurse beside him.

'I'm sorry,' Alex said, out of habit.

'We're here to do some obs on Amy,' Dr Haynes said, pushing his hands through his hair. 'We won't be long, perhaps you could wait in the nurse's office?'

'Oh, I don't think—' the nurse started to say, turning her back to Alex to gesture something with her eyes.

'Right. Yes, okay. Right, Alex, we'll go on to Natasha and then come back to Amy so you can have a little more time.'

'Okay, thanks.'

The nurse wheeled the machine away, deflated blood pressure bags flapping over multiple dead screens. Alex went to pick Amy's hand up again when she felt hot breath in her ear.

'I'm so sorry about leaving the other week,' Peter Haynes said, leaning over her.

'Please,' Alex whispered, 'don't mention it.'

'It was terribly unchivalrous of me. Especially after you invited me back so kindly.' He paused. 'You did invite me back.'

Alex stared at Amy's hands and whispered, 'Please, I said don't mention it.'

She waited for the footsteps to move away, and sighed so hard her body crumpled like a pile of clothes.

'Oh God,' she whispered to Amy, 'I did something so awful a couple of weeks ago.'

Amy, of course, did not reply.

'It's not even the first time I've done something like that. I mean, God, it's not even the tenth time I've done something like that, but I want to make it the last.'

Amy's index finger curled ever so slightly and her chest rose and fell, rose and fell. It just slowly and steadily kept doing what it always did. Alex wanted to curl up next to her on the bed. To brush Amy's hair out of the way and rest her own head on the pillow.

'I met your birth dad, Paul, the other day.' Alex squinted to see if she could make out a reaction. When she saw a slight quiver in Amy's chest, she didn't trust her eyes.

'I'd love to hear your side of that story because I don't trust him as far as I could throw him. I'm really...' Alex paused, unsure how much she wanted to say out loud. 'I don't know what to make of him, Amy. His story doesn't quite add up.'

Alex could hear Natasha's curtain being pulled back and more sticky slapping of shoes.

'I know you didn't tell the truth about how much you'd seen Paul,' she whispered fast. 'I'd love to know why. I'd really love to know why.'

'Okay, time's up,' the nurse said with a sing-song brightness that didn't match her eyes. She strapped the blood pressure bag quickly to Amy's arm and popped the heart rate monitor onto her finger, allowing her hand to fall back on the bed.

'Thanks for the extra time,' Alex said, gathering her bag and phone. As she patted her pockets down to check for her keys, she heard the nurse say something about an elevated heart rate. Alex shuffled out without meeting the doctor's eye.

Alex realized it was Amy she spoke to more than anyone else. And she had come to look forward to their shared, silent moments more than any other part of her week. When had her world become so narrow?

She wondered if Amy had any idea how narrow her own world had become. Those friendships that would have meant everything, would have felt so solid, broken by time and tragedy. No knowledge of the wider world her friends now occupied or the private worlds they had created for themselves.

The way Alex missed Matt was excruciating, but she missed more than that. She missed her own friends and having other people's worlds orbiting and overlapping with hers. She was no more a part of her old friends' worlds than Amy.

Dinners out, parties with friends, camaraderie in the Ladies, interviewing interesting people over Michelin-starred meals. Being behind the velvet rope. It had all disappeared.

After leaving *The Times* in a blaze of bile, she'd thought the world was at her feet.

She'd thought she had options.

She'd packed her best clippings into their beautiful baby-blue leather binder. She'd applied her eyeliner *exactly* how the last *Grazia* beauty segment had advised, gripping the basin with her other hand. She'd been certain that her attention to detail would be the cherry on the cake.

She'd lowered herself carefully into the car, adjusted the wing mirrors that were strangely off-balance and programmed her satnav. She'd taken a deep breath and a deeper gulp.

The perfume that had smelled so fresh when she bought it had mingled with the seeping, sour scent of bourbon. She'd popped another mint in, circled her fingertips around her temples and opened the window for a blast of fresh air. Finally she set off to London, squinting to stay steady on the correct side of the central reservation.

They will be thrilled, she'd thought.

Just a few months earlier, she'd turned down an offer to become associate editor of *Grazia*. Matt told her it was her decision, although he looked uneasy when she said no. 'But you can learn about fashion on the job,' he'd said. 'You always look nice to me.'

'It's not just the fashion stuff,' she'd tried to explain. 'It's a whole lifestyle change. And it's features and commissioning. I've not commissioned anything since I was at *Mizz*, I wouldn't know where to start. It just feels like a massive opportunity to fall on my arse.'

But Matt had been right. She should have accepted it. She could have learned on the job. Besides, instinct and creativity were what mattered. A more normal office setting, away from the filth of newspapers... maybe things would have been different. Maybe things could still be different, she'd told herself. *This will fix everything*, she'd thought.

Alex had reached the *Grazia* offices lock-jawed from the brutality of city driving, her ears ringing with the sounds of bus horns and pedestrian crossing signals. She'd parked right outside, pulling up onto the pavement so she didn't block the road.

Right in the middle of Shaftesbury Avenue wasn't strictly a parking area, but Alex had to go in then and there or her nerve would have left her on the floor.

Inside Endeavour House, she'd waited to speak to the receptionist who was talking excitedly to the security guard about something going on outside. The receptionist had a blunt-cut hairstyle that was as glossy as a maraschino cherry, and cartoon-red lips that must have required constant coatings.

Eventually she'd smiled at Alex, 'Can I help?'

'I'm Alex Dale and I'm here to see Melissa Craw,' she'd said, swapping her clippings folder to the crook of her other arm.

'Melissa Craw?' The receptionist had frowned a little and looked across at the security guard who looked entirely uninterested.

'Yes,' Alex said, sharply.

'Melissa left *Grazia* a little while back. Has she arranged to meet you here?'

'Oh. No, not exactly.'

'Do you have an appointment with the *Grazia* team? Perhaps I could call one of them?'

'Who is Melissa's replacement?' Alex had asked, shifting the weight from one leg to the other and feeling incredibly angry and betrayed, but she couldn't work out why and by whom.

'Who do you have an appointment with?' the receptionist had asked, with an urgency that bordered on irritation.

'I was offered a job here,' Alex had said a little louder than intended as she leaned into the desk. The security guard had finally taken his eyes off whatever was distracting him outside and he looked Alex up and down.

'I was offered a job and I turned it down but that was...' Alex had laughed and leaned further over the desk, trying to draw the receptionist in conspiratorially. 'That was a mistake, as it turns out. I'd meant to accept the job, and I very much do accept the job and I just need to do the decent thing and let them know in person.'

The receptionist had smiled but looked uneasily at the guard.

Eventually, the receptionist had picked up the phone and jabbed a couple of buttons.

'Hi, Debbie, is Annabelle with anyone at the moment? Uh-huh. Uh-huh. Okay, I have a...' She'd clasped her hand over the receiver. 'Sorry, what was your name again?'

'Alex Dale,' Alex had whispered back.

'I have an Alex Dale down here, she had – yes, that's right, Alex Dale. She had asked to see Melissa so I've explained that Melissa has left, but she says she's here to accept a job? Does that sound— Yes, yes, okay. Thanks, Debbie.'

The receiver had clicked back into place.

'I just spoke with the editor's PA and she's going to speak to the editor now and give me a call back. Could you wait over there, please?'

Alex had shuffled into one of the plush seats in the window and studiously checked her phone. No new text messages. She'd used the screen's reflection to wipe away the grit of make-up that had made its way back under her eyes during the drive.

She could hear horns from outside and rolled her eyes. *London.*

After a short time, the receptionist had been back on the phone, her eyes darting between Alex and the security guard.

'You need to leave now,' the guard had said.

'I'm still waiting for someone to have the decency to come and see me,' Alex had said, fighting back tears and crossing her arms over the binder in her lap.

'Miss,' the guard had said, leaning in so his nose nearly touched hers, and without a scrap of kindness. 'You need to leave now.'

'But you don't understand!' Alex had yelled as the security guard pulled her arm up like a toddler mid-tantrum.

'You're making a huge mistake, you all are. God, this is so embarrassing!' she'd screeched as the guard pushed through the doors and deposited her firmly outside.

She'd fumbled in her bag for her keys, spotting a small crowd standing around her car which, she realized, had slightly kissed the barrier at the side of the pedestrian crossing.

'Is this your car?' the security guard had asked, eyebrows to the sky.

'Well, that's none of your business now. After you've been so rude to me!' Alex had yelled.

Tears and snot were smeared into Alex's blusher and she'd really felt that she deserved the dignity of leaving without further interrogation.

'You're hammered, darling, I can smell it from here.'

That's when Alex had spotted the traffic warden circling her car and flipping his pad open. His too-big Puffa jacket and cap had drowned him like a new school uniform.

Alex had wiped her face and slinked around to lean on the driver's door.

'There's no need for that,' she'd cooed at the expressionless warden. His high cheekbones, almond eyes and deep-black skin giving nothing away.

'How about this? You don't write that out and I just go on my way. No harm done,' she'd smiled, running her hand down the zip of his jacket. His face had been overrun with horror then.

Popping the door handle, Alex had licked her lips. 'Why don't I make it worth your while? Mmm? Why don't you get in the other side and we go somewhere and I make it worth your while?'

'This is entirely inappropriate,' the warden had said in a crisp but shaking voice that gave away his young age.

'Don't be a spoilsport,' Alex had purred, blowing a slight burp away from the corner of her mouth.

The warden had backed away for a moment, heading over to talk to the security guard who was shaking his head and staring at the car.

Then Alex had done the only thing she could think of and jumped into the driver's seat, jammed the key in the ignition, freed herself from the barrier and thundered down the bus lane.

She'd woken early the next day with absolutely no memory of the journey home. She had still been in her black dress-to-impress dress, her handbag spewing its contents all up the stairs. She'd trodden carefully, making her way outside to inspect her car, barefoot. The dents haunted her until the next drink, a few hours later.

She'd drunk the house dry.

When she finally came to from that blackout, she'd lost a couple of days and a lot of money. Nauseated and drenched in sweat, she'd started sending pitches to everyone she could think of, only stopping when the nausea got too much and she had to vomit.

CHAPTER FIFTY-ONE

Jacob

13 October 2010

Jacob rested his leg under Amy's hospital bed and leaned back in his chair. He said nothing and didn't pick up her hand. He rubbed his eyes deeply, grinding his knuckles into the sockets until they hurt.

He'd accepted a lift from his mother, who believed that he was going for a check-up on his leg and had tried her damnedest to accompany him inside. In the years since he'd left home, the memories had dulled, but now he remembered vividly how his mother had accompanied him everywhere, insisted on being designated driver right up until he left home. It was out of care, protection, but it could feel like hands on his throat at times.

She'd been the same with Tom, probably Simon too when he'd been young, although he was often off in their father's car going to the court or on this mission or that.

Amy's breathing was so quiet that you had to strain to hear it, like trying to pick up a tiny thread from a thick carpet.

Jacob tried to shut the noise of his thoughts out. He looked at Amy, oblivious Amy. Her skin almost translucent, her head suspended on the plasticky pillow, in the kind of deep sleep Jacob could only daydream about.

After languishing in his own arrested development for so many years, how had things unravelled so quickly over the last few weeks? Was this always on the cards, Jacob wondered. It's not like he'd ever really given marriage his all, not if he was brutally honest.

He'd always prided himself on being A Nice Guy. A decent bloke who would do the right thing, put the right people first and stay loyal. To the bitter end. He'd told himself that for years. Would Fiona describe him as a nice guy? Would his child think he was putting the right people first?

The more important she should have become, the further down the list of priorities Fiona had slipped. Fiona who was out there, walking, talking and living. Who was carrying his child and had treated him like the man he is and not the boy he was.

He looked at Amy, eyes open and hair freshly brushed. Her skin was as milky and smooth as a child's, no ravages of time played out on this face. Amy was like a doll, like a photograph. A different beauty to Fiona.

When Jacob had looked in the mirror after his uncomfortable, propped-up shower that morning, he'd seen some cartoonified old guy emerging through the steam. An approximation of him. Saggier, greyer, sadder. When he sat with Amy he felt fifteen again, but if she'd opened her eyes then and there, she wouldn't have recognized him.

None of this stuff touched Amy. He could dress it up and say he *knew*, he just *knew*, that she benefited from his visits. That his dogged determination to just keep plodding on was having some positive effect. He had believed that at first, before years passed without any obvious change for the better. Whereas his sneaking around and inside-out priorities had held his own life underwater. No wonder Fiona had changed.

Fiona had been so cool at first. Not cool in the hip way she tried to be with her band T-shirts and art student hair, but cool in the way she'd never tried to change him. Yes, she pushed for things they didn't need and she was bossy about housework. But she hadn't pushed for him to be anyone but himself and to spend time with her. She'd always wanted to spend time with him, until now.

Jacob took one last long look at the bed and left without sitting in any other cubicles, swinging his crutches as quietly as he could.

As promised, his mum was waiting in the car park. No radio on, just sitting and waiting, deep in thought.

'That was quick,' she said as Jacob popped the passenger door handle.

'Yeah,' he said. 'I'm healing fine.'

Sue started the car but took her hands back off the wheel and turned to him.

'We should pop in to see Fiona while we're here.'

'I don't think so, Mum.'

'We love having you to stay but you've got to sort this out before the baby comes.'

'I know, Mum.'

'Jacob, whatever the problem is, it can be overcome. If there are kids involved, you'd be surprised what horrors you can put behind you. But you have to show up.'

It had been a long time since Jacob had heard his mother talk with anything other than a disappointed acceptance. The disapproval cut him.

'You don't understand, I tried to talk to her the other day and she didn't want to know.'

'You're right, I don't understand. You've got a wonderful woman you loved enough to marry and a precious baby on the way. Nothing is more important than that. I know Fiona is a firecracker at the moment, but she's heavily pregnant. Not to mention tired, hormonal and in need of support. Even, *Jacob, look at me*, even if she says she doesn't need you – she does. And you need to be there when she realizes that. Darling, nothing is unfixable. You just need to be a man about this.'

After a stunned silence, Jacob said carefully, 'I guess we could see if she's in. Right now she doesn't want to know me, and I said some things I didn't mean that haven't helped. But I should try to talk to her again, you're right.'

'For goodness sake, Jacob, stop being so wishy-washy. You have a baby to think about. It's not about whether you make each other happy, it's about putting things right for your child.'

'Let me call her first. She hates people turning up unannounced.'

'You're not people, you're her husband, and it's your house too. Problems need fixing, by hook or by crook. It sounds like you're putting this off because it's hard.'

'You have to let me do things my way, Mum.'

'Apparently so.'

'Fiona, I'm just around the corner and we really need to talk.'

'No. I can't handle this right now.'

Jacob cupped his hand around the phone, wishing he'd hobbled out of the car to make the call.

'Look, we both said some things we didn't mean—'

'I meant them, I wish I hadn't but I did.'

'Well I meant them too, at the time.'

'Did you just phone up to start a row with me?'

'No, that's not what I want at all. Look, let me come round and let's just talk. We really need to get everything out in the open. I know I've not been open enough with you,' Jacob side-eyed his mother and stopped talking.

'You haven't been remotely open with me, J. I think the first honest thing you said to me was that you wanted to break up.'

'That's not what I said.'

'Well that's what I heard. So what's the problem, you thought you had somewhere to go but she's turned you down?'

'No!' Jacob turned awkwardly in the passenger seat to face out of the window. 'For the millionth time, I'm not having an affair.'

He lowered his voice, 'I've never cheated on you, I never would.'

As he spoke, his mother unbuckled her seatbelt and opened the door to get out.

'I'll be out here,' she said as Jacob cringed.

'Who was that? Are you there with her?'

'It was just Mum.'

'Your mother was listening to this? What the fuck is wrong with you lot?'

'She gave me a lift and we were in the car, she wasn't really listening.'

'Have you heard yourself, Jacob?' Fiona sighed. 'We do have things to sort out. We have the baby to make arrangements for, there's house stuff to talk through and things like maintenance money. I'll talk about that with you. But until you're ready to tell me the truth, the whole truth and nothing but the bloody truth, you don't get to talk to me about anything else.'

Jacob waved for his mum to get back in the car. 'It didn't go well,' he said, without looking up.

'You just have to keep trying. Jacob, if you only knew the problems I've had to fix in my time. This is nothing.'

'Problems with Dad?'

'Nothing you need to worry about. Just believe me that when you become a parent, you need to be willing to confront *anything*, to clean up any mess and keep on smiling while you do it.'

Sue started the car again.

'Mum, could you drop me at a friend's house, it's just around the corner?'

'Which friend?'

'A woman called Alex. We're helping each other with something.'

'Oh, Jacob, don't tell me Fiona's right?'

'No, Mum,' Jacob frowned. 'I'd never cheat on Fiona, I'd never cheat on anyone. I just need to put some old stuff to bed that needs to be put to bed.'

'I don't know what you're talking about, but I can tell you this: no good comes from wallowing in the past, you need to accept that what's happened has happened, box it up, bury it and don't look back.'

CHAPTER FIFTY-TWO

Alex

13 October 2010

A sharp knock came at the front door.

'Oh, hi,' Alex said.

'Hi.'

'Come in. Let me help you.'

'I'm sorry to come here like this, but I don't know what to do. Everything's a mess.'

'Has something happened?'

'Nothing new. My wife thinks I'm having an affair and I can't bear being in Edenbridge.'

'I'm sorry,' Alex said, patting Jacob's arm uneasily.

'I thought that perhaps I might be able to help you some more, while I still have a couple of days off work,' Jacob added. 'Maybe I could work some of this stuff out and then, I don't know, put it to bed and move on. I need to come clean to Fiona and I need to be fully hers – "fully present" she calls it.

'To be fully there for Fiona, I need to say goodbye to Amy but I can't when I still don't have any answers. I know I can't because I've tried and failed before.'

Alex helped him into the living room.

'My baby's due soon. I can't be separated from my wife, that's not how this is supposed to go. No matter how badly we're getting on.'

'How long does she have left?'

'It really could be any day now.'

Alex tried to forget the smile that had spread across Matt's face as he digested what she'd told him. 'We're going to have a baby?' he'd said, eyes wide. 'Really?'

'Yes, really,' she'd nodded, smiling with relief at his reaction.

He'd grabbed her hands in his, stared wide-eyed at her and drank in the news. Good news, finally. Weeks after losing her mother. And he'd squeezed her, wringing out every drop of what she'd just told him. A secret she'd held for many weeks.

Then she'd handed him a glass of champagne, offered her own glass to toast.

'It's fine in moderation,' she'd protested. 'The French...'

'You're not fucking French, Alex.'

She really did scale it back then, to moderation. Or somewhere near.

Maybe Matt's new baby had been born already. She'd tried not to think about it and hadn't asked. Babies stopped things dead.

'I was going to call you later anyway,' Alex told Jacob.

She'd been mulling over whether to share her concerns about Paul with him. In many ways it was too soon; it was just a theory and not a watertight one. But it didn't feel right withholding anything, and Paul had originally crossed her desk because of Jacob.

Alex waited for him to settle, a look of disquiet creeping through his face. She wished she could offer him a drink and throw one back herself, but she only had a few servings on the plan for the day and not for many, many hours yet.

'What is it? You're worrying me.'

Alex took a deep breath. 'It might be nothing. But some stuff has come to light and there's a slim chance we might know who did it and why.'

'Shit, really?'

'Yeah, maybe. It's only a maybe.'

'Who?' Jacob stared expectantly.

'Paul. Paul Wheeler.'

'Paul Wheeler?' Jacob sat back for a moment, then sprang forward in his seat. 'Seriously? You really think he's capable of that? Why? You didn't think that the other day.' Jacob looked absolutely horrified. Sweat collected on his temples and his eyes were wild. Alex wondered how on earth to tell him the possible motive.

CHAPTER FIFTY-THREE

Amy

Sometime in 2010

I had the dream again. I don't think it can technically be called a nightmare because it starts so nicely, but it is 'nightmarish' by the end.

In the dream, it's finally happening. I'm lying flat on my back and I'm trying to remember the bit in *Forever* by Judy Blume where Katherine has sex with Michael for the first time. He's done it before but she hasn't. And I'm trying to remember the details and how she got through it but I can't because all I can think about is how much it hurts. I can't feel any other part of my body except where it hurts, and the pain is radiating through the rest of me with every heartbeat. In the dream, he seems to get heavier with every move of his hips. And he doesn't seem to notice, or maybe doesn't care, that I'm holding my breath and screwing my eyes shut.

I knew it would hurt because we're told it will hurt, just like you know it will hurt when you have a baby because your mum still complains about it years later. But I'm sure that when I actually have a baby, it'll still be a surprise and I'll probably yell at everyone, including my mum.

The pain of him blinds me, right through the dream and out the other side. And I'm thinking about how you see pictures in *More* magazine of women wrapped around men, sitting on chairs to do it or throwing their hips around without a care in the world, no grimace on their face. But all I can do is lie frozen and try not to cry. I can't imagine this ever being easy, never mind feeling nice. I can't picture myself ever becoming a *More* magazine woman.

Even in the dream, I feel sad knowing that the story I'll tell my best friends about this will be full of lies. If I even tell them. And if I don't, I can't bask in the glory of getting there first. Which sounds pathetic and is pathetic but it's also true.

And as soon as it's over, every single time I have this dream, I realize I've made some kind of mistake. Sometimes, I'm in the wrong place. Other times I realize I'm running late for something really important. Or there's someone else there. One time I dreamed that my mum was calling me from outside the door. This time there was someone else actually in the room, a woman. I don't know who she was but she was saying things like, 'It's not your fault, Amy, it's not your fault he changed,' things like that. And I was trying to whisper to her to get out before he sees her but she wasn't listening. Before I realized it, I was screaming and *she* was screaming and then everything went black.

When I woke up this time, the dream was still hanging around me, caught in my sheets and my hair. I could feel the echo of the sting, the weight of him on my chest. I could almost smell his breath in my ear as it turned to wet drips of condensation.

That's it now, I'm never going to shake these dreams and how realistic they are. Robbed of the real thing by a stupid dream. It doesn't matter that it didn't really happen because my body, my brain and now my memory all think otherwise. It's so unfair that I start to cry, but no sound comes out.

CHAPTER FIFTY-FOUR

Jacob

13 October 2010

Jacob was in the passenger seat, pushed as far back as possible to give his leg space as Alex drove him back to Edenbridge. He'd barely spoken for the last twenty minutes, while Alex had barely stopped.

His girlfriend. His sweet, fun, *normal* girlfriend, sleeping with her own father? No. There was just no way. Alex's latest idea was plain wrong. Not necessarily wrong about Paul Wheeler hurting Amy, he could well believe that, but way off-piste about the rest. She had to be.

'What happens next?' he interrupted. 'Are you going to the police about this?'

'Not formally, no. Not at this stage, anyway. It's such a serious crime to accuse someone of and, like I've said a few times,' Alex looked at him briefly, 'it's just a theory, one of several.'

Jacob nodded and looked dead straight at the road.

'I've asked Matt to look into it to see if there's anything more on Paul's record that might be relevant.'

'Okay.' Jacob ground his teeth as he watched his home town creep into the windscreen and along the sides of the car.

Amy's step-family set-up had always been a bit alien to him. He knew it was one of the many things that his mum looked down on about the Stevensons, even if she'd never openly admitted it. In his mum's world, marriage was for ever, no matter what. It wouldn't have mattered what his own dad had done or not done; Jacob knew full well the Arlingtons would have remained resolutely together to the bitter end.

He wondered what his parents really made of his own predicament. How far down the line from fracture to permanent break did they think he and Fiona were? How far down the line *were* they, for that matter? Would someone else end up as weekday dad to his child? He shuddered with a bolt of unexpected anger.

Alex's black Polo had just passed Edenbridge Town station when her phone rang in its cradle. Jacob watched her fumble to answer it on loudspeaker. She seemed almost ditzy, which was new to him.

'Hi, Matt.'

'Hi, Alex, can you talk?'

Jacob looked at Alex, who looked at the phone.

'I have someone in the car with me at the moment,' she said. Silence from the other end. 'Hang on,' she added, 'I'll pull over and get out.'

CHAPTER FIFTY-FIVE

Alex

13 October 2010

Alex pulled into the station's overflow car park and swung across two spaces. She yanked the phone from the cradle, crushing it to her ear as she climbed out of the idling car.

'Hey, what's up?'

'Well, I have something concrete but you might not like it.'

'Oh?'

'Paul Wheeler didn't do it, Alex.'

'Are you sure?'

'Yes, I am.'

Matt had perfected the policeman's monotone delivery, Alex realized. Good news, bad news, the same flattened voice announced it. Even to her; maybe especially to her? Did he speak to Jane in the same low rumble? Alex didn't remember his soft voice sounding so toneless before. And she thought she remembered everything.

'You sound very certain.'

'I'm totally certain, because he was in prison at the time.'

'You're kidding me! But he said he'd been—'

'I'm sorry, Alex, it looks like he was puffing up his involvement for some reason. But he couldn't have been anywhere near the school when he said he was.'

'What was he in prison for?'

'Shoplifting.'

'Seriously?'

'Yep. He'd been caught for it a couple of times already so he got three months. He went in a couple of days before your girl went missing.'

'Shoplifting.' Alex shook her head.

On some level, it was a relief. The idea of Paul and Amy locked in some kind of doomed love affair was repulsive at best. But that didn't make Amy any less attacked then or any less alone now. Despite her reservations about Paul being the culprit, it still felt like a setback.

'Of all the pathetic things, Matt. God.' Matt's voice in her ear offered little in the way of consolation.

'I'm sorry, Al.'

Al. She hadn't been called that in years and it knotted her chest.

'Well, thank you anyway. I appreciate you taking the time to look,' she said, in an echo of his emotionless tone.

Matt paused. She could hear him breathe heavily. 'Are you okay?'

'Yeah, I'm fine. It's not like I *wanted* it to be him, I just wish I was a little closer to some kind of resolution,' she said, giving more away than she'd hoped. 'For Amy, I mean.'

'Don't give up, will you?'

'Of course not,' she said, pursing her lips. 'I told you, I'm dead set on finishing what I started.'

'I'm glad to hear that.' For a moment, it sounded like he had more to add but, after a few seconds, he said, 'Take care.'

'Thanks. And you.'

Fuck.

She propped herself on the bonnet and sighed. That rotten, slimy bastard had been willing to string her along for a few quid. Just to blag some cash for an interview full of lies. Selling out

Amy's memory when he'd never given her anything.

Bob was right not to want him in Amy's life.

Bloody Paul Wheeler.

She needed to get Jacob home, and then back to her kitchen. Her story still had no conclusion; she was kicking up dirt and getting nowhere. What on earth was she thinking, really? A lifestyle journalist whose recent idea of research was a hasty Wikipedia search or copying and pasting from a press release. Even as a columnist the details were extracted from the depths of her head, just memories or observations. You couldn't get those wrong.

She looked across at Jacob in the passenger seat, who was clearly nervous about what she might have just been told. 'It wasn't Paul after all.'

'Is it wrong to be glad?' he asked.

She shook her head. 'Not even slightly. But it does mean there's more work to be done.'

CHAPTER FIFTY-SIX

Amy

Sometime in 2010

There's a woman here. She's introduced herself as Alex and I think she might think I'm someone else, although she knows my name is Amy. Maybe there's another Amy here, wherever 'here' is.

I don't put her straight, I just bite my tongue because it's nice to have a visitor. I hope Other Amy isn't missing out too much because of me.

I know it's selfish but I'm just so lonely; the days and weeks are blending into a wide black sea and it's rare that I see land. And the land that I glimpse doesn't really satisfy me. I miss my mum. I know it's been a long while since I saw her or Bob but I can't let myself dwell on that. I tell myself that their work is in the way, but something in the pit of my tummy knows it's worse than that. I let it stay there. I feel weak and scared right now. So I'd rather be lied to than told a difficult truth.

Alex's voice sounds familiar, like I've heard it years ago or maybe she sounds like one of my mum's friends or the ladies she works with in the shop. It sounds like a posher version of my voice. It's soft and quiet but you know that she really means everything she says, like she's planned each word and they all matter. I like people who are decisive and know what they want to say or do. That's how I want to be.

She's a journalist too. I mean, I'm not yet, but I want to be. And at one time she must have wanted to be, and now she is. Sometimes it works out that way. Maybe it'll work out that way for me. Maybe if Alex keeps coming back to see me, she could help me get what I want. I'd work for it. I'll tell her how hard I'd work for it.

In the background, while Alex talks, I can hear music. It sounds like Oasis but it's not a song I know. There's been talk of a new album for a while.

Liam Gallagher is singing about a "wonder wall", and about being saved.

Alex says she likes it, but I'm too into Blur to admit that I quite like the sound of it too. It lulls me like a nursery rhyme and I start to feel sleepy again.

When I wake up, she's gone. For a minute, I'm not sure if I dreamed her up all along until another voice – the one that sings like my mum – mentions me having a visitor.

'It's nice to have a new friend, isn't it?' she says. But I don't reply.

The lyrics I heard earlier with Alex keep drifting back to me in snatches as the other woman washes my face.

I hope Alex comes back.

CHAPTER FIFTY-SEVEN

Jacob

14 October 2010

'Hi, Alex,' Jacob answered foggily, holding his phone loosely to his ear. His other hand covered his scrunched-up eyes.

'Did I wake you?' Her voice sounded distant and watery.

'No, well yeah, you did, but it's fine. I need to get used to early mornings again. What's up?'

'I just... I guess now that Paul is ruled out, I wanted to look at what's left to explore,' Alex said, her voice without any of the adrenaline of the previous day.

'I guess there's nothing else you can do.' Jacob always felt uneasy when Alex took pains to explain her process to him.

'Right. Well Paul may have lied about his own timeline with Amy, but that doesn't mean he lied about everything. There's still the claim that he saw her with another guy one time.'

Jacob was silent for a few beats; he didn't want to give this thought any oxygen. He sat up slowly and blinked a couple of times. A tatty toy box caught his eye and he felt a sudden pang of nostalgia. He half-expected to hear a Game Boy through the wall, or even the awful depressive music Tom had turned to in his teens.

'I don't buy it.'

'I know you don't and I know it's hard for you to even consider.

But knowing that Amy probably had consensual—'

Jacob cut her off. 'Please, I don't need to hear this again.'

'Sorry, it's just, if there was someone else,' Alex asked carefully, 'who would she have told?'

'Probably Jenny.'

'Jenny threatened to have me arrested when I tried to talk to her.'

'That doesn't surprise me,' Jacob said.

'When was the last time you saw Jenny?'

'My last day at school, fifteen years ago.'

'Did you get on?'

'We got on okay, I guess. She was quite brash and full-on, not my kind of person, but she was a decent enough girl. I think she was quite a good friend to Amy.'

'So if you were to, say, call her up out of the blue, how do you think she'd react?'

'Oh God, I can see where this is going.'

Jacob had expected some reticence, so Jenny's eagerness to meet him had made him uneasy all over again.

On the phone, she'd offered to meet first thing the next day and he'd felt his bravado instantly seep away.

Now Jacob sat squirming in the back of a café tucked disconcertingly around the corner from their old school.

The café door swung inwards and the first thing Jacob noticed was how big Jenny was. Not just chubby or overweight, she was really very fat. Jacob could clearly see the familiar face, but it was floating on a much larger face.

She had thick fingers, a gold ring cutting deeply into one of them. And she looked far older than thirty.

They hugged an awkward, squashy hello after she made her way over.

'Don't worry, Jake, I know you're in with that journalist.'

Jacob raised his eyebrows in surprise.

'Come on, I've not heard from you for fifteen years and then just after she tries to pull a number on me, you get in touch. I'm not daft.'

'You're right. But I think you've got her a bit wrong.'

'Hmn, well, whatever, I'm not interested in her. How are you?'

'I'm okay, thanks. I'm married now and expecting my first baby any day. How are you?'

'It's okay, Jake, I'm not going to try it on with you, you're safe.'

Jacob smiled, and immediately worried about the depth of relief he'd shown.

'I'm loved up too, and we have a little girl,' Jenny said.

'Well congratulations to you both. How old is she?'

'She's three.'

'Oh, lovely. Not long until school then. What's her name?'

'She's due to start next September, yeah. It's flown by.' Jenny hesitated. 'And, um, she's called Amy.'

Jacob stirred his tea without looking up. Eventually he complimented her on the choice of name.

'My partner suggested it. He knows all about our Amy, obviously. I wasn't sure at first but... it really suits her.'

'It's nice that you could do that,' Jacob swallowed. 'Jenny, I know you're not impressed by Alex's methods, but she's beginning to get somewhere. She's starting to find answers and I know I've still got lots of questions. Haven't you?'

'You need to be careful with journalists, Jake. And she's a sneaky one.'

Jacob frowned. 'Look, I don't like saying this, but Alex thinks that maybe Amy um...' He cleared his throat. 'That Amy might have been seeing someone else before she went missing and it turned sour. Do you know anything about that?'

Jenny opened her mouth to say something but looked down.

'I'm really sorry,' she said. 'That journalist told you about the virginity thing, didn't she? I'm so sorry, it really wasn't—'

'What virginity thing?' Jacob heard his heartbeat over his voice.

Jenny's eyes searched his face. 'It was just stupid, I mean I didn't think she'd take it seriously. I didn't even consider it at the time.'

'Jenny,' Jacob lowered his voice and stared into her eyes, which were filling with tears. 'You're really freaking me out. Can you please tell me what you're talking about?'

Jenny exhaled and sucked her lips in for a moment as if she had completely deflated.

'God. Okay, so me, Amy and Becky had this stupid game going to see who could lose their virginity first.'

'Amy did?'

'Yeah, all three of us did. It was just a bit of fun, it was silly. It didn't change anything. I didn't do anything because of it and I hadn't thought Amy took it seriously.'

'Hadn't thought?'

'The journalist. She said Amy wasn't a virgin when she was attacked. She said Amy had, y'know, done it. I didn't know whether to believe her or not.'

'Believe her,' Jacob said quietly.

'Shit. Look, I didn't know. I really didn't know. If I had, I would have told the police.'

'Told the police what?'

'About the other bloke.'

The walls of the café seemed to pulse and loom in as Jacob gripped the table. He felt the blood drain from his head.

'I don't want to upset you.'

'Jesus Christ, Jenny, we're beyond that now.'

A cold sweat crept up Jacob's neck as Jenny described holding back Amy's hair in The Sleeper pub toilets a few weeks before she went missing.

'She was pretty pissed, and even when she was throwing up she was babbling away. At the time I thought it was just the drink talking and I wasn't exactly sober either but, y'know, maybe there was more to it.' Jenny looked up and opened her eyes wide. 'If I'd known how far it'd gone, I'd have told the police. I just didn't think anything of it.'

'Didn't think anything of what, Jenny?' Jacob said impatiently.

'She said she was feeling guilty. 'Cos she was interested in someone else and he was interested in her.'

Jacob sat back like he'd been yanked by the hair.

'I'm really sorry. She loved you to bits but she was confused. I asked who it was but she wouldn't tell me.'

'You have no idea?'

'She said that it was someone close to you. And that's why she felt so bad. Please don't look angry, she said nothing had happened and she never mentioned it again. I should have asked her about it when she was sober but I didn't.'

'Why not?' Jacob asked, his face clammy.

Jenny looked down, 'Because I didn't want to know. I didn't like the idea of her doing that to you.'

Jacob couldn't feel his legs. He started to fire out every school friend's name he could remember. Jenny blinked away tears and held up her hand.

'I don't know. I'm really sorry, Jake.'

'I don't know what to say. I shouldn't be angry with her now, but that's exactly how I feel.'

'She loved you, Jake. Whatever else happened, she loved you. I just hope she didn't do anything stupid to win that pathetic bet.'

'I can't believe she'd be so casual about it. I really thought it mattered to her.'

'It did, Jake.'

'No, Jenny, it really fucking didn't. And if you knew how long I waited for her.'

'I'm so sorry.'

'So am I.'

CHAPTER FIFTY-EIGHT

Alex

15 October 2010

'I'm going on paternity leave soon so I don't have much time,' Matt said as Alex's hand shook slightly, holding the phone to her ear.

Paternity leave. It was all so very proper for him this time, so real. Matt announced his upcoming leave in the same police tones that he'd told her about Paul Wheeler's alibi.

When Matt's name had popped up on her phone's screen, she'd almost sent the call to voicemail, embarrassed that she was no further along. But to see that he was calling, to know his fingers had found her name on his phone, that he'd found a place to hide while he spoke to her, had carved a sliver of time just for her, meant she had to answer.

'Alex, I know the Paul Wheeler idea was a non-starter, but I remembered you'd asked me to look into similar cases, do you remember?'

'Of course I do.' *I remember everything, Matt. I review our conversations over and over in my head until I feel sick.*

'I've finally passed over some of my cases so I had a chance to look into this yesterday. And I found something that could be relevant.'

'Oh?' Alex sat down heavily on her sofa, wet running things

leaving an instant dark patch. The rain whipped at the old kitchen window, an angry wind whistled down the chimney and knocked at the grate to get in. Could there really be something new, some gift from Matt to kick things up a notch?

'Don't get your hopes up, but it's safer if we talk in person.'

Alex sat up straight. 'I'd love to. How about today? How soon can you meet?'

She had two hours to get ready, drive to the train station, park and buy a ticket. Two hours in which to stay out of the kitchen, two hours in which to avoid Dutch courage. She looked down, she was still shivering in her wet running tights and hoodie. Her hair was ridged with sweat, and her cheeks were mottled.

She scrambled into the shower, rinsing shampoo into her eyes in haste and nicking her leg with the razor.

It was lucky that time was so short. Any longer and she may have sat paralysed, barely able to breathe at the thought of seeing him again. Now, for the first time in years, she would be so close to his skin that she'd smell his aftershave. Perhaps he was grey now. Grey would suit him.

Had she had days to worry and panic, she might have ordered ten or so outfits to try on and discard in tears, sinking more and more red wine to quell the panic and blur the mirror. With half of her clothes in the wash and a quarter of them drying in the warmest corner of the kitchen, she had little choice.

She pulled on matching underwear, embarrassed while she selected it. She chose her cleanest jeans and a close-fitting Jack Wills jumper that she hoped was a little more flattering than her other options. She blasted her hair on the highest setting of the hair dryer. Her hands shook as she applied make-up clumsily, and then washed it all off again. She would do it on the train when her heart rate was a little closer to the normal range.

'You look well,' Matt lied.

'You look great,' Alex replied.

He really did look great. And he smelled great too. Musky, woody and luxurious. For a moment, she just stood and drank him in. Matt was wearing his thirties well; relaxed laughter lines around the eyes, the lightest of silver touches to his stubble. He looked well-worn and expensive, like a prized leather Chesterfield.

Alex displayed the accoutrements of a good thirty. A great bag, expensive make-up. A decent mask.

On the plus side, she reasoned, she probably did look markedly better than the last time he saw her. How could she not?

'I don't have long.' Matt clearly didn't feel the need to explain. 'So let's get down to it.'

'Sure.'

'You first,' Matt pointed.

'Me? Oh, okay... Well Amy's boyfriend from the time has been helping me.'

'Woah, that's great!'

The positive shock on Matt's face was a little too much. *Yes, Matt, I'm not completely useless. I do finish some of the things I start. The important things. Well, y'know, some of them.*

'How did you find him?'

He broke into my house.

'Journalistic excellence.'

Matt smiled.

The Greenwich coffee shop was surprisingly quiet. Perhaps the clouds had chased the crowds away, or perhaps Matt knew this place as a particularly private rendezvous point.

In the corner, a handful of overdressed students tried too hard and laughed too loud, mocking the plastic menus and tomato-shaped sauce bottle – which would have been considered kitsch and cool when Alex and Matt were their age.

By the door, a father in crumpled clothes gave up trying to read the ketchup-splattered paper as his twin toddlers rocked back and forth, toast soldiers pulverised by their pudgy palms.

Alex told Matt about Jacob. She mentioned Jenny and her rebuttal, that Jacob was talking to her as they spoke. She described the eye strain from combing through hundreds of articles. She whizzed through the field trip to see where Amy was found, the conversations with Becky and the mad dash to Devon to accost Bob.

'I've got to be honest, you've done more than I thought you would have. No offence.'

'That is slightly offensive, Matt.' Alex rolled her eyes. It was hard to know if he was being playful or genuinely thought she was useless.

Then Matt smiled. Oh God, that smile. The one where the deepest dimples opened up from cheekbone to chin, ready for her to fall in and float away. That smile that used to be hers whenever she took the time to tease it out. Now it belonged to Jane, who was 'thirty-eight weeks and four days, not long now!' and thought he was 'doing overtime and I feel shitty about it, so...'

'Look, like I said, I don't want to get your hopes up but there is something I found and it doesn't sit easily with me. It's just too close to ignore.'

'What is it, Matt?' Alex felt her heart race and she tried not to look too eager.

'In early July 1995, a very drunk sixteen-year-old girl was chatted up on a late bus in Edenbridge. The young guy talking to her convinced her to get off at the edge of town and, well, you and I would say he raped her.'

'Who wouldn't say that?'

'There are some grey areas in the case file. She got off the bus with him willingly, she was intending to sleep with the guy. We'd deal with it very differently now.'

'Who was the guy?'

'He was never tracked down but, going from her statement, he was somewhere between mid-teens and mid-thirties, which isn't very helpful but perhaps shows just how pissed she was. He was at least six foot, with dark hair and a deep voice. Hang on, is this off the record?'

'If it needs to be.'

'Don't give this to your editor or anything, not yet.'

'I won't, Matt, what is it?' She wanted to grab his jacket and shake him along.

'He said his name was Graham.'

'Graham.' Alex rolled the name around on her tongue and wrote it down in her notepad. It didn't mean anything to her.

'So this "Graham" chats the girl up and convinces her to get off the bus, share the bottle he had, have some fun on the common.'

'Okay. All sounds very sleazy.'

'It was. Like I said, she was drunk and she changed her mind and asked him to walk her home instead. He didn't let her go. He tied her hands up and had sex with her.'

'Raped her,' corrected Alex.

'Yeah. Her statement says he put his hands on her throat afterwards and threatened to kill her.'

'That's awful,' Alex said, angrily. 'And no-one's ever been done for it?'

'There wasn't a lot to go on,' Matt said, defensively.

'It definitely feels connected. What do you think?'

'Well, it's not a million miles off what happened to Amy. Don't get too excited though, Alex. At the time she was seen as a flaky witness due to her circumstances.'

'What circumstances?'

Matt exhaled. 'She had a difficult background. And given how pissed she was at the time, the case probably wouldn't have been brought by the CPS *even* if they'd had a suspect.'

'So despite someone who was basically a kid being brave enough to come forward to give a statement, this guy was allowed to carry on, and probably get worse? Possibly go on to attack Amy?'

'Tread carefully, Alex. This isn't a case of us letting a bad guy slip the net. The case wouldn't have held up.'

'Matt, I'm not out for police blood. I couldn't give a crap about that. I'm just trying to look at anything that might help Amy.'

'Okay. But just remember that this is off the record, and you definitely didn't get it from me.'

'How realistic is it to ask if I can talk to the girl that reported the rape?'

Matt cocked his head, raised his eyebrows and said nothing.

'Absolutely out of the question?' Alex helped.

'Yep. There is literally no way that I can pass a victim's name on to a member of the press for no reason.'

'And I guess you can't get in touch with her?'

'I really can't, Alex. I know that's not what you want to hear, but how could I justify it?'

'Because I want you to?' They both smiled.

'Alex, if you bring me a reason to open this up again, then I can pass it on. But it would need to be really solid, more than just a hunch. I know it sounds uptight but you remember how it is.'

'I remember everything, Matt.'

'I know.'

'I miss you,' she whispered.

'I have to go.'
'I know you do.'

Graham. It was a pseudonym, of course; no-one who plans a sex attack blurts out their real name during the preamble.

This tall, dark young man calling himself Graham *had* to be Amy's attacker. From what little Matt had shared, the man sounded entirely in control. He must have planned things, or at least had a plan ready to go for whenever he spotted a potential victim. That must be something that takes years to work towards, thought Alex, there must have been some baby steps along the way. Or maybe he was guided by someone else.

Alex had been on the brink of giving up and sinking into a deep red several hours early, and several glasses too many, and now Matt of all people had placed her slap bang back on track.

She had a name.

She had a similar case. Just weeks before Amy was abducted.

She had a story. She really had a story.

She was so excited that until the train pulled into Tunbridge Wells station, she thought solely about Amy and didn't dwell on the way Matt's scent lingered on her clothes and how beautifully his eyes still danced over her face when she spoke.

CHAPTER FIFTY-NINE

Amy

Sometime in 2010

Alex came to see me again today and it wasn't as nice as the other times.

I must have been dozing when she got here, and I missed the first part of what she was saying so all I heard was some pretty weird stuff. I don't know if this was because she thought she was talking to a different Amy, an Amy who's had a bit of a rough time, but I couldn't really make sense of it.

She started saying something about dating older men and getting hurt by them. I mean, it felt inappropriate, but maybe she doesn't have anyone else to talk to about this stuff.

I've definitely noticed people open up to me more and more now. A woman the other day, I think she said she was a nurse, was talking about getting divorced because her husband had been sleeping with their neighbour. And then another one, who sounded pretty old, was talking about her boyfriend from when she was a teenager. How she still missed him and wondered what he was up to.

The woman who sings to me while she's washing my hair is here. She's telling me about someone who comes in and 'sits', whatever that means, about how he's broken his leg and his wife is having a baby. And I'm like, okay, so? I don't mean to be rude, but I don't know this man so I find it hard to care about his leg or his baby.

It feels like forever since I've spoken to Jenny or Becky or got any gossip from school. Screw broken legs and babies, what about the school disco and who's snogging who? Has Jenny worn down Steve yet or is she still making desperate eyes at him across the bunsen burners? What about Becky, is she still having those dreams about Mr Parker? Ha-ha, she never should have told us about that, what did she expect us to do? *Not* take the piss about it relentlessly?

Anyway, Alex was going on and on and it started to freak me out a little bit. It was almost like I was being accused of something. I don't know, I didn't like it and I tried to tell her. I don't know what happened, or if I offended her, but she just suddenly stopped talking.

I still hope she comes back.

CHAPTER SIXTY

Alex

15 October 2010

Matt's impending paternity leave brought another deadline into sharp focus. Jacob's wife could have his baby at any time and, as soon as she did, he would be a dead end. No matter what he might say in the run-up, he wouldn't have the time or the inclination to help from the moment the first contraction kicked in.

Alex knew she was juggling with flaming tar, but instead of staying home with her teatime jug and her medicinal measure, she drove to the office where Jacob had said he worked.

She sat in the car park listening to the car radio and willing him to get a move on. It was some kind of afternoon drivetime show where people phoned in with their requests. It poked a little hole in her ego to hear 'Waterfalls' by TLC being placed in the 'golden oldies' category.

Eventually, the smoky-brown double doors were shoved open and Jacob, flanked by a younger man with dark hair and drop-waisted jeans pottered out. They walked slowly to a black Audi A3, Jacob reaching for the passenger door. *Shit, of course he'd get a lift home.*

Alex popped her door open, key still in the ignition. As she leaned out, she waved and called his name.

Jacob and his colleague both span around and Jacob gave her a look that couldn't possibly have meant anything other than 'What the fuck?' His friend leaned on his car door watching curiously as Jacob made his slow progress across to Alex.

'What are you doing here?' he asked, aghast.

'I wanted to hear how it went with Jenny. I thought I could give you a lift home while you told me.'

'You should have called me. I could have met you around the corner.'

'I'm sorry, I didn't think.'

'I'll have to explain to Marc who you are now.'

'Just say I'm a friend.'

'Like that doesn't sound dodgy.'

'Say I'm your cousin then, there's nothing dodgy about a cousin.'

'Hmn.'

'Did he buy it?' Alex asked as Jacob clambered awkwardly into the passenger seat.

'I think he had to.'

She crawled out of the car park and into the rush-hour traffic. Alex wanted to cut straight to the point and ask what Jenny had said, but slowed herself down to ask about his first day back.

'It was okay, very busy.'

'So how did it go with Jenny?'

Jacob paused and flexed his hands. 'Well, Amy was cheating on me, Alex, so you were right there.'

Alex braked with more force than she intended and looked at Jacob, raising her eyebrows.

'Apparently Amy had got drunk a few weeks before she was attacked and she told Jenny that she'd fallen for someone else.'

The sides of Jacob's mouth twitched downwards.

'Hmn,' said Alex.

'What does *that* mean? I thought you'd be pleased that you were right.'

'I'm not pleased about any of it and I'm sorry that you thought I would be. I don't know quite what to say. Are you okay?'

'I guess. I mean, it's not like Jenny told me my wife was cheating or anything...' Jacob trailed off.

'Did she actually say Amy had done anything with this person?' Alex was trying to stay patient.

'No. She said that Amy liked someone else and he liked her. And she said that Amy was confused about what to do. Jenny didn't know for sure that anything had happened, but she didn't know it hadn't, either. She just hadn't asked.'

'When did Amy tell her this?'

'A few weeks before she went missing.'

God, I wish Jenny would let me interview her, thought Alex. Her memories could clearly unpick some of the knots in the story and it was increasingly obvious just how clueless and dopey Jacob had been back then.

'Did Jenny have any idea who this other person was?'

Jacob took a deep breath. 'That's what's driving me mad. She said it was someone close to me. It must have been one of my school friends, but surely they'd have come forward?'

'Not if they thought they'd get in trouble. Did you ever have any suspicions about Amy and your mates?'

'No, never. She didn't seem to like any of them.' Jacob swivelled to face her. 'Jenny said Amy had been in some sort of competition to lose her virginity, and you knew about it.'

'Did she?' Alex kept her eyes on the road but could feel Jacob looking at her.

'Yes, she did.'

'Okay, Becky told me about it but I didn't want to mention it unless I really had to. I knew how much it would upset you. And to be completely honest, I put even less stock in it while I thought there was any chance Paul could be the culprit.'

'I just can't believe she'd be so flippant. I knew she was keen to, y'know, but not like that. I thought she wanted to take that step with me, not just with anyone that would have her. Do you think she did something stupid because of it?'

'Hand on heart, I don't think this silly competition meant anything. I think most teenagers are in the same race, openly or not. I don't think Amy would have done anything rash just to beat her friends at something they were all going to exaggerate anyway.'

'I hope not, but she did sleep with someone, that's not pie in the sky, however much I hate to consider it. You told me that was a cold medical fact.'

'Yeah, it is. And we don't have enough facts for my liking. I really think Jenny is the key to this, she's the only one that we know Amy confided in. Do you think she might talk to me if you were there?'

'I don't know, maybe. I can ask.'

'There's one other thing that still confuses me. Do you have *any* idea why your brother Tom might have gone to see Amy a few years ago?'

'No,' Jacob said wearily, 'I still have no idea. I mean, he's a caring guy and I can imagine him wanting to see if she was okay. Maybe. But even that's a bit...' he trailed off. 'Look, he really didn't know her that well. It just happened around him.'

'But it must have affected him,' Alex said, gently. 'Your parents would have been distracted, you were interviewed by police, he even had to move school. All that stuff must have taken its toll.'

'Yeah, but he wouldn't be the first kid to move school or have disruptions in his life. I can't see it bothering him after all this time.'

'Did he like his new school?'

'No, but anyone would have hated it. St Cuthbert's was a super-religious private school. Small and very strict. And it was all boys too, very different to the grammar.'

'So, basically, the only effect all this had on Tom was a bad one. He had to leave a school he liked to go to a gloomy boys' school.'

'Alex...'

'But he didn't complain? He didn't rage at you about this? *Your* girlfriend gets attacked but *he's* the one that has to move schools, and he didn't moan?'

'He's always been a good guy, Alex, he's just not a complainer.'

'Or he felt responsible. He felt like he deserved to be punished.' She gripped the steering wheel and stared dead ahead, afraid to see the anger creeping up Jacob's neck, afraid that she'd stop and apologize.

'You're way off, Alex, you're crossing a line.'

'And then, on top of all this easy-going, understanding acceptance of something shitty happening to him, he then – as an *adult* – goes to see Amy. The girl that caused all of this upheaval. You don't see how that's suspicious?' She could feel him staring at her, glowing hot and red in the passenger seat, but she stared resolutely at the black road.

'Hold it right there, Alex. I can see what you're doing and I don't like it. This is my family we're talking about, not some dodgy bloke like Paul Wheeler.'

Alex chewed her lip, waiting for him to finish. 'Jacob,' she said, tersely. 'Right now, there are still some strange coincidences involving your brother. That doesn't mean he did anything wrong, but you must be able to see why I have to ask.'

'You're heading in the wrong direction.' Jacob paused and took a deep breath. 'Come and speak to my mum. Come and ask her why she and Tom visited Amy, because I'm blowed if I know.'

'Really?'

'Believe me, this is the last thing I want to do, but this needs to be nipped in the bud and I don't have any answers. There'll be a perfectly reasonable explanation and, once you've heard it, you can get on with working out what really happened.'

Sue apologized for the non-existent mess: 'If I'd known we'd have company...' and buzzed around the kitchen in a way that made Alex incredibly nervous.

'Mum, don't worry, I'll make the tea,' Jacob said to the back of her head.

'I'm sorry to come here unannounced,' Alex called after her, still blushing from the way Sue had eyed her up and down when they first walked in. Like she knew Alex from somewhere. And not in a warm way, more like she'd seen her throwing up in the river or rowing in the street. Both of which were possible once upon a time.

'It's fine,' Sue said curtly. Perhaps thinking better of it, she turned around and smiled. 'It's kind of you to drop him home.'

'Mum, I know you've not met Alex before but she's a friend from Tunbridge Wells. You dropped me at her house recently.'

'I thought so.'

Jacob blushed.

'You do know, I hope, that Jacob is married?' Sue said to Alex as she poured thin amber tea into the tea cups.

'It's nothing like that,' Alex started to say, looking at Jacob.

'Alex is just a friend, Mum.' Jacob looked at his feet.

'Married men don't spend this much time with women who aren't their wives, Jacob. No wonder Fiona's so cross.'

'I shouldn't have come here,' Alex said, picking her car keys back off the sideboard. 'I'm sorry.'

'No, wait,' Jacob said, holding his palm up and then folding it back to his side.

'Mum, there's more I've not told you.'

Sue crossed her arms over her chest and stared hard at Alex.

'Alex is a journalist, Mum, and she's writing about Amy.'

'Amy?'

'Amy Stevenson, my old girlfriend from school.'

'I know who Amy is,' Sue said.

'Mrs Arlington, I'm writing an article for *The Times* about the work they do on Bramble Ward at the Tunbridge Wells Royal Infirmary.'

'Oh?'

'I've been focusing on Amy's story.'

'I see.'

'And I've been talking to people like Jacob who knew Amy before she was attacked, and he thought you might be able to help.'

'Did he?'

Sue held Jacob's eye until he looked back down at his feet.

'Well, that was all a very long time ago so I can't imagine I'd have anything useful to tell you.'

'You'll have a different perspective on it to her friends or to Jacob. You worked at Amy's school, for example?'

'I didn't have anything to do with the pupils. I really don't like the idea of being interviewed.'

'Would you mind trying, Mum? Alex's article might help me and her other friends come to terms with what happened.'

'Oh for goodness sake, I'm sure you all came to terms with it years ago.'

Jacob said nothing.

———

'Yes,' agreed Sue, 'Amy was a lovely girl. I didn't know her well, but she certainly seemed to have a spark about her.'

Alex pushed the iPhone closer along the pine kitchen table. Sue fiddled with a coaster and flicked her eyes at Jacob, scrunched next to her in a matching pine chair. Alex wondered if these were the chairs he'd grown taller in, in which he'd learned to use a knife and fork.

'All the school staff were affected, of course. People don't realize it, but teachers feel these things very keenly. They spend years with these youngsters, getting to know them.'

'And how about you, how did you feel?'

'Awful, of course. I felt dreadful for Jacob. I was powerless to help him, which is a horrible feeling as a mother. And we were devastated for her family. Your child being hurt is every parent's worst nightmare. You'll do anything to prevent that.'

'So you and Amy got along?' asked Alex.

'Amy was a lovely girl,' Sue repeated, stirring another cup of tea.

'Did she spend much time at your house?'

'A little. She and Jacob were going steady for a while, so she came round from time to time.'

'Did Amy get on with your son Tom as well?'

Sue frowned. 'She wasn't friends with Tom.'

'But she must have met him?'

'Yes, of course, once or twice. But they weren't friends. Tom had plenty of his own friends.'

'Mrs Arlington, when Amy went missing, the police interviewed Jacob.'

'Yes, they did. It was terrible.'

'Were you frightened?'

'I wasn't frightened, because I knew he hadn't done anything wrong. But it was horrible to watch him go through that upset.'

'You weren't worried the police might think Jacob was involved?'

'No, of course not.' Sue looked horrified. 'Besides, he'd been with me when Amy went missing so I knew there was no reason for them to doubt him. I could see the police were just going through the motions.'

'How did Tom react when Amy was found?' Alex asked.

'Why do you keep asking about Tom?'

Alex looked at Jacob. How far could she go?

'Mum, why did you and Tom go to visit Amy after my wedding?'

Sue's eyes widened and as she opened her mouth, the front door lock rattled and footsteps hit the hall. Sue closed her mouth and looked up at her husband in the doorway.

'Alex, this is my father, Graham,' Jacob said, warily.

Alex's stomach lurched. *Graham.*

'Pleased to meet you,' Alex said, turning to offer her hand. As she looked up, she was surprised to see a tall, handsome man standing in front of her. He looked a good ten years younger than Sue, although that did not add up. His eyes sparkled but his lips barely smiled.

'Likewise,' Graham said, keeping his gaze on Alex until she had to look away. 'I could have collected you, Jacob,' he said as he walked over to the counter and splashed whiskey over a neat pile of ice. He wore tennis whites and his green eyes were framed by weather-tanned skin. The whole room seemed to hold its breath for him.

'Dad, Alex brought me home...' Jacob started, looking at his mother for reassurance.

'Alex is here to grill me, I'm afraid,' Sue interrupted. 'She's a journalist, Graham. She's writing about Amy Stevenson and seems to think I can help.'

'A journalist?' Graham said, his voice measured and in control. 'Well, that's disappointing.' He took a long look at Alex and a deep sip of amber liquid. Alex felt her own thirst tighten in her throat.

She realized Jacob wasn't going to say anything more and started to explain. 'I'm not trying to make anyone uncomfortable, but I'd like people to understand what happened to Amy and what she's going through.'

'Well,' said Graham with the soft and steady patter of a diplomat. 'She's not going through anything now, mercifully.' He poured himself another drink, steadily and without comment from his family. Alex suspected this was how most afternoons unfolded in this kitchen.

'What happened was unfortunate,' Graham continued, his eyes briefly expressing compassion, 'but that was many years ago and she's been gone for a long time now.'

Jacob's phone rang on the table and he picked it up quickly. 'I'm sorry, it's my boss. I have to take this.'

Alex watched him walk lopsidedly out of the kitchen.

Lowering her voice, Alex said, 'Amy hasn't gone anywhere, far from it. She's communicating. I've seen it myself. She may be able to tell us what happened soon.'

'Okay,' soothed Graham, 'Jacob has a call now and I think it's time you left. My wife has helped you more than enough, I'm sure.'

'Why *did* you take Tom to visit Amy, Mrs Arlington?'

'Okay, let's go,' Graham interjected, placing a hand gently on the small of Alex's back and applying just a little pressure.

'Fine,' Alex exhaled, tired from hitting a brick wall. 'Could I please just use the bathroom before I go?'

'I really think you should just—' Graham started.

'Yes, if you must,' sighed Sue. 'Last door down the hall.'

Sue watched in silence as Alex made her way out of the kitchen.

When Alex emerged from the little room, she could see Sue's back to her in the kitchen, and through the window Graham sitting rigid on a bench in the back garden, looking into the trees and sipping from his tumbler. Alex darted into the lounge, as quietly as she could.

She could hear Jacob upstairs and, as she crept closer to the archway into the kitchen, she could hear Sue speaking quickly and quietly into the phone.

Alex held her breath to listen.

'Tom, it's Mum. There's something I need to tell you and it's not good. Call me back when you get this message. It's urgent, darling.'

Alex's heart jumped in her chest. Tom. *It had to be Tom, using his father's name as what? A hastily chosen cover name? Paul must have been bullshitting about the older guy.* Alex kept her eyes trained on Sue. She could hear Jacob making his way slowly down the stairs. As quickly as possible, she used her phone's camera to snap as many of the family photos on the mantelpiece as she could. School photos, holiday pictures, those awful posed studio snaps of reluctant children in ties and waistcoats. She snapped without looking, thumbing the camera button on her screen as many times as possible. She'd tidy them up later.

'What are you doing?'

Alex swung around to see Jacob in the kitchen doorway as she stuffed her phone back into her pocket.

'Just going back to get my bag,' she said, feeling the tips of her ears burning. Jacob went ahead and swooped her bag from under the kitchen table, thrusting it at her, cheeks and ears blushing.

'I'd better show you out,' he said, apologetically.

CHAPTER SIXTY-ONE

Jacob

15 October 2010

Jacob walked Alex to the front door and with a low voice said, 'I'm sorry. I guess that was a bad idea after all.'

'I'm sorry too, I didn't want to upset your mum.' Alex said, although her eyes were dancing with something. Maybe adrenaline.

Jacob stepped outside with her, leaving the door on the latch.

'I'll try talking to her again when Dad's not here.'

'Could you meet tomorrow? There are a few things I'd still really like to talk through.'

They arranged to meet the next morning at the hospital café. Alex left without turning back and Jacob's shoulders sagged as he sloped back into his parents' hallway.

'We're having casserole for supper, I hope that's okay.' Sue clattered the oven door open with her lemon-coloured oven mitts and bent down to extract the pot.

'Mum, I'm sorry.' Jacob hovered awkwardly in the doorway.

'Could you get the pickled red cabbage out, please? It's in the narrow cupboard with the pull-out bit.'

'I know I shouldn't have put you on the spot like that.'

Sue closed the oven door gently with her slippered foot and placed the casserole on the hob.

'Oh, Jacob,' she exclaimed, putting her right hand on her forehead. 'I didn't put the broccoli on to boil.'

'It's fine without, Mum, don't worry.'

'Don't be ridiculous,' Sue snapped, reopening the oven door and pushing the pot back into its empty belly.

She filled an orange Le Creuset saucepan with water, which gushed a little too energetically from the tap and splashed her pale-blue jumper.

'Oh, for—!' she exclaimed and stood for a moment as if she was surveying a scene of utter chaos.

Jacob stood back nervously as Sue took a deep breath and closed her eyes for just a moment.

'Jacob, can you please put this broccoli on to boil and can you *please* get the pickled red cabbage out? I need to change my top.'

'Sure,' Jacob said and watched his mother walk briskly from the room, stealing a glance at the teapot as she went.

Jacob excused himself after a silent dinner and went up to his small bedroom. There was nothing to do, but he couldn't stand to be around his mother, who seemed to be as hurt as she was anxious. His father, as ever, remained icily reserved.

The sounds of the kitchen bubbled up as they always had.

'I'm concerned about what happened today, Sue,' said his father's low, steady voice.

'He shouldn't have brought her here but you know he doesn't mean any harm, Graham.'

'I just don't really understand why you would take it upon yourself to go and visit that girl?'

Sue was either silent or speaking too quietly for the sound to rise.

'Why would you deliberately insert yourself *and Tom* into this situation? Years after everyone has moved on?'

'You know Tom, he worries about everyone.'

'And why are you indulging him?'

'Tom and I were just showing a little human kindness, that's all. Is that a crime?'

Jacob could precisely picture the expression that would have spread across Graham's face. One of restrained contempt.

'*That's* not a crime, no. But a crime was committed once, and have you forgotten the police coming to call?'

'Oh, now you're being ridiculous, Graham,' sighed Sue. 'You wouldn't understand, you never have. You don't know anything about those boys.'

'Oh, that old chestnut. I'm not in the mood for this, I'm going to find something on the box.'

'Of course you are.'

Jacob heard his father flick on the TV in the other room, the flipping channels creating a montage of nonsense that seeped up through the floorboards.

He heard his mother's phone ring and the tell-tale scrape of the patio door, his mum slipping out to smoke one of the Silk Cuts he had always known were in the teapot.

CHAPTER SIXTY-TWO

Amy

Sometime in 2010

Alex came to see me yesterday and it was nice again this time. She brought music with her and I was like, *God, I can't believe no-one's done this before.* It was like coming home. 'Buddy Holly' by Weezer, tonnes of Pulp and Blur, Iggy Pop, the Stone Roses, Smashing Pumpkins, REM, Portishead. All my favourites, plus a couple of bands I'm not too keen on, like Stiltskin who did the jeans advert song, and Nine Inch Nails. Although I do like 'Hurt', 'cos who doesn't?

But even hearing songs I'm not bothered about was blissful. To just feel drums in my chest and guitars down my back and to know every single word like a friend, it was the kindest thing anyone has done for me in a long time. I wonder if my mum sent Alex. I wonder if Alex can tell me where Mum is. I wish I could ask, but the words just get stuck in my throat.

After Alex left, I could still hear the music. I felt this weird and welcome mix of calm and excitement. And I felt a bit more like myself, and a bit more ready to 'find' the rest of myself. If that doesn't sound too pretentious.

It's hard to describe how I feel at the moment. I guess it's like being stuck really far down a well. Being able to see a bit of sunlight out of the top, but being too far from it to be heard. I feel warm; cocooned but separated. Maybe this is what it feels like to be a baby in the womb, not that anyone could remember to confirm that or not. I had felt safe too, but something has dented that recently and I can't put my finger on what it is. So maybe I'm just getting a bit further up the well and closer to sunlight? I don't know if that's wishful thinking or not.

Hearing my music earlier helped pull me up. But one particular song keeps coming back to me over and over again and it's adding to this unsettled feeling. 'Do You Remember the First Time?' by Pulp. I love that song, y'know, it gets me every time. It's so persuasive and witty and cheeky. But I don't know if it's because of this bloody dream I keep having, literally about my first time, or because of this general anxiety, but the more I try to shake the earworm, the more uncomfortable I feel.

I have that 'dark alley' feeling, like when you know something's behind you, or it's a quiet bit of a horror film and you can tell something bad's about to happen. But obviously nothing has happened and nothing's going to happen. I just can't get rid of it.

I know that they'll be around to give me my medicine soon, and then sleep will put a line through it. I just hope bad dreams aren't waiting on the other side of that line.

CHAPTER SIXTY-THREE

Alex

16 October 2010

She'd been awake for hours, but Alex was still yawning as she approached the café doors.

It was harder than ever to sleep these days, and the few drops of wine in her system did more to agitate than relax her. Last night, thoughts of Tom and his dad's name and Jenny and, as ever, Amy, circled around like the ghosts and witches of Macbeth. The family photos she'd hastily snatched had flickered through her eventual dreams like a flipbook, the pages chattering like teeth.

She'd fallen asleep late but woken long before the sun.

As Alex pushed the door to the café open, she spotted a new bruise on her forearm and self-consciously tugged at her sleeve. Bruises were no longer a product of one-off drunken mishaps, now they were a creeping reminder of the deeper damage done to her system.

The busy widows that made up the 'Friends of the Hospital' ran a tight ship. Café doors opened at 7 a.m. sharp and were shut tight at 3 p.m. From Monday to Saturday, a series of eager older ladies in deck shoes and tabards provided hot drinks in uniform china cups. They carved thick slices of sponge cake and stuffed sandwiches with a range of timeless fillings. Egg and cress. Cheese and pickle. Ham and wet tomato.

Jacob was already seated when she arrived, two mugs of tea on the table.

'Thanks, I need this.'

Alex laid her iPhone out in front of her and held her pen over her notepad. The name 'Graham' was dancing on her tongue but she had to bide her time, pump everything out of Jacob before silencing him with this latest information.

'So I'd like to hear more about what Jenny said. Don't worry about repeating yourself, just start from the beginning. Even if you don't think it's important, just talk and I'll make notes.'

Jacob nodded wearily. 'Okay.' And then suddenly looked up. 'Fiona!'

Alex span around to see a heavily pregnant woman staring at her, nostrils flaring and chest rising and falling fast. She wore shapeless maternity pyjama bottoms, a woollen cardigan and a thin white vest that made her look like a dusty lightbulb. But while she looked tired, and her lips were pursed, her eyes were pretty and her cheekbones were flushed. Her auburn hair was glossy and pulled back into a ponytail, and her index finger was pointing straight at Alex.

'Is this her?' Fiona said to Jacob.

'I'm sorry?' Alex asked.

'Is the baby okay?' Jacob stood up sharply and hobbled towards Fiona, who was leaning on the back of a chair. 'What are you doing here? Is everything okay?'

She ignored Jacob's questions, continuing to stare at Alex. 'Is this her? Is this your other woman?'

'I don't understand,' Alex said as she looked to Jacob to explain.

'Alex, this is my wife, Fiona.' Jacob looked down at his hands.

'Hi,' Alex said uneasily as Jacob turned back to his wife who finally looked him directly in the eye, angrily wiping tears away.

'Fiona, I know this looks bad and I'm sorry, I'm so sorry.'

Fiona's eyes blazed but she said nothing.

'I'm a journalist,' Alex said carefully, 'and your husband's been helping me with a story.'

At this, Fiona leaned on a chair for support and half-smiled. 'A journalist, right,' she said eventually.

Jacob stepped towards his wife as slowly as a bomb disposal expert.

'Fi,' he said, reaching out for her hands, which she snatched out of the way.

'Fi, I'm so sorry. I have lied to you and then I've denied it and made things worse. But I promise I've never cheated on you, I never would.'

'Bullshit.'

'Please, Fiona, sit down.'

Fiona sat on the hard chair with a humph and winced.

'I think I should leave you two to talk,' Alex attempted, and Fiona shot her a look. 'You're not squirming out of this.'

Fiona put one hand on the small of her back for support. 'Don't look at me like that, Jacob, I'm not going to drop any second. Now start at the beginning.'

'It's a very, very long story,' Jacob said gently.

'You'd best get going then, because this baby is going to be born at some point soon and I need to know what the fuck it's father has been up to.'

Jacob cast an eye at Fiona's bump and took a deep breath. 'When I was at school I was going out with a girl called Amy Stevenson.' He paused for a moment but Fiona didn't react.

'We were both fifteen and I was very fond of her. We'd been going out for quite a while when Amy was abducted after school one day. She was attacked and left in a coma. Alex is a reporter, she's been investigating what happened to Amy.'

'None of this makes any sense. If this was true, why wouldn't you have just told me? Why wouldn't I have known all along?'

'I don't know,' Jacob answered, reaching out to touch her leg, pulling his hand back as she slithered away from him. 'I should have told you right at the start, but the longer it went on and the more time passed, I don't know... it sounds stupid now.'

'You never know, Jacob. You never have a proper answer for anything. This fucking – I don't even know what – this fucking *fairy tale* that you've concocted or she has...' she glared at Alex. 'It just doesn't add up. Just please, Jacob, please tell me the truth.'

'Jacob,' Alex said quietly, 'why don't we show her the truth?'

'Amy?' Jacob grimaced.

'Why not?'

Jacob paused. 'Fiona,' he said, shaking his head in disbelief. 'I don't know if this is a good idea or not, but if you come up to the ward, you can see Amy for yourself.'

Fiona's eyes widened.

'You're both fucking mental.'

Fiona stood up with a groan. 'I'm going, I don't have time for this crap.'

Jacob scrambled to his feet, 'I'm sorry, Fi, I'm really sorry.'

'I just need to go now.'

'Let me walk you out at least.'

'No,' Fiona snapped. 'Just,' she took a deep breath. 'Just let me go, Jacob.' Alex and Jacob watched as Fiona pushed her way angrily out of the café, the door swinging back towards them.

CHAPTER SIXTY-FOUR

Sue

Sometime in 2008

Closing the patio door softly behind her, Sue stepped onto the deck quietly, the fur on her slippers ruffling in the summer breeze. Disgusting habit, she told herself. Just as she did every time. Closing her eyes to enjoy the minuscule fizz of the tobacco catching light, she dragged the warm, sweet smoke through the stem of the cigarette, between her lips and deep into her chest.

She hoped all of her boys had avoided this filthy habit in adulthood. She'd gone to great pains to hide her own smoking from them throughout their lives. Thomas was the only one she'd ever caught, although she had no doubt that Simon had had his moments too, he was just more cunning. She really wasn't sure about Jacob. He was a stickler for following the rules.

Thomas had been fifteen when she'd caught him. Always such a good boy, such an easy, happy child. Until St Cuthbert's, anyway. From the moment he started at that school, he'd become enveloped in a black cloud. Everything seemed to pain or offend him. Suddenly he was wringing his hands over every perceived injustice, feeling guilty about the family's nice things and declaring himself vegetarian until Sue had to put a stop to that. He was wasting away.

He would wear T-shirts with naive political statements on and spend hours in his room listening to bands with names like The Manic Street Preachers. And then one day she'd had enough of the miserable music pouring over the top of *Coronation Street* and had gone upstairs and knocked sharply on Thomas's door. When no reply came, Sue had gone in. At first, she'd thought the room was empty with the music left on, which was bad enough. Then she'd seen the curtains flapping, the window wide open. As she'd gone closer, the shape of her youngest son had come into view. He was outside the window, sitting in a heap on the roof of the bay below. She'd cried out in surprise, startling him so he span around, a rolled-up cigarette dangling forlornly from his lips.

He'd stubbed it out on a roof tile and scrambled back through the window, standing in front of her with his head down and his hair flopping over his eyes.

'You should ground me, Mum,' he said.

'But you don't go anywhere, Thomas, what good would that do?'

'It's what I deserve, I s'pose,' he'd said and sat heavily on his single bed.

She'd left the room without another word. She'd not caught him again after that, but she'd not exactly tried.

She blamed that blasted school, but she couldn't uproot him another time. She regretted that decision in hindsight. The three years he spent at St Cuthbert's hollowed out her happy-go-lucky boy, replacing him with an anxious, guilt-ridden ghost. He'd become preoccupied with darkness, driven by an obsessive need to seek out the grubby and try to clean it. It set him on a path that had taken him further and further away from her.

Given how much he hated that school, it wasn't a surprise when Thomas chose to leave and take his A-levels at college instead. But it was a surprise, actually a terrible shock, that he was adamant that he wanted to go to college in a deprived area of London. For

God's sake. Some wretched need to expose himself to those less fortunate. And less moral and trustworthy.

After a few months of two-hour round trips on the train, he'd lugged his belongings all the way to a bedsit in a grotty corner of New Cross, refusing his parents' help. He'd spent his evenings stacking shelves to pay his way.

Was it a surprise that he'd continued creeping away? After university in the Midlands, he'd got his first social work job in one of those old industrial towns that had dominated the news once upon a time and was now full of single mothers, undesirables and feral kids with no moral compass.

Ever since St Cuthbert's, Tom had embarked on a series of thankless tasks. And now he wanted to come clean, to undergo the ultimate in thankless endeavours. Just as Jacob was finally moving on and getting married. Sue had stood aside for a long time, allowed him to make his own mistakes, to fall on his own swords, but this latest plan... well, it wasn't just *his* head on the block. It wasn't just his guilt.

If Tom spoke up, the family would be permanently fractured, and Sue wasn't about to let that happen. Whatever it took. She'd sooner die.

CHAPTER SIXTY-FIVE

Alex

21 October 2010

'So, does your editor like what you've done so far?' Matt tested.

'I've not shown him yet. I promised you, remember?'

The brute force of a baby crying in the background came down the line. 'I can't really talk for long, Alex. I'm looking after Ava while Jane's sleeping.'

For a moment, Alex said nothing. Too long a moment. She swallowed and pushed away the image of Matt gazing into the tiny face of a newborn. A newborn whose features she would recognize. She wished it was possible to have her evening nightcap now, without that throwing everything out of whack. Instead, she sat on her free hand as if it was likely to run into the kitchen of its own accord and pop open a bottle.

'Sorry, I'll try to be quick. It's just that I'm getting a serious sinking feeling about Jacob's brother, Tom. He just seems to be in the shadows everywhere I look. Metaphorically, I mean. He knew Amy, obviously, and he's kind of a loner, works with vulnerable kids.'

'Okay, I mean it's not against the law to be a loner. We'd have our work cut out if it was. Does he have an alibi?'

'I don't know. I know Jacob and his mum were out, and his Dad worked long hours in London so I'm guessing he was on his own for a few hours.'

'Well you can't guess that, he might have been at a friend's house or playing football or something.'

'Yeah, I know that,' she snapped before she could stop herself.

'Okay, I'm running out of time here, what do you need?'

'Sorry. Look, I found something else out. It could be a coincidence, but the Edenbridge pervert shares a name with Tom and Jacob's dad, Graham.'

'If Tom is involved, that would be one hell of a fuck-up. It seems way too obvious.'

'He was only thirteen though, he would have been a novice, or maybe he was just an apprentice. Maybe his dad is involved somehow.'

'Look, the description of "Graham" said he was mid-teens to mid-thirties, would a thirteen-year-old even be classed as mid-teens to most people? And as for his dad being involved, that seems like quite a leap.'

'Jacob's a big guy, really tall. I guess his brother probably is too. How drunk was the bus girl – what did you say her name was?'

'Nice try.'

'Alright, but you said she was really drunk. How reliable is her attempt to put an age on him?'

'If you start going down that route. How reliable is any of what she said?'

'But maybe that's it, we don't know what's right and what was the drink obscuring things. If I could just talk to her.'

'Absolutely not.'

'What if I could show her a picture of Tom, find out once and for all?'

'Alex, I can't give you her details. Besides the fact that those details are well out of date, she lived in a halfway house for Barnado's kids, so she won't still be there.'

'A halfway house? You mean she was from a kids' home?'

'Shit, I shouldn't have told you that. I'm so exhausted I don't know what I'm saying. Don't take advantage.'

'I'm not trying to take advantage of you. Jesus.'

'I'm sorry, Alex, I can't give you her details, I just can't.'

'It happens all the time, Matt, police sources are the backbone of newspapers. It's when money changes hands that it's a problem. You'd just be giving me a name, that's all. Please think about it.'

'I don't need to think about it. My baby is three days old. I can't take risks with my job; the stakes are too high.'

'Look at your baby daughter, Matt. Amy was Jo and Bob's little daughter. This girl was someone's baby.'

'Don't you dare.'

'Matt, please, just a name. I'm from around here, aren't I? I could say I heard what happened from a friend of a friend. She would have told people at the time. I could say I had a friend at the children's home.'

'Jesus, Alex, I don't know. About any of it. I need to go. I can't think straight.'

Alex sat on her knees on the sofa, her chest resting against the back, staring out of the window like a dog in the boot of a car. Her days stretched three times as long now that the first drink on her self-imposed timetable was right before bed. Not that it was helping her sleep when did finally get to that point.

It seemed too much to try to make notes when there was nothing new to say. As she started the afternoon's internal monologue, *just one won't hurt/no, no, no,* her phone vibrated off the sofa cushion. She flipped it around to see a text message from Matt:

Caroline Mortimer. Delete this. Please.

Alex leaped up from the sofa and span around, not quite sure what to do. Should she even reply? Would she wake the baby? The phone would still be in his hand:

Thanks x

She pretended to herself that the kiss was a mistake. And waited for a reply that never came.

She scurried over to her Mac to visit 192.com and search for Caroline Mortimer in Tunbridge Wells. There it was. Electoral roll, 1997. So Caroline hung around long enough to register, but left before the next election. Or died. Or went to prison. Or left the country. Or just didn't bother. Alex tried not to think about dead ends.

Eventually, after paying to access the complete records across every site she could think of, Alex reached the end of the digital breadcrumb trail. Caroline Mortimer registered to vote in 2010 in Malmesbury Mews, Greenwich.

'Found you, Caroline.'

CHAPTER SIXTY-SIX

Amy

Sometime in 2010

I'm asleep more than I'm awake these days. Like a cat, dozing. One eye lazily opening to consider the world, then slipping back under, unimpressed. But I don't particularly want to sleep, I just find myself waking up before I even realize I'm falling.

I'm getting rapid-fire dreams, flooding in one after the other. I swear I was dreamless for a good long while and now there's nothing I can do to stop them. It's like *A Clockwork Orange*, where they pin his eyelids back and he has to watch film after film after film.

There are recurring dreams too. One in particular I'm having more often than not right now. I had it again yesterday, after Alex left. It's the one where I'm finally losing my virginity. It was so painful this most recent time that it still hurt between my legs when I woke up.

When I first started having this dream, there was a nice bit at the start and it built up from there. I wanted it to happen, I was relieved it was finally happening. But there was nothing nice in the run-up this time, we just hurtled straight in. It's more of a recurring nightmare now.

Each time I have it, he hurts me more. I don't see his face and when he finishes, he turns his back. His shoulders shake as he laughs dismissively and tells me to clean myself up, even though he's left no trace. I hear him peeling the rubber away and dropping it into a carrier bag, and then I see him reach for a pack of baby wipes and I can make out that he's cleaning himself.

And then suddenly I want to go so much that my chest starts to pound. I sit up and straighten my clothes and try to leave, but he won't let me go. It's like that unique dream thing where you can't move; you're heavy like lead and you've forgotten how to walk or run except he's the one controlling my movements – he won't let me out and he won't say why. And even though nothing more happens, I know it's really bad. I know the dream has a bad ending, and I don't think I've seen the worst of it yet.

I'm scared to go to sleep, I'm scared to see his face. I think I know who it is, but I don't want it to be him. I don't want him to have done that to me, not like that, even when it's just in my head.

I hope it's just in my head.

CHAPTER SIXTY-SEVEN

Jacob

21 October 2010

Finally Fiona knew about Amy. The cat was out of the bag; he'd said it all, everything he should have drip-fed through their years together had tumbled out like a huge boulder and knocked everything down. She was no less fed up with him; his wife just had the specifics of the lies he'd told, rather than his denials. It didn't feel like progress, it felt like a spotlight had been shone on what a massive balls-up he'd made.

Fiona hadn't answered his calls, hadn't replied to any of his text messages. For all he knew, she could have had their baby and been making arrangements to move back to Lancashire without him. Or somewhere else, somewhere he'd never be able to find them. Even in 2010, it was possible to disappear.

Jacob had spent the whole day at work with his phone in his hand, willing something to change. But when Fiona's number flashed up, it still took him by surprise.

'Hello?' Jacob answered, making no effort to hide his panic. 'Are you okay? What's happening?'

'J,' she panted. 'Come out into the car park.'

'I needed to speak to you,' Fiona started to say, and was immediately folded over by a contraction.

'How close are they?' Jacob asked, rubbing Fiona's back gingerly as she leaned forward against her car.

'I don't know,' Fiona said, unfolding and breathing deeply. 'I was trying to drive, I couldn't time them.'

Jacob set the stopwatch on his phone.

'I needed to talk to you about Amy, J. I didn't know what to think, I mean I *don't* know what to think.' She breathed deeply.

'Look, I googled Amy,' Fiona said as she caught her breath. 'So I know some of what you said was true. But then I got here and my waters broke.' She breathed for a moment and wiped her eyes again. 'And then, hmn,' Fiona hunkered back down, both hands on her belly.

It had felt so alien to hear Amy's name coming from Fiona's mouth, but there were more important matters in hand. Jacob was so relieved to be involved that thoughts of Amy flew away in an instant.

'That was two minutes,' he said urgently. 'We need to go to the hospital. Right now.'

'Oh God, we're going to have a baby,' panted Fiona.

'We're going to have a baby,' echoed Jacob, allowing himself a brief smile.

CHAPTER SIXTY-EIGHT

Alex

22 October 2010

Alex jumped in a taxi at North Greenwich station. She roughly knew where Malmesbury Mews sat along the thick, grey snake of Blackwall Lane, but it still took her by surprise when the driver swung suddenly into the gateway.

She buzzed the door number and the gates groaned open onto the mews courtyard.

'Alex?'

As Alex approached, Caroline Mortimer opened her red door as far as the door chain would allow.

'Hi, Caroline.'

'Hold on one sec.' Caroline deftly closed the door, jingled the chain and threw the door wide open. As she did, Alex could see she was slim with a pixie hairstyle and tight-fitting jeans. She reached out to shake Alex's hand with a wide smile.

'Hi, come right in. Would you like a coffee or tea?'

Caroline wasn't what Alex was expecting. Far from a vulnerable, unreliable young girl, she was confident and clearly spoken.

'I've been thinking about this since you called,' Caroline had said apropos of nothing as she boiled the kettle, 'and I would be happy to be named. I mean, "happy" isn't the right word, but I'm not ashamed. Name me in your article if it helps.'

The two women sat in the small living room, scrunched onto a two-seater sofa with brightly coloured cushions, the iPhone recording on Alex's knee.

'I thought after I gave my statement that I'd help them do a drawing of his face,' Caroline laughed bitterly. 'You know, like they do in films. But they gave me my bus fare and said they'd call if they found him.'

'Did they ever call?'

'No,' Caroline said, shaking her head. 'I never heard anything else. Until you got in touch, anyway.'

'I'm surprised no-one connected you and Amy before now. It seems like there are some obvious parallels to me. Even if they were coincidental, they should have been looked at.'

'Yeah, but she was a nice grammar school girl, and I was a kids' home reject who got drunk and went to the common with boys. No parallels there.'

'You seem so together though, I'd never have guessed you had a troubled past.'

'Well thank you, that's been hard-fought, believe me. If you'd seen me back then you wouldn't have thought so. I lost some years. Drugs, the wrong men, the usual stuff. Having Toby changed everything. He was my chance to do things properly.'

Caroline reached to the bookshelf behind and showed Alex a picture of a smiling little boy in school uniform.

'How old is he?'

'Six. He's amazing, I'm really lucky.'

'Do you work?'

'Yes,' Caroline said crisply. 'I work with sex workers. Women and men.'

'Oh wow, do you help them get out of prostitution?'

'No, not exactly. I'm not a miracle worker. But I mentor them, help them access medical help, fill in housing forms, work with social services when their kids come under care orders.' She flashed her eyes briefly at Toby's happy little face. 'It's bloody hard but every shift is worth it.'

'Caroline, I know it's painful, but could you take me through what happened that night?'

'Of course. I knew I'd need to. It's not like I've ever forgotten it anyway. Not really. So what do you want to know?'

'Start at the beginning. Where did you meet him?'

'I'd been to the Kings on the high street in Edenbridge playing pool and drinking handouts. I was pretty drunk. That counted against me, you know. It always does with girls. I walked down the high street towards the railway station and caught a bus. He got on afterwards and sat in front of me.'

'Where were you headed?'

'Out to Hever. I had temporary accommodation there and it was too far to walk in the dark.'

'Did you know where he was going?'

'No, he didn't tell me,' Caroline looked down. 'Or I don't remember. He'd been sitting there for a minute or two and he turned around and smiled at me. He asked me my name and I told him it was Charlotte. That was the name of one of the girls I'd shared a room with. I honestly don't know why I lied. He told me his name was Graham.'

Caroline winced.

'It's such a cliché, but one thing led to another. I hate that expression, but it's true. He came to sit next to me on my seat and slid right up close to me. He was very handsome and he had a nice smile. There wasn't anything dodgy about him at all. He was really tall, I don't know how tall exactly, but a lot taller than me and a lot stronger.'

'Did he tell you anything about himself?' Alex asked. 'Anything you remember, even if it seems trivial?'

'I know we talked about work at first. I told him I worked in a shop and he said he wanted to help people. That sounds really cheesy now, but I was very young. That made him seem like a good person. He had booze with him, a bottle of whiskey in his jacket pocket, and that was enough for me. We had a snog while we were still on the bus. I remember thinking he was gentle and relaxed.'

Caroline's eyed filled with tears. 'It was nice to have that type of attention. I thought he was really kind for offering to share his drink. And then we got off the bus and I realized we weren't where I thought we were. The fresh air must have sobered me up because I realized it was a bad idea and I asked him to walk me home.'

'And what did he say?'

'He was really calm and he just said, "No, Charlotte, we need to finish what we've started."'

'I'm not saying you should have, but did you try to run away?'

'I didn't want to make a fuss,' Caroline said with a damp laugh. 'I didn't know which way to go and felt like I'd done something wrong by changing my mind. I kept apologizing. I said I was sorry, but I really needed to go. And that's when he went for me.'

'It's okay, take your time,' Alex said.

'I don't really know exactly what he did because it was so dark, but he was very fast and heavier than he looked. I was on the floor before I knew what was happening. I could feel him tying my hands behind my back and it really hurt. I said, "No, you don't need to do that, I'll do it." You know, "I'll do it with you, just don't hurt me." But he just laughed and carried on. Then my jeans were off and he was on top of me. He seemed to like it most when I struggled so I struggled more so he'd finish quicker.'

'Oh God,' Alex said before she could stop herself.

'I know. You develop a strange logic, but it worked. It was all over quite fast. He told me to stay there or he'd hunt me down and kill me. I believed him.'

Caroline took a deep breath.

'He put his hands on my throat and left them there for a really long time, not squeezing or anything. Then he just cut my hands free. I could hear him stepping away and the bracken snapping under his weight. I was too scared to look around but I heard a car engine—'

'A car engine? Did you tell the police that?'

'I think so. It was quite close by, so either someone was waiting for him or he'd left his car there. I guess it could have been someone unconnected, but I don't know why anyone would have been there that late.'

Alex thought again about Graham and Tom; could she have been looking for one person when it was two all along? She remembered Matt saying how unlikely that was. But unlikely was not the same thing as impossible.

'I'm so sorry you went through this on your own, especially when you were so young. How long did you stay there?'

'All night. I even slept a little bit, curled up next to a big tree with a load of bracken over me like something out of *The Jungle Book*. The sun came up and I started to hear cars nearby so I made my way to the road. I was too scared to thumb a lift in case he was in one of the cars, checking up on me. I managed to walk home and sat in the bath for hours, trying to work out what to do. I didn't have anyone to ask for advice so I flipped a coin and decided I'd go to the police.

'By the time I got there I was shaking violently. I felt really ill by then too, sort of hollowed out and freezing cold. I must have looked a state. I mean, I had soaking wet hair and make-up all down my face. The policeman behind the desk took one look at me and ushered me into this little room with a towel for my head and a cup of tea but I was shaking too much to drink it, it just spilled everywhere.'

'I'm glad someone looked after you at least,' Alex said.

'I wouldn't say that. He sort of threw the towel at me and rolled his eyes. I waited for a long time, maybe an hour, and then two different policemen came in.'

'No female officers?'

'They said I could ask for one but it could be hours. I decided to tough it out.'

'Were you examined?'

'No, they said there was no point as I'd had a bath and he'd used a condom.'

Alex shook her head and thought of Matt, the debates they'd had over expensive dinners. Him forever championing the force, the strength of character and moral rigidity of his colleagues. Her sloshing £12 glasses of wine as she'd argued with him. They'd usually end up laughing about something else.

'It's over fifteen years ago,' Caroline said carefully, 'and some of it is so hazy that I don't know if I've rewritten it in my head. I couldn't tell you how long I sat in the bath, or which day of the week this all happened on. I couldn't tell you the exact order of things or even some of the details about *him*. But there are some things that are razor sharp, so sharp I try to forget them but they pull me up short and hit me out of nowhere. Like his eyes,' Caroline continued, turning to look at Alex. 'I'll never forget his eyes.'

'Caroline, if I showed you a picture, do you think you'd recognize him?'

Caroline looked panicked, as if Alex had said he was standing outside the door.

'Yes. I'm absolutely certain I'd recognize him; I've never forgotten, no matter how hard I've tried. Hang on, do you know who he is?'

'I don't know for sure, but there's someone I have a funny feeling about. He could be totally unrelated though. Sorry the photos are a bit dodgy, they were taken in a rush.'

'Who is he? Do you know if he's done this kind of thing again? Is he the one you think hurt your victim?'

'He's just someone that's come to my attention while I've been researching this story. To be honest, I almost hope it's not him. Can I show you?' Alex asked.

'Okay.' Caroline inched away slightly as Alex picked her phone back up.

Alex opened her phone's photo gallery and found the batch of pictures she'd snapped hastily in Sue and Graham's living room.

'Most of these probably aren't clear enough as I took them in such a hurry, but I've left them all in just in case there's anything useful. Just scroll through in your own time and tell me if you recognize him. I don't want to lead you in anyway.'

Caroline scrolled with shaking hands, squinting at the pictures, some of which were obscured by the flash bouncing off the frames.

At the last one, she narrowed her eyes and suddenly recoiled and stood up, still holding the phone. She pointed to the screen, eyes wide in terror.

'That's him. Oh my God, that's him.'

CHAPTER SIXTY-NINE

Amy

Sometime in 2010

Well, I know how the dream ends now. It wasn't a surprise, really. The writing has been on the wall with every previous 'showing', but that didn't make it any less horrible.

It was like I was watching it happen to someone else, like a horror film. And I was screaming 'Run!' 'No!' But my voice just bounced off like there was a glass screen in the way. For all my screaming, it changed nothing.

Now it's clinging to me like a stink. I can't shake it like a normal dream and maybe I shouldn't shake it just yet. Maybe I need to face it. Problem is, I'm just too scared to face it alone and I don't have anyone to help me.

CHAPTER SEVENTY

Jacob

22 October 2010

'He's so perfect, I just want to eat him,' Fiona said, sleepily.

Jacob held his new son like he was woven from tiny twine and could unravel at any moment. 'I didn't think anything could be so tiny and beautiful,' he said, eyes welling up again.

'And so hungry.' Fiona closed her eyes and sank her head into the hospital pillow.

Jacob smiled and traced his son's round, pink cheek with the tip of his finger. He looked across at his wife. He'd never seen anyone do anything so brave before. He loved Fiona, liked her too, but he'd never stopped to consider her as strong until he watched her deliver their child into the world, almost in silence save for a low, rumbling moan.

He felt like he'd been pulled into the present and anchored there by the tiny little fist wrapped around his smallest finger.

'I can't believe how many times you've been in this hospital before,' Fiona said, suddenly. 'I wish you'd told me. I would have understood, you know. I really would have.'

'I just couldn't risk it. I couldn't risk losing you,' he said, kissing his baby's light-blue knitted bonnet, which was slipping down over his scrunched-up eyes. 'I don't know if this makes any sense,' Jacob said quietly as his son fell back to sleep. 'But the more I fell for you, the more guilty I felt. Like, I was getting to move on and she wasn't and it wasn't her fault.'

'Do you still love her?' Fiona asked.

'You never forget your first love,' Jacob answered carefully. 'But I never loved her like I love you. It was different, it was kids' stuff, I just didn't let it go when I should have and then I thought I was all she had.'

'I can't keep sharing you, J, not like before. Not now.'

'I know you can't. I don't want you to. I just want to be with you and this guy. I don't even want to go to the loo without him.'

Fiona smiled. 'You don't have to not see her again, but just, I don't know, just from time to time. What do you think? Can you do that?'

'I think I should have done that a long time ago.'

'Listen,' Fiona said, propping herself up. 'You're here in the hospital anyway. He's sleeping now and won't be doing much of that soon, so why don't you go and tell Amy your news while you have the chance? Tell her about the baby and explain that things need to change. Explain that you won't be back so often, like maybe, a couple of times a year.'

'I don't know, Fi, I think I need to make a clean break. Alex is visiting Amy regularly and trying to get some kind of justice for her. I can't help with any of that so I should just leave Amy in her hands. Amy doesn't actually need me, but you both do.'

Jacob lay his tiny baby in the transparent cot at Fiona's side. A burst of warmth in his chest nearly knocked him over. He kissed Fiona on the lips for longer than he had in months, maybe years.

'I love you so much,' he said.

'We love you too,' she answered, already half asleep.

CHAPTER SEVENTY-ONE

Alex

22 October 2010

Alex called Matt from the train to Tunbridge Wells. *Please answer, please answer, please answer...* she chanted, silently.

He didn't seem entirely surprised to hear from her.

'I spoke to Caroline,' she said, excitedly.

'Alex,' he whispered, 'be careful with that name, please.'

'But you need to hear this, Matt. I know who did it. I know who did it for sure.'

'Is this another hunch?'

'No. This is cast iron and I'm certain that the same person who attacked Amy also attacked Caroline. Caroline's willing to identify him, but only if you'll handle the case. She doesn't want anything to do with the local police but I've convinced her that she can trust you.'

A door clicked, the sound of the outside came whistling down the line.

'Okay,' he said, 'tell me everything.'

———

Matt was due to come to Tunbridge Wells the next day, once he had taken Caroline's statement. Now Alex had to reach Jacob and fill him in before anyone else did.

She'd called Jacob's mobile six times and left three messages, but no reply.

There was only one place he could be. Alex got in her car at the station and broke every speed limit on the way to the hospital.

CHAPTER SEVENTY-TWO

Jacob

22 October 2010

Jacob took the steps two at a time up towards Bramble Ward, adrenaline pumping through his still wonky leg. He passed the spot where he'd fallen weeks before and rushed on.

Amy's cubicle curtains were closed and there were no nurses on reception. In the background, the radio babbled with the sounds of old pop music. It was No Doubt or someone like that, someone he wasn't sure at the time if he should like, and hadn't had Amy around to ask.

The office door was shut tight and Jacob was about to knock when he saw a man's black shoes and black trousers through the gap under Amy's curtain. His heart thumped and his head span a little, thick with the exhaustion of a new parent.

He coughed but no-one came. He watched the black legs and feet. No orderly or nurse wore black, he slowly realized, they all wore scrubs of different colours. Suddenly he saw the feet walk quickly in the direction of Amy's head. Jacob instinctively strode over and pulled back the curtain to see a dark-haired man leaning far too close to Amy, his hands denting the pillow heavily on either side of her face.

CHAPTER SEVENTY-THREE

Amy

22 October 2010

I'm still running over the dream in my head when a familiar voice breaks my thoughts.

It's low, too deep to be a boy's voice, but soft for a man. At first, I can't make out what he's saying. I want to say to him, 'Take a deep breath and speak clearly,' but I can't. So I have to concentrate really hard to cut out background sounds like swooshes and beeps that I've barely noticed before.

Coating everything is the sound of music, a song I don't know, with lyrics that are interfering with the man's voice and crowding out my own thoughts.

I finally manage to focus a little on what he's saying. I think I must have missed the most important bit – the bit that explains what on earth he's on about.

'I shouldn't have let it happen,' he's saying. 'It should never have gone that far.'

'Can you hear me? I don't know if you can hear me,' he adds, sounding worried but still whispering.

Who are you? I can't place you.

'Amy, I'm just... I'm so sorry I didn't stop it before it went that far,' he's saying. 'I knew deep down what would happen, I just didn't* *want to face up to it. And now look where we are.'*

I wish someone would turn the bloody radio off. He stops talking for a bit, and even over the radio I can hear him breathing. His breaths are almost louder than his words. Maybe I should concentrate on his breathing instead, try to make sense of that. Why is he breathing hard? Why do people breathe hard? Exertion, maybe he ran here? Or excitement, but he doesn't sound excited. Fear? Why would he be scared? I'm not scared. Maybe I should be scared.

'They said you might be able to talk soon.'

Who are 'they'? And how do they know I can't talk? Oh God, I really can't talk.

'And I wanted you to know that, if you can talk, you should say—'

Why can't I talk? Why the hell can't I talk?

'Amy, you need to tell—'

I can hear curtains whooshing open and a man starts to yell loudly.

But what do I need to tell? Who do I need to tell it to? What the hell is going on on the other side of my eyes?

CHAPTER SEVENTY-FOUR

Jacob

22 October 2010

'What are you doing?' Jacob said, grabbing the man's shoulder and twisting it round.

'Jacob!' said his brother Tom, open-mouthed and red-faced. Jacob staggered back and repeated the question. 'What the fuck are you doing? What were you doing to her?'

'I wasn't doing anything to her. I was just talking to her, I needed her to understand.'

'Understand what?'

'How sorry I am.'

Jacob's stomach lurched. 'It was you,' he said quietly. 'Holy shit, it was you!' Jacob pulled Tom up by his black jacket and lunged at him, nearly knocking him onto Amy's bed. He took a wild swing, which missed. Tom covered his face and ducked, knocking the chair so it sat tangled in the curtain.

'My own brother!' Jacob yelled as Tom cowered in the corner. The curtains opened suddenly and Dr Haynes and a nurse were standing aghast. The radio had been abruptly switched off and, after a second or two, Dr Haynes said loudly, 'Out, now, or I'll call Security.'

Tom scrambled to his feet and ran towards the door. Jacob

stumbled after him, calling, 'Don't you dare, don't you dare run away again.'

The brothers burst out into the corridor and Tom headed for the stairs but Jacob grabbed him and pulled him back, holding him above the stairwell so his dark hair flapped over the steep drop below.

'You tried to kill her,' Jacob spat, tears streaming from his eyes and hands tightening on Tom's shoulders.

'Tried to kill who?' Tom cried. 'What are you talking about?'

'Amy! You bastard, you jealous little bastard, you tried to kill Amy.'

Tom's eyes widened, his pale face clammy. 'No, no, you've got it all wrong.'

'Did someone help you? Who was she seeing? Was that you as well?' Jacob's words ran into each other as Tom shook his head furiously, mouth open but wordless. 'You were jealous. You wanted a girlfriend like Amy, you always wanted whatever I had.'

'You're so wrong, it wasn't me, I swear!'

'You're a liar!' Jacob's hands were creeping further around his brother's neck when he heard the lift doors judder open and a voice cry: 'Stop, it's not him!'

CHAPTER SEVENTY-FIVE

Alex

22 October 2010

The brothers looked dazed and Jacob was panting heavily. Tom slumped to the floor in front of Alex's feet and sat with his back to the stairwell balustrade, head in his hands.

'He was trying to kill Amy,' Jacob spluttered, swaying on the spot lopsidedly.

'No, I wasn't,' Tom said quietly. 'I was talking to Amy. I was apologizing to her.'

'Apologizing for what?' demanded Jacob.

'You knew all along?' Alex asked Tom, walking a few steps to put her hand on Jacob's arm to try to calm him down. He shook it off.

'Are you Alex?' Tom asked.

'Yes, how did you know?' Alex answered, looking between the two men.

'My mum told me,' Tom said. 'She said you were close to figuring it out.'

'Mum?' Jacob repeated, staggering back. 'What the hell is going on?'

'Jacob, Tom didn't attack Amy,' Alex said. 'But I think he knows who did.'

Tom put his head in his hands and sobbed. Jacob crouched

down next to him. 'What the hell do you know, Tom? Tell me now.'

'I didn't know for sure but I don't know who else it could be.'

'Were you there?' asked Alex.

'No. But I'd seen them together. I saw them together that afternoon and he took her away in his car. Then she never came back.'

'Who?' Jacob yelled and pushed Tom into the balustrade. 'Who?' he yelled angrily.

CHAPTER SEVENTY-SIX

Amy

22 October 2010

Simon. My secret, Simon. So it's true.

It wasn't Simon talking, I knew that. But it took a while to realize who it was and that Tom was talking about what had happened. About Simon going too far. Which is, really, the foulest understatement in the world.

If it wasn't for last night's dream – nightmare, whatever – I would have thought Tom was wrong. That the 'too far' he talked about was Simon flirting with me. Or me with him. Or maybe, just maybe, he was the other side of the door or watching through the kitchen window when we had kissed.

But no. Last night, the dream reached the end. At the time, I still thought it was just a dream. But that didn't make it any less terrifying. It was still seeping away when Tom's voice sounded in my ear.

Everything is silent now. No-one is here to explain what's happening. No Mum, no Alex, no singing woman that washes my face. I'm totally on my own again. Alone with my memories.

If I could feel cold, I would feel cold. If I could have started to shake, I would still be shaking. Perhaps I am, but there's just no-one here to tell me that. The dream, the memories, the inevitable ending. Why I hadn't realized until now that it was a memory, I don't know. There's so much I don't know. I think Alex might know. I think this might be why she's been coming here. I'd like to hear her voice explain it to me. Mostly though, I just really want my mum.

CHAPTER SEVENTY-SEVEN

Jacob

22 October 2010

Jacob sat in the wing-back chair of his wife's cubicle holding his tiny baby son and staring into space. Tears welled slowly before skidding down his cheeks, all colour drained from his face.

Fiona kept one hand on Jacob's arm while Tom sat at the very end of the bed.

'You knew all this time,' Jacob said eventually, without moving his eyes from his son. 'You knew that Simon had attacked Amy and you didn't say anything.'

'I wanted to tell you,' said Tom. 'I wanted to say something straight away but you were in pieces. I told Mum everything and she said not to say a word. She said there was no reason to think Simon was involved. Mum was convinced it was a coincidence that they'd been together and it would devastate you to think Amy had cheated. She said it would break up the family.'

'And is that what you thought too?'

'I didn't want to break up the family but that's happened anyway. Deep down I think I knew it was him, though I didn't want to believe it. I handled it wrong. So did Mum, but I should have stood up to her.'

Jacob looked across at Tom, who looked down.

'Even if you didn't know for sure what happened at the end, you knew he'd swooped in on my girlfriend, my underage girlfriend, that he'd had it in him to do that,' Jacob spat. 'That's not what normal people do. Normal people don't sleep with their brother's fifteen-year-old girlfriend and then disappear without a trace just before she's found almost dead.'

'I've got no excuse, J.'

Fiona sat up. 'Why did you go to see Amy today, Tom?'

'Mum said she'd started to communicate,' Tom said.

'That's not true,' Jacob said, looking at Fiona. 'That's not true at all.'

'She didn't say she was talking, just that she'd started to show signs of communication or something. She thought Amy might eventually be able to tell people what had happened with Simon.'

Tom caught Jacob's eye. 'No, J,' he said, 'she didn't think Simon had attacked Amy. But she was worried people would jump to conclusions. She was worried how you'd cope.'

'Huh,' Jacob muttered. 'Right.'

'I just wanted to tell Amy how sorry I was for not doing anything. I thought if she was in there somewhere, she might hear me and understand. I wanted to tell her that if she could hear and if it was Simon that hurt her, then she had to let people know.'

'Did she respond?' Fiona asked.

'No, not at all, but I had to say it. I came once before,' Tom said, apologetically. 'And I didn't say a word to her. It was a few years ago, around the time you got married. I'd decided enough was enough, I had to tell the police what I'd seen and let them handle it. Mum brought me here to convince me that telling the police wouldn't make any difference to Amy. I was weak and it worked. I lost my nerve.'

'What exactly did you see that day?' asked Jacob. 'I mean, really?'

Tom looked up, rubbed his eyes and ran his fingers through his floppy dark hair.

'I'd seen Simon looking at Amy, when she came over and things. I thought he liked her. Or fancied her, or whatever.'

'Really? I never noticed anything.' Jacob said.

'Amy noticed. I didn't realize she had, but then I saw them in the kitchen once. You were in your room and they didn't know I was in the hall. I heard Amy and Simon laughing and I looked through the crack in the door. I don't even know why I looked but she was standing really close to him, playing with her hair. His hand was on her waist and then I saw him kiss her. On the lips. Just really quickly, not a full-blown kiss, just... I don't know, not an okay kiss.'

'Seriously?' Jacob asked. 'You saw Simon kissing my girlfriend and you didn't say anything?'

'I'm really sorry, I didn't know what to do. I just crept upstairs and then walked back down really noisily so they'd hear me and stop what they were doing.'

'Did you see anything else like that?'

'Not until the afternoon she went missing,' Tom said quietly.

'It was while you were at judo club. Simon said he had to collect something so I was at home in my room. After a while I heard Simon's car pull up.'

Tom took a deep breath. 'I heard the front door go, and I could tell he wasn't alone 'cos I could hear a girl's voice. I heard them coming up the stairs but I didn't realize who the girl was.'

'And what happened when they came upstairs?'

Tom looked down. 'They went into your room.'

'My room?' Jacob's face folded in shock.

'Do you remember how messy Simon's room was then? He was packing all his stuff and I thought he must have used yours because it was tidier. I still didn't realize who he had with him, I just thought it was rude to go in your room, that's all.'

'Why was Simon packing?' Fiona asked.

'He was going volunteering, going to work in Africa,' Tom said.

'Simon's such a good person,' spat Jacob. 'Such a good person that he slept with my girlfriend and then beat her to a pulp.'

'Did you know for sure that they'd slept together, Tom?' asked Fiona.

'Yeah, I did. Jake, I'm so sorry. I heard Simon say "Amy", but I hoped it was a coincidence. I crept out of my room and listened outside and I could hear them in there.'

'In Jacob's bedroom?' Fiona asked.

Tom nodded, blushing. 'I just hovered in my bedroom doorway, I didn't know what to do.'

'Tom,' Fiona said, reaching with her fingertips to touch his hand briefly. 'You were both so young then, you were just a boy. This isn't your fault.'

Tom looked briefly at Jacob. 'What happened then?' Jacob asked quietly, looking down at his sleeping baby.

'Simon came out smirking and I saw Amy straightening her clothes. The look on her face.' Tom shook his head.

'She just burst into tears. I scarpered back to my room, I didn't know what to do. They went downstairs and I could hear them arguing. I couldn't hear what they were saying but Amy was getting louder and louder. She said she'd made a mistake and that they shouldn't have done this. She was getting more and more hysterical. I don't know what he said or did but she grew quieter and then I heard the patio door go. I came downstairs and couldn't see them anywhere so I went back up to my room and tried to forget about it.'

'And then they were gone?' Jacob asked.

'And then they were gone,' said Tom. 'I'm so sorry.'

Jacob kissed his son's tiny nose. He looked at Fiona, and then finally made eye contact with Tom. 'I know you are, mate,' he said, 'I know you are.'

CHAPTER SEVENTY-EIGHT

Alex

22 March 2011

Alex woke up early. The crisp spring day nibbled at her toes as she took a lungful of morning breath.

The starched sheets were still tightly swaddled around her, but she dragged herself out into the chilly air and splashed her face with warm water from the basin.

She carefully packed her medicines into the side pocket of her holdall and placed her folded clothes into the belly of it.

Alex tucked her letters of apology into the other side pocket of her bag and crept into the residents' lounge for breakfast. She drank several cups of peppermint tea and picked at a slice of toast and marmalade, smiling politely at the hum of conversation all around, accepting a few hugs.

She loaded her bag into the taxi and asked to be taken straight to the hospital in Tunbridge Wells. The taxi had been arranged by reception, and the taxi drivers knew not to ask any questions. Alex wondered how many 'graduates' spilled their stories anyway, programmed from weeks of group therapy.

———

Matt was waiting for her in the café, cradling a cup of grey coffee, her article folded in front of him. He rose when she came in, stepping forward to meet her. For a moment, she just stood and stared, waiting for her heart to settle. He stared back, running his eyes down from the top of her head.

'You look great,' he said emphatically.

'So do you.' He always did.

They hugged lightly, quickly.

'How was treatment?' he asked.

'Oh, you know.' Alex shrugged, unsure if he actually wanted to know.

'I really don't know.' He looked apologetic.

'Well, it worked. It helped. I don't really want to...'

'No, of course, I'm sorry.' He gestured to the newspaper. 'You did so well,' he said.

'I couldn't have done it without my police source,' she replied, and smiled.

The four-page article had been published while Alex was in treatment and she had yet to see a copy. Her byline sat in bold type at the top, above a tiny head and shoulder shot. In the centre of the first double-page spread was a picture of Amy, her arms around Becky and Jenny. All three girls were laughing wildly.

A close-up of Simon, now wiry and greying, had been dropped into the second page of the article. He was definitely handsome, but Alex was surprised by how scrawny and wild-eyed he'd looked when she finally got to see him. He had arrived in court with a black eye and swollen nose. He almost looked pitiful.

It had taken weeks to extradite him. He was wanted in several countries on sexual assault and rape charges under his alias – Graham Barnes. Father's first name, mother's maiden name.

Highly unoriginal but highly effective for fifteen years.

The prosecution had Tom and Caroline as witnesses, but Amy's school bag had never been found and Simon's old car had long been sold for scrap.

A conviction might still have been uncertain were it not for the trial's star witness.

Amy.

Because of the trauma Amy experienced during her previous 'tennis test', it was agreed by the judge and her medical team that there would be a limit of ten questions, and the session would be stopped if Amy became distressed. The defence and prosecution were each permitted five questions, to be submitted in advance.

There was absolute silence in the court as the video was played. In the background, Amy lay flat in an MRI chamber while in the foreground Dr Peter Haynes and his team sat pensively in the control room, screens showing Amy's brain dormant above them.

With a slightly shaky voice, Peter explained the rules to Amy. She was to imagine herself playing tennis if the answer was 'yes' and to imagine herself relaxed and floating in warm water if the answer was 'no'.

To check the process, Peter asked quietly, 'Are you Amy Stevenson?'

The 'tennis' part of Amy's brain lit up red with a halo of orange and yellow surrounding it like the licks of a flame. The court seemed to hold its collective breath.

The defence questions were read crisply by the doctor, leaving a long pause between each one.

'Do you know where you are?'

No.

'Do you know how old you are?'

No.

364

'Do you know what year it is?'

No.

'Are you in any pain?'

No.

'Do you know who attacked you on July the eighteenth in nineteen ninety-five?'

A pause. *Tennis.*

After the defence had tried to discredit the confused, damaged witness, the prosecution took a different approach.

'Amy,' Peter read from the agreed piece of paper. 'For the next series of five questions you must continue to imagine yourself playing tennis for yes, or 'affirmative', and imagine yourself relaxing in warm water the rest of the time. Okay.'

There was a short pause and then Peter's voice came over the courtroom speakers louder and more decisive than before.

'Amy, we are now going to ask you to spell out the name of your attacker. First question, what is the first letter of your attacker's name? A, B, C, D, E, F, G, H, I, J, K, L, M...'

As the doctor got further through the alphabet, Alex had watched the members of the public gallery leaning towards the screens.

'N, O, P, Q, R, S—'

Tennis.

An audible gasp shot from the collective mouths of the court. Sitting flanked by his defence barrister and solicitor, Simon hung his head.

'Next letter,' the video voice continued, undisturbed by the reaction of the court.

'A, B, C, D, E, F, G, H, I—'

Tennis.

It seemed for all but Sue Arlington, the writing was on the wall. And it spelled Simon.

The following week, after a long silence, the jury foreman had side-eyed Simon and finally spoken: 'We find the defendant guilty.'

Jacob had squeezed Fiona's hand to the right, Jenny Cross's to the left. Becky Limm had hugged Alex, and Bob had put his head in his hands and sobbed, his wife Judy by his side. Tom couldn't bear to be in the room once he'd given evidence and had spent the final days of the court hearing looking after his little nephew.

Throughout the trial, Sue had been sitting at the front of the public gallery with a hollow-eyed Graham. When the verdict was read out, she'd made a sound like an animal's howl, temporarily bringing the courtroom to a standstill.

Matt picked up a salt shaker and stared at it intently.

'Are you okay?' Alex asked.

'Not really. God, Alex, your timing has always been lousy.'

'What do you mean?' Alex asked, her chest hurting at the thought of what he might say. She considered standing up and leaving, checking out of anything even close to emotional.

'You finally managed it,' Matt said, reaching for her hand. She moved it away, the thought of his touch too painful to contemplate.

'Don't, Matt, please. I'm not strong enough.'

'You're stronger than either of us knew.'

'I'm so sorry,' she swallowed. 'I wish I'd managed this before. In time,' Alex tangled her breathing up in the beginning of a sob and stopped.

'I wish you had too. Half of me hates you for not managing it back then,' Matt said, still fiddling with the salt shaker, avoiding her eye.

'And the other half?' Alex asked quietly, regaining some composure.

'You know how the other half feels.'

'The whole of me feels the same.' Alex looked down and watched the thick teardrops splashing onto her jeans in clumsy patterns.

Matt's own scant tears had fallen onto the newspaper, a couple of thick black dots speckling the words she'd written.

'Oh shit, I'm sorry,' Matt said, rubbing the damp spots and spreading them further. 'I'll try to get you another copy. Or maybe it will still be online?'

'Don't worry, I can ask them to send me one.'

They both wiped their eyes, cleared their throats, sipped their tepid drinks.

'So what are you going to do now? Is this your new direction?' Matt asked, his eyes still mauve around the edges, a unique colour she hadn't seen since the day he left their home.

'Well, *The Times* are taking me back on. I'm going to do a new column and they're considering a series on forgotten crimes so, you know, we'll see.'

'Will you call if I can help again?' Matt looked hopeful, and Alex found herself inhaling sharply.

'Well, I... do you think that's a good idea?'

'Probably not,' he smiled apologetically. 'But I'd like it if you did.'

Alex chewed her bottom lip. Her heart hurt like it was burning her from the inside out. She took a deep breath, worried she might leap across the table, grab him and never let go.

'You know, Matt, I'm going to do the next one alone. I mean, I'm going to leave you alone. With Jane,' she smiled, and fresh tears trickled a zigzagged path over her cheekbones. 'And with Ava.'

Matt looked away and breathed deeply. He rubbed his hand over his face and shook his head.

'Thank you.'

Bramble Ward was empty and the nurse's station abandoned. The radio was off, there were no other visitors and the only sound was the distant hum of the machines and the quiet orchestra of patients' breaths.

Alex checked her reflection for leaking mascara, signed herself in and walked slowly over to the corner cubicle. She sat lightly in the chair.

'Hi, Amy, it's Alex. How have you been?'

She picked up Amy's weightless hand, warming it between her own and holding it lightly to her cheek.

Alex moved from the visitor's chair and sat on the bed. Then she lay down next to Amy, still gripping her hand. She popped one earphone into Amy's left ear, the other into her own right ear, closed her eyes and pressed play.

CHAPTER SEVENTY-NINE

'Finding Alex'

Sunday Times Magazine

3 April 2011

The last time I wrote a column for this newspaper was in 2007. At the time, I was married and expecting a baby. I was also a barely functioning alcoholic who drank bourbon from one of those ceramic novelty mugs that look like a Starbucks takeaway cup.

I wish I could say that losing my baby was my rock bottom. I'm an overachiever. I managed to find several other rock bottoms.

When my husband finally walked out on me and my pickled womb, I tried to write my way out of the hole. Instead, I wrote my way out of a job and into a pub. Have you heard the one about the national newspaper columnist who bangs a busboy in a bar crowded with contemporaries? Don't worry, *Private Eye* did.

After being thrown out of my own publisher's building, I also managed the spectacular feat of being thrown out of a publisher's office where I did not work. It was only fair. I'd turned up, booze steaming from my skin like a geyser, demanding a job I'd turned down months before. A job that had long been filled.

I lost days, I lost weeks. I lost everything.

I woke up with strangers, unconscious in the bed I'd once shared with my husband. I hallucinated, counting glass spiders on my ceiling and willing them to cut me to pieces. I lost every single friend. Irretrievably. Imagine just how badly you'd need to behave to lose every single friend. *Irretrievably.*

Eventually, I managed to pull my head above water. Just. For eighteen months I kicked wildly until my legs were so tired I was ready to be carried out to sea.

'If you don't stop drinking,' my family doctor told me, 'you'll be dead in a year.' I drank that night.

And now I sit with bourbon-free coffee in my mug, liver damage controlled with pills, nursing the blinding clarity that comes with sobriety. That vicious clarity that alcoholics like me try our damnedest to avoid. To my surprise I realize that, rather than grinding towards the inevitable ending of my own story, I'm still in the middle.

So what changed? I found a friend.

Amy Stevenson isn't an ordinary friend. She's a girl who everyone has heard of, but she's likely unaware of her fame. She's a girl who was also stuck in a deep rut.

The difference between Amy and me, is that she hadn't dug the rut herself, and she refused to lie down and die in it. When she could have given in and given up, she kicked and screamed and used every drop of strength she had. I saw in Amy someone with no second chance, fighting like fury to create one. And when you see that fight take place in front of you, you recognize your own second chance.

It's time for me to take it. To be grateful for it. To earn it and to own it. I have no idea where my second chance leads. All I know is that I need to put one foot in front of the other, every day, for ever. And to dedicate every step to my friend, Amy.

ACKNOWLEDGEMENTS

I used a lot of artistic licence in dealing with Amy's condition, but the Royal Hospital for Neuro-disability is a brilliant organization doing groundbreaking work, so check them out if you're interested in learning facts rather than my fictionalized account.

So many people helped bring this book to life, and I'm sorry to anyone I've overlooked, but firstly I have to thank Nicola Barr, my awesome agent. Her patience, insight, cheerleading, un-Scooby Dooing and brunches can never be repaid. Everyone at Greene & Heaton is wonderful, actually, but I'd also like to thank the brilliant Kate Rizzo.

My editors on both sides of the Atlantic have helped shape this book into something of which I'm so proud, I can't even articulate it (not great form for a writer). Sara O'Keeffe and Maddie West from Corvus/Atlantic, Linda Marrow from Ballantine/Penguin Random House, thank you so very much.

To Ilana, for showing me how it's done, you frickin' trailblazer. To Sarah, a brilliant writer herself and a very patient and encouraging reader.

My best friend Carole, who is nothing like Amy's friends, although she did once shave an undercut into my hair on a park bench and we did used to drink Archers and lemonade together. The Midlanders, whose enduring friendship is a source of huge pride as well as belly-hurting laughter. Our playlists helped, I love you guys. To my pals from News International and Associated, thanks for the memories. And thank you to Romi, for the cuppas and hugs.

I was very lucky to have a mum and dad who never did things the boring way and never said I should just get a sensible job. Cristy and Vik, who are my friends as well as my sisters. And Rich, who I dearly wish had been around to see this, and whose strength, wisdom and *Futurama* quotes I thought about a lot while writing this. He was alright.

And, of course, infinite thank yous to the love of my life, James, and our swarm of funny, loving, rude-song-singing, adventurous and ridiculous kids: Pops, Bear, Little Legs and Fu.